Fae by the Bay

Research with Rivals

Jillian Witt

Cover Artwork by Flourishing Fables

Map by Holly Dunn

Editing by Adie Hart

Copy Edit by Isla Elrick

Published by Myth and Magic Book Club

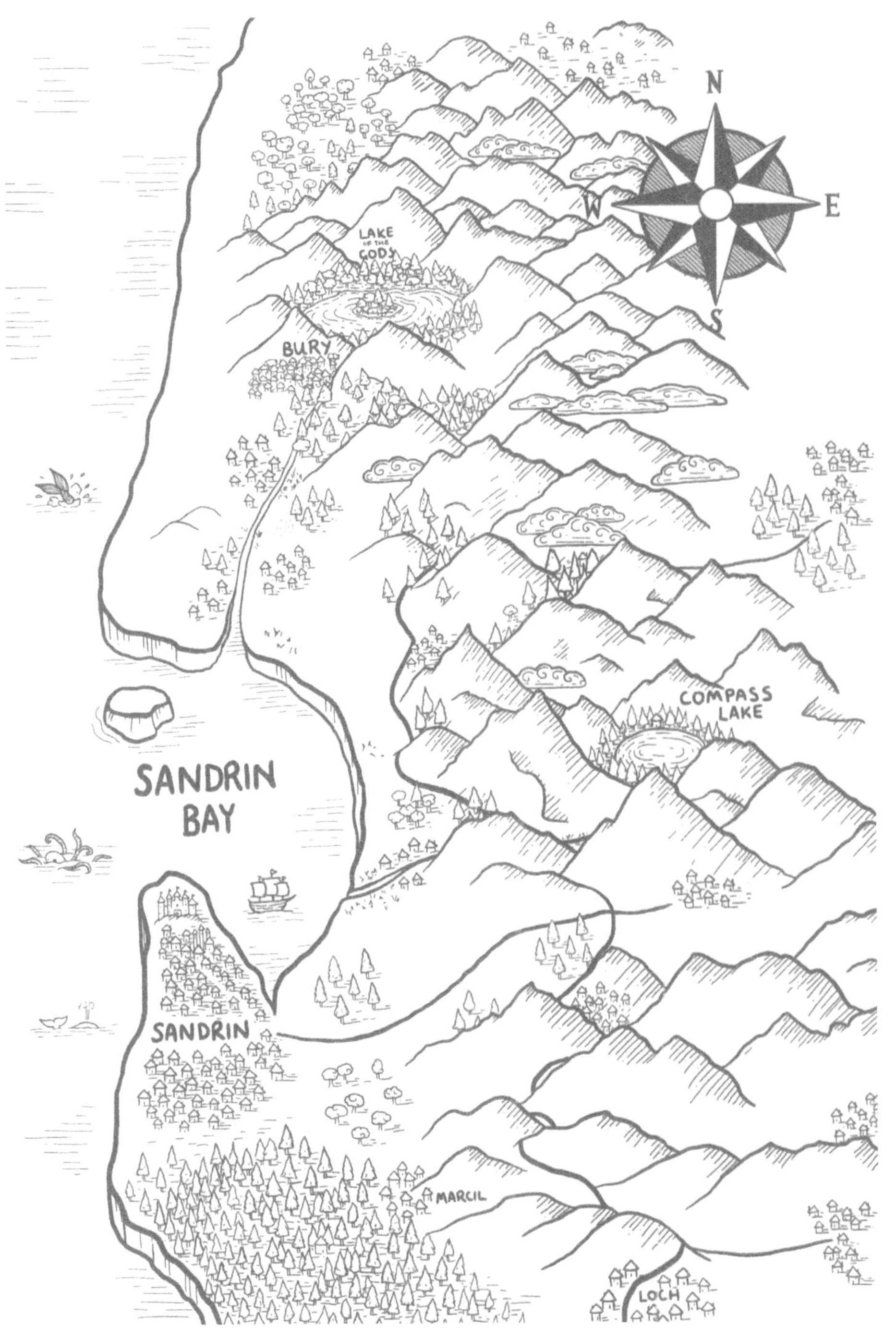
N
W
E
S
LAKE OF THE GODS
BURY
COMPASS LAKE
SANDRIN BAY
SANDRIN
MARCIL
LOCH

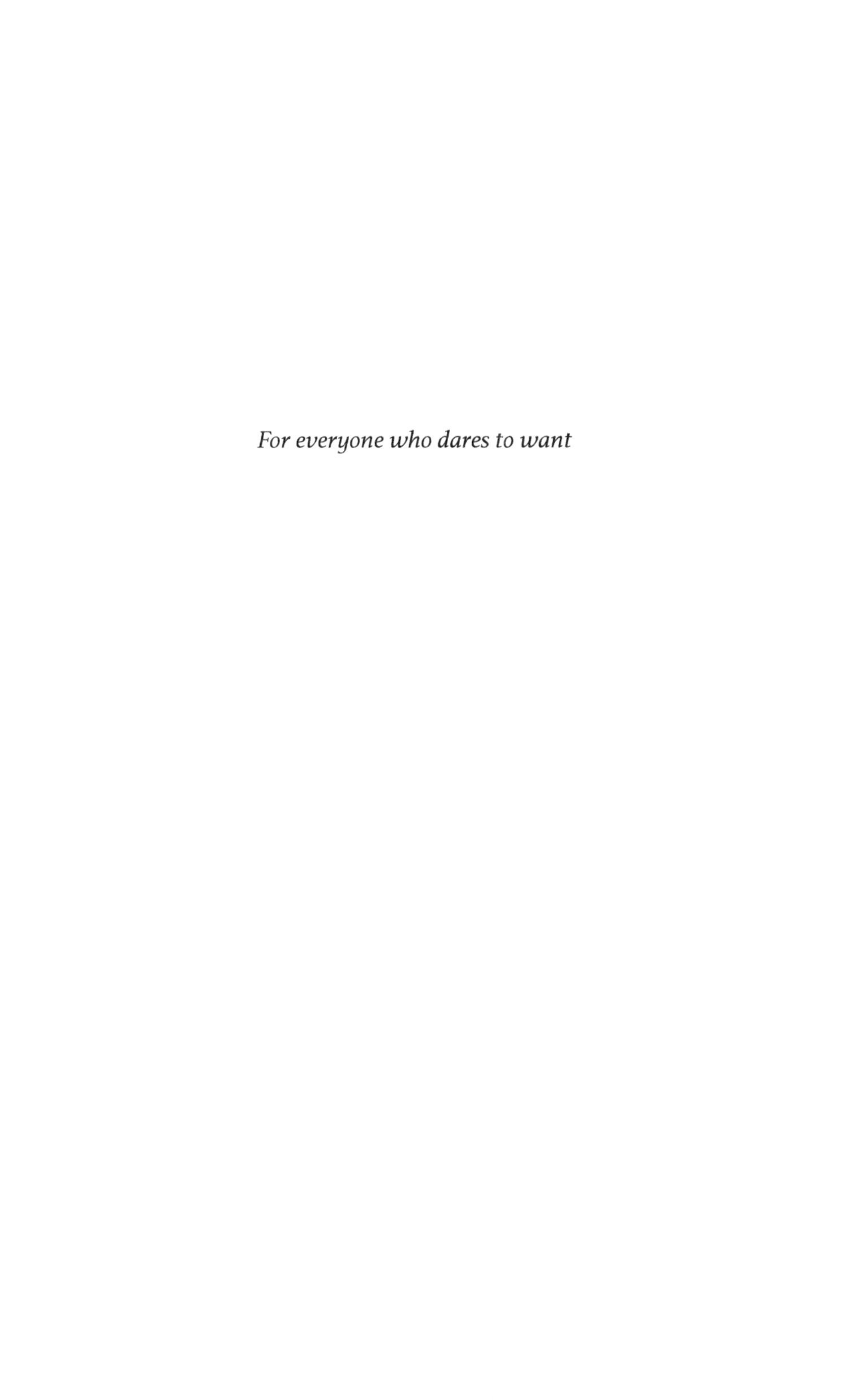

For everyone who dares to want

1

Evelyn

Having a favorite study carrel in the Vesten Library might have said more about me than I'd liked, but honestly, I never thought I'd be allowed in, so small things still felt like huge accomplishments.

Now, if only I could reach said study carrel without the utter embarrassment of being seen by my fellow researchers in the other aisle.

"What's she doing over there? Are we in danger?" Tatyana's voice drifted over the dark wooden shelf. Unfortunately, I was stuck here on the opposite side crouched next to all five volumes of *Sandrin's Floral Encyclopedia* and *A History of Fae and Fauna*. More unfortunately, Tatyana and Landon were speaking of my experiment.

"It's blood magic, tested on living things. In the middle of the Great Room. Of course, we're in danger. Anything could happen," Landon replied.

He wasn't wrong, precisely, but I didn't appreciate his tone. I'd taken every precaution for this experiment. Not that my desk particularly *looked* safe right now. From his vantage point, one could see seemingly random items spread atop it: my notebook and pencil, a ceramic pot with two incompatible flowers planted in the dirt, and a small knife.

"And she's not even there overseeing it," Landon droned on.

I refrained from letting out a sigh or making my presence known. I had only slipped away to grab a textbook. That had been my second mistake.

My first mistake was thinking the Vesten would ever accept my research.

My area of study, blood magic, was not new but had recently gained popularity. Fae society had previously looked down on the magic; some still did, but one advantage of growing up outside of the courts was that I'd never known that. I tested what I pleased without risk of ostracization. Spoiler alert: I was already ostracized. It wasn't until I'd started working at the library that I realized how vehemently other researchers disagreed with my approach.

"We should tell Ambrose, he'll put a stop to it," Tatyana said.

There was a touch of awe in her voice, like a common citizen calling on a fabled knight to save her. I wanted to gag. Ambrose was the only other researcher in the library who studied blood magic. But he had been studying history in the library for much longer. He was unfortunately decent at both. I bit my lip as I acknowledged that was an understatement. As Tatyana's inflection indicated, he was the library's golden boy. He knew everything and solved all their problems.

I was one of those problems, so they had him deal with me frequently.

Ambrose considered my research methods dangerous at

best and reckless at worst. Thankfully, the head librarian disagreed. Still, it made working with Ambrose challenging. Our communications were like two people speaking different languages, and we didn't have the luxury to fall back on small words and gestures to bridge the many gaps. Yet, somehow, we'd ended up the only two in our discipline.

The shuffle of feet drew my attention. Were they actually going to get him? What children. I shouldn't be surprised, but still fury bubbled inside of me. It was literally my job to conduct these experiments. I yanked the book I needed off the shelf, *Sandrin's Floral Encyclopedia - Part IV*, and gripped it tightly, before remembering that their absence was precisely what I needed to make my escape from the stacks without notice.

Instead of standing from where I was crouched in the next aisle, I glanced across the room to where Ambrose stood reshelving a book. Tatyana and Landon strode toward him like soldiers on a mission. Ambrose would disapprove of my test. If he had his way, we would never test blood magic on any living thing—not even plants.

Again, I silently acknowledged that blood magic *was* dangerous. What no one seemed to grasp was that *all* blood magic was dangerous. If danger was the line we couldn't cross, then neither mine, nor Ambrose's position should exist.

I'd never dared hope for this position. It hadn't even been an option I considered. Until six months ago, the courts liked to pretend half-fae didn't exist. And they tried *hard*. They didn't allow my name in the court record book. I couldn't attend school with the other Vesten children. No one would teach me about our magic.

When I was a kid, Mom didn't have a lot of spare money, so sometimes, I'd watch other children at the sweets store in town. They would come out with brightly colored lollipops, fantastically shaped chocolates, and these small red balls of hard candy that smelled like cinnamon. Unsurprisingly, the Vesten who exited the shop ignored me. Even worse, the human children I saw every day at the school I was allowed to attend did the same. I thought maybe if I had the candy, it would make them include me, but I couldn't even have that. So, I'd press my nose right up to the storefront's glass window, thinking maybe I could smell it—maybe that would be enough.

It was never enough.

It wasn't even about wanting the candy, though I did. It was about wanting to belong to one of the groups in the shop. The fae didn't think me fae enough to be one of them, and the humans thought me too fae to be theirs. What did that leave me?

Eventually, I learned not to want any of it.

Wanting was fuel to the fire of disappointment. If I didn't want the sweets, at least I wouldn't get a stomachache. If I didn't want my father to return, then maybe I wouldn't care that he left us. And maybe if I didn't want this position in the library so badly, it wouldn't be a big deal when Ambrose finally convinced the head librarian to change his mind about my employment.

Unfortunately, my gaze lingered on Ambrose across the room. I'd need a ladder to reach the shelf onto which he effortlessly slid a book. No one needed to be that tall or that broad. And no one needed their clothes to fit that well. Even through his customary layers—a white shirt, with an earth-tone vest—the definition of his arms was clear. We spent all our time in a library, reading books. When did he have time to exercise?

My eyes narrowed as Tatyana and Landon reached him. I was out of time. Finally, I stood from behind the shelf and scuttled toward my study carrel by the fire. The Great Room was always so cold. One of the benefits of this particular spot was proximity to the heat.

The items on my desk hadn't moved, but I took my seat and unnecessarily tidied them while sneaking covert glances across the room. Ambrose, hands on his hips, nodded along to whatever fears Tatyana and Landon espoused about me and my research.

I gritted my teeth. It wasn't just that he had an impossible physique. He always looked so confident, so at home in this library. I, on the other hand, held my books tight to my chest in hopes no one would take them away. Scurrying away from shelves where others gossiped about me wasn't a one-time occurrence.

Lines had been drawn quickly on the correct and incorrect ways to experiment with blood magic. Testing on living things, even plants as I did, was in the minority. Ambrose, on the other hand, tested only on inanimate objects.

I tried repeatedly to explain that intent mattered most—more than test subjects. The only one who appeared to listen was the head librarian. I guessed that was enough to retain my employment, but it was isolating.

Across the room, Landon gestured toward me and Ambrose's gaze followed. I flinched and tried to find the section of the book I'd been interested in.

Core to my understanding of the magic was that the intent of the wielder drives everything. It wasn't so different from other forms of magic. Each of the four fae courts wielded an element, and, as we continued to learn, additional magical gifts. I might have been only half-Vesten, but I inherited the gifts of my court. Vesten had fire magic, and when I called it, it answered. I might not have flashy control over it like other Vesten, but I blamed my missing father for that, not the magic.

I leaned onto the table top and held out my palm. With little more than a thought, it filled with a lonely flame. The light flickered against the papers and plants on my carrel. I sighed and watched how it danced with my breath before dousing it. If only the other Vesten magic I'd inherited were that easy to control.

My shoulders tensed as something unruly inside me awakened at the thought of my *other* gift. Honestly, my emotions had been all over the place in the last few minutes. I was surprised she hadn't made herself known sooner.

With a deep breath, I chose to ignore that particular problem, as well as the one unfolding across the room where the trio continued to talk. I was hired to conduct blood magic experiments and I would do so.

Setting aside my book, I picked up the knife and glanced again at the ceramic pot. This was the next test in a series about blood magic and bindings. I had tested with inanimate objects, but the core of this test was to determine if two things that didn't like each other could be made to stay together. To truly test it, I needed to test something that had a preference. A rock didn't care if it was placed in a stream or next to another rock. Living things had opinions.

Like me, for example, I didn't like anyone using the study carrel across from mine, so I hid the chair in the closet every morning.

For this test, I found two plants that didn't particularly like growing together, and the experiment would try to force them to do so. The rose and the morning glory fought over nutrients, and it was common for morning glories to overshadow roses, starving them of sunlight. This experiment would bind them in this pot. It would be a success if both plants flourished—but without magical intervention, the rose should be dead in a week. This was a low-risk test with living things. It wasn't like I was experimenting on humans or fae.

Only a few drops of blood were necessary, rather than a full vial for something particularly complex. The magic just wanted proof of the wielder's investment. The walls of my carrel shielded me from view as I pressed the knife against the tip of my finger and spoke. "Bind. I want these flowers to grow together, to coexist in this habitat."

The blade pierced my skin, and a small bead of blood welled to the surface. I turned my finger over, holding it near the dirt. Slowly, but surely, a single drop slipped from my finger.

"Evelyn—"

"Eeep." I squeaked as I jumped at the interruption. My solitary study carrel wasn't enough to keep him away.

"What are you doing?"

I scowled up at Ambrose, who stood beside my desk, and grabbed a cloth for my finger in the process. My face pinched further at my interrupted experiment. I wasn't even sure how much of my blood had landed on the soil. Had my intent been clear?

"Announce yourself before you stalk over here," I hissed.

Ambrose's lip twitched, almost like he wanted to smirk. But that wasn't us; we didn't smirk at each other. We begrudgingly read each other's papers and passively-aggressively commented on the method of experimentation and resulting conclusions.

"This is not me stalking," he said.

Something inside me warmed, and I shifted in my seat. His words begged the question of what it was like to be stalked by him—to be his prey. Would he give immediate chase? Or would he prowl and take his time?

My cheeks heated. *Where had that come from?* I might have a guess, as the thing inside me—the second magic of the Vesten fae—fully woke from her slumber.

And now I was thinking about his shifter form.

In addition to wielding fire, most Vesten could change into animals, but you weren't supposed to ask what kind. My mom and I learned firsthand how rude the Vesten found the question. With my father gone, my human mom attempted to find me a Vesten mentor. She was turned away by everyone she approached. Some slammed doors in her face. Only one had the decency to explain that asking about such things was taboo. You learned from your family, that was how it went. They did not offer suggestions for those with no Vesten family members in the picture.

I took a deep breath to collect myself and push the unwelcome thoughts away. "Do you need something?"

Landon and Tatyana made no effort to hide as they watched the encounter from across the room. I may know why Ambrose was here, but I certainly wouldn't make this easy for him.

Ambrose glanced over my obvious experiment and frowned. "Have you had this test reviewed?"

His forearms were exposed as he leaned over the wooden wall surrounding the desk. Whatever he had been researching before Landon and Tatyana's interruption must have had him stumped. Ambrose was always annoyingly put-together, except when his studies overtook him. When that happened, he messily rolled up the sleeves of his white shirt. I cataloged his frustrations as small wins for myself.

I pulled my gaze from the exposed pale skin and met bright hazel eyes and the slightest upward tilt of his lip. It was gone before I could name it.

"I'm not sure it's any of your concern."

He straightened, and his arms fell to his sides. "It's everyone in the library's concern if those plants grow so large they block the exits and trap us in here."

Quickly, I checked the plants to see if something unexpected occurred. The two flowers looked unaffected. "I assure you, I followed procedures and took the utmost care in my experiment."

His eyes narrowed suspiciously at the plants, and he mumbled. "Not sure it helps when living things are involved."

My spine straightened, and the beast in my mind showed

her teeth. I dug my nails into my palms beneath the desk to stop the change from happening.

Not here.

My nostrils flared through a deep breath. Calming. Centering. "I was hired to learn about blood magic. You are well aware of the information lacking in Vesten history. This is how I intend to do it."

His ears pinkened. He was an expert on Vesten history, so distinguished that he'd taken on researching blood magic when no one else would. "Yes, well." He glanced across my desk again. "I look forward to your paper detailing the experiment and the conclusions."

Liar.

He hadn't reviewed the paper I submitted yesterday yet. I glanced back at the plants. Hopefully, we were done here and he would leave. I'd calmed the animal in my mind only momentarily. She would be a problem if this conversation continued. I needed to leave anyway. I had started my experiment, but the results would take time.

"Could you read my work on anchors?" he asked, as he shuffled the papers in his hand.

I'd never tell him, but I was eager to read this paper. He'd been researching anchors, or objects of significance to specific instances of blood magic. They were physical representations of the magic, helping to focus the wielder's intent. Ambrose hypothesized that they did more than focus intent; they might house it. Unfortunately, I didn't have time to read the paper right now. The clock on the wall announced I had to leave for my second job soon.

"Not tonight. Maybe if you had arrived earlier to ask, I could have fit you in."

In hindsight, I could have done without tacking on the last part of my response. My comment wasn't really fair. Ambrose had been here for hours, but something about the way he'd casually strolled into the Great Room mid-morning raised my not-so-metaphorical hackles. Those who didn't claw for every scrap of respect they received were difficult to trust.

His eyes widened in surprise, then narrowed. "We can't all obsess over blood magic all the time."

My hand balled into a fist. The animal I'd almost suppressed scratched again to break free. Not here. Not now. Deep breaths. In through the nose, out through the nose.

Ambrose Yarrow had an inexplicable ability to get under my skin. I needed him gone.

"Fine. Give it to me. I'll finish it before you arrive tomorrow."

I'm sure this conversation was giving him whiplash, but he could join the club.

Ambrose stared at me. "You just said—"

"I know." I took another deep breath to calm the raging animal inside me. "Please leave the papers on my desk. You can go now."

My internal temperature was rising with my beast's desire to break free. Sweat would drip from my brow momentarily if I continued to push her down.

It was unpredictable how fae magic would materialize in someone like me. Some half-fae had magic just like their fae parent. Others had none at all. Many had something in between.

As Ambrose considered my statement, but still didn't leave, I began to count backward from one hundred. It was these moments, which were unfortunately increasing in frequency, when I secretly wished my father hadn't run out on us. I wished someone could teach me how to handle the animal that fought so hard against me.

Everyone assumed that because I hadn't had uncontrollable shifts as a child, I'd never have them. I had thought that the case, too, until a few months ago.

If only it were still true.

Ninety-nine, ninety-eight, ninety-seven. It would be inconvenient for my shift to make itself known now.

The animal and I didn't get along well. She was too separate, too unpredictable, and honestly, too unfathomable to comprehend. I didn't know how to control her. Usually, I was at her mercy—when she wanted out, she freed herself. I couldn't let it happen here, though.

"Evelyn?"

I'd missed whatever Ambrose had said. Why was he still here? Reason drove all aspects of my life, except for my shift and my interactions with Ambrose Yarrow. The two things shouldn't mix.

Concern lingered with Ambrose's furrowed brow. The knuckles of his fingers were white where they gripped the wooden carrel as if he clung to it for dear life. "Are you—"

"I'm fine," I said quietly. *Ninety-six, ninety-five, ninety-four.* My heart rate steadied with another breath.

I dared a glance, but he hadn't yet turned to leave. Our gazes locked, and I couldn't quite fathom what I read there.

Some would say I'd made a hobby of studying Ambrose Yarrow. I would say that I liked to know my competition, and he was the only one in this library who knew anything about blood magic. But the near feral look on his usually stoic face didn't sit well with me. He must think I'd pushed blood magic too far and tested it on myself. Maybe this was what would finally get me fired.

Ninety-three, ninety-two, ninety-one. The heat retreated as quickly as it had come. Thus was the animalistic response. My mouth opened. What did I tell him? That I was fine again?

Any explanation was interrupted as a high-pitched caw echoed through the Great Room. The rustle of flapping wings drew my focus to the large black raven entering. The bird had yet to reach us when it shifted into a male, landing on two feet without breaking forward momentum.

Clumsily, I stood, dipping my chin with such force that a strand of my dark brown hair fell from my braid into my face. "Lord Arctos."

He was tall, like Ambrose, but wiry instead of broad. His blond hair was shoulder length, and while he had the beauty of the fae, there was an undefined sharpness to him, probably due to him being one of the four gods who'd created the continent. I hadn't given much thought to my belief in the gods until Lord Arctos showed up at the library a few days ago. Then he had surprised me further by staying at my friend Luna's inn. The Vesten God didn't put on airs, but I still had no idea what to make of him.

He glanced between me and Ambrose. "Good, I'm glad you're both here."

When Lord Arctos had arrived in Sandrin, he asked me directly for research help with a project. This had been yet another sore point between Ambrose and me. Ambrose assumed I was already hard at work on whatever the Vesten God needed. In reality, since he'd asked for my help, he'd told me nothing else about it.

Lord Arctos shook briefly, like he was adjusting to the feeling of the light brown tunic and dark trousers that had appeared with him. "Miss Knowles, I've already asked for your expertise on my project. Gabriel has pointed out that you work quite well with Mr. Yarrow."

He glanced between us again as if looking for confirmation. Neither of us made a move of acknowledgement.

"Well, he asked that I include you both in the briefing, and he does run this library, so I will cede to his wishes."

Lord Arctos didn't sound like he was ceding to anything. His eyes sparkled as if he had decided this entire project would provide infinite amusement. Maybe it would. For *him*.

"What will we be working on?" Ambrose asked with a dismissive glance at me. I'm sure he assumed I already knew.

The god's brow pinched as he focused on Ambrose. "You'll find that out at the briefing."

Ambrose dipped his head in acknowledgment, though I couldn't be sure he was chastened.

"Should we meet in Gabriel's office?" I asked and peered at the clock. Seraphina understood when things came up, but I hated to be late.

"Yes." Lord Arctos gestured between us. He didn't seem to miss anything. "Is five minutes enough time to wrap whatever this is up?"

The assessment was disconcerting, but I nodded, mumbling to myself. "The faster you leave, the faster we'll finish."

The Vesten God tilted his head slightly, like he might have heard. I gulped as I realized the words were not quiet enough. Today was really not my best.

Instead of responding, he smiled and clapped his hands together. "Wonderful. I can't wait."

Shifting again, he flew out an open window on the other side of the room.

Ambrose studied me in a way that I would never grow accustomed to. "Do you think he knows Gabriel's office is the other way?"

"I'm not sure he cares."

There was another almost twitch of his lip at that, then something changed, and the lines of his mouth flattened, his arms folding over his chest. "So we'll be working together on his project. Did you know?"

"The Vesten God doesn't share his plans with me." I closed my notebook and slid it neatly into the corner of the table, then placed the pot for my flower experiment on the windowsill.

"Do you know what the project is?" he pressed.

Outwardly, I sighed in exasperation, but Ambrose's tenacity was, begrudgingly, my favorite thing about him. Unfortunately, he was an excellent researcher. He wouldn't let this go until he understood the problem and had a solution in mind.

His hazel eyes met mine at the sound. "What?"

I shook my head and echoed the Vesten God's words. "We'll have to attend the briefing to find out."

2

Evelyn

Gabriel ran the Vesten Library, not so much with an iron fist as with a warm heart and inquisitive mind. He'd hired me, the first Vesten to take a chance on me after the new court leaders accepted the existence of half-fae.

When I'd worked at the Sandrin Records Office, the researchers had taken turns working the reception desk. That was where I'd been sitting when Gabriel walked in the day he offered me a job. He'd walked right up and spoken to me like he knew I was a researcher. Honestly, he'd spoken to me with more respect than the humans in the Records Office ever did. My colleagues there avoided me at best and gave me extra time at the reception desk when ignoring me didn't work. To them, I was too other, too fae.

Too bad the fae didn't believe that.

That day, the head librarian had shaken my hand and asked me about blood magic. He wanted to know what I had studied, what my methods included, and what my plans for the future were. The way his warm brown eyes searched the Records Office almost sadly said he knew I wasn't allowed to conduct my tests there. He could have knocked me over with a feather when he then asked if I wanted to work for him at the Vesten Library.

It had taken everything within me not to grasp at the offer immediately, but I knew the opportunity wasn't for me. It was for someone fully Vesten. When I'd told him I wasn't, he tilted his head in question. I'd clarified my half-fae heritage. Saying that I was half-fae had kept me from every Vesten school I applied to. Gabriel had looked thoughtful, but then he repeated his offer.

I started working for him the following week.

The warm and relaxed head librarian was not quite the Gabriel we found when we entered his office.

His long blond hair was tied in a messy knot at the base of his neck. So many strands were slipping free that it was clear he'd spent the morning scratching his forehead. His clothes were rumpled, like maybe he'd been here all night.

Still, he managed a smile. "Ah, Evelyn, Ambrose, so glad you're here."

"Everything alright, sir?" Ambrose asked.

Gabriel waved him off. "Fine, fine. Have you seen Lord Arctos?"

"He said he'd meet us here," I replied.

The office was small, but Gabriel had to stand to reach a tea service that looked fresh. "Wonderful. Would either of you care for something while we wait?"

I accepted, taking a seat in front of the desk as I tried to determine the problem. The office looked the same as it had for the last few months of my employment. The large wooden desk occupied half the space, and papers were scattered messily across it. A few shelves filled with books decorated the wall behind Gabriel. Some appeared to be in review, lying open on the desk.

Ambrose took the chair next to me. Concern was evident in his furrowed brow, but he seemed to understand we wouldn't get information until Gabriel decided to share. He ran his fingers through his auburn hair while we waited.

As another question formed on my lips, the familiar black bird flew into the office. He perched in the corner of the room and shifted so his fae form leaned against a small end table. Then he crossed his arms over his chest like he'd been waiting for us all this time.

Gabriel glanced at him, showing no surprise at the shift or positioning. He had a cup of tea ready and handed it to the god.

Lord Arctos gestured for Gabriel to proceed. "Please, let's get started. Time is short."

It struck me as an odd thing for a god to say. I was new to Vesten history, but I'd studied a lot in a short period. Lack of knowledge would not be the reason this position slipped through my fingers. All the texts indicated that the fae had been created hundreds of years ago. No records detailed how long the continent and humans had existed before that. All this to say, I assumed time was quite long for Lord Arctos, one of the continent's four creators.

"Well." Gabriel cleared his throat. "We have a project that I believe requires both of your expertise."

"I'm sorry for the intrusion, dear, but I'm about to do something distasteful and decided you deserve a warning."

The voice in my head somehow matched the piercing green eyes of the god staring at me from the corner of the room. It was wild and unpredictable, like an unexplored forest. I had no means of response. Gabriel was still speaking.

"I'm going to say some things about half-fae. Please know that I do not believe any of them. I need to test our friend here"—he nodded at Ambrose—*"before allowing him to work on this."*

Again, I had no way to object. I could have told him that Ambrose didn't need testing. Ambrose was an academic through and through, no matter his family. He didn't care about one's lineage—he only cared about their intelligence and ideas. He didn't dislike me because I was half-fae; he disliked me because of my methods and beliefs about blood magic. With no way to communicate such things, I shrugged.

Gabriel finished by impressing the secrecy of this project. "I know I can count on both of you, but just so there are no misunderstandings, only those in this room know the details of what you'll be researching."

"I can't believe we don't even have real fae researching information so critical to the fae courts," Lord Arctos said as he took a sip of his tea.

He had warned me, but still, I flinched at the words. The animal in my mind roared to life at my discomfort. For years, half-fae or fae born of multiple courts had had to hide themselves. The new Norden Point, or water fae leader, had changed everything. She'd brought acceptance to the courts. However, there were plenty of fae who believed exactly what the god had voiced.

Ambrose noticed my reaction. To his credit, he didn't hesitate. "Excuse me—"

Lord Arctos continued. "Are you sure this is the correct team for this project, Gabriel?"

Gabriel rested his elbows on the desk, and his head fell into his hands, leaving me to wonder if he, too, received a warning about Lord Arctos's behavior, which he was unable to challenge.

The chair beside me scraped the floor as it was hastily slid back. Ambrose was on his feet now. "You may be a god, but you are surprisingly uneducated about your creations."

I wanted to roll my eyes, but I was too off balance by this

encounter. Only Ambrose would think to insult a god by calling him uneducated.

"No one knows more about blood magic than Evelyn does," he added.

The animal inside me liked that. If she weren't already so upset, I thought she might purr. My cheeks heated, and something uncomfortable twisted in my chest.

Lord Arctos's eyes widened, and his lip curled into a smirk. "I see what you mean now, Gabriel." The god folded his hands in his lap, like he'd finished his move and it was now someone else's turn. "Fine. Mr. Yarrow can work on the project."

Ambrose sputtered. "What?" He glanced at me in confusion. My expression must have matched his. Quickly, he sat. And he must have finally registered what he'd said to the god, because his face went white as a sheet.

I was already tired, and we hadn't even heard the description of the work we needed to do. While Gabriel attempted to explain the situation to Ambrose, I wrestled my animal into submission. Even when she was happy, she was a handful.

This beast was so inconvenient. I'd gone twenty-six years without so much as a flicker of an animal form. Then, a few months ago, that had changed. The first time I shifted and caught a glimpse of my reflection in the sea, I panicked. All I could think was that this couldn't be happening. It couldn't be possible. This animal was a myth.

I'd shifted several times since then. None of the shifts were within my control. She took charge every time. At least she kept us away from others when she emerged.

Gabriel waved his hand as if wishing to wipe away the last few minutes of conversation. "Lord Arctos was determined to test you, Ambrose. I'm sorry. I couldn't stop him. He wanted to make sure you were a fit for the work."

I was a little impressed that Gabriel would speak of Lord Arctos as if he were a trying toddler while sitting beside him. It probably helped that Gabriel's son was the head of our court, the Vesten Point.

All court and godly drama paled in comparison to Gabriel's pride in his son. He went to great lengths to ensure Carter had what he needed to run the Vesten Court effectively. His fatherly devotion was delightfully nauseating at times. Occasionally, it made me wish I believed Mom's story about my father. She didn't think he had left us. I clenched my teeth, thinking of how badly she wanted him to come home. She was convinced something terrible had happened to prevent his return. I could have believed that in the first few weeks, maybe even months, but twenty years was an awful long absence to explain.

I shook myself free from the thought as Gabriel moved on to the relevant details of the project.

"There is an unknown magical connection between each of the gods and their Compass Point." The Compass Points were the four fae leaders, named such because the seats of their magic sat like cardinal points on a compass of the perfectly circular Compass Lake.

I leaned forward, finally interested in the conversation. "What are the symptoms of this connection?"

Gabriel smiled, but it didn't meet his eyes like usual. "Under the right conditions, they can share magic."

"In both directions?" Ambrose had a notebook in hand and a pencil poised to write. He always had it with him. It was easy to know when something intrigued him. If it did, his notebook and pencil were mysteriously present within seconds. I was convinced this was the sole reason he wore one of those vests every day—for the pockets.

His gaze snagged on me staring at the notepad. It was his turn to flush. I might have commented about it once or twice. He explained himself unnecessarily. "You never know when you'll need to record your findings."

I rolled my eyes, having heard that answer before.

Lord Arctos looked delighted, then answered Ambrose's question. "Yes, in both directions."

Ambrose made a note and gave me a sideways glance that had me itching to cross my arms over my chest.

"And you want to know what? About the connection in general?" I asked.

Gabriel glanced at Lord Arctos. "We want to know if there is any precedent for it. And, in particular, if there is a way to undo it."

"To undo it..." Ambrose seemed like he would ask another question. I had a feeling it was the same one I had. *Why do they want to undo it?*

"We want you both to work on this. Your combined knowledge of history and blood magic is unparalleled in any of the courts. Ambrose, you have used your knowledge of history to better understand blood magic anchors, and Evelyn, though you're new, your understanding of the discipline and your intuition for the magic are unmatched. You two are equally paced in your research paper submissions, and they are all of the utmost quality. Quite honestly, there is no one else in your league."

My cheeks warmed. This was news to me. I'd been under the impression that Ambrose, the library's golden boy, was in a league of his own.

Gabriel continued. "As Lord Arctos has said, we are short on time. So, to incentivize you both, whoever can explain the connection first will receive a promotion."

Ambrose's mouth opened just as mine did, but Gabriel cut us both off.

"The promotion will be to Vesten historian, the top research position for the court, working for the Vesten Point."

My mouth hung open, now for a different reason. Ambrose's teeth clicked together with force as his snapped shut.

I started, "That position—"

"Hasn't been filled since Carter had it, yes," Lord Arctos said.

Carter was Gabriel's son. The current leader of our court had been the best researcher this library had before he was called to the position of Vesten Point. That hadn't been what I was going to ask, but I was glad for the god's interruption. The real thought that had crossed my mind was that a *half-fae* had never held that position.

Gabriel kept speaking, and I hung on his every word. "Carter has a new vision for the position. Its name will remain the same, but given the trajectory of magic on the continent, he requires any future holders of the title to be as adept with blood magic as they are with Vesten history." The head librarian glanced between us. "If I could melt you two together, you would be the perfect candidate. As it stands, Evelyn is stronger with blood magic, and Ambrose is stronger with history. But you're each making remarkable strides with your weaker subject."

I bristled. The only reason I wasn't an expert in Vesten history was that I hadn't been allowed in the library until a few months ago. If I'd had the opportunity to study it prior, I would have mastered it. What was Ambrose's excuse? What fae snobbery drove his hesitancy with blood magic?

It didn't matter. My mind was already exploring the possibilities of me in the Vesten historian position. I could change the way blood magic was studied. My research could open unlimited possibilities for those born without magic. The position had seemed so far out of my reach that wanting it hadn't even crossed my mind. Now I wasn't sure I could let it go. I could elevate the profile of half-fae in all the courts by winning. To realize that Gabriel thought me qualified made something warm swell in my chest, and I didn't quite know what to do with the emotion.

My excitement had my animal reaching for the reins again. This time, thinking of her only spurred me along. This could be the key to solving the conundrum of my shift. The position would provide access to the information I needed. I was still in a daze as Gabriel continued.

"We will help you in any way we can"—he gestured between himself and the god in the corner—"but please know information on this magical connection is incredibly limited." He glanced again at Lord Arctos. "The gods and Compass Points only recently became aware of it."

"So, we need to find out what the magic is and why it exists?" I asked.

Lord Arctos bristled. "We have some idea of what it is."

Ambrose was scribbling furiously in his notebook. "Can you share?"

"Let's see how you do with the first piece of information Carter has for you."

The beast inside me tried to shake my tenuous hold. She didn't like that this seemed like a test, that we weren't receiving all the answers the god had. "Do you know if it's blood magic?"

The fae drew a clear line between elemental magic and blood magic. They considered their elements the pinnacle of magic, and anything else was a cheap replica. It was part of what had drawn me to blood magic—the idea that anyone could use it. I didn't know what the gods thought of it. Lord Arctos was the first I'd met.

The god studied me. He tilted his head, and I could easily imagine his bird form replicating the motion. "I don't know. Such distinctions don't occur to me. Magic simply is."

My shoulders relaxed slightly at that. At least this response made sense to me.

"Carter believes that it is blood magic," Gabriel added.

"Do you have any details of the connections?" Ambrose asked.

Gabriel nodded. “Lord Arctos and Carter tested the magic themselves.”

Ambrose sucked in a breath, and even I had to agree with his show of concern. Testing an unknown magic between a fae and a god was as risky as it got.

“Lord Arctos will explain the details when he deems it appropriate.” Gabriel pushed a book toward us. “This is a journal of two human girls, daughters of a governor of a small village hundreds of years ago. Not directly related, but Carter thought it explained blood magic’s ability to ... take control.”

Intent was tricky, I knew that, but this sounded worse. Ambrose took the journal, and I pushed back my beast’s snapping teeth at the presumption that he would read it first. Begrudgingly, I told myself it was fine. I had work at the tavern. Perhaps there was a way for me to collect the journal tonight when I was done.

“Anything else we need to know?” I asked, as I stood to leave.

Lord Arctos replied, “Not at the moment. I’ll tell you what I know tomorrow. Review this in the meantime.”

3

Ambrose

My scholarly instinct was to finish my notes about the project, but with each passing moment, Evelyn got further away. It was late afternoon, and in all likelihood, she was leaving for her work at the tavern now. We needed to talk. I stood to chase after her as she left Gabriel's office.

"Ambrose," Gabriel interrupted my progress. "A moment."

Lord Arctos had disappeared again. He must have shifted and flown from the office when Evelyn left. With just the two of us, Gabriel's small office felt cozy rather than cramped. I still wasn't at ease, but I sat. He was the head librarian, after all.

"Your father messaged to say he would stop by the library this afternoon."

I sat up straighter. Father hadn't said anything to me this morning. He couldn't have known about the meeting and potential promotion, could he?

I must have asked that last part aloud because Gabriel

responded. "No, he was unaware. He simply asked to meet with me, but he will know when he gets here. That's what I wanted to prepare you for."

My father had been Vesten historian before Carter. He'd retired, but it wasn't a secret that, since he had, he didn't like the direction the library's research was taking. That was where I came in. I was his second chance at the position. He'd trained me my entire life to do what he couldn't, to fix the path the library was on, to bring our research back to things that mattered—or at least what he thought mattered. History.

"The rest of the library may not know what you're researching, but the rumor mill will quickly pick up on the competition for the Vesten historian position."

"How?" I asked. If it had only been the four of us in that room, how would anyone else know?

Gabriel massaged his forehead. "I'm sure Lord Arctos is saying something too loudly in front of other researchers now. He enjoys the dramatics."

I held in a snort. First, I couldn't believe Gabriel spoke about the Vesten God in such a way. Second, I couldn't believe I tended to agree with him after our brief interactions. My ears heated as I thought about what Arctos had said about Evelyn.

Gabriel must have noticed. "I won't tell you he didn't mean offense by his questions, he probably did. The only thing I can say is that you passed his test just as both Evelyn and I knew you would."

"You can't know what she thought," I said.

Gabriel's smile was soft. "I recognized the exasperated shake of her head when Lord Arctos revealed his plan to her. It was the same one I gave him. Still, he proceeded."

I wasn't sure that made me feel better, but it reminded me I needed to find Evelyn. "Thanks for the heads up about my father. I have something to take care of before he arrives."

The head librarian gave me a smile that indicated he knew

precisely what that was, though I wasn't sure how. With the journal he'd given us in hand and my notebook tucked safely back in my pocket, I went in search of her.

My wolf perked up as we left the office. *This isn't a hunt*, I told the large gray animal pacing back and forth in my mind. He didn't seem to agree, but he let me carry on without much input.

I found Evelyn in the Great Room. She walked through an aisle of bookshelves, but her steps seemed slow, hesitant. I approached and was about to tap her shoulder when suddenly she turned, rounding on me.

"Yeep!" She squealed and jumped into the air. I must have truly startled her, because her gaze roamed my height and width unchecked. My wolf insisted she found us attractive. Up until this moment, I hadn't been so sure. The apples of her cheeks pinkened when she realized I'd noticed her perusal.

A smirk curled my lip. "Did you yeep at me again?"

"You should wear a bell."

My wolf preened. Honestly, I didn't try to sneak up on her. My connection with my wolf meant that I was always light on my feet. A brief thought flashed through my mind, that she might not know that. Since she didn't shift, I had no idea how much instruction she'd had about shifted forms. The Vesten were a secretive bunch when it came to our animals.

Her mumbled words drew me from my thoughts. "I needed to talk to you about this and the journal before I left for the day." She held up the paper I'd left on her desk.

"Are you going to continue work on your ... other project?" I turned quickly to glance at the windowsill by her study carrel.

She shrugged, following my gaze to the plants. "I started the experiment, so I must monitor the results." Something shifted as her focus returned to me. Her tone grew brisker as she continued. "Can you leave the journal on my desk when you're done for the day? I'll collect it tonight."

I nodded, and she continued. "I'll try to read your paper as I agreed, but it will be a lower priority to the journal."

With that, she nodded, effectively dismissing me. I held my ground, blocking her escape as she moved to walk by. We hadn't discussed anything we needed to. The problem was that I didn't know how to start.

I scratched the back of my neck. "I'm sorry for Lord Arctos's comments. I'm sorry Gabriel allowed them." It was wholly insufficient for what the god had put her through. Things were changing for half-fae in the courts, but that didn't mean some fae didn't hold the beliefs that Lord Arctos had spouted.

"Lord Arctos warned me." She shook her head. "Has he ever spoken into your mind? It was ... disconcerting."

Her look of defeat roused my anger anew. It reminded me of how she'd flinched with the god's first sentence on the subject of half-fae. I knew it wasn't the first time she'd heard such a thing. My insides twisted at the thought. "It doesn't matter. He still didn't need to do it. If he wanted to know how I felt about hierarchy in the fae courts, he didn't need to perpetuate baseless claims to do so."

She nodded, but I wasn't entirely sure she heard me. Her arms wrapped around herself in protection, as if she were attempting to keep everything inside secure. Evelyn was usually so sure of herself with me. She was quick to tell me I was wrong. Truth be told, I couldn't help but do the same to her when the opportunity presented itself. But mostly, I just wanted her to be safe. I wanted to work with her. We'd recently helped our friends break a blood magic spell on an inn. It had been the most challenging but most satisfying work I'd done in a long time, and I knew without a doubt that Evelyn was the reason why. She'd more than fascinated me when we first met, and every interaction since had only stoked my interest.

Words were tumbling from my mouth before I could stop

them. "I just wanted to say that I'm glad we're both working on this, together."

I winced, knowing that we weren't quite collaborating on this project. We were competing. Maybe she wouldn't notice...

"This isn't the same as with Luna's inn," Evelyn said.

Internally, my wolf was satisfied that her thoughts had gone to the same place mine had. Outwardly, I tilted my head in question. But mostly, I was glad Evelyn was annoyed enough with me to speak so directly. It was a stark contrast to how small she'd looked in Gabriel's office when Lord Arctos spoke of half-fae being less than.

"Yes, we worked well together, but that was when there was nothing to claim. I just wanted to help my friend's inn succeed."

I studied her thoroughly. Evelyn was never one to speak about what she wanted. I'd asked her goals and aims on multiple occasions, simply trying to get to know her better. She'd never shared them. Something about this moment made me wonder if she finally would.

"What do you want now?" My instinct said she wanted the position. She wanted to be Vesten historian. I hadn't even finished the thought when the words were out of her mouth.

"I want the Vesten historian position." Her eyes widened immediately at the admission. It looked like she had to physically stop herself from lifting her hand to cover her mouth.

I, too, was surprised she'd actually said it. Instead of being horrified, I was delighted. She'd told me something about herself. But the excitement only lasted for a second before the pieces slipped into place and I realized what this meant.

Of course she wanted the position. She had a chip on her shoulder the size of a small mountain. Not that it hadn't formed from the fae's constant dismissal of her as a half-fae. And not that she didn't deserve the Vesten historian position. If everything Gabriel said about the way Carter wanted to evolve the position was true, Evelyn stood as much of a chance of winning it as I did—maybe more.

My father would have thoughts on that. I sobered. "I see."

It was the wrong thing to say. Her gaze snapped back to mine and narrowed. I could have sworn a snarl escaped her lips before she spoke. "Did you just assume the position would go to you?"

"That's—"

"Ambrose!" Landon called.

I briefly closed my eyes, fighting my frustration at the interruption. My wolf whined in my mind, and I silently agreed with him. This had gone off track, but Tatyana and Landon were the last people Evelyn would want to speak to.

She made her escape, and this time, I let her slip by me. Landon and Tatyana didn't even acknowledge her when she passed them in the aisle.

"Ambrose, did you really have a project briefing with Lord Arctos?" Tatyana asked. "The library is buzzing about it."

I didn't care about library gossip, but at this point, all I could do was watch Evelyn walk away.

"I can't believe you're going to be Vesten historian," Landon added.

My hackles rose at the comment. It wasn't true. Not with the criteria Gabriel had shared. My feelings on the matter were complicated, and I didn't want to discuss them with these two. Regardless, I knew Landon's voice was too loud. Evelyn had absolutely heard it.

"You know they'd never put a half-fae in the position, no matter the changes at Compass Lake. It'd be unheard of..." Landon trailed off as he looked up and noticed Evelyn was still within earshot.

I met and held Evelyn's gaze across the room. She couldn't think that I believed this nonsense, could she? What had

Gabriel said in his office? She knew I didn't need to be tested. But how could he know that? I'd apologized to her for Lord Arctos's words, but had I clarified that I'd never thought that way about her? Not even for a second?

The moment extended between us. I opened my mouth to speak, but she clutched my paper to her chest and fled.

As if the day could get worse, Evelyn hadn't been gone for more than a few minutes when my father entered the Great Room. He didn't come to the library often, but as soon as Landon caught a glimpse of him entering through the large double doors, he stopped mid-sentence.

"We should get back to work," Tatyana said, but with little energy. She knew she didn't have enough time to escape without appearing rude.

I knew neither Landon nor Tatyana cared about getting back to a specific project as much as they cared not to be with me when my father approached. He had earned a reputation with even the newest researchers.

"Ambrose," Father called as he made his way to me. A cane preceded him as he walked. He slid it back and forth with each step to ensure nothing was in his way. His eyesight wasn't entirely gone, but it was severely impaired.

He paused upon reaching me and turned his head imperiously toward Tatyana and Landon. "Don't you two have work you should be doing, instead of gossiping?" He shook his head in distaste and dismissal.

"Yes, of course, Mr. Yarrow," Landon murmured, and the pair disappeared.

They most certainly weren't out of earshot when Father added, "Maybe if those two spent half as much time learning our history as they do spreading rumors, they might make something of themselves."

I cleared my throat. It was rude, but honestly, I was still upset with them about what they'd said regarding Evelyn and the historian position. I hadn't had a chance to correct them with my father's arrival. I would try to do so before I left for the day. The entire library needed to stop speaking carelessly about half-fae.

"And what about you, my boy? What do you have to say for yourself? Standing around here when I know you have work to do."

I clutched the journal tighter. I did need to start reading this, I just didn't think Father would care for its contents. "You're right, I have work to do. Did you need something before I begin?"

He tilted his head in consideration. "Good, good. It's good that the competition for Vesten historian isn't the first thing out of your mouth. It shows you're going to work hard even though you're guaranteed to win."

I stood up straighter. "That's not—"

He waved away my objection. "I know you'll win, given everything I've taught you. You know the history and you have the legacy for the position, but it doesn't serve to act like it's a done deal."

My nostrils flared as I responded. "Evelyn is the best blood magic researcher this library has ever seen. I don't in any way think it's a done deal."

Father waved his hand in another dismissal. "I just spoke with Gabriel—he knows the future of the Vesten Court is with its history, not with blood magic. I know he'll make the right choice."

I couldn't imagine what discussion my father thought he'd had. Everything about this conversation seemed pointless, but still, I continued. "It's not Gabriel's choice. It's the Vesten Point's, and he seems to prize the study of blood magic greatly."

"Yes, yes, that's because it's new and flashy. He's young. He'll learn soon enough the dangers. He'll realize that only history can truly be trusted to guide us."

My lips threatened to curve into a smile as I considered the book I held in my hand. It was over five hundred years old. There was no question that it *was* history. Yet Gabriel, Carter, and Lord Arctos thought it held information about blood magic that we needed to know. Maybe blood magic and history were more interconnected than we all thought. I wouldn't share that information with Father. It was classified, and at this point, his opinion was so entrenched that I wasn't sure facts would sway him.

He didn't notice my pause. "I'll let you get back to work. I'm on my way to pick up Sasha and Timothy. I just wanted to tell you I'm proud of you. This is everything we've been working for."

And like that, I deflated. There was no winning here. Father's words were just as rare as Evelyn telling me what she wanted. The only problem was that Father's approval was only given if I followed directly in his footsteps.

I didn't want to do everything precisely as he had. It wasn't that I didn't want the Vesten historian position. On the contrary, I did. I wanted the opportunity to shape our court's research. I wanted to make an impact, especially under the direction of the current Vesten Point. But doing everything that Father had done was like a suit two sizes too small; it didn't fit right. It was why I'd dipped my toe into the study of blood magic to begin with. Father still didn't know about that, though.

"I'll see you for the evening meal," he said.

I swallowed, unsure how to proceed with so many conflicting thoughts circling in my head. "Yes, Father," barely made it past my lips before he left. I had decisions to make, and the only thing that would help was thoroughly documenting the pros and cons. My notebook was already in my hand, a habit that required little thought, as I returned to my desk and started writing.

4

Evelyn

I loved my work at the library, but days like today reminded me why Parkview Tavern was my sanctuary. It was in the exact center of Sandrin, nestled into the largest stretch of greenery within the city. A small moat surrounded the old wooden building, making it feel like you were truly venturing away from the hustle and bustle to enjoy a drink.

The best part was, no one here cared if you were human or fae—or some blend of the two. No one cared what you did outside of the tavern. Seraphina, the owner, cultivated a community where none of that mattered.

As I slipped in the back door to start my shift, I smiled at the dull roar of noise emanating from the main room. It was strange to think that Seraphina had considered closing this place only a few months ago. Now, it was always packed with patrons.

My apron hung on the hook by the kitchen. I secured it and

took a deep breath, ridding myself of my day at the library. My beast had relaxed. She seemed to be back in her cage now that I had distance from so many stressors.

"Evelyn!" Seraphina jumped as she came around the corner from the kitchen, almost running into me. Hastily, she crumpled a note clutched in her hand.

When I attempted to flash her a smile, she put her hands on her hips. My internal pep talk must not have worked as well as I hoped.

Her shoulders fell in recognition of a trying day. "Ah, so it's like that with you, too."

"Everything alright?" I asked.

Her fist closed more tightly around the paper. "It's fine. Nothing I can't handle. What about you?"

"Maybe the same? I plan to forget about it for a while, but I'll let you know if I fail."

Seraphina smiled. "Acceptable. I'll check in before you leave. Luna said she'd be here for the evening meal, so maybe we can sneak out and stand in the moat or whatever she does to calm down."

I nodded. "Sounds like a plan."

Tucking the note in her pocket, Seraphina ran her fingers through her long blond ponytail. "Ready to get out there?"

"Are you?"

"Ready as I'll ever be." She ushered me down the hallway, which opened into the tavern's main room. It was an older building, with dark wood beams and paneling. The bar was to my right, and Seraphina slipped behind it as I walked past.

Mina, another server, was already on the floor. She smiled at me and nodded toward the left side of the room, which tended to be how we split the tables. A couple had just sat down by the window. I approached them to take their order and put everything else behind me.

Focusing on what advantages Ambrose might already have

in our competition would get me nowhere. Still, I couldn't quite rid myself of the scene in the library, when I'd blurted out that I wanted this position—to him, of all people.

What if I didn't get it? Ambrose would be unbearable. My skin felt too tight as I relived my most embarrassing moment of the day. The beast I'd thought calm awoke with my discomfort. *Deep breath in through my nose and back out through my nose.* It felt like my every spare thought was spent trying to control my shift.

Fortunately, this familiar routine demanded my attention. Unfortunately, I was an expert multitasker. My brain ran a mile a minute, so even as I took orders and delivered meals, I cycled through my troubles at the library. Luna and Vincent's arrival a few hours later was my only signal that time had passed.

"Two Solstice Sips?" Seraphina asked as they took seats at the bar.

I was collecting another order nearby and couldn't help but smile. "They're getting a little predictable, aren't they?"

Luna tucked one of her silver strands behind her ear. "I still love hearing Vincent order it. Please don't take that from me. He gets so excited—and a little pretentious—when requesting the drink he helped create."

Vincent's cheeks pinkened, but he smiled with nothing but adoration for Luna. "I live to make you smile with my slightly pretentious comments."

Seraphina mock-vomited from behind the bar, but her own smile was wide from their banter. They might have met through a tangled bargain, but their romance had bloomed like unchecked wildflowers anyway. Luna's head fell onto Vincent's shoulder, and his wind magic rustled her hair while his arm slipped around her waist. She deserved nothing less than the worship he and his magic continued to heap upon her.

"Deliver that order, Evelyn," Seraphina said. "Then Vincent

can cover for me a moment while we slip out. I don't think you've made it out of your funk."

I picked up the drinks and nodded. These females had done so much for me. I hated to ask them to listen to me whine, but they'd recently reminded me that friends wanted to know things about each other. I had promised to do better at sharing parts of my life, especially those at the library.

With a quick wave to Mina, I slipped out of the main room and down the hallway to the employee entrance. When I pushed open the door, Luna was already taking off her shoes and gesturing to Seraphina to do the same.

Seraphina's lip twitched into a smile even as she asked, "Is this necessary?"

"Very," Luna responded as she hopped into the moat. "You'll join me, right, Evelyn?"

I wasn't sure about the science behind standing in the water to relieve stress. It might help Luna because she was half-Norden, or water fae, but mostly, I thought she just enjoyed it. I shrugged and took off my boots, too.

Seraphina was doing the same when I hopped from the small ledge into the river surrounding the tavern. "Well, this is a fun new tradition for consulting on a bad day."

"What's up, Evelyn?" Luna asked. Her bright blue eyes were wide and inviting. She was one of the most selfless people I knew, besides Seraphina, although Seraphina did her best to hide her nature.

I sighed. "I guess I didn't let everything go as much as I'd hoped."

Seraphina chuckled. "I think you only took it out on the returned dishes, but..." She shrugged. "We'd love to hear if you want to talk."

"I was invited to work on a special project today."

"The one the Vesten God is here for?" Luna asked.

They already knew this part because Lord Arctos was a

guest at Luna's inn, so I nodded. "He and Gabriel only selected two researchers, and the work is well within my specialty. They said that whoever finds the answer they're looking for will be promoted to Vesten historian."

Luna was smiling, like she assumed I already had the promotion.

Seraphina was more cautious. "Who is the other researcher?"

Even Luna's face fell when she realized what Seraphina was asking.

"Ambrose Yarrow."

Luna's lips pressed into a thin line. "Wasn't his father big in the library, too?"

Ambrose was one of Vincent's closest friends. I wasn't surprised she knew a little about his family. I nodded. "The current Vesten Point, Carter, was the last one to hold the Vesten historian position. He retired to take on court leadership, but Ambrose's father was the historian before that."

"But that doesn't matter if you do the research better, right?" Luna asked.

Seraphina patted Luna's shoulder like she didn't want to spoil her view of the world. Luna scowled and swatted at her. "Lord Arctos seems fair. He wouldn't make it a competition if it weren't one."

"I do think Lord Arctos and Gabriel have the best intentions," I said.

"You want to win, right?" Seraphina asked.

Somehow, she always found the right question. Now that I'd admitted as much to my rival, I should be able to admit it to my closest friends. Still, I hesitated. Desire was like wisps of smoke, unattainable and better left to blow away.

Seraphina saw more than I realized as she rephrased. "This position would help with your sh—"

"Yes." I winced, taking the metaphorical olive branch she

handed me. This might not have been the whole truth, but it was relevant. I didn't like discussing my animal. Like maybe if I never spoke of it, then it wouldn't exist. Luna and Seraphina saw right through that. I could tell by the narrowing of Seraphina's eyes that she already knew what I planned to do if I got the position.

"Have you told your mom?" she asked.

I sighed but shook my head. "I just found out this afternoon. I don't want to hurt her, but when it comes to questions about my father, I can't seem to help it." I glanced around. No one was with us. The only noise was the gurgle of the river flowing and the soft sounds of the city on the other side of the park. "My shift is getting more insistent. I need to learn more about it. It ... it's unmanageable."

Luna pursed her lips. "I know Vesten are cagey about their shifts, but what about talking to someone like Gabriel? He seems approachable."

"No," I said without hesitation. "Yes, I need to learn how to shift, if possible, but my problem is also about what I shift into. It ... well, the animal shouldn't exist."

My voice had dropped to a whisper. Since my beast was in total control of my shifts, neither of them had seen her. I couldn't bring myself to say the animal's name, but it was enough to know she shouldn't be real. She was nothing more than a bedtime story that both fae and humans told their children.

I sighed, circling back to why Seraphina mentioned my mom. The Vesten shift was hereditary. My unfathomable form was just another thing that was my father's fault. And given the restrictions of Vesten society, he was also the only one who could explain it to me. If I was right and he'd left us rather than something bad happening to him, the Vesten historian position would be my key to finding him.

Unfortunately, finding him alive and well would probably break Mom's heart.

"You know we'll always tell you to do what you need to for yourself," Seraphina said. "Your mom will understand, though."

The worst part was that she was right. Mom would understand; she'd even encourage me. I just felt guilty that I'd be searching for a father who'd abandoned us. I'd be searching for a way to crush Mom's dreams. It would be different if he had only abandoned me, but he had left Mom, too. She didn't speak about it often, but I could tell it wasn't a pain easily forgotten. Months after he'd left, we'd eventually moved from a small village in the north to Sandrin. It was as if Mom forced herself to take steps forward.

"What if your mom is right and you can't find him?" Seraphina asked.

I folded my arms over my chest. "It's a possibility, I guess. I think it's unlikely."

Seraphina must have seen my resolve. She nodded and let it drop.

"What about Ambrose?" Luna asked. "You two worked so well together. Now you're, what? Competing?"

I shrugged. Confronting these emotions had drained me, but at least my beast behaved with Luna and Seraphina. "I assume so. Though he doesn't see it that way. He thinks the position is already his."

Luna opened her mouth like she'd respond, but Seraphina elbowed her, and she closed it.

"What? He does. His friends were already joking about it when I left today."

They shared a glance and nodded.

I put my hands on my hips again. "Yes, working with him on Luna's inn was ... not terrible. But this is different. Not only because I want the position for my own reasons"—I swallowed around the partial admission—"but also because the position should not go to a fae who expects to have it handed to him."

Luna looked like she'd interrupt again, but Seraphina's hand slipped to her wrist and squeezed.

"I may not have the *Vesten* qualifications on history, but I do have qualifications. Gabriel took a chance on me as a half-fae, and I haven't let him down. I know I can do this."

I wanted so badly to keep going, to add *and how amazing would it be for the Vesten Court to have a half-fae in such an important position? It will only help them to understand that we're not less than them.* The words just wouldn't come out. Even with my closest friends, with females who were also half-fae struggling to find their place between human and fae society, I couldn't bring myself to voice the want.

My breaths were heavy. Luna stepped forward, placing her hands on my shoulders. "We're on your side. Always." She glanced at Seraphina and added, "Maybe let Ambrose speak for himself, but do what you need to do to achieve your goals."

A long exhale escaped my lips as they both invaded my space and hugged me. Some part of me wanted to cry over the unconditional support. Another part of me wanted to rage about how unfair it was that the fae courts didn't see these females as perfect just the way they were.

WE RETURNED to the busy tavern, and my heart was a little lighter. I wished I could speak as freely and confidently as Luna and Seraphina. Their words made all my concerns seem a little less bad—at least for the moment.

I hung my apron back on the hook and prepared to leave. As I perused the tables a final time, I stopped on a middle-aged brunette who hadn't been there before I went outside. She was alone with a book propped against the table, unaware as I approached.

"Mom, what are you doing here?"

Her bright green eyes blinked up at me. They were one of our few features that didn't match. My eyes were dark brown, almost black like my hair.

Mom took her time pulling herself from whatever fantastical story she read. I got my love of books from her. She'd seldom been without one when I was a child. While her taste veered toward the fictitious and the happily-ever-after, as I grew older, mine gravitated toward history and fact.

Her button nose twitched as she took in the scent of stew at the table next to her. Then her bow-shaped lips curved into a smile. "Hi, honey. I thought we could eat our evening meal here when you finished working."

"Sure. I just finished. Let me put in our order and tell Mina we're staying."

Once the task was complete, I returned to the table with Mom. "How was your day?"

She set the book aside and gave me her full attention, which she was almost religious about. We had a meal together whenever possible, and no distractions were accepted. "Oh, fine. A lot of visitors from Long Night are still in town. So we had a lot of customers browsing the book shop."

The recent winter solstice holiday had been the busiest in Sandrin in my lifetime. Until recently, the continent had been plagued by a mist that left those caught within suspended in a sleeplike trance. Now that the fae court leaders had removed the plague and restored those affected to their rightful state, the world seemed much more populated.

Mom bit the inside of her lip. "Not the visitor I guess I'm looking for, but..." She shrugged and trailed off. It was as if she handed me the conversation on a silver platter.

When I was younger, I wanted to believe Mom's story about

my father, but eventually, I'd decided to face facts: he'd left us, and he wasn't coming back. The need to shift rippled beneath my skin. While I still didn't particularly want to find him, my beast made things complicated. Plus, it would put to rest once and for all Mom's ludicrous belief that he was coming back.

"Mom."

She waved me off. "I don't need a lecture tonight, honey. I know what you think about my hope."

I sat up straighter in my chair. "Mom, I need to tell you something."

"What is it?"

"I am competing for a promotion at work."

"A promotion! Oh, sweetie, that's incredible. You haven't even been there that long. Congratulations."

I ran my hand over my braid, suddenly feeling like Ambrose with how he always made his own hair untidy when he was uncomfortable. Why would I think of Ambrose now, of all times? I guessed he was my competition. I pushed the stray thought away and focused on Mom.

"Remember how we used to talk about moving to Compass Lake?"

It was a village nestled in the mountains. The very heart of fae politics, and the one place Mom and I had never belonged. I think that was why she'd suggested it. She had wanted so desperately for me to find peace with my fae side, maybe even more than she wanted my father to return.

She smiled a little sadly. "I remember. Your father always talked about the lake's beauty. But what does that have to do with the promotion?"

"The position is Vesten historian. The historian works very closely with the Vesten Point, so those in the position can choose to live in Sandrin or Compass Lake Village."

Mom looked thoughtful. "I would love to live there. But would you?"

She knew me too well, seeing things I thought no one did. Maybe I was only fooling myself that I hid them in the first place.

"I think I could do some good there." I paused and pressed forward with the subject I needed to broach. "At the very least, it would give me access to the Vesten Court records."

Mom's face fell.

"It would give me access to find my father once and for all."

She folded her arms over her chest. "Is that the only reason you want the promotion? To prove me wrong? To tell me I've been a fool all these years for waiting for him?"

"What? No. Mom. I need answers about my..." Something sizzled beneath my skin, and I cut myself off to focus on my deep breathing exercise.

Mom pressed, "Your shift?"

I nodded through an inhale but also hid a wince. Like with Luna and Seraphina, I only told Mom half of the story. For her, it was the more relevant part—the part with an opportunity to cause her pain, but still...

Why had I been able to spout my wants so freely to Ambrose this afternoon?

Mom worried her lip. "I'm sorry, I don't know what his animal was. That sounds silly, doesn't it? He just always seemed so private about his shift. I never watched him do it."

It wasn't much to go on, but perhaps my father was extra secretive about his shift because his animal form was unusual. I wouldn't know until I talked to him about it. Some part of me felt bad that I required my father for this. Mom had done everything she could for me. She'd loved me unconditionally, had been there for me through the human changes and the Vesten even though, as a human herself, she did not know the Vesten ways. I never wanted her to feel like she hadn't met my needs. She'd never failed me. It was always him who had.

"It's alright, Mom." I downplayed the animal that pushed to

the forefront with my emotions. "I'm managing. But I'd like to worry about it less. I think he could answer some of those questions for me."

"What makes you think you can find him? When he hasn't been able to find us?"

I sighed. It seemed too harsh to remind her that I didn't think he was looking for us. Mom and I would disagree on that fact until we heard it from the male's mouth. "The Vesten historian is responsible for the court record keeping. At the very least, there is an annual census."

She gave me a searching look as our food was delivered.

"Thanks, Mina," I said.

"You two need anything else?"

I shook my head. "This looks great."

As Mina walked away, Mom reached for me, placing her hand over mine. "If you're sure this is what you want, you don't have to worry about me. I will be fine with whatever you learn. You've never been one to give up on a question that was hard to answer. This is no different. I have no doubt you'll get the promotion."

With a quick squeeze, she removed her hand, and I dipped a chunk of homemade bread into the vegetable stew while it cooled. "Thanks, Mom." I had never doubted her support. It was the hope lingering in her eyes that worried me.

"Now," she said, cutting into her meat pie and watching the steam escape. "Who are you competing against for the promotion? Is it that handsome Ambrose boy? Tell me everything."

I took a bite of the stew-soaked bread and raised an eyebrow at Mom.

"What? We're not ignoring facts, are we? We can beat him while also acknowledging that his appearance is quite appealing."

I rolled my eyes. "Yes, Mom, of course it's Ambrose. He's the only one in the library who stands a chance." I said it with a confidence I wasn't sure I felt, leaving off what I'd discussed with Seraphina and Luna about Ambrose's father. I didn't want to hear Mom's well-intentioned platitudes.

Tonight, I wanted to imagine that I could find the information Lord Arctos required before Ambrose did. I wanted to imagine that my unique skill set and thorough understanding of blood magic would help solve the god's problem. I wanted to imagine that I'd be awarded the promotion because of my accomplishments, regardless of who my competition was.

5

Ambrose

Of course she was here. I had rearranged my morning to get to the library early, and it still wasn't early enough. Evelyn was hunched over a book—the journal, which I'd left on her desk as requested—aggressively taking notes about what she read. Just once, I wished I could arrive before her and find out where the chair for the carrel across from hers went. My usual seat on the other side of the room mocked me as I strode to it.

I still couldn't fathom what we'd heard yesterday, and couldn't wait for Lord Arctos's explanation. The Vesten God and Vesten Point had tested an unknown blood magic connection between themselves. It was reckless—the epitome of everything Father feared. It reminded me of ... I glanced across the room at Evelyn. Well, it reminded me of someone else I knew. Evelyn's research had always part fascinated and part terrified me.

Most days, I wasn't sure if it was her courage or my caution that was more troublesome.

Evelyn had been a mystery I wanted to unravel from the first moment I met her. I wanted to know what she loved, what she hated, why she spent so much time on blood magic, and what made her so good at it.

We'd first met when Gabriel sent me to the Records Office, where the human officials of Sandrin kept their history. We'd needed to cross-reference some of our dates with theirs. The problem was that no one in the Records Office cared about fae records. I had approached the reception desk with little hope. The female sitting there stared at me, pre-annoyed by my arrival. I would have gone to anyone else, but she was the only one there, as if she'd drawn the short straw.

Not only had she been able to help me, she'd been able to tell me which of the human record books I would need to cross-reference with my fae ones. The organization was different. It was the way she described the human and the fae books that made me realize she didn't consider herself a part of either group. My wolf had discreetly sniffed in an attempt to determine what kind of fae she was.

Apparently, I wasn't as discreet as I thought. She reprimanded me for my presumption, but no lessons were learned on my part, as she also gave me the information I sought. She was half-Vesten. While she showed me the books I needed, she said I needed to tell her about myself, since I'd been so rude as to try and smell her magic. I was so intrigued with her I didn't mind sharing. My work at the library had recently changed, so I told her about my research on blood magic. It was brand new, and I was still terrified of it. The first career decision I had made without my father's approval, although I didn't share that part; it was too personal. Instead, I told her the Vesten Point prized information on blood magic, and very little of it was available. I could prove myself invaluable if I made progress in this area. She didn't stop me as I pointed out that the only other researcher with published work on the topic wasn't associated with any of the fae courts. They published everything independently.

Only then did I notice she had stopped in place. I turned to check on her, and her cheeks were pink. She tilted her head as if trying to solve a puzzle, then she surprised me completely when she whispered, "You can't be Ambrose Yarrow."

My mind couldn't work fast enough to keep up with how she had arrived at my identity. Then she introduced herself. Evelyn Knowles. She was the independent researcher—E. Knowles.

When I realized who she was, the work she did outside of the Sandrin Records Office, I'd asked her why she worked here. Immediately, I'd known I said the wrong thing. She had pointed to the books I needed, and then she was gone.

Still, I had mentioned her to Gabriel that afternoon at the library. He'd needed to know there was a brilliant magic researcher stuck in the Records Office. We hadn't spoken about it again, but Evelyn had started at the library a week later.

Evelyn and I had never made it past that first impression, though.

I shook myself from the memory and changed course, walking toward her.

She didn't acknowledge me, even when I arrived at her desk. I cleared my throat.

"Oh!" Her hand went to her chest as she jumped in her seat. "Ambrose. You scared me."

My wolf preened. I tried to disguise my smirk with a frown. "Sorry. I thought I'd check when you wanted to hunt down Lord Arctos for the information he promised. Have you finished with the journal?"

I glanced at the plants she'd experimented with yesterday. A rose, and ... was that a morning glory? They didn't usually do well together in a garden. Evelyn had told Gabriel about them a few weeks ago. She'd mentioned that she'd planted them beside each other in her own garden. The roses had never bloomed; the morning glories strangled them out. What could Evelyn be testing with them both in the same pot?

I'd been staring too long at the plants, so I shifted my focus to Evelyn. Her eyes narrowed; clearly, she'd noticed my attention on her experiment. She thought me too critical of her tests, I knew.

"Now works for me," she said.

Her tone was polite, but it felt closed off. I hated that this project set us against each other. No one had ever challenged my hypotheses or conclusions as much as she did. Well, my father did, but his approach was to tell me what I should be doing, not to ideate with me. Evelyn seemed genuinely interested in brainstorming together—when she wasn't angry with me.

Unfortunately for Evelyn, competing against her would only motivate me to strive for further improvement. A motivation based solely on the fact that I didn't want to seem like an idiot to her.

The defiant expression on her face yesterday made my wolf want to howl. *I want the Vesten historian position.* She had said it so boldly, so proudly. I wanted that kind of conviction. I wondered how few people she showed hers to.

"Should we try Gabriel's office?" she prodded as she stood, reminding me we were supposed to be searching for Lord Arctos.

"Yes, good idea."

We began to walk together toward the Great Room's large double doors. I grasped for something, anything, to fill the silence. "Anything of note in your readthrough?"

She hesitated. Her brow furrowed as if she were at war with herself. I knew the struggle. The desire to discuss what I'd found was at odds with the fact that we were theoretically competing on the outcome of this research. I would tell her about my findings anyway. They would never sway her conclusions. If anything, she would reread with my interpretation in mind, probably to try to prove me wrong. My wolf sighed, telling me that I sounded pathetic. While true, I didn't care; I just wanted to discuss the ideas with her.

"It's not like I haven't read it myself," I pressed.

She crossed her arms over her chest as we made it to the door. Just when I thought she wouldn't indulge the desire, she spoke. "These two human sisters practiced blood magic ... recklessly, as you would say."

I paused with my hand on the doorknob. "Yes, but I think almost all practice of blood magic is reckless."

She raised a brow at the admission. I was a little surprised by it myself. It was complicated to separate my views of blood magic from my father's experience. Evelyn's experience with blood magic was utterly different, though. I wanted to know more about it. Before I could ask, her expression soured. Something about what she wanted to say next clearly made her very uncomfortable.

"What is it?" I asked. I'd pulled the door open, but we both stood still.

Her nose twitched again, like she was trying to inhale deeply to calm herself. Now I really wanted to know what she thought.

"When the sisters turn into veil cats..." She paused and glanced at me. Her sharp features were guarded, like she dared me to object, but there was curiosity there, too.

"I read it, Evelyn. I'm also familiar with the animals. They shepherd spirits to the afterlife."

She scanned the surrounding space, as if checking to see who else could hear us. "You are?"

"I previously considered them only a children's story. I

know others believed they were extinct, but I think our illustrious leader would contest both facts."

She looked confused.

"The Vesten Point, he's a veil cat shifter," I elaborated.

I wasn't sure she was breathing.

"How do you know that?" she asked.

Now she had me questioning it. There was very little that Evelyn didn't know. I couldn't believe she was unaware of this. Although I did get the sense that, as a half-fae, she didn't pay much attention to court politics.

"He took the form regularly when waking those impacted by the sleeping plague." I scratched the back of my neck. "He didn't make a formal announcement, but it's out there."

She cleared her throat. "Not only do the sisters shift into veil cats in the journal. One of them forms a blood magic bond ... unintentionally."

That was the most terrifying part of the book to me. "Yeah, I caught that, too."

Evelyn ran her hand down the length of her braid. "I knew intent could ... twist. It hadn't occurred to me that intent didn't have to be acknowledged by the wielder."

Before I could respond, the black bird—who was becoming a little too familiar—flew through the door I held open and landed on Evelyn's shoulder.

"*Are you two ready to hear the details of mine and Carter's test?*"

Evelyn was right; I didn't care for the way the Vesten God's voice slid into my mind. It wasn't something I would ever get used to.

"We were on our way to look for you," she said.

"*Yes.*" He glanced at where we stood in the middle of the doorway. "*It looks like it.*"

Heat rose to the tips of my ears, but before either of us could say more, Lord Arctos flew back toward Evelyn's desk, and we had no choice but to follow. I pulled my notebook and pencil from my pocket as we walked.

Lord Arctos spoke from his perch on the study carrel as soon as we arrived. "*Carter and I confirmed that the connection is there, and that it works.*"

"You told us that," Evelyn replied as she retook her seat. The second chair was still missing, so I stood.

"*I'm just warming up. Give me a moment.*"

I was in awe of their rapport. She spoke to him the same way she talked to me, but through her annoyance with the god's antics, I detected a bit of fondness for him. That part was missing in our relationship.

"*We suspected the connection but needed to confirm it.*"

"So, you're saying this magical connection between the Compass Points and gods is similar to that of the human woman in this journal? That you didn't wield blood magic specifically to create it? It just happened?" I was still having a hard time believing this.

Lord Arctos ignored my question and kept speaking into our minds. "*The ceremony required us to be in a place of great magic, with an object of significance. We had to share a drop of blood each and open ourselves to each other. I believe you call this intent.*" He nodded to Evelyn.

"You shouldn't ignore Ambrose's question," Evelyn said. "It's important."

Lord Arctos ruffled his feathers. "*Some of the gods may have known. I did not. But yes, that is why we wanted you to understand that this magic seems able to understand intent even if it's not specifically voiced.*"

Well, that was terrifying. I'd already been scared of the magic when I thought it was able to twist spoken intent, not conjure intent from the wielder's thoughts.

"What happened when you did the ceremony?" I asked.

"Carter shared his power with me. I shifted into his veil cat form and called his fire."

Evelyn froze at the mention of the veil cat—like maybe she could have ignored what I had said about the Vesten Point, but she couldn't ignore the god of our court stating it as a fact. She seemed to collect herself to ask, "Anything else?"

The bird's black eyes narrowed on her. "*Yes, but you haven't earned it yet. Let me know when you have some ideas on how to break this connection.*"

With that, he flew away.

6

Evelyn

Ambrose had disappeared along with Lord Arctos, so I reread the journal. The animal—*the veil cat*—inside me perked up each time I read about veil cat shifters. I was still in shock over my conversation about them with Ambrose. Lord Arctos's casual mention of the Vesten Point's form had been a bridge too far.

Until reading the journal, I had been among the group who believed the veil cats were little more than a children's story. In my defense, animals that shepherd the spirits of the dead across realms seemed a little far-fetched, even if the animal in my head happened to be one of them.

The Vesten Point was a veil cat shifter, too.

How had I missed that piece of information?

Luna and Seraphina always teased me about not following popular culture. I guessed this was my lesson.

What did it mean? If the animals were hereditary, was I related to the Vesten Point?

Luna's comment that I should talk to Gabriel was looking less and less foolish with this new information. I dismissed the idea again. If I told Gabriel, he would tell Carter, and I could not risk looking like an idiot in front of the male who would decide my fate with the Vesten historian position. I didn't even know how to control my shift, for gods' sakes. As an adult Vesten, it was embarrassing.

I flipped the page in the journal more aggressively than intended. What was I looking for? Lord Arctos treating this whole thing like a game wasn't helping. There was so much to learn from these pages detailing the sisters' blood magic experiments. Still, other than the revelation we'd made with Lord Arctos, I wasn't sure this text would help hypothesize how to break the connection between a Compass Point and a god. It talked only of how connections were formed without explicitly spoken intent, not how to unform them.

The paper Ambrose had asked me to read yesterday was still on my desk. I had read it once last night. Unfortunately, it was worth another read. If Ambrose's hypothesis was correct, if an anchor held part of the magic, destroying the anchor could destroy the magic. Lord Arctos had referenced an "object of importance" in the test he'd done with Carter, but was that object also part of the original connection being forged? I pulled Ambrose's paper toward me to read it once more. It was something to go on, at least.

Hours later, I startled as a wrapped sandwich fell onto the corner of my desk. Blinking, I glanced up at Ambrose, his sleeves rolled back and forearms on display as he leaned over my carrel. "That bell, we discussed?"

The way his lip twitched felt ... playful. A shiver ran down my spine.

I wasn't sure what to make of that, so I picked up the rolled sandwich and sniffed. "What's this?"

"A veggie sandwich. It's past time for an evening meal. I figured you were hungry." He held a second one in his hand.

Too many thoughts crossed my mind at once. How did he know what I liked on my sandwich? Did he want to ... eat together?

His words were factual, like so much of what Ambrose said to me, but I could sense something beneath them. I tilted my head, unsure if I was evaluating him or the food.

Mom had been correct. Ambrose was handsome, in a completely unexpected way. While he had all the usual traits of a researcher, never without his vest or a notepad, the rest of him didn't fit the stereotype. He followed rules—he didn't like risk—but there was some small sliver of him that was *wild*. It was increasingly visible in the gold of his irises. I guessed that wasn't so odd for a Vesten. It was likely the animal beneath the surface.

He was my competition, though, no matter how intriguing I found him. Sharing a meal would be a mistake. He'd dismissed my stupid slip about wanting the position yesterday. Hadn't he? His friends had all but shouted that a half-fae would never be the Vesten historian.

Luna and Seraphina's words crossed my mind. *Maybe let Ambrose speak for himself.* All he had said in response to my slip was, "I see." His friends had said stupid things, but that wasn't new. It was almost common. At the very least, if I asked him to sit, I could confirm my understanding of anchors.

Perhaps a meal together wouldn't be so bad.

He couldn't very well stand there, leaning over the carrel while I ate. Though I was convinced I would regret this at some point, I stood and walked around the corner to the closet.

"Evelyn ... did I—"

I pulled out the hidden chair and brought it to Ambrose.

"What is this?"

It occurred to me then that I hadn't confirmed his amiability to my idea before making this gesture. "Would you like to sit?" I pointed to the sandwiches. "And eat?"

My voice sounded less certain than usual, and my second skin was twitching to be free. Discomfort coated my every move, but I was far too committed to back out.

Maybe he would say no.

He arched a brow, then took a seat quickly, like maybe he feared I'd snatch it away. Instead of sliding it into place in the carrel across from mine, he pulled it right up to the corner of my desk. "I've been looking for this chair."

I cleared my throat. "You can never tell where the maid is going to stash it."

He glanced up, studying me. "Indeed."

His lip twitched, and I knew he didn't believe me, but there was nothing I could do about that now. I needed to know how we were both meant to use my desk as a table. Ambrose regarded me and my empty chair, and I knew I must look ridiculous. But he was so tall, so broad, I wasn't sure there was space for us both crowded around my favorite study carrel.

My attention drifted to the flowers in the pot as I took a seat. I wasn't sure their bind had worked yet, but they looked good together. While there was still a chance for the morning glory to dominate the pot, I thought this was promising—an unlikely pair, growing together, sharing too small a space. The metaphor felt too apt, but I decided Ambrose and I could do the same—at least for the duration of this meal.

"Thank you," I said as I picked up the sandwich again.

He only grunted as he unwrapped his own and took a large bite.

"What do you think of the information Lord Arctos shared?"

He chewed, but his brow furrowed. I guessed I already knew his answer. He thought the test was reckless. When he swallowed and opened his mouth to respond, I asked a different question.

"What about the object of significance he mentioned? Do you think it's an anchor?"

"It's possible, but we'd need more information about the object. We know nothing about the genesis of the connection—that's when anchors are formed." He paused, as if realizing what my question meant. "You read my paper?"

I cleared my throat. "You asked me to."

He smiled briefly, then pressed his lips into a thin line. His thoughts must have grown more serious. Maybe he didn't want to share information that he thought gave him an advantage. "Have you considered the origin of the magic?"

Fae history might not have been my expertise, but there was only one occasion that had brought together all four gods and all four Compass Points. "It had to be the creation of the fae, right?"

"I think so, too. I wish Lord Arctos would tell us. Clearly, he knows more than he's sharing." He looked toward the window, like he was thinking about something else. "I just can't believe anyone would so recklessly apply blood magic to ... fae and gods. That's beyond even plants."

The words landed like a backhanded compliment. "All blood magic is dangerous."

His lips pressed into a thin line, as if he wished to do anything but continue this conversation. He still had half a sandwich left. This whole meal had been his idea. Now it just felt awkward and uncomfortable.

Unsure how to proceed, I unwrapped my sandwich. As I peeled back the paper, I caught my finger, slicing it. "Ouch."

Ambrose set down his partial sandwich and reached for me. "Let me help with—"

Blood was already welling in the small slice across my

pointer finger. His large hand engulfed mine as the first drop fell. He quickly wrapped a napkin around the cut.

Every instinct told me to yank my hand back. I could take care of myself. Why was Ambrose doing this? But something about the way his hand fully surrounded mine was … nice.

I liked it. It almost silenced the near-constant press of my veil cat against my skin.

It had been a long time since someone held my hand like this. Since my shift started, I'd been too scared to let anyone in. The last man who'd tried to touch me, even with my consent, set my veil cat off in a way that had me fleeing the restaurant and never looking back. I hadn't tried to date again.

This was different. A warmth spread through me as Ambrose pressed the napkin to the cut.

Not that this was a date.

I sucked in a breath. "Thank you."

Our gazes locked. My heart was galloping like a herd of horses breaking loose their ties. This was worse than the cut itself. I might not have known what kind of shifter he was, but I knew he had an animal form. His elevated senses would ensure he could hear my body's overreaction to him.

Could he hear my rapid heartbeat? My pulse pounding? Should I pull my hand back?

"If only all our interactions were this easy," he said, interrupting my spiral of panic.

Easy? This interaction had me on the brink of hyperventilating and he still hadn't let go of my hand. Did I want him to?

As he held the napkin to the cut, a purr in the back of my mind said no.

I grasped for reason. "What do you mean?" My brain spun. I wanted to talk about magic, not the complexities of every conversation the two of us had. His warmth was distracting. How could one produce so much heat in this drafty library?

"Just that neither of us has stormed off yet. Maybe we should have meals together more often," he said.

My heart stopped. That sounded like...

The only acknowledgment that he heard the implication, too, was the pink at the tips of his ears and his resolute glance out the window—unable to make eye contact. He spoke again, and it was so far from the same topic that I wasn't sure what to make of it. "There is something inherently unstructured in blood magic ... like—"

Finally, he dropped my hand, and I felt its absence immediately. That warmth from his touch consolidated in my fingertip, where blood continued to well beneath the napkin. It felt like something in me was almost reaching for him.

I found myself waiting for the end of the sentence. I thought I knew where he was going. There was no time I felt more untethered from the daily flow of my life than when I shifted. Ambrose flushed, and I realized he wouldn't complete his thought.

"What? I'm interested in the comparison." I gestured for him to continue.

His ears pinkened again with his further discomfort.

"What is it?" I asked.

He cleared his throat. "I was going to compare the lack of structure to that of shifting. Apologies, I know that's not..."

I almost wanted to let him continue down this uncomfortable path. He sounded like I had when I'd brought forth the chair. I didn't know why Vesten were so hesitant to talk about their shifts, but I had never spoken to other Vesten about it. I was desperate for more perspective.

"Please, continue with whatever part you're comfortable sharing. I'm not even fully Vesten, so you're not offending my sense of propriety by discussing it."

This made him look even more scandalized, but something

in my face also must have convinced him to continue. "My animal and I are inherently one. He's always with me, but I feel things so much more intensely in the ... form. My actions can be instinctive instead of thoroughly considered. Like when I'm running, sometimes I don't know where I'm headed until I arrive."

He picked up his sandwich like he needed something to distract himself. "Anyway. What was I saying? Concerning blood magic, it seems similar—the instinctual aspect."

While I seemed to instinctively understand blood magic, that was the furthest from my experience with my shift. Perhaps that was what made my shift so disconcerting. I might have liked pushing boundaries or finding unique ways to learn, but I didn't consider myself reckless. Things had to follow a logical path in my mind. That hadn't been the case so far with my shift. She was uncontrollable.

I wiggled uncomfortably in my seat just thinking about it. How much longer until I shifted again? With how on edge I was, I'd assumed it would happen last night, but it hadn't. If only there were a way to choose when it occurred. Ambrose said he and his shift were one? I wasn't sure my veil cat and I could ever see eye to eye long enough to achieve that.

"Thank you for sharing," I said as a more comfortable silence than I'd anticipated hung between us.

"Of course. Did your cut stop bleeding?"

I glanced down. "It looks like it."

He was wiping at something on his own finger. "What is it?" I reached for his hand as he had mine. There was a cut there. It looked like... "Oh my gods, did I bleed on you?"

His eyes were wide when I looked up. Then I realized how close I was to him. I'd entered his space, our faces so near now that we almost shared breaths. I cleared my throat and leaned back.

He took a moment to compose himself. "I ... I'm not sure." He glanced back at his hand. "It looks like my cut from this morning reopened, but I can't say for sure if any of your blood touched me."

He picked up another napkin and pressed it against his finger. Had we just bled on each other? A single drop of blood was enough to enact blood magic. An inappropriate giggle bubbled up my throat. His brow furrowed while he tended his wound.

"How incredibly foolish for two blood magic researchers to be so careless with their blood," I said. The journal evidenced how easily the magic could unfold, even without spoken intent.

He looked stricken. We both froze—and it was almost as if we both waited for *something* to happen.

"I don't feel anything," he said into the silence.

"Of course not." I wiped the concern away with an authority I wasn't sure I felt. "As you would usually point out, we should be more cautious in the future."

His brow furrowed again, deep in thought.

In my panic, I returned to inspecting the flowers. I had asked him to sit. Maybe to ask about anchors, maybe just for a moment of peace. He was right, we had mostly made it through this meal intact. The morning glory and rose looked peaceful together, too. Could Ambrose and I co-exist like they did? Could we grow together when we usually struggled to share space? It might be nice.

One meal discussing concepts of blood magic didn't make us friends. I sat up straighter, putting more distance between myself and Ambrose. The cut on my finger pulsed as if in objection.

Is this blood magic taking root?

No. It was an inconvenient admission, but I acknowledged I was always a little bit aware of Ambrose. A huff escaped from my lips. I laughed a little at how I'd worked myself up. This wasn't blood magic. It was a crush. One I couldn't abide.

There was still only one historian position. That was a fact, no matter how nice the idea of us growing together, like my plant experiment, sounded.

7

Evelyn

My logic might not have made sense to some people, but it made perfect sense to me. I worked outside convention, I tested blood magic with living things, but it was all carefully planned and well within my control. The alternative was too messy.

The alternative was all I felt in my veil cat form.

Ambrose had called it *instinctual.* To me, it was an incomplete analysis. It was running in any direction without a clear destination. It was like the cat wanted to escape the city, escape anything that might tether us to this continent.

I hated it.

This, however, was how I found myself on the northern side of Sandrin Bay, tearing through the woods, restless and unaware of what I sought, before sunrise the following morning.

As the pads of my paws pressed against the dirt and the tree trunks and low bushes flew by, my heart raced. It beat with the excitement of exploring something new—something undiscovered.

I didn't know what led me, and that might have been the worst sin of this form. As all four of my legs propelled me forward, my mind seemed intent on conjuring images of a certain researcher and his vest and his stupid notebook.

What was that about?

He had been on my mind since we'd separated last night. It probably had to do with the confusing mix of emotions he evoked. When he wasn't calling my research dangerous, conversations with him were the most stimulating I'd ever had.

Letting him tend my cut had been a mistake.

That tiny, barely there scab on my finger throbbed like it was a broken bone. The feeling had worked its way into my chest. A constant pulse that had woken me in the early morning hours and finally—finally—sent me curling in on myself and dropping to all fours in my veil cat form.

Again, I asked—what was that about?

Some might inquire, *Evelyn, isn't your shifter form inherently you? Can't you control it?*

I didn't know. Maybe? It wasn't as if I'd taken How to Shift 101. I'd had precisely zero help in figuring out how to cohabitate with this beast. And this fixation on Ambrose was new—well, new outside of the library.

Apparently, I was being uncharacteristically honest in my self-reflection this morning.

My breath heaved as I ran, but my veil cat assured me we were fine. She pressed onward with no hesitation. It had been hours since I shifted, and there seemed to be no end in sight.

Greenery surrounded me: bushes, trees, the hard-packed dirt beneath my paws, and nothing else. I'd paid enough attention to realize we were north of the city. In the months since I'd started shifting, this was usually where I ended up. So far, I hadn't run into another shifter.

I had a lot on my mind. Managing my shift was not going well. Determining how the animal itself fit into the political landscape of the continent, now that I knew the Vesten Point also changed into a veil cat, seemed impossible. Any hope I had of competing for the Vesten historian position relied on it remaining my priority focus. The unhelpful thoughts of my competition's abnormally large frame or the comforting heat of his touch notwithstanding.

This list didn't even touch on the sensation that felt like a pinging in my chest as I pressed forward toward ... something.

I needed something else to think about for a while. This must be why my thoughts cycled to my father. I rarely thought about the day he left. It was a scene I'd replayed incessantly as a child, when I was young and foolish and had still thought he might return.

We had been playing in the yard. The three of us lived in a small log cabin just outside one of the northwestern villages. My fire magic had manifested very early. At five, my father was already teaching me how to call and dismiss the flame. We played a game where he set up candles along the top of the fence, and I lit them from increasingly farther distances.

It annoyed me to think about how happy the scene was. He would smile broadly every time I succeeded. He would even shout encouragement and correction when I made a mistake. We could have had thousands of nights like that. He could have been there the first time I shifted. He could have reassured me. Perhaps he could have helped me control the change instead of letting it control me.

But he hadn't been around for any of that.

The evening before he left, another shifter had arrived. The only other one I'd seen at our cottage. Or, at least, the only one I remember. A bear lumbered out of the forest, and while my father put himself between me and the animal, he didn't pick me up—we didn't run. He waited patiently for the bear to change into a fae male.

My father glanced over his shoulder at me, nodding with something that tried to look like reassurance. His chin lifted in a gesture toward the back door of the cabin. He wanted me to go inside. I did as I was told, but the rapidly whispered words with sharp inflection behind me were indicative of anger. It drew my attention like a moth to flame. The other male shook his head, his lips curling in distaste. Seconds before my father realized I hadn't left yet, I understood that anger, that ... disgust was directed at me.

Father shooed me inside then. I ran directly into Mom's arms. She picked me up and pressed my head to her shoulder. It occurred to me later that she'd watched the rest of the scene unfold outside the window. I relished the comfort of her arms when the look on the fae's face had made the world outside suddenly seem so cold.

Father had left for work the next morning as he usually did. But that time was different—that time he never returned.

Now, I knew the other fae's opinion of me wasn't uncommon. Half-fae hadn't been accepted at that time. Mom, Father, and I had lived in relative isolation. The bear shifter's arrival signaled that the real world had caught up with us. No matter Father's feelings for Mom, or the little fantasy he thought he could live out in the woods, that moment had reminded him that wasn't the continent's reality.

I'd pointed this out to Mom a hundred times. I'd clarify that it wasn't her—it was me. Fae could slum it with humans, but they couldn't have children with them. Mom stubbornly refused to hear any of it.

I cleared the depressing thoughts from my head as the sparkling blue water of Sandrin Bay finally came into view. This northern part of the bay was familiar to me. I wasn't far from the ferry that crossed to the city. Maybe the veil cat would shift me back so that I could ride it again this morning.

That pressure still pulsed in my chest. I ran in the same direction—until the pulsing slowed, and the pressure lifted slightly. Something warm and insistent cascaded through me. Fire burned, not unpleasantly. This was it; the shift was finally done. I knew the change was complete as my hand reached to rub against my sternum. The sensation wasn't ... painful ... but the discomfort lingered.

My fur was gone. My hand pressed against skin. I'd shifted into the tank top and shorts I had been wearing to sleep. Though not particularly the outfit I wanted to wear on a ferry ride across the bay, I had to admit it was better than shifting nude.

The shift was disorienting, and I didn't know if there was a way to make it easier. I took a few shaky steps as I readjusted to my half-fae form.

I hadn't stumbled far on two legs when I realized I was headed in the wrong direction. A pressure in my chest seemed to tug me off track. I rubbed my sternum in an attempt to ease it, then turned—and came face to face with an enormous wolf.

No one could fault the squeak that escaped my lips. This wolf was the largest I'd ever seen. I was no longer in animal form and had no means of defending myself against such a predator. If things got dire, I wasn't even sure I could command the shift to help.

My heart raced as I stared at the wolf, but maybe more concerning than my reaction was my veil cat's. She curled up inside my mind like her work here was done. While the wolf wasn't attacking, I found my veil cat's lack of concern appalling, especially since just about every perceived infraction angered her. On all fours, this wolf still came to the height of my chest, but upon further inspection, I guessed its light gray fur did look soft in the early morning light.

The wolf stretched its paws forward, although *paws* was too generous a term—they had large claws that looked like they could do damage if he was provoked. But for now, the wolf lay down, and its tail ticked back and forth as if waiting for something.

"What is happening?" I wondered aloud.

None of this made sense.

I needed to get past this wolf. If it wasn't going to kill me, I had a boat to catch. The ferry wasn't known for being punctual, but once gone, it didn't return quickly. If I missed this early morning ride, I'd be waiting a while.

The wolf was still prostrate. If I didn't know better, I'd say its tail was now wagging. Did it want to play?

"I am going to walk around you, Wolfy. Please don't eat me."

I received no confirmation of my plan, but since I had no other options, I proceeded anyway. Everything I'd ever learned about predators was flashing through my head. Move slowly—no sudden changes. Keep your breaths even.

I was failing at the last one, but I hoped to control the first two.

My gaze locked with the wolf's golden eyes. The color was so unique. It was the same hue as the innermost circle of Ambrose's irises.

Where had that thought come from?

I returned my attention to the wolf. Wasn't I supposed to show submission or something? My veil cat growled at that thought. I cataloged the reaction as visceral disagreement. Then, I continued around the wolf with slow steps.

It didn't move as I inched past it. Finally, on the other side, I wondered how to make my escape. Give it my back? That didn't feel like a good idea. Take slow steps backward? That seemed silly. I glanced around. There was no one here to see.

"I'm going to walk away slowly. Please continue not to eat me."

Why I narrated my moves to this wild animal was beyond me, but I did. Every step I took away from the wolf brought back the pang in my chest. It had to be anxiety over the situation. Still, the wolf didn't move.

When I took my last step onto the path, the wolf whined low in its throat.

The noise tore at something deep in my chest, but I was far enough away to make a break to the dock. I didn't hesitate. Turning, I fled down the path and ran the entire way to the dock.

The pang in my chest didn't resolve itself even with distance from the wolf; if anything, it might have gotten worse. It wasn't my top worry. When my nerves calmed from the encounter, I was sure it would disappear. At least that's what I told myself as I boarded the ferry that would return me to Sandrin.

8

Ambrose

Nothing about the morning had gone according to plan.

My run had turned into a hunt. Senses that had yet to fail me led me toward an unknown target. Finally, I neared the finish line. The twisting in my chest loosened as I approached my prize, telling me we were close. My stomach dropped like a free fall when I caught my first glimpse of Evelyn.

Her dark brown hair was in a messy braid that made me wonder about her morning. Before she noticed me, her hand massaged her sternum, as if there was some itch there she couldn't quite scratch. It was an action I understood well.

What was she doing here?

Something in the back of my mind reminded me that her head tilts were a little too familiar, and there was a steadily increasing sharpness to her that was a little too wild, even for the researcher who tested blood magic on living things.

It had crossed my mind only yesterday that maybe she had

more Vesten magic than she led us all to believe. Well, I guessed that would be incorrect. She didn't lead her colleagues to believe anything about her. She let us draw our own conclusions, didn't she? So, I had only myself to blame if I'd underestimated her.

I hadn't seen her in an animal form, but shifting was the only reason a Vesten would be here in the early morning hours. While I hadn't completely forgotten the way she'd chastised me the first time I tried to smell her magic, she hadn't noticed me yet, so I decided to risk it.

The scent was strong; I must have just missed her change. She smelled ... feline. While the image of Evelyn hissing and swiping the claws of an angry house cat was mildly entertaining, I knew it didn't fit. We were miles outside of the city. She wore pajamas, meaning she must be on a morning run, fresh from sleep. I refused to catalog how much skin her pajamas exposed. If she'd made it this far north in a few hours, she was a larger cat. A wild cat.

Finally, she caught sight of me and froze in what I had to assume was fear. I didn't think, only acted on instinct as my wolf stretched forward in a bow. My tail flipped back and forth like I was asking her to play a game. Like maybe the hunt I'd been on this morning could be more of a mutual chase, and interesting things could happen if she let me catch her.

The problem was that Evelyn stared at me as if I were a predator. I guessed I was. My only rebuttal was that I had no illusion she wasn't one as well.

Her hands raised in a defensive posture as she crept around me. The slow, careful steps finally made me realize she had no idea who I was. For all that she must have shifted moments ago, it hadn't crossed her mind that I, too, was a shifter—one she knew.

When she turned to run down the path, my whole body

shook. It was like I tried to rid my fur of raindrops, except it wasn't raining and I was completely dry.

The pang in my chest was back. Each time her feet hit the ground, putting more distance between us, I winced.

Wait. What?

I might have had a bit of a crush on Evelyn Knowles, but I wasn't some lovesick teenager. Just because she found me repulsive didn't mean my world would end. I was not in physical pain due to her rejection of my wolf.

She didn't reject us. She didn't even know it was us.

My wolf had a good point.

Still, it couldn't be my focus right now. I needed to understand the pang in my chest, the knot tightening as the distance between us lengthened. Why was I physically affected by Evelyn?

My paw came up to scratch my ear in a move that echoed the way I ran my fingers through my hair in fae form. This didn't make sense.

I had thought about her a lot last night. Unfortunately, that wasn't unusual, but it seemed like we'd had a breakthrough when we shared a meal at her study carrel. We'd discussed theories as if we'd forgotten we were competing on this project. She had read my paper. Yes, I had asked her to, but then we received the new assignment, and I didn't expect her to care. I couldn't believe she wanted my opinion on anchors. It was a brilliant idea to consider them. Maybe I would have if we could brainstorm ideas that easily all the time.

The worst part was that I did try to talk to her. Most of the time, I ended up saying something to offend her. Every time we discussed magic, my father's voice was in my head, saying her work was dangerous. At least I'd ignored it last night.

I winced as I considered my father's thoughts on both of our cuts opening during our meal. Now who was being reckless?

An errant thought ran through my mind. This pang, this physical need, it couldn't be blood magic, could it?

No, no, neither of us had spoken anything. We didn't declare any intent, even if our blood did spill on each other.

That didn't matter in the journal Gabriel gave us.

Beyond the trees, the ferry captain shouted the last call for boarding. I shook myself free from my far-fetched thoughts of blood magic, even though the clenching feeling burned through my chest. Every instinct told me I needed to be on that boat, and I listened. Quickly, I shifted into my fae form and sprinted to the dock.

The captain's eyes narrowed as I slid aboard just before he pushed off. "Cutting it close."

I nodded in acknowledgement, but I was already searching the handful of passengers trying to find ... Evelyn.

She stood near the front. I was momentarily captivated by her hair. She usually kept it braided. It had been a disaster when I'd found her, pieces falling out, leaves and twigs sticking out in every direction. She must have decided the braid was a lost cause because now it was long and wild. Something I didn't quite understand had me wanting to stick my nose in it and soak up the scent.

That would be awkward. I pushed down what I could only assume were my wolf's urges and took slow steps toward her.

Steam curled from a cup she clutched in both hands. The captain must have had hot drinks for those who boarded early. Her whole body curled toward the heat, as if every inch of her skin that touched the cup was better off. She wore a black tank top and shorts, and the way she shook as the boat started to move told me she didn't know how to use her Vesten heat.

Her chosen study carrel in the library also made me question this. No other Vesten wanted the seat by the fire because most of us ran hot. Evelyn had fire magic. I had seen it with my own eyes, but she didn't use it to warm herself. My hackles rose as I realized what that meant.

No one had taught her.

Given Evelyn's age, it wasn't altogether uncommon to think her fae parent wasn't in her life. The stigma in fae society about half-fae was changing slowly, but fae could be stupid in their beliefs. That was one of the reasons I was so happy to work at the library. Gabriel didn't have those prejudices. When I had told him about Evelyn working in the Sandrin Records Office, his only question had been if I'd finally met my match.

Crossing the bay was a short boat ride, but it certainly wouldn't make her any warmer. Again, I moved without thought. It seemed to be a pattern with Evelyn. I had multiple layers on. Since I hadn't known where my wolf would take me this morning, I'd prepared for all environments before shifting. My sweater was over my head and I had my hand outstretched to Evelyn before any form of greeting left my lips.

Her eyes widened, and she scanned the boat as if looking for escape, like she wasn't at all happy to see me. "Ambrose. What are you doing here?"

I offered the sweater again as the boat began to move. "Do you want to wear this? The rest of the ride will be chilly."

She refused to look at me. Instead, she glared at the sweater like it offended her, before clutching the paper cup tighter. With a final glance, she seemed to calculate the distance between us and Sandrin's dock. The moment she grabbed the garment, apparently deciding that accepting my help was a reasonable cost for comfort, my lip tilted.

I wanted to teach her how to warm herself—to ensure she was never in need of doing something so distasteful as accepting my sweater again—but magic was a sensitive topic between us. At the very least, I had learned to tread carefully with it. The last thing I wanted was to seem like I was shoving my fae heritage in her face.

My questions when she'd first arrived at the library had been more offensive than I'd intended. I learned quickly after that. Little things like asking where she trained or asking what school she'd gone to were hidden traps for explosions of resentment toward the fae.

I couldn't blame her. Her responses reminded me she wasn't allowed in the school I'd gone to, and hadn't had the opportunity to read anything in the Vesten Library. Part of me liked that she'd showed us by besting us all with her knowledge of blood magic anyway. Mostly, I wished fae society was more accepting.

As she pulled my sweater over her head, a flame fanned to life in my chest.

What is happening?

"What are you doing here, Ambrose?"

I didn't see much point in hiding it. It was as good an introduction to talk about Vesten magic as any. She looked at me with those big brown eyes that I was now confident hid something animalistic. They narrowed with apprehension.

If there was one thing I was good at, it was learning from history. That was my specialty, after all. My experiences with Evelyn, especially when it came to traditional fae attributes like magic, led me to understand that it was best to offer her information first and see if she wanted to reciprocate.

"I was running in my shifted form." I cleared my throat, preparing to share something I wasn't sure I had ever said to anyone outside my family. All Vesten children were taught not to speak about our animals with others. I pushed aside my father's disappointment to offer Evelyn a little information about myself. "The wolf you just encountered on the path was me. I apologize if I startled you."

Her breathing hitched at my lack of evasiveness, and my wolf preened at finally understanding some part of Evelyn Knowles.

Let's not congratulate ourselves too early.

"You were big."

I choked on wherever I thought the conversation had been headed next. This was not it. "Excuse me?"

She flushed. I was absolutely delighted by this turn of events, but I had no idea what to do with it.

"Your wolf," she clarified. "It was large."

I couldn't even imagine the look I must have given her as she complimented my size. She continued to ramble, and I thought it was maybe the most perfect start to a day that I had yet to experience.

"You didn't scare me. You were just ... unexpected." Then her brow furrowed as another thought must have flashed through her mind. "When did you get there?"

I heard what she didn't ask. *What did you see?*

That was enough of an admission for me. If I'd had any doubts left—I didn't—this response was proof she had a shifter form. One she didn't want me to know about.

"When you saw me," I reassured her. "That was when I arrived."

She let out a shaky exhale and took a bracing sip of the tea in her hands. Her gaze finally met mine, and that warmth in my chest extended to my limbs.

This is decidedly not normal. The wolf in my head seemed to revel in whatever it was.

"You're not going to ask me what I was doing over there?" She glanced toward Sandrin's approaching shore.

"I would love to know, if you have any interest in sharing."

She appraised me. "I was taking a walk." She glanced down at her long, exposed legs and clutched her cup tighter. I was sure she was realizing how silly that sounded, given her dress.

"I see."

"You don't believe me?"

I almost laughed. "What I believe is irrelevant. I saw you walking in the woods. It matches your story."

Her brown eyes had me rapt. I didn't dare glance down at the length of her legs, the definition of her calves and thighs likely a result of many morning runs just like the one I was sure she'd been on today.

"Fine," she said.

I tried not to stare, but she didn't seem to have the same restraint. She seemed to study my arms, which were exposed since I had given her my sweater. At least I still had an undershirt on.

"You don't look cold." It was more of a statement than a question.

If the wolf in my head were a representation of my inner thoughts, he would be licking his lips at this perfect opening she'd handed me. "Vesten fire can warm from the inside." I tried to state the fact with no hesitation. If I left no room for interpretation, maybe she wouldn't see the information as a condemnation of her upbringing. My following words were more hesitant. "I could explain it if you haven't read about it."

She looked cautious, like a wild animal about to bolt from a hunter's carefully laid trap. Then her nostrils flared, and I knew the part of her that craved information had won out. "If you don't mind." She gestured to the distance between us and the shore. "We don't have anything else to do."

I pulled a hard candy from my pocket. They were bright red and tasted like cinnamon. I used them with my younger siblings to teach them about our magic. "Are you familiar with this candy?"

Something in her eyes lit up. "I've never had one."

The part she didn't say but was there in her face was that she'd always wanted one. I handed it to her. "Something about the taste, the cinnamon and sugar, is a good training tool for

Vesten fire magic. I had them all the time when I was learning to control mine."

She took it carefully, sniffing in a way that screamed Vesten. I didn't know if it was whatever had brought me to her this morning or the wolf in my head, but either way, I was enthralled with the action.

"Have one, and you can feel the heat build here." I pointed to my chest. "From there, you can do all sorts of things with it. Like spread it out to your limbs for warmth."

Her attention was still fixed on the candy. Briefly, she glanced at the nearing shore, then back to me. "Thank you."

I nodded, hopeful she would test it out later. We'd dock soon, and it occurred to me that I didn't want to separate. The awareness inside me seemed intent on her presence. While my wolf agreed with the sentiment, this was a new development.

"Hey—Ambrose." Her words pulled my focus. "You weren't ... looking for me ... were you?"

Was I? I considered it, but I didn't think it was that simple. The question didn't feel like a trap, like she wanted to know if I was stalking her. If it were, there would probably be a lot more teeth and claws and a lot less of me standing here like an idiot as I tried to determine my reply.

I shrugged. "I'm not sure."

She took a final, deep sip of her tea, emptying the cup. "I see."

"Yes. Well." I should have realized then what she was asking —why she was asking.

The captain's voice echoed across the deck, asking everyone aboard to disembark as the boat docked in Sandrin.

"I should get home and change." She looked down at my sweater again. "Is it alright if I bring this to you at the library today?"

"Of course." I didn't have a chance to say more before she

slipped off the boat and into the crowd of people near the docks.

The pang in my chest returned, the same as it had on the path. It tightened with each step she took away from me, telling me I was in trouble.

9

Evelyn

Something was wrong, and I was sure it was Ambrose's fault. The crowd thinned as I escaped the busy docks and walked toward my and Mom's apartment. The city was quiet; most still hadn't started their day. Unfortunately, that left only my thoughts for company.

I had tried to keep it together when he approached me on the ferry, arm outstretched with an offering he knew I could use. My entire body had shivered at the scent of the sweater. I might have asked what he was doing there, but the rapid beat of my heart suggested I already knew the answer before he shared it.

He was the wolf.

He hadn't seen me shift, had he? Judging from that slightly furrowed brow and the too-relaxed pose he held the rest of the cruise across the bay, he wasn't buying my morning walk excuse. He might not have seen my shift, but he suspected that I had.

Maybe it would be alright. Maybe the Vesten Library's golden boy, who wanted me and my method of blood magic gone, would let this go. I shook my head at the thought, even though he hadn't pressed for information when he clearly knew I was lying. Even more confusingly, he'd slipped me information about Vesten. He had been more than kind to not only share his sweater, but to teach me how to warm myself in the future. Surprisingly, he'd managed it without condescension.

His apparent kindness didn't make sense. Although if he hadn't seen my shift, he had nothing to hold over me. It wasn't my fault everyone assumed I didn't have one. I'd be in real trouble if he knew what I was. No matter how things had seemed between us last night, no matter the crush I couldn't seem to tamp down, if Ambrose Yarrow knew I was a veil cat and that I was unable to control my shift, he would use the information against me.

I focused on this because I didn't want to acknowledge that the twisting in my chest was back. It had returned the moment I left Ambrose's side. The wolf, my secret, Vesten magic—all these issues paled in comparison to the fact that my body was physically reacting to something, and I was afraid that something was Ambrose's presence.

For now, the sensation was uncomfortable but not unbearable, so I decided to ignore it as I arrived at our apartment and let myself in. Everything was as I had left it. Mom was still sleeping in her bedroom. I was glad, since I hadn't had a way to leave her a note before the change happened.

Our home was simple, two bedrooms and a shared living space with the kitchen. We overlapped less than we'd like with our busy work schedules, but it also gave us both our privacy. I went into my room to change before leaving for the library.

More reluctantly than I'd ever admit, I removed the warm sweater. I stared at the candy he'd given me. Ambrose's instructions on self-warming were simple. I was sure there had to be more to it.

I tried not to think too hard about how long I'd wanted one of these candies as I popped the red ball of sugar into my mouth. The snap of cinnamon on my tongue was a sweet zing, followed by an intense flare of heat. It built quickly, like the candy itself was a ball of flame instead of sugar. With Ambrose's instruction in my head, I distributed the core of heat to my limbs. They warmed almost immediately.

Is this why no one else in the library was bothered by the chill?

Cheeks warm in embarrassment, I changed, wrote Mom a quick note, and left for the library. It was such a simple thing—likely something that every Vesten parent taught their child. I'd still been learning to call the magic on command when my father left. We hadn't gotten to any of these more practical tricks. Embarrassment turned to a churning anger. This was yet another sin to lay at his feet. I pushed down the part of me that wanted so badly to have had someone to teach me these things. How did I end up at the mercy of Ambrose Yarrow for tips about Vesten magic?

He was still on my mind when I arrived at the library. The twinge was still there in my chest as I got to work. Today, I would learn all I could about the creation of the fae. I'd read a few texts on the matter, but I was sure the historian extraordinaire Ambrose Yarrow knew more.

If I were to impress Lord Arctos with the right questions about his project, I needed to know what to ask. I pulled a few history texts from the shelves to start with, but the restricted section of the library drew my attention. The best resources about the creation of the fae were there, but you needed special permission to access them. I clenched my jaw as I carried a stack of texts to my desk, sure Ambrose already knew the secrets that room held.

The library was still empty as I started reading. No matter how I tried to focus on the text, I couldn't help but contemplate the sweater folded neatly and placed in the corner of my carrel.

It was as if that twisting spring inside me was momentarily released when I thought—or looked at—something that reminded me of Ambrose.

The longer we remained separated, the worse it got. Tension stretched across every part of me. I tried to make myself small to ward off the discomfort. Then the creak of the Great Room's massive door signaled what my body seemed to already know. My breath released, dropping my shoulders from where they had crept up by my ears. I didn't have to look up to know it was him. Ambrose had arrived.

This was a problem.

Ignoring it was my only plan. What was I supposed to do? Walk up to Ambrose and tell him I was obsessed with him? No. All other options felt unacceptable, so I ducked back into my carrel and kept reading.

"Eep!" I squeaked as something pressed down on my shoulder.

"*Any updates?*" That same unknowable voice spoke directly into my mind. The large black bird accompanied it: Lord Arctos.

"I'm reading about the creation of the fae." I snuck a glance at him to see if he indicated this was a good idea or not. He didn't. "Ambrose and I also discussed anchors last night. Are you familiar with the concept? What was the object you and the Vesten Point used when you tested the magic?"

"*You and Ambrose, huh?*" Lord Arctos's wings flapped against the side of my face as his beak turned toward where Ambrose sat across the Great Room.

"It would help if you would tell us everything you know."

"*Now it's us?*"

I sighed. "This isn't the part where we differentiate

ourselves. This is still information you should have given us in the briefing." I turned my head to glare at him.

He looked resolutely in the opposite direction.

Was I really challenging a god here?

His feathers flicked against my face again as he fidgeted in what I could only imagine was agitation. "*You're probably right.*"

"Excuse me?"

My response was louder than the rest of the conversation. Ambrose's head lifted, and our gazes locked across the room. The slight arch of his brow was his only response to the black bird perched on my shoulder. Then, before I could decide if it was a good thing or a bad thing, he pushed back his chair and strode toward us.

"Everything alright, Evelyn?" he asked, glancing briefly at the bird.

I nodded, uncomfortable with how my breath seemed to come easier with each step of his approach. That unfortunate piece of information would be relegated to the back of my mind for later. "Lord Arctos was about to explain himself."

"*You're sure you want to share what I was about to tell you? He is the competition, after all.*" His tone was pure mischief with a hint of mirth. It reminded me of a child who had put a thumb tack on an empty chair and was now waiting for me to sit on it.

Ambrose's eyes widened, which I took to mean that the Vesten God was now speaking into both of our minds.

I shrugged. "You owe us what you know."

"*Fine. I'll tell you how to learn more about the connection we're asking you to break. You're on the right track, Evelyn, reading about the creation of the fae, but you won't find the information you need in that text.*"

Still seated on my shoulder, his wings poked at me as they ruffled. Why couldn't he have picked Ambrose's shoulder for his little tantrums?

"*The best information I can give you is in the restricted section of the library. You should read the journals of the first Vesten Point, Kenna. She was there at the creation of the fae, and the language she recorded is what Carter believes indicates blood magic was used to create the fae."*

Vindication rushed through me. I was on my feet immediately, and Lord Arctos's wing was flapping against my face again as I jostled him. "Excellent."

"But only the Vesten historian is allowed in the restricted section," Ambrose replied. It seemed almost automatic. He looked wistfully over his shoulder at the closed door that led to that particular section.

Had he really never been in there? Another crack formed in the image I had of Ambrose. It was comforting that his rules applied to himself, too. Maybe even more comforting that he gave Lord Arctos as hard a time about the rules as he usually gave me, but still. "I think we'll be alright if the literal god of our court is telling us to go in there."

Ambrose's hand balled into a fist, and his brow pinched. "It really wouldn't take that long to request permission from Gabriel."

I smirked, and it felt dangerously close to toying with him. The awareness of him flared to life in my chest, a sensation of heat tingling down my spine. It caught me off guard. This wasn't what Ambrose and I did. Still, the words slipped out, as if they, too, didn't require permission. "Where is the fun in that?"

My chair scraped against the wood floor as I pushed it in beneath my desk. I knew it would make Ambrose's hair stand on end.

"Evelyn," he said, his hands moving to his hips. "It will take ten minutes at most to get Gabriel's approval."

"Which seems like a waste of ten minutes."

Lord Arctos's head swiveled back and forth between us as we needlessly debated this next step.

"If anything happens to us, he'll have the record of what text we thought relevant."

"What's going to happen to us, Ambrose?" I tilted my head in consideration, feeling like I had untangled an entire ball of yarn but was unsure what to do with the accomplishment.

"Never mind," he said before doubling down on his original point. "Let's just get permission."

"He told us time was of the essence. We're doing as he requested." Heat flared inside me as Ambrose's ears reddened in frustration. I decided then and there that I liked pushing him in this way. What did he have to worry about? He was a full Vesten fae, his father retired from a position of honor in the court. Ambrose was renowned for his knowledge of the court's history. He could do whatever he wanted without consequence.

That's not what I saw on his face.

For the first time, it occurred to me that maybe he didn't see himself the way I saw him. Maybe he didn't think everything was within his grasp. The next question bubbled up the same way the awareness of him had—why didn't he believe that?

I didn't have time to consider it before he turned and walked away. "I'll be a moment. Just wait here."

The Great Room door hadn't fully closed behind him when the Vesten God swept into my mind. He was all condescending authority, speaking the information I'd been intent to ignore. "*When are you going to tell him that the two of you are magically bound?*"

10

Ambrose

My shoulders tensed as I heard her whisper something to the Vesten God. I was almost out of the room, but I had excellent hearing thanks to my wolf. The words were too whispered to decipher, but she did not sound happy.

Some part of me was pulled back toward the hiss of her voice, like maybe she required me for whatever debate they were having. The urge was stronger than I cared to admit.

Another part of me heard my father's voice in my head, warning me of the dangers of the restricted section. The least I could do was tell Gabriel our plan. I nodded to myself and proceeded toward his office.

Evelyn hadn't asked for my help. I had no idea where this protective instinct was coming from. Likely from the same part of me that didn't want to be away from her. Every step I took twisted that knot in my chest a little tighter.

So, I focused on something else.

At least if Lord Arctos and Evelyn spent the next ten minutes arguing, they couldn't sneak into the restricted section while I got permission. As I took the stairs two at a time, I was torn between hoping they argued a while longer and marveling at the audacity of Evelyn to fight that way with the Vesten God.

I remembered coming to the library to visit my father as a child. He had often been behind the roped-off area. I was never allowed in. When I questioned him, he'd say that some things shouldn't be known. The words had never sat well with me, especially from someone who worked in a position where knowledge was key. Even as I questioned them, they remained in my mind. It occurred to me that he hadn't heeded his own words, and it had cost him.

Now, here I was, years later, with Evelyn's taunts replaying in my mind, wondering if Father's reason was good enough. What if the knowledge was handled with care and caution? I considered the reckless test the Vesten Point had conducted with Lord Arctos. Might there be situations in which it was more dangerous not to know? Maybe the best we could do was learn what we could to prepare for any eventuality.

My hand swept through my hair before I could stop it. I was halfway to Gabriel's office but wondered if it wouldn't be so bad if I didn't get permission. What if I just walked into the restricted section and grabbed whatever books I wanted? What if Lord Arctos sat on my shoulder and directed me to whichever journal of Kenna's he wanted us to read?

Should I be concerned that he'd started the conversation with Evelyn instead of me? We were competing for the position of Vesten historian, after all.

At the thought of Evelyn, the uncomfortable twist in my chest was back. This insistent tug in her direction was becoming increasingly inconvenient. I'd felt her distance when she left the ferry this morning. Felt every step that she put between herself and me as I stood on the boat.

What was going on? And why did she seem so unaffected?

Yes, I found her attractive. My wolf certainly liked her, but that didn't warrant this type of behavior. She'd never done anything but express exasperation and general dislike of me.

I guessed that wasn't true. She seemed to enjoy discussing theories with me, like I did with her. That glow she seemed to effuse as we solved a problem, the excitement just below the surface every time we agreed on a hypothesis, that wasn't faked.

But now there was this contest. We were pitted against each other for a position my father had trained me for. Worse, she wanted it, too.

I sighed, having arrived outside of Gabriel's office. My hand raised to knock before I could consider how silly my explanation might sound.

"Come in."

Gabriel sat behind his desk. His hair was mussed, and his shirt was wrinkled. I wondered when he'd last left the library. He'd looked ragged for days. It made sense that he was working long hours, given that his beloved son required this information. Gabriel would do anything for him.

The head librarian peered up at me from behind whatever book he was reading. He must have asked something that I missed, as silence hung between us.

"Sorry, what did you say?" I asked, running my hand through my hair again.

He chuckled. "I know the feeling. My question was along the lines of, how can I help you, Mr. Yarrow?"

"Ah, right." I was suddenly nervous, as if the whole trip had been the wrong decision. There was no way Gabriel would say no, right? I scratched the back of my neck as I found the words. "Lord Arctos thought we might gain some insights from reading one of Kenna's journals in the restricted section. I wanted to make sure you knew."

Gabriel's smile was one of pity. "We?"

I swallowed, realizing my mistake. "Yes, me and Ms. Knowles."

"And you think that the god of our court and the researcher you claim pushes every boundary waited for you to get approval before walking into the restricted section?"

His eyes twinkled with fondness, even though his smirk was slightly condescending. I knew I was being ridiculous; his pointing it out was unnecessary. But Father had paid a high price for not heeding his own warnings. The least I could do was keep them in mind in my research. The rules were there to protect us and those around us.

My justifications were weak, even to myself.

"Alright, then. You have my approval," Gabriel said.

His response was so easy. It only made me feel more foolish. I turned to leave, ready to see how much I'd missed in the Great Room. They'd probably already read the entire journal and were on to some new part of the investigation.

Gabriel cleared his throat behind me. "Ambrose."

I glanced at him over my shoulder.

"I didn't hire you because of who your father is." He tapped his fingers on the desk as if unsure how to proceed. "Did you ever wonder why I approached you to research blood magic?"

The question was one I had almost asked a hundred times. I just wasn't sure I wanted to know the answer. Gabriel knew my father's view on blood magic. He should have expected me to say no to his request immediately. Yet I hadn't.

Gabriel didn't wait for my answer. "You are our best historian. You know every date, and you understand the historical context of every era. Why not leave you to what you're good at?"

"Did you think I'd say no?"

The small smile that crossed his lips was brief as he shook his head. "I hoped you wouldn't. You are diligent, inquisitive, and make connections throughout history that others miss. I knew you'd apply the same skills to this new critical study, if you could get past ... well, if you could get past what your father thinks about blood magic."

The words washed over me, but it felt like a fire was crackling in my ears, stopping the words from truly soaking in. Father had always claimed he was the one who got me hired. He said his word still carried weight at the library. It sounded like Gabriel had hired me despite my father.

"Thank you for the opportunity, sir."

With that, I hurried back to the Great Room. Evelyn stood next to the study carrel that I had claimed today. Even though I now knew where the chair for the desk across from hers was hidden, its location sent a clear message about whether I was welcome. I folded my arms over my chest as I approached.

She looked ... sheepish was the best word I could come up with. Her foot dragged back and forth across the floor, and she didn't make eye contact when I entered the room. Her shoulders hunched forward slightly, at odds with the fierce posture with which she usually carried herself.

My wolf awakened then. All senses were on high alert, even though nothing seemed quite so bad now that Evelyn was back in my sights.

I need to address this line of thought sooner rather than later.

The black bird was gone. Something was wrong. I could see it in the way she held herself, in the slow movement of her foot, and the slight downturn of her lips. Had she tried to get into the restricted section and something had happened? She didn't look hurt. My pace quickened, closing the distance between us. I reached out and touched her arm to get her attention. "Evelyn. What's wrong?"

Finally, on a deep breath, she looked up at me through long lashes. I was momentarily speechless at the sight.

"Did something happen? Did you try to get the journal?"

Her brow furrowed in confusion. Then she slowly shook her head, pointing to a book I hadn't noticed yet on the desk of my study carrel. "Lord Arctos showed me which book to get while you got permission." The hint of a smile was there and gone on her lips.

"Then what's the problem?"

Her foot swept back and forth again across the floor. I remembered taking the same posture when I was a child and accidentally broke one of Mother's vases the first time I shifted.

"Evelyn. You're worrying me." That ... whatever it was twisted in my chest, even though she stood right in front of me.

"You said you were looking for me this morning in the woods."

I nodded, not sure where this was going.

"And is that unusual for you? To be looking for me?"

What an odd question, though it was one I'd mentally been avoiding. Yes, I liked seeing her at the library. Yes, I thought about her more often than was probably considered normal. Her question was valid, though. It was *unusual* for me to try to find her.

My wolf paced back and forth in my head as I admitted, "It was unusual, yes."

My hand ran through my hair again of its own accord. The move appeared to tug her lip into a small smile. At least she wasn't threatening to report me for stalking.

"I can sense when you're not near me," she said.

Heat flooded my body at the words. She didn't just say that, did she? She sensed my presence?

"Something inside me is rather insistently drawn to you."

Well, this was completely unexpected. I'd been under the impression that my feelings were entirely unrequited. What was she saying? Was I dreaming? My wolf's tail flicked back and forth in my head with excitement, a sign that I was very much awake.

Before my mind wandered too far, I remembered the look on her face when this conversation had started. The way she'd been waiting rather nervously by my desk. My stomach plummeted like a stone sinking in the bay.

I don't know how I put it together, but before the words were past her bow-shaped lips, I knew what she would say. My whole body flushed as I pushed every idiotic part of me that had secretly hoped this was some declaration of her feelings back into the box tucked deep inside my chest.

Then the words came.

The reason for this tug in her direction.

The slight, inexplicable twisting in my chest when she wasn't near. It could be explained—I just hadn't wanted to consider it. The cut on her finger when we'd shared a meal yesterday. The wound from my run reopening. This information pointed to a single conclusion.

I couldn't believe my stupidity.

Part of me wanted to stop her. Once she said the words, we couldn't ignore them. But Evelyn was so much braver than I was.

"We accidentally bound ourselves together last night."

11

Evelyn

Getting the words out was hard enough. The way Ambrose stared as I tried to assemble the sentence was unbearable. But once Lord Arctos had unceremoniously shared the information my brain was protecting me from, I could no longer avoid it.

I had bound us together with my stupidity.

It should have been obvious that something had happened last night given my reaction to his hand on mine. But no, I'd been convinced it was a useless crush. Well, apparently, it was both.

I tried to explain—the meal together, the cut, none of it came out right. I wanted him to know this wasn't some reckless test. This was blood magic inferring intent, which I now decided it had no business doing.

His attention while I spoke left me hot and cold in equal parts, a problem not even Vesten fire magic could fix. After I blurted out the necessary information, he just continued to stand there beside his study carrel. Unblinking.

I'm not entirely sure how I decided what to do next. Ambrose was no help at all. Somehow, I convinced him that we needed to discuss this outside of the library. We needed a drink, maybe a few, and Parkview Tavern was the perfect option. We could have selected a closer tavern, but I was comfortable at the Parkview, and hopefully, Ambrose would think twice about shouting at me in such a public setting. It would keep things civil while we unpacked what I had done.

Or, at least, that was the plan.

His hand hadn't stopped running through his hair on the walk. Well, it had stopped long enough for him to roll up his shirtsleeves and pluck his pencil and notepad from his vest pocket. He scribbled the rest of the way there.

Now we sat at a table as far from the bar and Seraphina's prying ears as we could get. His gaze bored into mine like I was some kind of experiment. I guessed now I was.

How was I going to undo this?

Mina was working the floor, but Seraphina's eagle eyes spotted us, and she slipped from behind the bar to approach our table.

"Evelyn. Ambrose." Her voice was absent its usual warmth as she attempted to assess what this outing was exactly. The last time I'd seen her, I told her Ambrose was my rival for a promotion.

Ambrose startled at her voice. "Ah, Seraphina, hi."

Her eyes narrowed in my direction. I shrugged helplessly. The words had barely come out when I confessed to Ambrose. There was no chance I could repeat them for her now.

"What can I get you two, then?" she asked into my silence.

"Ale," I said.

Ambrose studied me. "I'll have what she's having."

Seraphina arched an eyebrow at me, and I steadfastly

refused to make eye contact. I barely caught her nod before she walked away to take care of our drinks. I knew we'd have words later, but right now, I needed to focus.

What were we going to do?

My unacknowledged suspicion had been growing in confidence all day. Every time he left my sight, something in me ached. It wasn't enough to have eyes on him, like I usually did from my corner; the discomfort in my chest pressed for more. It wanted proximity. It wanted connection. It wanted a whole lot of things I'd rather not consider right now.

Then Lord Arctos put into words precisely what I'd been avoiding. He'd seemed rather giddy about it, too. I didn't care what people said; the Vesten God was an unholy terror.

Ambrose's hazel eyes stared into the middle distance. A flash of gold expanded and contracted across his irises before he dropped his attention to his notebook. The gold ring reminded me how his eyes had looked this morning in wolf form.

How off-balance was he? Was he going to shift in the middle of this tavern? I'd ask him, but he was still studiously taking notes.

For once, my veil cat kept quiet. If I didn't know any better, I'd think she was enjoying this.

Seraphina returned with the drinks. She wordlessly set them on the table, gave me another look that conveyed that we would be discussing this later, and sauntered back to the bar.

"Are you sure?" Ambrose asked, breaking from his stupor. He set down his notebook and pencil to reach for his ale.

I nodded.

"How do you know?"

I took a long gulp of my drink, considering my response. It was rather embarrassing to discuss, but it had to be done. I would lay out the facts, even if they were huge, embarrassing facts that made me seem like a stalker pining after Ambrose

Yarrow. "I first noticed this morning. Everything made me think of you. It was like I couldn't get you out of my mind."

My cheeks heated. Maybe that wasn't the best place to start.

Ambrose took a sip of his drink and swallowed as if bracing for terrible news. That's what this was to him.

I sighed. This whole thing was uncomfortable, but it was blood magic. Sometimes, I felt like this particular magic reveled in discomfort.

No use stopping now. I continued recounting the morning.

"Then I felt ... led—I think that's the right word, led—to the woods where I ran into you."

"How so?" he asked.

I was so excited to talk about anything other than my magical obsession with Ambrose, I didn't think about my following words. "My shift. It's new, and it was quite insistent this morning in my journey to you."

When I realized what I'd said, I pressed my lips together tightly as if to keep any more information from slipping free. It was too late.

Ambrose's eyes widened. "Your shift is new?"

He did not seem surprised that I had a shift, more so that it was a recent change. I guessed I couldn't blame him for assuming after this morning. My cover story was weak.

"Yes," I said, and grabbed my glass again for a steadying sip.

I'm not sure when it had happened, but at some point in the last exchange, his notepad and quill had made their way back into his hand. As I shook my head, I decided this, at least, was promising.

"When did the shift begin?" His pencil was poised to take notes. I should have been affronted, given everything going on between us at the moment—this magic, the research project, our general differences in opinion—that he wanted to study me and my shift.

The worst part was that I wanted to answer him. I had

wanted to talk to another Vesten about this for months. But that wasn't why we were here.

While in most situations, Ambrose was an academic first, in this particular scenario, I couldn't trust that he wouldn't use my shift against me. The fact that I couldn't control it was easy evidence that I was unqualified for the Vesten historian position.

"We're getting off track."

He set the pencil down and ran his hand through his hair. "Right."

I cleared my throat. "Anyway, all afternoon, I could sense where you were in the library. It was uncomfortable when you left the room—"

"Why didn't you say something?"

I narrowed my eyes at him. "I did, eventually."

"What took you so long?" he pressed.

"I didn't see you asking about it earlier. What have you been experiencing, by the way? Maybe it's time you shared."

That straightened his spine almost like a slap across the face. "You said you were sure that this was evidence of a magical connection. What made you so certain?"

He was evading my question. Heat flooded my body, and I reached for my glass. Maybe his symptoms weren't as bad as mine. Maybe he didn't feel anything at all. How would I explain this if it was one-sided?

No, he hadn't hesitated when he said he'd been looking for me. He admitted it was abnormal. Why else would he admit something like that unless magic was involved?

"Lord Arctos confirmed it."

That finally reassured him. He'd probably been raised with a reverent respect for the Vesten God. He probably accepted everything the god said as fact. Although ... that wasn't quite right. He had challenged Lord Arctos in Gabriel's office on my behalf.

I shook my head. That was beside the point.

Some part of me was waiting for Ambrose to jump in like he did on every other project I hadn't asked his opinion on. I wanted him to press for every detail I knew and challenge every fact I stated.

He didn't, and I found it incredibly disappointing.

This whole thing was a lot, I understood that, but I hadn't thought anything could stop Ambrose Yarrow from his methods. Maybe I'd broken him.

"Our question is now the same as our project for Lord Arctos. How do we break a blood magic connection?" I returned to the facts. Hoping for Ambrose to jump in only reminded me that it was useless to want things. It always left me feeling empty.

He glanced up at my words. "Remember when we worked on the inn?"

The question was out of nowhere. Of course I remembered. "What does that have to do with—"

"We found a loophole in the intent."

Something in me warmed as he leaned forward to explain. A glimpse of that inquisitive mind making itself known, even though the idea of being magically bound to me seemed to be sending all his usual processes into chaos. He tapped his finger on the table in thought. "What if we did the same here?"

I was a little embarrassed that I hadn't considered it. The way we solved the problem at the inn had been my idea, but I hadn't considered it in relation to this yet. Ambrose's brain loved history. I imagined it was like a file cabinet, with labels for each subject, ensuring ease of access when he needed it.

If we could pinpoint the intent we used, maybe we could fulfill it, and the connection would release.

"Do we know the intent of the magic we used?" he asked.

These were the words I'd been unable to get out correctly at the library. I'd made it this far; it wasn't worth shying away from the fact that this was all my fault. Ambrose would scold me, he'd point out that this was the danger of blood magic in practice—that I never should have been so careless.

I swallowed and prepared to face his reaction to my mistake. "I know the intent."

Confusion crossed his face as his brow furrowed and his nostrils flared. He opened his mouth, but before he could speak, a head of brown hair with two silver streaks at the front lunged for me, and Luna's arms wrapped around my shoulders.

"Evelyn! I'm so glad to see you."

I shouldn't have been surprised that Luna's boyfriend, Vincent, walked up next to Ambrose and patted him on the shoulder. He had a sly smile on his face.

"I knew you would finally work up the nerve," Vincent said conspiratorially.

Ambrose's ears turned red, and he mumbled something under his breath.

Vincent's words seemed to mean something to Luna, and she glanced back and forth between me and Ambrose.

"What are you two doing here?" Luna's tone was much more cautious than Vincent's.

I sighed. We needed to finish this, or I would lose my nerve. "We're discussing something for work. I don't mean to be rude, but we need a few more minutes, then maybe Ambrose can come join you."

Luna shot me a look that said I was crazy if I thought I was getting out of the tavern without speaking to her.

"Fine," I said on another sigh. "Please. We only need a moment."

Ambrose didn't help with the explanation. Luna at least understood that something was happening and ushered Vincent toward the bar.

The ring of gold in Ambrose's hazel eyes expanded again as they fixed on me. The veil cat in my mind purred at the attention. I shook myself free of the connection as I remembered the last thing I'd said to him before Luna and Vincent's interruption—the conversation we needed to finish.

"As I was saying, the intent is the same as the plants by my desk. The goal is for the rose and the morning glory to grow together. They usually don't. The morning glory strangles the rose's resources." I cleared my throat, remembering that Ambrose had warned me off the experiment. He'd told me it was dangerous and could cost everyone in the library. At least the scale had been incorrect, but the overall spirit of his lecture felt accurate at this point.

I slouched in my chair, defeated as I finished. "I was thinking about them, about the experiment. And I thought it was ... I don't know ... an interesting allegory for our work together. I guess I wondered what it would be like if we grew together instead of getting in each other's way. And then I bled on you."

My hand reached for my glass, only to find it empty. Figured.

When I finally brought my attention back to Ambrose, it wasn't clear if he was breathing. Something finally shook free, and he scratched the back of his neck. "You were thinking about that when you bled?"

His voice was almost soft. He didn't look like he was about to explode, and his tone didn't hold the telltale sign of an impending lecture. His resignation might have been worse. I nodded and let my head hang.

"I need another drink," Ambrose said, glancing down at his empty glass. This conversation had apparently been stressful for both of us.

The awkwardness was unbearable. Ambrose had given me a good idea. I could fix this. I'd done what I needed to and alerted him to the issue. Working to dissolve our bond would significantly set me back in my research for Lord Arctos and

Gabriel, but this was my mistake. It would be my priority to correct.

"I'll get out of your hair, then." I stood.

Ambrose blinked slowly as I spoke.

"The loophole is a good idea. I take full responsibility for the mistake. I'll start work on this immediately and have more ideas first thing in the morning."

I didn't wait for a response. The coins ready in my palm clanged onto the table as I dropped them and turned to flee the tavern.

12

Ambrose

"Stupid. Stupid. Stupid."

I punctuated each word with the beat of my forehead against the bar top. Vincent sat next to me and patted my shoulder while Luna's brow furrowed with concern. The rest of the tavern's patrons carried on around us at a dull roar, not having witnessed my colossal failure with Evelyn.

It had gone so much worse than I could have imagined.

"Do you want to talk about it?" Vincent asked.

I hadn't wanted to talk about it when I sat down next to him and ordered another drink. I didn't really want to talk about it now, but the way Seraphina was side-eyeing me from behind the bar told me my time bemoaning my current predicament was almost up.

The full glass of ale was cool in my hand. I held it against my forehead as I considered what to say. Except for Vincent, these were Evelyn's friends. I wasn't sure how much I should tell them.

"We already know you're competing for the position of Vesten historian." Luna must have suspected my hesitation.

That, unfortunately, hadn't crossed my mind at all this morning, which was a different problem. One that I did not have the mental capacity for at the moment.

Seraphina and Luna were protective of Evelyn. I'd seen it multiple times. Most recently in the way they'd attempted to assess what was bothering her. Evelyn might have left without answering their questions, but there was no way she'd make it more than a day without telling them what was going on. They appeared ready to hunt her down if necessary. That idea gave me some sense of relief as I spilled our shared secret.

"Evelyn and I accidentally bound ourselves together using blood magic."

Vincent spat the drink of his Solstice Sip he'd just taken. His eyes widened as he turned to me. "You what?"

Luna rubbed his shoulder, but behind the bar, Seraphina looked contemplative. She reached for a rag and began wiping down the already pristine counter as if to find something to do with her hands.

"What does that mean?" she asked.

"It means I can feel her absence right now." And I could. There was a distinctly uncomfortable pressure in my chest that had begun the moment she walked out the door. "It means being apart is a strain on each of us in its own way. It means we have to work together to find a way to either break the magic, which I'm not sure has ever been done, or circumvent it, like we did with Luna's inn."

Three sets of eyes stared at me. I couldn't bring myself to meet any of them.

Vincent was the first to clear his throat. His words were hesitant; he was likely unsure of their reception by the females around us. "Isn't this ... exactly the kind of excuse you were looking for to work together again?"

He looked sheepish even mentioning it.

My hands were waving emphatically before I could think about how loud I was. "I did not magically bind us together so that I could spend more time with her! That is the epitome of recklessness."

Seraphina's hands were on her hips now. "What you seem to accuse her of quite frequently."

I did do that. And I could admit that I had been no less reckless than she was with this. My real failure wasn't that we were bound together, or that my best friend seemed to think I'd done it on purpose because I needed an excuse to spend time with my colleague who hated me. No, my real sin here was that I'd let her think it was all her fault.

It wasn't.

Vincent apologized to Luna. "No, of course, I don't think he'd do it on purpose to try and trap Evelyn. That's not what I meant. I was just saying he could make lemons out of lemonade."

"From the way she stormed out of here, it doesn't seem like Evelyn wants to work with him on this at all." Seraphina tossed the rag into the sink behind the bar and folded her arms across her chest.

My head hung. I needed to say something. I needed to do something. It was so distracting to have this emptiness—this awareness—pulsing in my chest. It was teetering on the edge of pain. That couldn't be a good sign.

"She doesn't have all the information. I have to tell her what I know, then she can make a more informed choice on whether she wants help."

I couldn't believe I'd sat silently while she spoke. It was clear she was embarrassed about her feelings, even when they were beyond her control. Mine, on the other hand. Mine were what got us into this mess. I remembered so distinctly sitting in the chair she'd offered me at her carrel. The chair she had kept hidden from me as one who might impose upon her quiet workspace with my inane questions about her tests.

Sometimes I annoyed myself with my worries.

Even as I questioned her work, I envied it. It would be a little intoxicating to be the focus of her attention like that. I'd been thinking how lucky those two flowers were to be bound together in that pot under her watchful eye. As much as I pressed Evelyn on the details of her research using living things, I knew she was careful. But my father had been careful, too.

Her position on the dangers of blood magic made more sense than I cared to admit. All of it was dangerous, since it hinged on intent. My father's voice flooded my mind as I considered it. He always said it was more dangerous with living things because you were managing your intent *and* the test subjects. There were more variables to consider.

And wasn't my current predicament proof that my father was correct?

A throat cleared. Seraphina, Luna, and Vincent were all staring at me. They must have asked me a question. I hadn't heard it.

"What?"

"What do you need to tell her? What information do you have?" Luna asked. It might have been Luna's question, but I couldn't help but notice the way Seraphina watched me. Her hand curled into a fist like one incorrect answer would get me thrown out of the tavern. Honestly, I had no doubt she could if she wanted to.

"I think I need to tell Evelyn first. But I promise I will do it first thing tomorrow." I lifted my glass to my lips and tipped it back, emptying it. The slight rush the alcohol brought wasn't near enough to clear my head of the cycle it was fixated on. My wolf growled in my head, but this time, I was pretty sure it was me he was angry at.

You did this. It's your fault. And you let her think otherwise.

Letting her work with faulty assumptions was more dangerous than any of the tests I'd accused her of doing in the library. Maybe I needed to find her tonight. That tightness in my chest constricted. Finding her wouldn't be a problem.

Luna and Seraphina shared a glance, likely deciding whether or not my answer was sufficient. It must have been. Or, at least, they could give me a day to try things myself. Surely, they would come after me with pitchforks should I fail to provide Evelyn with the necessary information promptly.

I pulled out some coins and left them on the counter as I stood. "I'll take care of it."

The words were more for me than anyone else.

"I'll walk you out." Vincent stood and gave Luna an endearing smile before following me through the busy tavern.

He pulled me to the side of the building as soon as we exited. "Are you alright?"

I considered my response as I took in the cool night around me. Parkview Tavern was aptly named, surrounded by greenery. The scent of the forest filled my nose as I took in a deep breath. The twisting in my chest was still there, but it wasn't getting worse. I wondered if that meant Evelyn had made it home.

"I'm fine." I sighed heavily as Vincent rolled his eyes at my reply. He wouldn't let me leave without more information. "I was just embarrassed speaking with Evelyn earlier. She said she thought about me all the time. I thought she was..." I couldn't bring myself to say it, even to Vincent, and he'd heard me say that I believed the Vesten God was a myth.

"You thought she was interested in you?" He somehow knew what I was hiding without my awkward attempt at an explanation. "You thought she was telling you she had feelings for you, like you do for her."

I swiped my hand listlessly through the air. "It doesn't

matter. She confessed to a lot of feelings, none of which were under her control."

"Don't jump to conclusions, Ambrose. If everything you've said is true, you have both magic and real feelings floating around in there somewhere." He gestured to my chest. "Don't presume to know about hers until you ask her about them directly."

I shrugged.

As if realizing he'd get no more acknowledgment from me, he switched to an even less cheery topic.

"What did your father say about the competition?"

I ran my hand through my hair. "You are a bright spot in my day, Vincent," I said with a heavy dose of sarcasm.

"So, he took it well, then."

"He just assumed I would win. And somehow my keeping up the appearances made him proud."

I wished I could sort through my own feelings on the matter, but I was at my wits' end with everything else. Father's opinions were colored by his accident. Until then, he'd been as avid a blood magic researcher as Evelyn. And honestly, not as good. Yes, he had reason to be scared, but I wasn't sure that warranted dismissing the subject entirely.

If the Vesten Point and Lord Arctos were to be believed, they had needed to know about their blood magic connection in order to save the continent. That made learning about it seem a worthwhile investment to me.

Unfortunately, Lord Arctos's problem and the competition for Vesten historian also weren't at the top of my priority list. My bond with Evelyn was twisting me in knots. I needed to get some rest. Hopefully, that would clear my head, and we could start fresh in the morning.

"This will all work out," Vincent said, giving me a small smile. "I'm sure of it."

On one hand, I wanted to believe him. I considered him an

expert in love now. Things had worked out so well for him. He'd gotten the girl *and* the job. Though not the position he'd originally wanted, his current one fit him even better.

When he'd originally made that stupid bargain with Luna, I told him he was biting off more than he could chew, especially when his wind magic took note of her. Clearly, I had been wrong.

But just because it worked out for him, that didn't mean my disaster would have any silver lining. Evelyn and I were competing for the same position. One she wanted. One I had been training for most of my life. We had to research a magical connection that was hundreds of years old, one that no one had even realized existed until recently. On top of that, now we had to take a break from that work to find a way to sever the bond we'd accidentally formed between ourselves. And I hadn't even confessed the whole truth about how it was formed.

So, yeah, I was in a much worse place than Vincent had been when he struck his bargain with Luna. I'd be lucky if Evelyn still spoke to me if we made it out of this at all.

13

Evelyn

Movement was uncomfortable. It was the same unwieldy feeling of my shift, like being in my own body was not where I belonged, but I knew this one wasn't my veil cat's fault. Every step through the forest that forced me away from Ambrose was another tightening in my chest.

This was ... bad.

I was sure it was worse than bad, but my brain couldn't find a better descriptor as my baser instincts slid to the forefront.

One of my favorite things about Parkview Tavern was that it was located in a lush, green wood that ran from the city center to the sea. Unfortunately, the tavern's placement precisely in the center of the city meant there were no easy paths to my usual escape routes. My fraying nerves about this bond, the project, and Ambrose released some of the careful hold I attempted to keep on my shift. I laughed at my hope. My veil cat was in control when she wanted to be, and it seemed she was choosing now to take over.

It was sheer luck that most of my shifts had been so early in the morning that no one had seen me run through the streets as a giant, reddish-brown cat. I wouldn't be that lucky forever. As my claws fought to extend and gooseflesh rose on my arms, I didn't think I would be that lucky now.

Sandrin was packed. The sun was low in the sky, and it was less than a week after the largest winter solstice celebration this city had seen in years. Locals were leaving work for the day, families were gathering for a meal, and tourists were searching for new adventures within the city's limits.

If I shifted, I was screwed.

When I glanced down at my hand, it was almost entirely paw. My fur grew and disappeared as I struggled to regain control over myself. I sucked in a few deep breaths, but nothing worked.

"Not now. Please, not now," I whispered to myself, even though attempting to reason with my veil cat had yet to help me.

The only good thing about this veil cat takeover was that at least I wasn't thinking about Ambrose.

And then I was thinking about Ambrose again.

I stopped walking and looked around. A few couples meandered in the park ahead of me, but I had a little space. The discomfort was too much, though. The risk of losing this battle against myself was too great. With each step farther away from the tavern—from him—I lost a little more control. There was no way I made it all the way home. I ducked behind some bushes into a small copse of trees to get hold of myself.

With a thick tree trunk at my back, I sucked in more deep breaths. *In through the nose, out through the nose.* I could do this. I didn't need to be near Ambrose. He didn't want me near him, anyway. He was utterly embarrassed by everything I'd shared at the tavern.

It was the height of irony that I'd had to admit to him that one of my tests, which he considered so reckless, was responsible for our current predicament.

Maybe he was right. Maybe any blood magic was too dangerous.

I didn't believe that. Blood magic was the only magic available to those not fully fae. It could be life-changing to those born without magic. The story about the human sisters in the journal proved that. When natural disaster had driven the food supply to unpredictability, they used blood magic to feed their people.

One mistake didn't throw away all that potential.

Even if the one mistake had been a pretty big one.

My head ached as I sipped in another lungful of air in my hidden location. I let my body slide down the tree against which I leaned. My paw—hand—stopped shifting, and I wasn't sure why. It didn't feel like I had grasped some semblance of control, but the shift had stopped its progression. I dug my hand into the dirt, as if it were a lifeline.

The tightness in my chest loosened. My breathing exercises were working better than anticipated. I had never been able to stop the shift when it was so insistent.

Then I heard the rustling in the bushes.

No, no, no. I couldn't have a visitor in here. Maybe I'd wrangled a minute of control, but it wouldn't last if someone pressed in on my peace.

A fresh scent hit my nostrils, and it occurred to me why the twisting feeling had lessened. Ambrose smelled like old books and pencil shavings. They might have been mundane scents, but they suited him perfectly. His auburn hair peeked through the dark green bushes even in the shadows of the fading light.

"What are you doing here, Ambrose?" I asked, pushing myself up with the help of the tree. I didn't need to appear weaker than I was sure I already looked. He didn't need to see how badly this magical bond was affecting me, or how little control I had in this moment.

And he was the absolute last person in the world I needed to shift in front of.

"Evelyn? Your heart was racing. I thought you were in trouble." He slid the rest of the way through the bushes and stood up. His broad shoulders took up too much space in my small clearing.

Standing now, I still craned my neck to look up at him. "I'll be fine. Continue on your way."

His hazel eyes did a cursory full-body scan. It wasn't lingering, but it left me feeling raw and exposed all the same. I glanced down to see what he saw. More of me must have been partially shifting than just my paw. My pants and shirt were torn. A dark line of dirt covered my knee from where I'd fallen when clambering through the bushes myself. I felt twigs in my hair as I ran my fingers over it. In short, I was a mess.

He stepped toward me. "Let me help you."

"No." I held up my hands to stop his forward progress.

He halted at my movement. "Evelyn." He ran his fingers through his hair in exasperation. "We need to talk."

"Tomorrow would be best." My nostrils flared, but when I reached for another deep breath, all I could smell was Ambrose.

Wood shavings, probably freshly carved from the stupid pencil he kept in his pocket. I didn't know whether to laugh or cry. What was I doing? The scent was ridiculous, but he smelled good. My veil cat didn't press forward, but it was like she sat patiently in my head, biding her time while I made an idiot of myself all on my own.

His hair flopped unevenly from the constant tousle of his fingers, but instead of a messy disaster, it looked like he meant it to be that way. It was frankly unfair. My gaze raked over his shoulders, so big they seemed to take up all the space in my small sanctuary. I'd never understand how someone who spent as much time tucked into books as I did had such broad shoulders and unfortunately defined arm muscles.

What was wrong with me? Was I checking Ambrose out?

Ambrose tried to speak. "I need to—"

"If you must stay, give me a minute."

My nostrils flared, and Mom's teasing replayed in my head. *We're not ignoring facts, are we?* I had always known Ambrose was handsome. I thought my body and I had agreed we were ignoring that particular fact, since everything about me seemed off-putting to him.

I closed my eyes, taking another deep breath, trying to ignore his scent. Maybe if I didn't look at him, he wouldn't be so appealing. My veil cat's tail twitched in my head, like she knew better.

Another deep breath.

Nope, the stupid smell was still there. Musty books? Come on, how is that a turn-on? My cheeks flushed at the thought, because as much as I didn't want to admit it to myself, that was exactly what this was. My crush was progressing, because here I was considering how attractive Ambrose Yarrow was in my discombobulated state. I wasn't thinking clearly enough to remember why that fact was irrelevant.

Maybe this was just the magic. Yes, that sounded right.

But you'd noticed his physical attributes the first day you met him in the Records Office, and probably every day after that in the Vesten Library.

Before I had found my favorite study carrel, Ambrose used to sneak up on me often. Well, he still snuck up on me even with the study carrel, but now I blamed that firmly on his wolf. Once, though, just after I was hired, while I attempted an experiment with a huckleberry bush, I'd barely pricked my finger. He'd appeared behind me and told me it was against procedure to conduct any blood magic experiment with living things in the Great Room.

I'd jumped so high I'd fallen out of my chair. Then I'd asked him where he suggested I conduct the experiments, in that case. Only the interruption of Gabriel, oblivious to the tension between us, had stopped us from getting into a full-blown argument.

Ambrose's ears had pinkened then. It was the first time I'd seen it, and a stupid flutter somewhere in the vicinity of my chest had enjoyed the look. The slight look of concern on the too-self-assured fae's features was something I would forever crave. It had lasted only seconds before he'd turned and walked away from me.

I opened my eyes in the small clearing beyond the bushes. I wished he would walk away from me now, too, like he had then.

It used to be so easy to drive him away. Now he stood resolute and unmoving, like he'd make me hear whatever he'd decided he needed to say. Finally, I nodded. That seemed signal enough for him to proceed.

"I need to tell you something about the bond between us."

No. I shook my head. That was not a topic we needed to cover now. I was barely holding it together as it was. I couldn't listen to him lecture me about my recklessness—about my mistake.

"It's not as straightforward as you seem to think it is..."

Of course it wasn't. I was not an idiot; undoing or changing the shape of a blood magic bond was an unknown, maybe impossible task. It was why the Compass Points and gods had asked us for help in the first place. Hadn't I just told him that an hour ago? My temper flared, and whatever battle I had previously won against my veil cat was forgotten.

"Ambrose." I clenched my teeth as my veil cat finally lost patience with this whole scene. She must be done toying with me. Done waiting for me to make some ill-conceived move on my attraction to Ambrose.

The shift surged within me, and I couldn't hold it back.

"Evelyn?" The register of his voice elevated. He sounded worried, like when he thought I was doing a particularly risky experiment. Usually, he would run his hand through his hair when he used that tone of voice—further evidence of his nerves.

It occurred to me then that I could no longer see his face. I had fallen to the ground. On all fours, to be precise. My now paw didn't need to scratch my head to know that reddish-brown fur covered my body.

I shifted in front of Ambrose Yarrow.

14

Ambrose

My knees hit the packed dirt in front of Evelyn as I reached for her, attempting to catch her before she fell. I realized too late the danger I'd put myself in. She wasn't falling so much as collapsing into her shift. Now, her veil cat's yellow-green eyes pinned me in place.

They looked so different from Evelyn's deep brown. They were no less alluring. Gods, I needed to focus. The variance in color signaled that the animal might have been more in control of this particular shift than Evelyn was.

Evelyn was a veil cat shifter.

Puzzle pieces slammed together in my mind. How scared she'd been that I might have seen it. Her line of inquiry about the current Vesten Point's form. It was certainly not a common shift. The current Vesten Point was the only one in recent history.

More concerning than the type of animal she shifted into at this particular moment was the fact that she did not seem to have any control over the change. The cat stared at me for another moment, and then one paw moved toward me.

I wasn't sure if I should shift into my wolf or if that would only make things worse. My animal whined in my head with indecision.

"Evelyn," I tried.

The veil cat growled as the yellow-green eyes I stared into shifted to brown.

Interesting. Interesting and dangerous. Evelyn's growl showed off her sharp, lengthy teeth. Her ears went back, and her hackles raised. All the straightforward signs that I needed to give her space. Still on my knees, I shuffled farther back until my shoulders hit the bushes surrounding the small enclosure.

Evelyn was in control when the veil cat's eyes matched her own. I got the sense that Evelyn *in control* of her veil cat was worse for me. A strong, innate understanding told me that she wouldn't attack, but honestly, I had no idea where that confidence came from. My cowardice had allowed her to leave the tavern embarrassed and alone. I'd followed her into this secluded space, and now I'd seen the shift she was hiding.

She was probably pissed at me.

Before I could decide to crawl back through the bushes, her eyes shifted to yellow-green again. With the change in eye color came a significant reduction in her signs of aggression. Her movements were quick toward me, and I didn't have time to get away. Not that I wanted to at this point. I still hadn't told her what I needed to about our bond. And the way she kept losing control of her shift worried me. I didn't think she should be left alone.

I understood what was happening. Like with her not knowing how to use her fire magic to warm herself, she must not have had anyone to explain this to her, either. She was acting like a young Vesten first learning about their magic. Our court was blessed with both fire magic and the ability to shift forms. Most outside of the court didn't understand how the two magics went together, but we considered them two sides of the same coin. The flame ignited the change from fae to beast and back.

Once one understood that, they tended to realize that the animal itself wasn't separate from us. It was a part of us, just like our fire magic. Evelyn's eyes shifted color again, and the separation between her and her veil cat was evident. She was fighting too hard; she wasn't comfortable in this second skin.

How long had it been like this?

I knew nothing about Evelyn's fae father. Her mother had stopped by the library a few times for meals or to drop something off. I'd liked her immediately. My Vesten hearing came in handy when she was around. Her first question after asking Evelyn about her day, or whatever errand had brought her there, was always about me. A broad smile usually followed her asking where the handsome Ambrose boy was hiding. Her mother seemed to enjoy the way Evelyn's shoulders tensed at the mention of my name.

Admittedly, I liked it, too.

The veil cat's eyes shifted once again, and with the brown came a growl that should have scared me more than it did.

Anger flooded me that no one had taught Evelyn about her shift. Where had her father been? Where were any other Vesten fae who could have helped her? I counted myself as one of them, and something clenched in my chest at the thought. The feeling had nothing to do with the magic that bound us. My heart broke for Evelyn, and heat surged through my veins, arching my back like I, too, might shift uncontrollably.

I never lost control of my magic. Before exploring blood magic, I had trained for years to perfect my use of the Vesten flame and shift. Fire flared in my palm now as I wondered how anyone could consider Evelyn less than perfect.

She'd moved closer to me. Her steps paused as my fire

erupted, but she didn't flee. I held my breath as she leaned in even closer. The tip of her nose sniffed my flame. Her eyes were that yellow-green color.

Had no one taught her how to shift? Our Vesten customs to not discuss our shifted forms outside of family had boxed her out of learning—the same way our definitions of Vesten had kept her from our schools for so many years. It wasn't right. Even if, on some level, the shift was instinctual, it wasn't something I wished anyone to have to go through alone.

There was a comfort that came with having the shift explained. I'd found an internal acceptance when my father did so for me.

She licked my hand, unafraid that my flame would burn her.

It wouldn't—it'd be like my flame burning my own palm.

Evelyn the brown-eyed veil cat might not have wanted me around, but Evelyn entirely ceding control to her shifted animal seemed to like me. More than that, she seemed to trust me. I wasn't sure what to make of that.

Slowly, I stood and doused my flame. I warred with myself about how to proceed. There was nothing that truly angered Evelyn more than when I asked questions about her experimental method. It didn't seem to matter that I was trying to help—that I wanted her and everyone in the library to be safe. She saw it as an invasion. Those were the times I knew she truly disliked me. They were also, unfortunately, the questions I couldn't help but ask.

It felt similar to the decision I faced now. Evelyn was an adult; if she wanted to give herself over to the shift completely, that was her choice. My mind was ready with the rebuttal. *Is it her choice if she doesn't know how to stop it?*

The thought nagged at me. If no one had taught her, was this really her decision?

Her soft fur against the tips of my fingers had me glancing

down. She'd wrapped herself around my legs, her tail curled to hold me in place. The position was such that the scruff of her neck was beneath the hand hanging limp at my side.

That was ... intimate.

The tips of my ears went hot, and I was glad no one was around to see.

I didn't want to leave her like this, but hadn't she made it clear she didn't want to talk to me tonight?

In her veil cat form, she nuzzled my knee, while I ran my fingers through my hair with indecision.

Without warning, a growl ripped from her throat. She hissed, and her ears were back again as she turned to face me. The brown of Evelyn's eyes mixed with the yellow-green, and I didn't think the result would be good. Evelyn was fighting herself too hard. This wasn't going to end well.

"It's alright, Evelyn," I tried. "Breathe. The shift is you, you are the shift. Don't fight so hard against it."

It was obvious she didn't listen from the way her whole body started to shake. I couldn't leave her now. There was only one way this type of shift could end.

"You're alright. You're safe, Evelyn," I tried to soothe her, like my father had done to me with my first shift, but it didn't seem to help. Her lip arched to reveal even more teeth. Her hackles rose, and her massive, reddish-brown body shook even more intensely.

I held my hands out as if to prevent the burnout I knew she was barreling toward.

She shook again, and a yowl that chased down my spine like steel against steel slipped from her mouth. With it, she fell to the ground in a heap.

I dropped to my knees again beside her. Tentatively, I reached out to stroke her fur. "You're safe, Evelyn," I tried to reassure her, but her eyelids were closed. The slow, even rise and fall of the chest of her veil cat form made it clear she had passed out. I hoped it would only be a few moments before she naturally shifted back into her half-fae form. The change didn't come as expected.

The small shelter of bushes had served its purpose to preserve her privacy for the shift, but I couldn't leave her here.

She was a large, wild cat, not at all a tame kitten I could easily carry, but that didn't change my decision. I scooped her up in my arms. Her size was unwieldy, but physical strength had never been a problem for me. Getting back through the bushes without disturbing her required some maneuvering. From there, I only had one choice.

I didn't know where she lived. Full dark had fallen, and in no world would she want anyone else to see her in this form. This part of the park was relatively empty; anyone taking a stroll had found their way home or to their evening meal. I covered her with my jacket anyway.

Her feline head pressed against me, and I chose the only option available. We weren't far from my apartment. It was the closest place I could go to protect her privacy and keep her safe. If she didn't wake up until morning, it would be less than ideal, but I would cross that bridge when we got to it.

15

Evelyn

Metal clanged against metal in the distance. A pot, maybe? Noises were still fuzzy, the world around me not yet in focus. Wherever I was, it was warm, and I was wrapped in comfort. It smelled like something mundane, but fruitier scents wafted in from the doorway. I felt safe, and I wasn't ready to leave.

Voices stirred me to life—ones I didn't recognize. A young girl's voice floated to the room I had yet to identify. "But why is she in your bed?"

My eyes snapped open.

"My friend wasn't feeling well. She's just recovering."

I knew that voice. It was soft and low and reassuring. I'd heard that tone when we spoke of magic on the ferry.

Why was I waking up to Ambrose Yarrow's voice?

Scenes of last night flashed through my mind. The park. The clearing behind the bushes. Too-big Ambrose taking up too much space within it. Shifting. Fighting desperately for control with my veil cat. I winced.

I must have passed out. Carefully, I pushed myself to a seated position. The soft and warm comfort in which I had found myself moments earlier was, as the young girl described, Ambrose's bed.

It was large, but it looked like I'd taken up the entirety of the space. The bedroom was a bit sparse, but that didn't surprise me for Ambrose. The bedside table held a single book. The rest of the room featured light, neutral colors, mostly grays and whites. It reminded me of his wolf.

"Mom says sometimes when we don't feel well, we're just hungry."

This kitchen conversation was becoming increasingly confusing. Who was this girl? Ambrose couldn't possibly have a child, could he? My cheeks heated as I remembered how I'd reacted to his presence in the clearing—the worst possible time for attraction to strike.

"Sasha," his voice was so gentle. I wasn't sure I'd ever heard him use that tone before. "Mom is right, but in this case, my friend just needed rest."

Now I felt like I was intruding. I pushed myself out of the bed and tried to decide if I should make noise to alert them that I was awake.

"I'm going to help Timothy get ready. Will you be over with breakfast soon?" Sasha must have accepted his words as true. However, she didn't sound old enough to be wandering the streets by herself. She already knew I was here. I might as well make myself known so that Ambrose could go with her.

I cleared my throat as I took careful steps out of the room and down the hallway. Thankfully, even in the state I was in last night, I'd shifted back to my half-fae form fully clothed. Although I questioned my self-preservation instinct, since I'd shifted in front of Ambrose Yarrow.

I paused my steps as I considered what that meant.

He knew I could shift.

That isn't that bad. I knew he didn't believe my lies yesterday.

He knew I couldn't control my shift. That much had been obvious.

He also knew I was a veil cat shifter.

How would he use this information against me? Why had he brought me here?

I closed my eyes and let my head fall back as everything else rushed in. We were still competing for the position of Vesten historian. We were bound by blood magic—a mistake I'd made. I was supposed to have worked on the solution to that particular problem last night. Instead ... I glanced around ... this had happened.

I needed to get to the library. Sasha spoke of breakfast. It must be morning.

The deep breath I pulled in through my nose stood no chance of calming me with all of this racing through my mind, but I attempted it anyway.

I scanned the kitchen and living space as I exited the hallway. The little girl, Sasha, looked just like Ambrose. Her hair was a brighter red than his auburn, but they had matching aquiline noses and full lips.

"She's awake!" Sasha jumped for joy at my arrival. I was taken aback, having never been shown such enthusiasm for my simply existing.

Ambrose met and held my gaze. It might have been a trick of my eyes, but he seemed to move a little slower than he had moments before—as if afraid to spook me if he did something too fast.

He stood over a stove, a spatula primed in his hand over an iron skillet. A white mark of what I could only assume was flour smudged the side of his nose and splattered across the light blue apron he wore. It was oddly adorable.

That couldn't be right. My spine snapped straight as I tried to pull myself together. I shouldn't ogle Ambrose Yarrow on a typical day, for a whole host of reasons. If he also was partnered and had a child, that was an entirely different side of the coin I didn't need to deal with.

"Good ... morning," I said hesitantly.

His hazel eyes hadn't left mine. He nodded in reassurance, even if I wasn't sure what he was reassuring me about. That it was alright that I had exposed my secret to him? That I was intruding on his family's morning?

"Good morning, Evelyn," he said.

"I've been waiting for you to wake up," Sasha said, making sure we didn't forget about her, even though the way Ambrose snared my attention made that a challenge.

I can look away at any time.

Reminding myself of that fact didn't seem to help. My veil cat felt like a house cat curled up in front of a fire, which was the exact opposite of how my half-fae body was processing this experience. There was a rightness to this place, to my proximity to Ambrose and the unexpected domesticity of this moment. It felt warm, like I'd popped one of those hard red candies Ambrose had shared on the ferry yesterday.

Except I hadn't.

Reason slid back in. These must be symptoms of the blood magic. It wanted us to grow together. I needed to get to the library to figure out how to break it.

"Sasha was just going home," Ambrose seemed to remind her.

"Oh, yes." Her eyes widened as if surprised she'd forgotten. She moved to the counter to grab a stack of pancakes on a plate. "I'll take these. Bring the rest when you're finished." Turning on her heel, she walked to the door.

"Ambrose, do you need to..." I gestured toward her, the girl who couldn't be more than six, who he seemed ready to send out into the city on her own.

His attention hadn't left me. "She's alright. She's just going down the hall. You can watch her if you feel more comfortable." He tapped his nose. "I can scent if anyone else is in the hallway on her walk."

So Sasha didn't live here. That still didn't quite explain who she was. I opened the door since her hands were full with the plate of pancakes. As I was already at the door and didn't want to continue to stare at Ambrose like an idiot, I watched Sasha.

He was right, of course. She walked down two doors and opened the unlocked door on the opposite side of the hallway. She announced her entry and the arrival of breakfast with glee.

The noises in the kitchen behind me quieted. Ambrose must have finished his work. I turned to face him, finding him close.

I couldn't hide my jump, though I managed to keep the inevitable "yeep" in my mouth.

Ambrose's lip tilted into an almost-smile. "I know. A bell. I'll get one."

His familiar words left me wanting to smile in return, but I couldn't. I was in Ambrose's home. He knew too much. I needed to get away from whatever this was.

He opened his mouth to speak again, but I didn't want to hear whatever he'd say.

"Who is Sasha?"

His brow furrowed, then smoothed as he scratched the back of his neck. "My little sister."

My shoulders sagged in relief, and I didn't mull too long over why that might be.

"Your family lives down the hall?"

He nodded. "My mother travels quite a bit for work. And father could use the help with the twins."

I wasn't sure what I'd expected, but that was not it. A

hundred other questions filled my mind, each one more invasive than the last. Ambrose didn't make me ask any of them. He simply continued speaking. "My father's eyesight is severely impaired. I just like to help when my mother is traveling. Twins can be a handful no matter the circumstances."

This time, I didn't stop the slight curve of my lip, even though there was still a list of reasons I should.

Another thought occurred to me, making me wince. "Let me guess, you also get them to school?" That was why he was never as early to the library as I was.

"I do." He paused as if realizing why I asked the question. "They go early. I come into the library later because my father always has a hundred questions about what I'm doing with blood magic."

My head tilted automatically at the mention. "Did he ... work with blood magic when he was at the library?" As I finished the sentence, I felt like I was sliding across ice while it was fracturing beneath me. Something in the back of my mind yelled *danger*, but it was far too late to stop. I was already halfway across.

Ambrose sighed, not making eye contact, but continued to speak. "Blood magic is what affects his eyesight. It was a research project that didn't go as he anticipated."

I sucked in a breath. More puzzle pieces of Ambrose Yarrow snapped precisely into place. "Did he..." I didn't know how to finish the sentence.

"Did he test on living things? Yes, I suppose he did at one point. He certainly doesn't now. Some would say he championed the practice of only testing on inanimate objects as a safety measure. Most of the time, he's trying to shut down all research on blood magic."

"I see." And I did. I had always assumed Ambrose was raised with a love of learning, of testing. Those attributes were always so clear in him. I thought the constant poking at my experiments was reserved only for those whose methods he didn't trust. Was it possible that his incessant questions, his caution that implied irresponsibility on my part, were attributes he was raised with? How did his father feel about his current projects? I didn't have to wait to find out.

"He likes to review the experiments being conducted in the library. The documentation is public for Vesten." He scratched the back of his neck. "He has concerns with nearly all of them —with the safety risk they present."

Then my cheeks heated. Were his nagging questions misplaced anxiety? I didn't want to know that. This felt too private all of a sudden. I didn't want to know more about him and his family's history with blood magic. My veil cat uncurled in my head, perking up as if to say *liar.*

I needed to get a grip. I needed to get to the library. I needed to know what Ambrose was going to do with the information he had obtained last night.

"About—" I started.

"We should—" he said.

He gestured for me to go first.

Suddenly, I wasn't sure what to say. I took a deep breath and searched for words I was sure didn't exist. Should I thank him? Threaten him? Ask him what he was going to do now that he knew about my veil cat? About my lack of control? My indecision must have been written plainly on my face.

"I won't tell anyone about your shift." He ran his hand through his hair in a way that was oddly comforting. "I'm not sure why you keep it a secret, but no one will hear it from me."

A breath escaped my lungs. Was it that easy? My brow furrowed. "Why?"

He raised his hands in a gesture of peace. "I know what it's like not to understand your shift." He paused as if unsure how to proceed. He decided on something. "Do you want to know what works for me?"

"What ... works ... for you?"

I was confused. Were we really not talking about the fact that I was a veil cat shifter? A mythical animal? Was he offering information about shifting to me with no strings attached?

I couldn't take it anymore. "Are we not going to talk about the animal I shift into?"

He shrugged. "I told you a few days ago, it's not as crazy as you seem to think. If the Vesten Point can do it—most would see it as a sought-after shift."

I mulled that over. "And you don't want to be the one to point out that another veil cat shifter exists?"

"Your secret is safe with me, Evelyn. I don't know how else to express that." He held my gaze until I was the first to look away.

"I have to go. I'm sorry about whatever happened when I shifted, and that it meant I didn't spend the time working on this blood magic bond between us. I think it's putting more stress on my shift than usual."

He rubbed the back of his neck again. A blush tinted his cheeks. "Evelyn, we need to talk. I tried to tell you last night, but I don't think you heard me before you shifted." He gestured to the table between his kitchen and living space. "Will you have breakfast with me? I need to explain something about the magic binding us. You seem to think it's entirely your fault. I assure you, it isn't."

16

Ambrose

I was not one to hide from hard truths. My job was to bring them to the surface, to state facts that might otherwise have remained unaddressed. Why was I having such a hard time with this particular truth?

The wolf prowling in my head lay prostrate, covering his face with his paws as if to ask the same question.

It was embarrassing, sure, but it also wasn't that simple. Evelyn had been embarrassed when she'd confessed that she'd magically bound us together. If I were only embarrassed, I would have said something yesterday, so that Evelyn didn't feel so singularly stupid. So that she knew this wasn't only her fault.

And that was the problem.

I wasn't convinced that my feelings and actions were due to the blood magic.

My wolf went back to pacing in my head as I considered that. *I can't ignore that blood was spilled, that I had intent. The fact that I found her on the opposite side of the bay in wolf form is also suspicious. I hunted her, for all intents and purposes. That wasn't due to my attraction.*

On a heavy sigh, I returned to the kitchen to collect the stack of pancakes that Sasha hadn't taken. I separated them onto two plates while I boiled water for coffee.

Evelyn sat uncomfortably at the table. Her spine was straight, and she nervously tucked her hair behind her ears as she glanced around the apartment. What must she think of it? I tried to imagine it from her perspective. Morning light spilled in through the windows in the sitting room. The light gray sofa, the plain wood table, and a small collection of toys that the twins had brought but hadn't taken home with them. The space wasn't much, but it was mine. That had been my concession to myself when I decided to stick close to my parents' place to help with the twins.

As if the thought summoned them, another knock sounded at the door. I was unsurprised to see Timothy peek around the door as it opened. He hadn't quite learned to wait after the knock.

"You didn't bring the rest of the pancakes. Sasha said you probably got distracted. She said you couldn't stop staring at your friend."

I shook my head, wondering if my siblings had been created solely to torture me, even if his assertion wasn't far from the mark. I had forgotten to bring the rest of them. "Here they are, Tim." I offered him the plate with the remaining stack.

"Father asked if you needed him to take us to school."

I thought maybe Evelyn snorted from the table, but when I glanced over my shoulder, her face was as masked as it had been when she searched the room.

"I'll be there in a few minutes. Evelyn and I need to finish our discussion."

Timothy nodded and left with the plate. I poured hot water over the filter and grounds, making two cups of coffee to accompany our meal. While the coffee finished, I went to the porch to pick fresh berries from the plant I kept there.

"I really can just meet you at the library. It's clear you have a busy morning," Evelyn said.

I returned, rinsing the berries and delivering the plates and cups to the table. "I asked you to stay for breakfast. I need to get this out."

She nodded. "Thank you, this looks lovely. You cook for them every morning?"

I shrugged. "Most."

"You said your mother travels for work? What does she do?" She bit her lip as the question slipped out, like maybe she hadn't meant to show as much interest as she had. Or maybe she thought I'd find the question impertinent. Something in me was happy that she even cared to ask. I never knew where I stood with Evelyn. I wanted her to want to know more.

"She maintains a private library for one of the old fae families. She travels often to collect new items for them and verify their authenticity before purchase."

I cut into my breakfast. It also helped that this line of questioning would avoid the topic I so desperately needed to discuss with her.

My wolf flopped on the ground again in disappointment. I mentally argued with him: *just a few more minutes of peace.*

It was a testament to how much I wanted to avoid the main topic, that I continued to share information about my family—about our tenuous history with blood magic. My hands wrapped around the warm mug, bringing it to my lips, and I took a bracing sip before offering more information. "Mother took the job when Father retired. She'll never admit it, but I'm sure she's hoping to come across more texts on blood magic."

Evelyn's leg bounced beneath the table. I could feel the vibrations through the floor. For a minute, I thought she wouldn't ask. She bit her lip as if to keep the words in. I exhaled when they slipped out anyway. "Why?"

I found myself wanting her to know. Maybe it would help her understand why I was so thorough when it came to her experiments. "My father gave up on trying to break the magic that impairs his eyesight." I swallowed. "My mother hasn't. She thinks she'll find the information in a rare text someday."

Evelyn's eyes narrowed. "Why doesn't she ask you? You must have more information than any book she might find in an old fae collection."

A huff escaped through my lips. It was almost a defense of me—of my ability—even though I knew she didn't care for my cautious methods. In reality, my research was a constant battle against myself. A continuous need to learn, weighed against the need not to recreate an accident like my father's. And he warned me about it daily.

"Neither of them wants me to study blood magic. My father may want me to be Vesten historian, but he has his own plan for how I should do everything differently." I scratched the back of my neck, realizing we'd entered equally uncomfortable territory speaking about the Vesten historian position. "Not that I'm guaranteed it."

She tilted her head as she took a bite, chewing thoughtfully before speaking. "Is that what you want with the position?"

What a novel question, but for once, her hackles didn't rise with the discussion. She seemed genuinely interested. The way she had so purposefully told me she wanted the Vesten historian position a few days ago rang through my mind. That kind of conviction was intoxicating, although I still didn't know why she wanted it. I just knew with absolute certainty that she did.

Had anyone ever asked me why I wanted it? If I wanted it? Father had tried to convince me not to study blood magic when Gabriel offered. He'd tried to convince me to do anything else, even leave work at the library entirely. I was far too obsessed with history, and Gabriel's offer introduced me to a new field of study. Something terrifying, yes, but something inherently connected to the history I loved. It was only after Father's attempts to dissuade me failed that he'd focused on safer research procedures with blood magic. His requests had seemed reasonable until I met Evelyn.

"I want to learn from our past. I want to believe we can do better as a court, as a continent."

She nodded thoughtfully. "And what about blood magic? Where does that fit in?"

I sighed. "That answer changes by the day." My answer was too honest, but something felt unfiltered between us in this room. At my kitchen table, eating the breakfast I had made for my family, it felt different than every single one of our discussions in the library. "I want to believe experiments can be conducted safely."

She gestured between us, her cheeks bright red. "That's just not the way blood magic works."

Well, she had me there. I was aware that there would always be some risk. I was still having a hard time articulating my acceptable risk tolerance in discussions with my father. His tolerance was nonexistent, and I understood why, but I knew, as Evelyn said, that to learn more and make progress, there needed to be a middle ground.

"That's what I wanted to talk to you about." I ran my fingers through my hair. "About risks in conducting blood magic experiments." I let the words slip from my lips like the question had slipped from hers. "I think there was more risk than you realized the other day—"

Her posture, which seemed to have finally relaxed as she listened to me talk about my family, snapped back to attention. "You want to lecture me further on—"

I pushed the words out before she could misconstrue them. "I don't think it was only your intent that led to our bond."

Her fork stopped in its path to her mouth, and she gaped at me. In the next breath, it clanged against the plate as she set it down, or possibly dropped it. I wasn't sure because I didn't take my eyes from hers as they narrowed in my direction again.

"Excuse me?" she said.

I cleared my throat. The hardest part was out. "It wasn't only you. The risk I'm talking about is that you don't know all the details of that evening. You were thinking about your experiment and about us growing together like the flowers." I took a sip of my coffee. "But I was there, too—blood from my cut was also spilled. You, more than anyone, should recognize that there may be multiple intentions at play when living things are involved. That night, during our meal, I was thinking about how everything I say to you comes out wrong, and how it might help if we could understand each other better."

"Help what?" She looked so distrustful. Somehow, this entire thing was having the opposite effect I had hoped it would.

"Our relationship."

She choked on the sip of coffee she'd taken in my silence.

"Our working relationship," I clarified. "I just thought that maybe if we knew each other outside of the Vesten Library, if we spent time together like we did when we helped Vincent and Luna, that maybe our relationship wouldn't be so antagonistic."

She huffed out something that could have been a laugh—or a strangled snarl, I wasn't sure. "So, you think your intent blended with mine?"

I nodded.

She didn't look up as she took another bite of her breakfast. I wasn't sure what else to say. I'd admitted what I needed to. "I'll help find out how to undo it," I said. "We'll both take time away from Lord Arctos's project to fix this."

"Why didn't you say something earlier?" Her voice was

quiet, which in my experience with Evelyn meant that she desperately wanted the answer but wasn't prepared to say as much. I wanted to tell her, but how would that sound?

I wasn't sure my actions were from magic. I thought I was just obsessed with you.

Something in my face must have shown my hesitation.

Finally, she glanced up, looking around the room again instead of at me. "If this morning is any indication, I'd say the magic is getting its way."

Was this because of the magic? I hadn't felt any pressure in my chest when considering telling her about my family. Mostly, I had wanted her to know. To know me better, to know that my ticks, my quirks, weren't as hostile as she seemed to believe. I couldn't say that, either. Instead, I held her gaze. "The getting to know each other is a bit one-sided."

She laughed but didn't steer the conversation toward her or her family. "I think figuring out how to undo this"—she gestured between us—"will help us with Lord Arctos's project. At least if we work together on it, we'll remain on equal footing."

I dipped my chin. She pushed back from the table, taking our empty plates to the kitchen to clean. She did so seamlessly, as if it were the most natural thing in the world to use the soap and rag I had there. I only watched in fascination.

"Thank you for breakfast," she said at last. "And for sharing about your family. I'll let you take your siblings to school, and I'll meet you at the library?"

"Sure," I said, knowing she couldn't see my nod.

Finishing the dishes, she gave me a final glance and slipped out the door. The truths I had shared didn't stop the tug I felt as soon as she was out of sight.

17

Evelyn

The rose and the morning glory twisted together in the pot on the windowsill. These two plants that usually strangled each other's growth couldn't get enough of each other. Obviously, they were mocking me.

Grow together—was that what Ambrose and I were doing?

As if thinking of him reminded me of the tension building in my chest from our separation, I pressed down on my sternum.

Everything I say to you comes out wrong. It might help if we could understand each other better.

Ambrose's confession cycled through my thoughts. He really thought that? At the same time that we both spilled blood?

Growing together wasn't so different from understanding each other. If I were feeling more contemplative, I'd consider why our desires seemed so aligned in that. I tapped my finger against the desk in a steady rhythm. Ambrose still wasn't here.

It had been over an hour since I'd left his apartment. Where was he?

Then again, I didn't strictly need him to continue with either project. Why was I so fixated on him?

Magic, Evelyn. The answer is magic.

Honestly, I hoped that was the case. The soft morning light in his apartment had done mesmerizing things with the gold in his hazel eyes. It hadn't helped that he'd run his fingers through his hair every few minutes. He must have been nervous with all he shared, but toying with his hair also highlighted the blond strands hidden within the auburn, and I couldn't help that my stare lingered.

I wasn't sure if he'd realized it in the moment, but by the end of our conversation, it was clear that he was putting effort into us growing together. He had shared so much about his family and even a little of himself. Part of me wondered if he wanted to share everything that he had, or if it was another facet of the magic urging him to do so. Was it like the tightness in my chest that encouraged our proximity to each other? My stomach churned as I considered the magic forcing him to speak. I hoped that wasn't it. He hadn't looked to be in pain.

Either way, if he kept sharing like he had this morning, maybe we'd find our way through the blood magic connection. The magic wanted us to know each other better—it was making us uncomfortable to be apart. Ambrose had made a good suggestion: if we fulfilled the magic's desire—if we spent time together and got to know each other—it should break the connection.

The veil cat in my head purred at the thought.

We do not want *to spend more time with Ambrose Yarrow.*

Her tail swished in my mind as if to wipe away my thoughts, which she considered irrelevant. I hmphed to myself. Ambrose and I were colleagues. We knew each other professionally. The cat's tail flicked back and forth again as if waiting for me to continue. *Now I guess I also know about his father's experience with blood magic, his mother's search for an answer, and the way his younger siblings stare at him like he hung the moon.*

I sighed. Loudly.

"*I see you're making great progress.*" The familiar black bird landed on my shoulder.

I wanted to sigh again. I was not in the mood to deal with the Vesten God.

"*They say it helps with research when you ... have a book open.*"

"You know I have multiple problems to worry about at the moment." Even as I said so, I grabbed the book from the corner of my desk and flipped it open. It was the one I'd pulled from the restricted section. We had yet to dive into it, even after the hassle of collecting it.

"*Sometimes the best way out is through.*" The bird's wings flapped against my face.

I scrunched my nose. "You can't hear my thoughts, right?"

"*No, thank ... me. Who wants to hear you pine over Mr. Yarrow's forearms flexing? Not even I am that bored.*"

"I—" I was about to tell Lord Arctos off when I flushed, remembering exactly what I'd been thinking about before I passed out last night. I'd cataloged every inch of Ambrose as a veil cat. Or when I'd been fighting between it and my half-fae form. I bit my lip, knowing that I was past pretending I didn't find him attractive—particularly his forearms when he rolled up his sleeves.

"*Not even going to deny it? That's a plot twist.*"

"You are very sassy today. Can I help you with something?"

"*I thought I made that clear. You can help me by finding a way to break the blood magic connecting the gods and the Compass Points. Were you not listening in the briefing?*"

I sighed. "Are you always so ... exhausting?" I asked.

"*Rose says so.*" The bird tilted his head. "*Sometimes Aurora agrees with her.*"

A snort escaped. I was pretty sure he referred to the Norden Point and the Norden Goddess. "Maybe you should consider that feedback."

"*Maybe you should consider the book in front of you,*" he mocked.

My fingers slid over the pages as I flipped them. Kenna's journal was a mess of hurried scrawlings. Some were her thoughts, others were conversations as she remembered them. I wasn't sure exactly what I was looking for, but Lord Arctos sat on my shoulder and read with me, flitting his wing at the side of my face when he decided that I missed something.

He had me pause at the description of the Lake Refilling Ceremony. It happened once a year at Compass Lake. It was meant to commemorate the creation of the fae.

"The powers we bestow you with must intertwine—a bond that strengthens and does not break. They must be as united as the water in the lake, unable to tell which drop has touched which shoreline." Zrak looked at each fae leader. "Lest you think you can ignore us, we will never be far from you. Your power is connected to the lake. The land here will be your seat of power—this is where you will be strongest." He paused. "And we'll know if you weaken."

I snorted. "So, this is how you knew the Lost God did something ... shady?"

"*How do you know that?*" Lord Arctos asked.

"'We'll know if you weaken,' is a pretty good indicator. I know you're gods, but stating as much so boldly, it seems the understanding of another's power was something of which he had alternate assurances."

Lord Arctos huffed. "*We created the fae, we could be connected that way.*"

"Another fae created me," I said, "but he doesn't know what I'm capable of."

The black bird's head swiveled toward me. "*Is that so?*"

Well, I hadn't quite meant to get into family story time with the Vesten God, but I didn't see a way out of it now, since I'd been the one to bring it up. "My fae parent, my father, isn't in my life."

Lord Arctos made another huffing sound. "*And you're so sure he doesn't know anything about your magic?*"

The question gave me pause. Was I sure? I guessed not. My father had known I had fire magic before he left. I didn't think that whether I had magic or the amount had mattered to him. It was more likely the human stain in my blood that he'd run from.

"I can confirm, even if Evelyn can't, that my parents have no connection to my magic. I had to tell them the first time I shifted," Ambrose said in that calm and confident tone he used when speaking about a historical fact.

I jumped, squeaking as I glanced up to where Ambrose now stood, his arms draped over my study carrel as he leaned against it again. The sleeves of his white shirt were already rolled back, and there were ... forearms ... everywhere. I blamed Lord Arctos for my attention on the way his muscles flexed when he laced his fingers together so casually.

"Ambrose," I said through gritted teeth, about to tell him off again about sneaking up on me.

His smile was wolfish.

My heart flip-flopped in my chest, a feeling wholly separate from the tightness when he wasn't near. This might have been the first time he'd so obviously shown me his animal. Seated in my chair, with the Vesten God perched on my shoulder, I wasn't sure what to do with the intimacy. Then I realized Lord Arctos had been speaking into my mind, but Ambrose had answered the question.

"You were speaking to him, too?"

The black bird shrugged, which just meant more feathers flapped against my face. "*He was walking toward us anyway. I figured I'd give him the option to be useful.*"

Ambrose's hazel eyes narrowed at that comment, leading me to believe Lord Arctos's words continued to be for everyone. I tried to hide the blush overtaking my cheeks as I realized Ambrose must have heard what I said about my fae father.

I decided to ignore that fact and return us to the matter at hand. "So, if this is where the gods announce that they have done something to connect themselves to the fae, do we have any text about what they actually did?"

Lord Arctos sighed as if we were the most exhausting beings on the continent. "*I have a note from Zrak. He said only to give it to you if you got this far.*"

"This whole thing has been another test?!" My voice was higher pitched than I would have liked, but I couldn't help it. I was sick of how the Vesten God dropped pieces of information like pathway markers; you were never sure the next one was there until you were already upon it. We stood little chance of success this way.

"*The Osten God wanted to make sure you had some skill before you were to be trusted with the next piece.*"

Ambrose folded his arms over his chest. I hated how I noticed the flex of his biceps under his shirt. This was getting ridiculous, but I went ahead and mentally blamed it on the magic.

We needed to return to work on our own problem. I was no longer sure how Lord Arctos had tricked me into working on his thing when I'd been intent on separating Ambrose and me before proceeding.

"When will you bestow this new piece of information on us?" I asked.

"*I'd like you both to have a meal with me tonight.*"

"Where?" Ambrose asked before I could complain.

"*Let's meet at the tavern Evelyn is so fond of. Parkview, is it?*"

"We'll meet you there." Ambrose inexplicably took charge

of the rest of the conversation. "Now, Evelyn and I need the time before the evening meal to do a bit more work."

Lord Arctos snorted. "*You mean work on trying to break your connection before you break mine? I'd prefer you test your theories amongst yourselves anyway.*" He flapped his wings with newfound energy. "*Carry on. I'll see you in a few hours.*"

The way Ambrose studied me as Lord Arctos flew away made my heart race. I hadn't realized how much Lord Arctos's presence was calming me until he was gone.

As usual, Ambrose didn't seem to have the slightest understanding of how he affected me. He leaned a little farther across the carrel to touch the plants in the window.

"Sorry I took longer than anticipated," he said. "My mother returned from her most recent trip and... Well, I'm sorry for the delay." His lips flattened into a thin line as he spoke. What new books or intel had she brought home? Had it been well received?

I wondered what Ambrose's relationship with his parents was like. They were both in the picture, but he spoke about them as if they had their own expectations for his life. Did they ever ask him what he wanted? His eyes had widened drastically this morning when I'd posed the question. He also hadn't seemed sure in his response—like he was testing the words. I wasn't sure what to make of that.

"I didn't get much done before Lord Arctos showed up," I said. "I was considering the path through our connection."

Ambrose glanced around as if searching for ... a chair. I hadn't taken the time to hide the one across from me when I'd arrived today. It just wasn't worth my time. It certainly wasn't so that I could experience the corner of Ambrose's lip twitching when he noticed it. I'm also sure it wasn't so that his large form would crowd into my space as he pulled the chair over, the same way he had the night we unintentionally bound ourselves.

My veil cat purred at his proximity. I reminded myself that this was just an effect of the magic. But gods, I hoped he couldn't hear her.

Old books and pencil shavings filled my nose. He was so close. Then he pulled out that stupid notebook and pencil. That could not be a turn on. I refused to believe that. Still, I grasped for words. Magic. We were discussing blood magic and an approach to solving our predicament.

"So, through the magic," I said. "Yes? We should try to do what it wants? You appeared amenable to that approach this morning."

He scratched the back of his neck absent-mindedly as I spoke. "I am ... amenable," he said. "Are you?"

His question was hesitant. One, I wasn't sure how much had to do with the magic between us versus our history of ... how had he phrased it? Consistently misunderstanding each other. I didn't plan to share more than was necessary. I could tell him about my time at the Sandrin Records Office and some of the work I'd done there. Hopefully, that would soothe the magic between us.

It would be fine. I wasn't sure if I nodded to him or myself, but with it, we sealed our new approach.

18

Ambrose

Evelyn and I arrived at Parkview Tavern early. She'd agreed to my plan more easily than I anticipated, and that left me optimistic about its outcome. The blood magic wanted us to grow together, or for us to understand each other better. Either intent led to the same result: we needed to talk about ourselves without fighting about work if we hoped for the magic to release.

Though I had high hopes for the plan, when I pulled open the heavy wooden door, it felt like I was walking to my own execution. Seraphina stood behind the bar and crossed her arms over her chest as Evelyn and I entered. Clearly, she was still unsatisfied with my answers yesterday about our predicament.

We didn't even pretend at the privacy of a table in the corner this time. Evelyn marched us straight to the end of the bar and two open stools.

Seraphina's smile for Evelyn was warm, at least. "Everything alright? I didn't expect to see you tonight."

Evelyn nodded. "We're having a meal with Lord Arctos in a little bit. We came early to talk."

The fierce bartender's hands were on her hips in a moment. "That's what you said yesterday. Then you snuck out, upset."

It was as if an entirely different Evelyn appeared in that moment. She looked almost sheepish, an expression that, to me, seemed thoroughly foreign on her face. "I'm sorry, Seraphina. I needed to get out in a hurry."

Seraphina didn't hide her dismissive glance at me. "Need me to get rid of him?"

I let out a shaky breath as Evelyn's lip tipped into an almost-smile. "Not yet."

"Keep me posted," Seraphina said, turning toward the bottles behind her. "Two ales?"

Seraphina couldn't see Evelyn's nod with her back turned, but the owner appeared to take the lack of protest as acceptance and poured each of us a glass. As she slid mine into my hands, she gave me a final glare. She pointed to her usual perch just a few steps away. "I'll be watching from right over there."

I swallowed, more intimidated than I cared to admit.

"So..." Evelyn turned on her stool to face me. "What should we talk about?"

At least this question was something I'd considered. I retrieved my notebook to look at the list.

"You wrote down what we should learn about each other?" she asked.

I couldn't tell if she was in awe of the preparation or embarrassed by it. "I thought about every time you seemed angry at me after a conversation. Those seem like good places to start for understanding each other better."

"You don't think you could have just been an ass in that conversation? There has to be a deeper meaning to it?"

I laughed. "It's entirely possible that I was. In that case, I'd like to understand for future interactions."

She looked ... contemplative. I wasn't sure if that was a good or bad sign, but I pressed forward.

"How about the day we met?" We might as well start at the beginning.

"What was wrong with that?" She took a sip of her drink.

"You walked away in what some would consider the middle of a conversation." I paused.

She sighed, looking down into her glass as if deciding whether or not this approach was worth it. The way she rubbed her sternum made me wonder how the discomfort from the magic affected her. In the end, she pushed her shoulders back and continued. "I ... I had wanted to meet you since I read one of your papers. And there you were, admitting you knew who I was, too." She paused. "I thought I finally had someone to speak with about blood magic, someone who would care more about the research than ... the rest"—she waved her hand to illustrate the complexity and unfairness of fae society—"and the first thing you can think to ask is why I worked in the Records Office. As if I would work there if I had any other choice."

I was sure my ears were bright pink by now. "I'm sorry, Evelyn." The list in my notebook seemed irrelevant if this was the foot on which we'd started our entire relationship. She'd wanted me as a colleague, and I'd made her feel less than—just like everyone else.

My stomach churned, but I knew we needed to do this, not only for the magic.

"Before I even knew who you were, at the circulation desk, I already knew you were the most intelligent person I had ever met. When I realized who you actually were, someone whose every word I had read, it just didn't make sense." I took a long sip of my ale. "I assumed you would be one of the most sought-after researchers, and I know my ignorance only reinforced a lifetime of prejudice you have dealt with. All I can say is that I will do better in the future."

She nodded. Then, as if to distract her from my admission, she glanced down at my notebook again. "What about the test on the mulberries?"

I rubbed my forehead. "This one was also on me. I couldn't stop the reaction. Father's accident occurred when he was working with mulberries. He said he'd intended to see growth opportunities. I believed his theory was that the magic could guide us—we didn't have to come up with all the answers. I'm not sure if he had an alternate intent he was unaware of, or if the fact that there were few opportunities for growth meant there was little to see. But either way, when the magic took hold, his vision was severely impaired."

There was a large crease in her forehead, like she didn't quite understand.

"I was just worried. Scared. Anxious. I'm sure they were all fighting for top billing in my brain at the time."

"About me?" she asked with some wonder, as if she couldn't quite believe that was the case.

I tilted my head, now trying to comprehend her side of the question. "Of course."

The apples of her cheeks turned red, and I felt another layer of understanding peel away.

"Of course I was worried about you, Evelyn. That's always been my problem. I know you're capable. I know it doesn't come off to you this way, but I know you're careful, too. My father was both of those things. Accidents still happen."

She held my gaze, and something tugged between us at the understanding. I couldn't say if it had anything to do with the magic or not. My wolf paced in my head. All my senses were thrown off when it came to Evelyn Knowles.

"What about this one?" She pointed at another item on the list. "It was like you didn't want me hired."

A laugh slipped from my lips at that statement, and Evelyn, being Evelyn, narrowed in on it.

"You did want me hired?" she asked.

When I didn't reply, frozen, contemplating what to share, she pressed, "Why did the head librarian come to the Records Office, Ambrose?"

I let my head hang as my fingers wrapped around my glass. "Because I told him there was someone he should meet there for an open position."

Her mouth hung open, and I realized then how badly we'd needed this—blood magic or not.

"We only talked for a few minutes," she whispered.

"And I wished it had been a few hours. Gabriel hadn't read your papers. I shared one with him because I knew you were exactly what he was looking for. And then you were there, in the library, doing your tests. You were so ... sharp with your words and your mind. And Gabriel trusted you. That also doesn't happen often. I can't tell you how many researchers he leaves to their own devices."

"So you were jealous?" she asked. The question seemed so plain, so unfiltered—my answer was anything but.

"It's more complicated than that. I felt like I had been working forever to barely grasp what you intuitively understood."

Her soft laugh was music to my ears. I wanted to earn it more often. Part of me wondered if she was truly entertained or if her reactions to me were a result of our current predicament. My stomach dropped, and I took another long pull of my drink as I cataloged everything that entailed. For a moment, I dared to believe I was just here, at the tavern, having a drink with Evelyn. Maybe we were just discussing our day and our perspectives. We wouldn't always agree, but we could negotiate, perhaps meet in the middle, or learn a little from each other instead of assuming the other came from a place of judgment.

I wasn't sure where we would go from here, but I felt certain we were accomplishing some part of our goal.

When I glanced back up, she studied me. Her lips moved, but no sound came out. I took this to mean she was still formulating what she wanted to say. To the casual observer, Evelyn might have seemed rash, but I knew she was careful with her words. She knew the power of them and chose each one with care.

"I call you the library golden boy in my head," she admitted.

A loud laugh slipped from my lips. "It's not always in your head, Evelyn. I've heard it."

She didn't look chastened as she continued. "You've been studying this for years. You had a great teacher in learning Vesten history. You know the needs of the court inside and out. I'm stumbling along in the dark, trying to do my best."

"You don't think I'm doing the same?" I clutched my glass for something to hold on to. "Every day, I'm unsure about what I'm doing. I believe in my research, but I know it can't get us where we need to go. Some days, when I'm reading your papers, I know your vision for blood magic testing is correct." She sucked in a breath, but I continued. "But that is at war with my every instinct. Sometimes, I'm not sure if I love or hate that part of my work."

"The history—you love the history, though, right?"

I nodded.

"Is that why you stay? Even though the rest upsets you?"

The single question would have made my knees shaky if I weren't already perched on the barstool.

"It doesn't upset me." I tapped my fingers on the bar. "Don't you ever get nervous?"

Her smile was soft. "I do."

It didn't make me feel better, but it was a nice reminder that we had as many similarities as differences. I took another long drink. "My family agreed to stop testing, stop trying to find a remedy for Father's vision, but I can't help but..."

She nodded. "You can't help but think you can learn something new in the study of blood magic?"

I sighed. "Yes, I guess that sounds pathetic."

Her hand reached for mine, covering it where it lay on the bar top. "It doesn't. I do the same thing for my mom. In fact, it's part of why I want the Vesten historian position."

I sat up straighter, even though my attention was still locked on her hand where it lingered over mine before she removed it. We were no longer touching, but now only inches separated our fingertips.

I'd overheard the end of her conversation with Lord Arctos today. Her fae father wasn't in the picture. I had already assumed that from the lack of information she had on how to shift, but the confirmation made me irrationally angry.

"My story doesn't sound as altruistic as yours. It makes me sound like a terrible daughter, but I'm hoping you'll hear me out, and consider where I'm coming from, like we're supposed to be doing."

The way her finger wrapped around the end of her ponytail told me she wasn't sure she believed that. She wasn't making eye contact, but I nodded anyway.

"Mom and I have different thoughts on where my father is." She cleared her throat. "Mom thinks something ... happened to him." This time, she took a long drink before proceeding. "I think he left us."

I wasn't sure where this was going. "What would have happened to him?"

"Mom believes he was a victim of the mist plague."

The mist plague had put those affected into an endless

sleep. Whole villages had been taken, and it wasn't until recently that the Compass Points figured out how to awaken those impacted. "If that were the case ... wouldn't..."

"Yes," she nodded. "That's my point. If he had been impacted, he would have been home by now. It's been months since the Compass Points awakened the last village."

"I see." I did, but I didn't. The way she had spoken to Lord Arctos, it made the statement that her father left her seem like a fact, not something recently determined.

She understood the vague question in my statement. "Yes, I believed this well before I had proof of it. It never made sense that he happened to disappear to a random village the same day it was taken by the mist plague." She waved her hands in exasperation.

"If he were a shifter, he could have been, you know, shifting and running." I shrugged as she glared at me.

"I get it. It's possible. It's just not particularly likely, is all I'm saying."

"What does the position of Vesten historian have to do with protecting your mom?"

She sighed. "It would just be nice to be able to put the conversation to bed once and for all. Part of the record keeping is family trees."

I nodded. "You would find him?"

It was her turn to shrug. "I would for Mom's sake. She doesn't deserve to wonder what happened forever."

It must have been the empty glass sitting in front of me, but I leaned forward. "What about you? Don't you want something, too?"

Her eyes widened in surprise. She tried to hide it, but she wasn't fast enough for the way I studied her. "I learned a long time ago not to want anything from him. I would like to know if he's a ... if his shift is the same as mine. If he has any answers for me, I'd take them, then we could go our separate ways."

I opened my mouth to respond. Before I could speak, a large hand clasped my shoulder. I glanced up, and Lord Arctos stood behind us in his fae form.

His green eyes were filled with mischief. "Were you two starting without me?"

19

Evelyn

We relocated to a table with Lord Arctos. My spine straightened at the fact that everyone stared at us. Word had spread that the Vesten God was in Sandrin. Most still considered it a novelty that he appeared on the continent at all.

It did nothing to ease the tension that crept into my shoulders. The tavern had been near empty when Ambrose and I walked in. It had still been the end of the workday. Now, the whole place was filled. I hadn't even noticed. I'd been too invested in my conversation with Ambrose.

I couldn't believe all the ground we'd covered. His father's accident had occurred while experimenting with mulberries? He'd told Gabriel about me at the Records Office? The facts didn't overlay well with my picture of the library's golden boy who wanted to see me and my rogue experimentation methods gone.

Lord Arctos looked at me expectantly, holding out a chair at the table for me to sit. How long had he been waiting? The dull roar of patrons around us swallowed my "thank you" as I sat. While I was happy for Seraphina and her booming business, I wasn't sure this was the best location for this discussion. Anyone might have been listening. Ambrose and I needed information on the blood magic connection between the gods and their Compass Points.

It was supposedly a secret, but Lord Arctos didn't appear worried. He ordered a drink and food immediately from Mina like he'd been waiting all day for this very moment. "Luna has been raving about this place. It better be as good as she says."

"You had us come here because Luna recommended it?" I asked.

He nodded. "What else are you supposed to do in a new city?"

Ambrose cleared his throat. "This city isn't exactly ... new to you ... is it?"

Lord Arctos gave him a flat stare. "You may be surprised to learn that the dining establishments in a city change over hundreds of years."

I raised my glass to my lips to hide the smile that threatened when Ambrose's ears pinkened with the chastisement.

"So, what were you two discussing? Any progress on breaking your own little connection?" He looked directly at me.

I felt Ambrose's gaze on my cheek, and parts of our conversation flashed back through my mind, warming me from the inside. What was I supposed to say about our progress? I'd shared more than I intended—about Mom, and finding my father. How much had Ambrose meant to share? We wouldn't know if it worked until we physically separated.

"We're trying something."

Lord Arctos glanced dismissively at his fingernails. "What are we trying?"

On a deep sigh, I explained. "We are trying to work through

the magic. If we complete the magic's original objective, it won't be needed anymore."

Something lit in Lord Arctos's green eyes. They flicked to Ambrose. "And has everyone come clean about their intent?"

I honestly had no idea how he knew that, but I guessed it didn't surprise me that he did.

Ambrose, on the other hand, sputtered. "How do you know we both had intent?"

Lord Arctos leaned back in his chair in a sprawl that would have looked lazy on anyone else, but somehow Lord Arctos always appeared formal. "I'm a god."

This time, I glared at him. "It's a real question. The information could help us."

He sighed, clearly bored again with the conversation. "The magic connecting you, I can see it tied in the middle."

Ambrose and I stared at each other. My brain was stuck on the fact that Lord Arctos could see magic. Again, he was a god. Who knew what he was capable of? He seemed to enjoy dropping magical facts like little sprinkles of whimsy in a dull conversation. Either way, I was glad when Ambrose finally spoke.

"You can see the magic connecting us?"

He shrugged. "Yes, and if anything, the knot has tightened. I'm not sure what you're doing is working."

I opened my mouth to continue questioning that, but he cut me off.

"I asked you both here to talk about the next steps in my problem. Although it's not reassuring that you've failed to solve your own."

I rubbed my temples. This conversation was giving me a headache.

"The Osten God wanted me to share more information with you if you figured out where the magic was enacted on your own. Even with your own situation"—he waved his hand between us—"you were quick to identify the creation of the fae as the origin. So here is what I know: His intent was to share."

Lord Arctos spread his arms like he'd dropped some all-powerful truth at the table. Ambrose and I stared at each other, blinking. *His intent was to share.* I wasn't sure what to do with this particular piece of information.

"We need more," Ambrose said.

Lord Arctos pursed his lips. "Zrak is the one who concocted the magic to create the fae. I thought you were a history expert, but since that assumption is proving incorrect, let me hand you the details." He cleared his throat like he was preparing to enrapture us with storytime. "The gods created the fae to keep our power in check. It was about balance. We had made enough mistakes with our power, we needed a group on the continent that could—"

I rolled my eyes at the Vesten God and cut off his lecture. "Yes, yes, one doesn't have to be the library's golden boy to know this story. Even I know it. In addition to making the fae, you also sacrificed one of yourselves to further tip the scales in the continent's direction. Hence, our confusion at your referencing the Osten God. Wasn't he the one sacrificed?"

The Vesten God smirked. "Don't worry so much about the why or how of the message. Just know that the message is factual. Zrak was to sacrifice himself after the creation of the fae, and therefore, he intended for magic to continue to be shared between him and his creation when he was gone."

I guessed the spirit of the intent was what mattered. Lord Arctos indicated it was sharing. Yet, what he and Gabriel had described in the briefing was something more akin to taking. It wasn't an enormous leap to realize one of these beings with immense power must have sought more than Zrak's original intent. A god or a Compass Point must have wanted more power than they were allotted and so decided to leverage this seemingly benevolent connection to do so. The whole situation left me unsurprised and a little disappointed.

This was why we couldn't have nice things.

"So..." Ambrose attempted to pick up the thread. "If Zrak's intent was to share magic, do we know what each of the other gods' intent was? Presumably, you each gave some of your blood to create your fae courts?"

Ambrose was much kinder than I was. I had already concluded what had gone wrong in the magic—I assumed the worst of the participants. Though I was unfortunately confident in my assumption, as a researcher, I knew Ambrose's method was the right one. My hypothesis was just that until it was proven or disproven.

Lord Arctos looked unimpressed with the question. "We each followed Zrak's lead. He told us what to do, how to create the fae."

"Essentially, any one of you could have realized there was room for interpretation and shoved in your own intent?" I asked.

The tapping of Lord Arctos's fingers on the tabletop was his only response. Thankfully, our food was delivered, granting the Vesten God a brief moment of excitement at his first spoonful of beef stew before we had to return to the nefarious intent of one or more of his peers at the creation of the fae. "Luna was correct. This is delicious. She really should be the one writing that recommendation column, not Vincent."

I laughed. That recommendation column was her favorite thing to read. It was what had brought her and Vincent together in the most roundabout way. I was sure she'd love to hear Lord Arctos consider her an expert in recommendations.

Ambrose and I also tucked into the food we'd ordered. As we each took a moment of silence, I considered our options. If we didn't know the other gods' intents, could we try to work through the magic? If the hidden intent was ... intentionally to take ... was there a way to work through such magic at all? Furthermore, if Lord Arctos didn't think that what Ambrose and I attempted for our own magical connection was working, what chance did it have on the gods and Compass Points?

There was still another option.

"What about an anchor?" I asked. We hadn't fully explored that possibility. Lord Arctos had been incredibly ambiguous in our questions about the object used in his ceremony with the Vesten Point.

Ambrose's brows lifted. "We would need more information about the object used in your ceremony. What was it? Where is it now?"

"I want you two to go to Compass Lake," Lord Arctos said as he took another sip of his drink. "You'll find all the answers to your inane questions there."

"Excuse me?" Ambrose asked, pausing the progress of his spoon to his lips. Something twitched within me as I noticed how full they were. Unfortunately, he chose that precise moment to look at me. My gaze darted away, hoping he didn't notice I'd been staring.

"I want you two to go to Compass Lake. You have all the information you can find on this matter from the library. The Vesten Point can answer these questions for you. Then the only thing left to do is test. If I know anything about this magic, it's that location matters. A place of importance to the magic itself. That means we need to test at Compass Lake, where the creation of the fae happened."

"You're sending both of us?" I asked.

Lord Arctos smirked and seemed to glance at some imaginary thread between us, although it wasn't so imaginary to him. "I doubt you could separate even if you wanted to."

I crossed my arms over my chest and leaned back in my chair. "We'll test on you and the Vesten Point?"

He nodded, taking another bite of his stew. "It will give you both face time with Carter. Then he can decide who he wants as his historian."

I didn't appreciate Lord Arctos's smirk, given as if to remind us that the historian position still hung in the balance between us. He was enjoying this whole thing entirely too much.

"When do we leave?" Ambrose asked.

"Tonight. You should be able to make it to the Crossroads Inn this evening, and then I can meet you at Vesten House tomorrow. I'm assuming the two of you can move faster up and down the mountain leading to Compass Lake in your shifted forms than on horseback."

Ambrose was looking at me with a hint of concern. I shared his worry, but I didn't want to discuss it in front of Lord Arctos. My inability to call my veil cat on demand was not something the Vesten God needed to know. Ambrose must have read my determination in the hardening lines of my face. He glanced away, thoughtful.

All I could do was try. Either I would shift, or Ambrose would get to test the Vesten Point and Vesten God without me. I ignored the growing anxiety bubbling in my stomach. With a nod to Lord Arctos, I replied, "That works for me."

Ambrose rolled his eyes at me before he responded. "That works for me, too."

20

Ambrose

We parted briefly to pack for the trip. I hated that Lord Arctos was right. The thrum in my chest pulsed as we separated. I thought our conversation had gone well. She had told me her plans to find her fae father and how her mother considered him missing. The resolve in her features as she spoke, the sadness mixed in, it didn't take her admission to know she didn't share that with many. How could sharing it have done nothing to change the magic connecting us?

As I slipped into my parents' apartment, I rubbed my chest. The connection was just shy of discomfort. If our first attempt had failed, we would need to try again. At least we had time together to test alternative ideas.

It was about a two-day ride on horseback to Compass Lake. Lord Arctos was correct, though; we could be faster in our shifted forms. I wasn't confident that was an option for Evelyn. Her glare before we left the tavern tonight had not been reassuring. I pocketed more of the red cinnamon candies I had given her to help distribute her fire magic as heat to her limbs. If she let me, I could show her how to use the candy to help control her shift, too.

We'd cross that bridge when we came to it.

Father greeted me with a question from his seat on the couch as I entered. "Ambrose?"

"Ambrose, is that you?" Mother had returned from a trip earlier this morning. She and Father hadn't been happy to hear from the twins that Evelyn was at my apartment for breakfast. Part of sticking close to my family meant that I had the illusion of privacy—my own space—but that nothing was truly secret. Maybe the twins could be bribed to keep quiet when they got a little older.

Mother appeared, coming out of the kitchen. She was shorter than Father and me, and slimmer in stature. Her hair was a deeper brown than my auburn, but other than that, I could see my features in hers. She brought a cup of tea to Father while the twins, for once, entertained themselves quietly in the corner with some books.

"It's me. I came by to tell you I'll be out of town for a few days."

"Were you selected to meet the Vesten Point at Compass Lake?" Father clapped his hands together before accepting the tea. "That's as good as granting you the position."

I scratched the back of my neck. "Both Evelyn and I are going."

Mother's lips tipped into a smile, but they flattened immediately when she glanced at Father.

"Both? That can't be right." He took a sip of his tea. "Your mother was just at Compass Lake to collect some new pieces for Mr. Oliver. She said the Vesten Point was expecting the new historian to visit imminently. It can't be the half-fae girl."

My wolf's hackles raised automatically. "Her name is Evelyn."

He waved dismissively. "I meant no offense. It has nothing to do with her breeding and everything to do with her reckless testing—with her focus on blood magic above all else."

We'd had a similar conversation this morning. It had made me late to the library to meet Evelyn, but none of it seemed to have sunk in with my father. "I told you she's not reckless. She's studied the magic for years. Her tests are thoroughly considered. Yes, there is always risk with the magic, but she manages it the best she can."

"Ahh, but that's the problem, isn't it? The risk is always there." Father took another sip of his tea.

"We can't live in fear of what could happen. At some point, we have to consider the benefits of the magic." I winced. Was it cheesy to use the old fae tagline in this? Yes. But was it one Father respected? Unfortunately, also yes.

He hmphed in response.

"Anyway, Lord Arctos is sending us both. I have to go. I just wanted to let you know."

"That's wonderful," Mother said.

I had to hand it to her; she was a rock, weathering any of Father's storms. He had his own thoughts on who should have the position of Vesten historian—me—and how I should use it —to learn from history instead of testing new theories on blood magic. Mother, on the other hand, tried to see the best in everything. She never went against Father's wishes explicitly, but she consistently looked for the silver lining.

As I considered my parents, one of Evelyn's questions from this afternoon resurfaced: *Is that why you stay? Even though the rest upsets you.* Did either of my parents see my discomfort—my confusion—as clearly as Evelyn did? I wasn't sure her conclusion was correct. The magic didn't upset me, but the conflict between what I wanted to attempt and Father's warnings was constant. My internal struggle materialized into something Evelyn had noticed.

Did anyone else? Father, well, he stubbornly refused to see anything that didn't align with his plan for me. Mother, I think her glass-half-full attitude sometimes stopped her from noticing hard truths. It wasn't bad. I loved her optimism.

The history, you love the history, though, right? Evelyn saw that clearly. If I could find my way through my conflicting feelings on blood magic, I would be a lot happier. What did it say about me that someone who disliked me so strongly was the one who saw me so clearly?

Maybe it's not all dislike. My wolf paced with excitement.

I shook my head. "I should only be a few days."

"Go, go. We'll be fine without you," Mother said.

Father shot her a glare, but I didn't wait to see what he would say. I walked across the room to kiss my siblings on their foreheads, each one barely acknowledging my existence while they read their book. Then I left to pack.

EVELYN STOOD JUST OUTSIDE of town, waiting for me. Her arms were folded over her chest, and I couldn't help but notice that her foot tapped lightly against the ground. Was she ever late for anything?

I must have asked the question aloud because she responded: "My mom always said if you're not fifteen minutes early, you're late."

"Well, that clears up a lot about your opinion of my arrival time at the library." I shot her a smirk. "See, we're getting to know each other when we're not even trying."

Her cheeks pinkened, and her heartbeat accelerated. To my utter delight, that new development had started as soon as I was in sight. It was funny that her heart beat faster in my presence, and mine relaxed in hers. When I'd seen Evelyn standing on the edge of town, impatience a familiar cloak around her, the twist in my chest had loosened. I felt like I could breathe for the first time in hours.

I didn't mind her reaction to me, though. The twitch of my wolf's tail said he didn't mind her racing heart, either.

She bit the inside of her lip, sucking at it while she thought something through. I didn't care how long it took. My attention was glued to her mouth, wondering what it would be like to have the focus that corner of her lip currently had.

The tips of my ears grew warm. Then she was staring at me with the look she usually reserved for the researchers who told her blood magic wasn't real magic. I shook myself, sure that I had missed something.

"Did you hear me?" she asked.

"No."

"Well, that's fine. I apologized for imposing my time-keeping standards on you and your life, where they have no business. I won't do it again."

I huffed out a laugh. "Did that count as the apology?"

"No," she said flatly. "You missed that. All you get is the summary. Now, shall we go?" She gestured toward the road leading out of town.

I glanced around. We were just off the main path. We could easily step farther into the woods to shift. It was unlikely anyone would see her animal, as it was dark and the trees were thick between here and Compass Lake. She didn't wait for my response, though. Her question was rhetorical. She turned and walked toward our destination.

"It's a half-day's ride to the Crossroads Inn. You won't make it there tonight on foot."

"I can sleep on the side of the road," she called over her shoulder.

Impossible female. I pulled one of the cinnamon candies from my pocket. Sasha was learning how to shift, so I had plenty to share if Evelyn would let me. I jogged to catch up with her, turning so that I offered them in my palm as I walked backward in front of her. "You know there is another option."

She looked down at the candy. Something like surprise flashed across her face briefly.

Did she think I was going to shift and leave her to walk? "Why did you wait for me if you thought I was going to leave you here?" I asked.

She crossed her arms again. "Because I said I would."

My wolf growled within my chest as our picture of Evelyn became clearer. I'd been impressed at the library with how easily she stated what she wanted: the Vesten historian position. The more I studied her, the more I thought that was a fluke—an anomaly, said in a moment of anger toward me because of her belief that I'd considered the position mine from the start.

Setting aside that slip, her usual behavior was becoming much easier to understand. I suspected she didn't handle disappointments well. She said as much with how she'd spoken about her father this afternoon at the tavern. Her go-to was not to expect anything from me—not to set herself up for disappointment.

I wanted her to expect something from me.

I dropped the candies into her palm and reached for her shoulders to halt her progress. Surprisingly, she let me. "We can run together. I can ... help you."

She looked up at me through her lashes, and my heart skipped a beat. The look was there and gone so quickly I wondered if I imagined it. Her eyes narrowed instead, and she angled herself away, suspicion coloring her features. I let my hands fall from her shoulders as she crossed her arms over her chest again. "You don't know if it will work."

"You're right." I shrugged, but I knew she had used the hard candy I gave her yesterday. She wasn't wearing her sweater when I arrived at the library. "The candy worked for the heat, didn't it?"

She flushed. If she had figured that out, I was confident she could use the same method to force her shift.

"It will work for this, too." I paused. "It won't help you control it, though. You have to accept your veil cat on your own."

Her eyes narrowed further into slits. "I can—" She cut herself off, apparently not willing to attempt the lie that she could control her shift. I considered that progress between us. "What does it entail?" she asked.

The side of the road wasn't the right place for her to attempt this. I gestured toward the trees. "Let me show you."

"You want me to follow you into the dark wood?" At least she was openly mocking me now instead of glaring at me with suspicion. "You're a predator."

I couldn't express how quickly the wolf in my head was up and actively prowling in my mind. My lip curled. "I'll only chase you with permission."

Her spine straightened, and her heartbeat raced again. It had almost settled from when she first caught sight of me on the road. This, along with the dilation of her pupils, had my wolf pacing. She liked the idea of me chasing her.

It's just the blood magic.

The reminder was like ice water poured over my head. I couldn't flirt with her when there was this magical tether between us. Her reaction wasn't her own. I swallowed and tried again. "We should get off the road for when this works. We don't want anyone to see you shift."

She cleared her throat and nodded, leading us into the trees. Her bag hit the packed dirt with a thud. Thankfully, it was the type she could toss over her back when she shifted.

"I'll tell you what my father told me, what I tell the twins. Feel free to move me along if you've heard any of this before."

She chewed the inside of her lip again. I was sure she was trying to determine whether I was serious. The worst thing I could do was tell her something she already knew as if it was brand new information. I would start with the basics, because without her father, I feared no other Vesten would have shared them, but we had plenty of more advanced options available if needed.

"My father talked to me about flame and shift being two sides of the same coin. The flame burns away the old and makes new."

"The shifted form is new?" she asked. I could tell she didn't see her shifted form as a prize. To her, at least so far, it had only been a burden.

"Not necessarily. Because when you're in your shifted form, the fire also burns away the animal to bring back the fae, or half-fae," I corrected myself.

"I see."

I took a step closer to her. She craned her neck to look up at me, but she didn't step away. I held her gaze as my hand moved slowly—so slowly—toward her sternum. The pace gave her every opportunity to push me away.

Our breaths released in sync when my hand met her skin. A flame licked behind my own rib cage with the connection. I took a beat before studying her further. Did she feel this, too? I shook my head to focus. The flare couldn't distract me; she needed to hear this, needed to understand this for the shift to work.

"Your veil cat is part of you," I said, pressing my fingers against her. "The candy will help you access the heat, the flame of change inside. But for the shift to be on your terms, you have to believe that it's as much you in here"—I pressed again—"as your heart beating in your chest."

She sucked in an uneven breath. "How can—" She cut herself off and tried again. "What if it chose the wrong person?"

My eyes closed as anger flared to life within me. My wolf wanted to howl, a cold, lonely sound in honor of whatever Evelyn had experienced with the fae to make her voice the concern. "The animals are never wrong. Fae can be wrong. Fae can be stupid and prejudiced. But the animal can never be wrong."

"It's so unpredictable," she tried.

"Only because you aren't participating in the conversation. If the two of you communicate, I think you'll see that the veil cat's every action is carefully calculated, the same way the half-fae part of you would make a decision."

Her lip almost curled into a smile at that. She took a deep breath, letting her eyes close and her chest expand into my touch. When her eyes opened again, they found mine. "What do I do next?"

"You tried the candy from yesterday?"

She nodded slowly.

"Do the same. Instead of pushing the heat out to your limbs, let it consume you, like you're burning from the inside."

Her head tilted. "That sounds ... painful."

I let my head sway from side to side. "It's not. Have you felt pain when you've shifted before?"

She shook her head.

"This shouldn't be any different. Your fire doesn't burn you—it's a part of you. You already figured that part out. The candy is the fire starter, then apply that same thinking to your animal."

I'd seen Evelyn wield her fire magic, even if she didn't know how to do so with precision. That part, she had figured out more intuitively than the shift.

Finally, regretfully, I stepped away, letting my hand fall from her chest. My fingers were automatically cold. Every part of me wanted to rectify the situation by encroaching on her space once again.

But she needed to try this on her own.

She licked her lips like she did when she prepared to test some tricky magic. Then, she popped a candy in her mouth. I felt heat, even though I saw no flame. She was incandescent in the darkness. Her eyes narrowed, and I worried that she was trying too hard—that she was trying to force the cat into submission. Our gazes locked and held. In that moment, her chest fell, and she took in a breath so deep it was like she wasn't sure she'd ever inhale clean air again.

With a final, imperceptible nod in my direction, her body crumpled forward.

I took a step toward her instinctively. With Evelyn, I should have known my concern was unnecessary. Her reddish-brown fur filled my vision as she prowled forward in veil cat form.

21

Evelyn

For the first time, I shifted because I wanted to. The heat consumed me but didn't burn. I let it overtake me and create something new, just as Ambrose said. On the other side, my veil cat and I shared space.

Ambrose's words about making peace with my veil cat circled in my head. She and I weren't one, but we weren't fighting for control. I'd decided to shift, and she took charge afterward. Ambrose settled my pack on my back and then shifted himself. Within moments, my veil cat chased the large gray wolf through the woods.

At least it was a step in the right direction.

The simplicity was astounding. As I sprinted through the trees, faster than any horse I could have ridden, my hackles rose. This could have all been easily avoided if my father hadn't left. If he had taken five minutes of his life to tell me what Ambrose just did. But no, he hadn't had the decency to ensure I wasn't a danger to myself or others.

My veil cat growled, and we ran faster.

The gray wolf picked up speed just ahead, and I momentarily forgot my anger and pushed forward. If I didn't know better, I'd think he understood that chasing him—or racing him, as we'd taken turns doing on our journey—cleared my head. There was no room for anger at my father when I could challenge Ambrose to a sprint.

Dozens of miles later, we still played, taking turns with who was in the lead. My veil cat ran so fast we passed Ambrose, which meant, inadvertently or not, he was now making good on his promise to chase me. My entire body was alight, on fire, and it had nothing to do with my magic. Anticipation thrummed through me. What would he do if he caught me? Part of me wanted to find out.

This is just the blood magic. I have to ignore it.

I took a deep breath and sprinted faster. The night had grown fully dark, and the only light ahead was the entryway to the Crossroads Inn. It was newly built in the last few months, after the mist plague had been cleared and travel across the continent resumed. The inn was aptly named for its location. This junction was the crossroads of the continent. The road east and west led between Compass Lake, where the fae courts were situated, and Sandrin, the largest city on the continent. It was crossed by a road that ran north and south, connecting the continent's smaller settlements for trade and travel.

It was no surprise that the inn had been built here so quickly. Any proprietor would be lucky to have such a sought-after location. On our approach, a dull roar emanated from the building. Many travelers were returning home from the Long Night holiday in Sandrin, stopping here before returning to their northern or southern villages.

We didn't need to get any closer with me as a veil cat. I glanced at Ambrose in wolf form, who had also halted in the woods surrounding the inn. We needed to shift back.

Can I shift back?

The gray wolf nodded at me, as if insisting I go first. His nod was one of encouragement, like he was telling me that I knew what to do. Maybe now, thanks to Ambrose, I did. He had said the process was the same to return to my half-fae form. The real question was how to get the cinnamon candy when I was still a veil cat.

I glanced again at Ambrose. He waited patiently, the golden eyes of his wolf unblinking. It was like he wanted me to try on my own before he assisted. Unsure what to do, I searched myself for that all-consuming flame that had thrust me from half-fae to veil cat.

It wasn't there.

My body heated with something different: shame. What kind of Vesten was I, if I'd be forever dependent on candy to help with my magic?

Ambrose sensed my attempt and shifted. He pulled more candy from his bag and held one out to me. His palm was flat, offering the candy up with little fanfare. I could probably even grab it without touching his skin. My cat didn't want to. I licked the candy from his palm, and heat flared through me—whether at my behavior or the candy, I wasn't sure.

My fire consumed me, like a fuse that lit the shift back into my half-fae form. I was clear-headed and had no trouble shifting with my clothes on and my pack still on my back.

Before the fire could burn into anger again at the thought of how easily my father could have helped with this, Ambrose was in my line of sight. His brow pinched with concern briefly, then he gestured toward the inn's front door.

Only a few weeks ago, it was another inn that we had worked together to save. It had been the first time I realized that our investigative styles complemented each other. When we weren't arguing about the test subjects for blood magic, he was a fantastic brainstorming partner. I'd never had one before, unless we counted all the work we'd done together on this current project, which would be a different problem when it came to claiming the prize.

My mind wandered, and Ambrose strode ahead of me as I walked into the inn. It was warm and welcoming. Floor-to-ceiling dark wood was lit with the orange glow of lamps at the entry. Ambrose approached the desk, but off to the left was an ample open space set as a dining room. A fireplace crackled in the center, and tables and chairs circled it. Travelers filled the space. Overflowing from the seats, they stood in groups, engaged in conversations. I wondered how many of those travelers had known each other before this evening.

The inn felt like a place of new beginnings and infinite possibilities. Scents of cooked meat and roasted vegetables filled my nostrils. My stomach roared to life. The long run must have burned off my entire meal at the tavern. I'd say that was why I didn't hear Ambrose's alarmed words when he spoke.

Hand on my shoulder, he turned me back to him. I raised my chin so that I could meet his eyes, finally understanding that something was wrong. Concern filled my voice as I asked, "What is it?"

Ambrose held out a single key. "They are very full. I'm sorry."

Still, his panic didn't translate. My face must have reflected my confusion.

"They only had one room left." He paused. "For both of us."

We grabbed a light meal before the kitchen closed. The inn's owner was younger than I expected, or at least she looked young. It was impossible to tell if she could thank fae heritage for her ageless beauty. She apologized profusely for our situation, and added that she mentioned the lack of vacancy to the messenger Lord Arctos had sent ahead to secure the room. The proprietress made excuses, saying the Vesten God must not have received the message. I had my doubts about that assumption.

We lingered in the dining room. I tried to convince myself that it was the atmosphere here, but whatever I'd felt on entering the inn hadn't dissipated with the news of the room. There was something special about this place, and it felt like all the patrons were aware. The ideas of fae, old fae, and human didn't seem to matter here as they did in Sandrin.

An energy had existed on the continent since the mist plague was removed—one that couldn't be ignored. Here, the change felt real. I hoped it could be for the better. I hoped it could spread across the continent, with the tenacity of the all-consuming flame that now fueled my shift. I hoped, with something like the Vesten historian position, I could be part of that change.

My mind batted away the idea as soon as it sprang forth—a dream not worth considering, a hope not worth raising within my chest.

It was time to focus on our current predicament. No more stalling. We had to deal with the fact that Ambrose and I were sharing a bedroom tonight.

I gathered my pack from the back of the chair and stood. "I guess we should head up?"

Ambrose couldn't look more uncomfortable if he tried. He scratched the back of his neck and held out the key in his open palm as if it were a rodent he'd killed and he was now reluctantly offering me proof of its disposal.

Would staying in a room with me be so bad? He'd done it only last night, hadn't he?

Maybe that wasn't entirely accurate. I didn't know where he had actually slept in his apartment. Most likely, it had been on the couch in the living space, a whole room away from me.

We'd been close enough that the magic connecting us wasn't aggravated, but far enough away that he could still pretend at personal space. Given this was an inn, not an apartment, I guessed our room would provide no such illusion.

The key was solid and heavy as I plucked it from his hand. Turning, I trudged up the stairs. His footfalls behind me were soundless, but I was painfully aware that he followed. I processed every creak of the wood, every crooked painting hung, and every candle burnt down to the wick between us and the room we'd share.

My thoughts flashed back to last night—to Ambrose joining me in the small clearing I'd found in the park. His large presence had invaded the space when I felt most lost. I was angry at his arrival, terrified of discovery, but I was also comforted. There was a small release of pressure when he was near.

The comfort is only because of the magic.

Maybe. I'd been going over the magic all day. Specifically, I considered how attracted I'd been to Ambrose before I shifted. His presence had been so consuming. It was the only thing I'd seen clearly. When everything had changed around me, his strength grounded me. His size had only made the imagery more compelling. Crowding me in should have sent off warning bells; instead, it forced me to focus—it made everything but him a mere distraction.

I couldn't think about my shift itself without blushing. My veil cat had been so focused on him. She'd wanted him there, wanted to curl up in him the way a house cat curls up in a sliver of sun. I, on the other hand, had wanted to scratch out his hazel irises in hopes he wouldn't remember what he saw.

The animal always knows.

He'd said that before he taught me how to shift. Did he know what his words had meant to me? I considered what he'd confessed about his intent in our current predicament. It had been so similar to mine. We'd both wanted to stop this ...

antagonistic spark between us. I'd wanted to grow together. He'd wanted to understand each other. Neither required romance.

With each step, my heart raced faster as I ran out of ways to tell myself that I would sleep in the same room as Ambrose Yarrow, a male whom I was somehow magically connected to but was also attracted to. And I had to admit that attraction was wholly separate from, and even pre-dated, the blood magic.

Yesterday, I had convinced myself that the attraction sprung from nowhere and was therefore related to the magic. The more I considered it, the more I saw that for what it was—denial.

The first day I'd seen Ambrose, I'd been distracted by his appearance. Of course, the condescending words that had flowed from his mouth had made the attraction easier to ignore. Unfortunately, the more I got to know him due to the forced proximity of our connection, the more I understood where some of those quirks came from.

Maybe he wasn't so bad.

He was a dedicated son and a loving older brother. He was sharp, his mind a filing cabinet for historical details that he could always access. What I'd thought was an aversion to change was actually fear of repeating his father's mistakes. He was incapable of holding an opinion when new facts revealed that an alternative view might have merit. I was a walking confrontation of the beliefs he held—or at least the ones his father had taught him. No wonder he challenged me at every turn.

I swallowed thickly as I approached the door marked with the same number as the tag on the key. *Ambrose might be better than* not bad. *He might even be good.*

The brass key twisted in the lock under my feeble attempt at steady hands. I had no idea if I was hiding my nerves at all. Probably not. The sound of my heart racing was louder than the squeaks of the steps. Ambrose was kind enough not to comment.

As I twisted the handle, I closed my eyes, still afraid of how confined this space would be. Still worried that all these revelations would make sleeping in the same small room one hundred times harder. The magic might not have been affecting me, but I *liked* Ambrose, and I wasn't quite sure what to do with that information.

This was all only further complicated when I pushed the door open to find a tiny room—and one bed as its centerpiece.

There was little else on which to focus. A washroom to the right, but no desk, dresser, or bureau for clothes. Not that I would have used them, but it would be nice to scan anything else in the room.

Instead, I gaped at the bed. We entered the room, and I glanced back and forth between it and Ambrose. His shoulders were so broad; was there even room for us both to lie next to each other?

His ears pinkened as I silently continued my assessment.

My mind was racing, not at all connected with the words that spewed from my mouth. "I'm not sure we're both going to fit."

22

Evelyn

I'm not sure we're both going to fit? I wanted to smack my forehead like the idiot I was. Ambrose's mouth stretched to form words, but I could only assume that he, too, was overcome by my stupidity. We needed a safe topic, one to eradicate the fact that we were in this tiny room together for the night. One that could burn away the image my mind conjured of our limbs tangled together in the bed.

A lock of auburn hair fell over his face as he ran his fingers through it again. The ring of gold in his hazel eyes appeared to be thickening—shifting. His eyes held a fire that I hadn't seen before. Then, his body went rigid as the gold ring contracted.

My veil cat chose that moment to perk up. If I were in my animal form, my tail would be ticking back and forth, keeping time. Ambrose's hand flexed at his side before he balled it into a tight fist. And finally, I understood what was happening.

He was fighting his wolf. I hadn't seen it from this side, but the tension in his body was so obviously an attempt to control.

It surprised me that this—the shared room, the shared bed—set off his wolf. Hadn't he said he rarely lost control anymore? Was he so affected by the idea of a room shared with me?

I couldn't help but consider how my veil cat reacted to Ambrose. *The animal is never wrong.* Fine. I knew deep down it wasn't only my veil cat's reaction. Her goal was to be near him; she found peace with him—comfort—and I acknowledged that, lately, I did, too.

If he experienced something similar, we needed a topic to de-escalate this tension in the air between us.

My mind served up the perfect idea on a silver platter: Research. No one got into confusing, sexually charged situations while talking about research. Right?

I charged forward before I could mentally contradict myself.

"When I shifted today. When you ... touched my chest..." My cheeks heated. This was not headed in the direction I'd intended. The words got away from me, like they were two steps ahead, and I was jogging to reach them before the next ones slipped out.

Ambrose's spine straightened, and his knuckles turned white as he clenched his fists at his side.

I cleared my throat and tried again. "When you touched me, when you were explaining the shifting magic, my fire magic flared as if it knew what you were trying to tell me."

His head tilted, and he seemed to inspect both me and the bed, probably trying to understand how this story connected to our current predicament.

It didn't, but Ambrose was sharp. He'd catch up eventually.

"I'm sorry. I thought it was only me." Ambrose cleared his throat. "It must be an effect of the blood magic connecting us, something our skin-to-skin contact sets off."

I shook my head. "That's not..."

Wait. Did that mean his magic flared when he pressed his

palm against me in the woods? I set that piece of information aside to obsess over later.

My mind had wandered again. Ambrose waited for me to continue. "That's not what I meant to imply," I said. "It was good that you touched me."

His eyes widened.

Belatedly, I heard the words, but it was too late to take them back. I'd said what I said. As with our attempt to break the magic connecting us, the only way out was through. "When my fire magic flared, it flared toward you. It was almost like..." Here I was somewhat exploring the feeling verbally. I hadn't tried to describe it to myself, so I wasn't sure what words to use. It had been strong, something solid that wouldn't break, like Ambrose. It had also been flexible, fitting the shape we required. "It was like a rope ... of fire, leading toward you."

I didn't think he was breathing. "A rope," he repeated.

"Yes. Have you felt it?" I asked. Really, I just wanted to hear him speak a complete sentence.

He shook his head. "It has to be the magic connecting us ... What Lord Arctos described." His hands were in his hair again. "I'm so sorry, Evelyn. I don't know why it's presenting that way for you. The last thing I could have possibly wanted was for—" He straightened his spine and cut himself off. "We'll get rid of it. I'll put my entire focus on it."

I stepped into his space to halt his hands from further tousling his hair. It had fallen in a perfect swoop across his forehead. I liked it just the way it was.

When I looked up, I realized how close we were. I held both of his wrists in place, and mere inches separated us. I craned my neck to meet his hazel eyes. The gold ring around his pupils had receded to its usual size, but the flecks hidden in the green came alive in the lamplight.

"You're missing my point," I said. "I was sharing this because I think it's an interesting development for our research.

There was a physicality to the magic. Maybe with time, you'll feel it, too. Either way, the more tactile the magic is, the more possible it is to break."

A breath swept from his lips on a heavy exhale. His relief was palpable. His breath skimmed the top of my head, reminding me once again of our proximity and how much space he took up in this small room.

"I have no doubt you'll understand it better soon," he said.

I didn't have to look up at him to imagine the way his lip curled into that almost-smile. I did anyway. When I had seen this one previously, I assumed it was a condescending smile, one that said, *You're trying, and I can't bring myself to tell you all the ways that you're wrong.*

Maybe this was the work of the magic, but my time spent with Ambrose had made me realize that wasn't quite right. This was the smile he gave me when I mouthed off to Lord Arctos. Or when I came up with a new lead on a project, even when Landon told me it would never work. If I was willing to admit how long I had cataloged Ambrose's smiles, I might also have said it was the first one he gave me, the one in the Records Office when I'd told him which books he needed without being asked. With what I knew now, I wondered if this smile said something closer to, *You're amazing, and I can't quite bring myself to tell you.*

We'd been staring at each other for too long. If I had hoped to use talk about research to diffuse the weighty feeling in the room that pulled us together like a gravitational force, I'd failed miserably. I still held his wrist in place, and I found my fingers outside of my control as they slowly crept up his arm, pausing to fan out around the breadth of his biceps.

Seriously, does he do a thousand curls a day with the books in the Great Room?

His eyes tracked the movement of my hand. The gold in his irises thickened again, but this time, he didn't look tense—he looked focused. I moved slowly, giving him plenty of time to get away. But the way his eyes tracked me, I wondered who was the predator and who was the prey.

I found I didn't care, and for once, my veil cat didn't, either, as I raised onto my tiptoes. The distance between us closed, but he was too tall for me to reach his lips without his help. I stood there like an idiot again, fearing I'd miscalculated. He had to meet me here if he wanted this particular development between us. Seconds before I gave up and dropped back to my heels in mortification, his lips met mine.

A spark caught in my chest at the first press. It lit like tinder when he pulled me closer and nipped my lip in exploration. I didn't require encouragement as he coaxed my mouth open so his tongue could sweep inside.

The groan that built from my chest urged him on. As with our work together, he rose to my challenge. Our tongues tangled. It wasn't a battle of wills but a partnership to achieve the best results in this experiment. Whatever test we were conducting, I wanted to repeat it over and over.

He seemed to agree. His lips dropped to my neck, and explored the column of it as he trailed open-mouthed kisses against my skin. My head fell back, granting him all the access he needed. His arms moved from my waist to the backs of my thighs as he hoisted me up. I wrapped my legs around him like it was the most natural move in the world. On slow, steady steps, Ambrose walked us in an unknown direction. I didn't care so long as his lips were on me, especially on that space right behind my...

And then we were falling backward.

Ambrose caught us with a strong arm against the plush surface. His bicep flexed against my side. He'd tipped us onto the bed, his weight braced above me. For a moment, we stared at each other. Our hearts beat rapidly in time.

We were on the bed. The bed in our shared room for the night.

His gaze was hooded with desire. In this moment, I knew Ambrose Yarrow wanted me. If the way he tracked my every movement wasn't enough, the solid length pressed between us through his trousers was another giveaway.

I smiled as his large hand swept a loose strand of dark hair from my face. The touch sent that flare of fire between us again. I *wanted* more.

The thought was like a bucket of ice water poured over me.

Wanting things never ended well for me.

Something must have shifted in my face with my thoughts, because Ambrose's weight left as quickly as it had fallen against me. He cleared his throat and adjusted himself as he looked toward the washroom.

"My apologies, Evelyn." He could barely make eye contact. "Truly. I'm sorry. I think the ... magic ... got a little carried away."

A pit opened in my stomach as I made sense of his words. *He thinks the blood magic between us controls our emotions. This isn't real to him.* Somehow, that made it worse.

"Ambrose."

He waved me off. "No—"

I took a deep breath and tried again. I couldn't have him think this was some magical entanglement on my side. That wasn't fair. "Ambrose, I kissed you all on my own." I spoke clearly and directly, willing him to understand. "I think you're right, we shouldn't continue, but I won't have you thinking I was overcome by magic."

Momentarily, he looked startled. I wasn't sure if it was my directness or if I'd completely misread the situation. That didn't feel right. I might have started it, but he had kissed me, too.

Maybe he only thought he wanted you because of his misinterpretation of the magic.

The magic was not controlling our feelings. That wasn't what this was. Mutual attraction was neither of our intents.

But if he didn't know that, it wasn't any better than if the magic were controlling our emotions.

My cheeks heated, and I was suddenly exhausted, lost in the circles of what Ambrose might or might not have believed about what drew us together. It was better than the alternative, thinking about how much I had wanted things to continue.

I wiped my hand down my face. "I'm sorry, too." And before he could respond to that, I continued, "We should get some sleep. I'll take the floor."

His eyes narrowed at me. "If anyone is taking the floor, I will."

Stupid. Insufferable. My hands balled into fists at my sides. "Let's just share." I took matters into my own hands and propped a pillow in the center of the small bed, like a line in the sand between us. Then I curled on my side, leaving him plenty of space on the other half. I turned away from him, unable to witness his indecision.

It took longer than it should have to hear the groan of the mattress as it sagged under his weight. He, too, rolled onto his side to keep as much space between us as possible.

"Goodnight, Evelyn," he whispered.

I blinked into the darkness. My body still felt aflame from his touch, his kiss. It was a problem I would contemplate the rest of the night. I wiggled to try to find a comfortable position because there was no way I'd get a wink of sleep.

23

Evelyn

The soft glow of dawn spilled over my face, and birds sang their morning tunes outside the window. I blinked the world back into existence, feeling like I had dozed off only moments ago. It was not what I would call a restful night's sleep. My arms stretched out to relieve the tension in my shoulders, only for my left hand to abruptly hit something solid. I turned to investigate and found myself nearly face to face with Ambrose Yarrow.

Last night came pouring back in. Soft lips, tangled tongues, his body pressed against mine on top of the bed. The thoughts alone had a pool of warmth building within me.

Maybe the experiment bore repeating.

That thought doused the flame of the memory. I wiped my now clammy palms on the sheet as I considered him. Auburn hair fell across his face. His eyes were still closed, granting me shelter from the sifting gold and green that seemed to track my every movement. The lines of his sharp features were almost soft in the early sun's light.

Wanting Ambrose was a problem. He still thought the magic connecting us caused the desire we'd expressed last night. I winced. With each remembrance, my head sank deeper into the pillow, and I wished the soft bed could swallow me whole.

Usually, I enjoyed explaining theories about magic. In this case, I couldn't contemplate how embarrassing the clarification would be. How did I tell him that he was responsible for his own desire? *Sorry, Ambrose, the blood magic isn't responsible for the lust that overcame us last night. You're just attracted to me, at least physically, and haven't admitted it to yourself.*

Not really the romantic gesture of my dreams.

Not that I wanted a romantic gesture. I didn't. This was a physical attraction. No matter how considerate he had been in telling Gabriel of my research, or how caring he was with his siblings, or even the attention he paid to my magic use—the thoughtfulness he showed in teaching me basic Vesten tricks...

My body went rigid. I needed to get out of here. I turned to roll away and slip from the bed when I realized our fingers were linked beneath the pillow. The wall I'd built between us last night was still intact, but he'd captured my hand in sleep.

A soft sigh escaped my lips. It sounded more like longing than frustration. This was not good. When I pulled my fingers from his, my body felt cold in the morning's chill. I grabbed a few of the cinnamon candies I had stuffed in my pack and left the room.

Space was what I needed.

I crept down the staircase. It might have been my mind playing tricks on me, but there were no creaks to speak of from the steps today. As I slipped out the front door and into the woods, more tension eased from my body. Only a few steps farther from the inn, a new tightness emerged, or returned—a constricting in my chest with each step I took away from Ambrose.

The forest pushed the discomfort too far. Was the presence of the feeling increasing? The tether between us was shortening, the impacts of separation escalating. Lord Arctos was right; our attempts to understand each other better didn't appear to be working. I turned back to the inn's porch. The last thing I wanted to do was wake Ambrose with the discomfort.

With a heavy sigh, I closed my eyes and sat with my legs dangling beneath the railing. My head fell back, and I leaned against the base of a small wooden table as I searched for my fire magic. There was an ember there, and I knew I could call the flame to my hand, but I couldn't pull the more nuanced use Ambrose had taught me. I shivered and popped one of the cinnamon candies into my mouth. It took only a moment to suck the cinnamon away and find the heat at the center of the treat. The ember became a small flame.

It was easy, now, to push the heat to my limbs. As I did so, I took the chance to explore my magic—to get lost in it. It was no surprise that I found the connection I had tried to describe to Ambrose last night. My magic surrounded the spot. It felt like a physical thing beneath my breastbone. The more I explored it, the more I agreed with what I'd said last night. It was like a fiery rope that stretched between us.

With little thought, I sent my fire through it the same way I sent it to my fingers and toes to warm. It scorched a path across the connection, heading toward my target. The distance didn't feel as far as it should have. I quickly approached what I knew to be the midpoint. Just as I began to explore ... something ... I found there, the midpoint became three-quarters of the distance between us. The rope length shortened, confounding my progress.

I had only seconds to feel the center point before I heard

the familiar voice that set every hair on my body standing on end. "Everything alright, Evelyn?"

My eyes opened, and I looked up to find Ambrose straightening his shirt. He must have hurried from the room when I tested the connection. A slip of muscled abdomen disappeared as he shook the fabric. I had felt the shape of his frame last night, with his body pressed on top of mine, but this visual confirmation of sharp lines disappearing beneath... I jerked my gaze up to his face.

I wasn't sure I had ever studied the shifting colors of golds and greens in any pair of hazel eyes as much as I studied Ambrose's. I didn't know what I was looking for, but I searched them for ... something. Embarrassment at my blatant perusal? If anything, he looked a little smug. Anger from last night? I didn't see it. Dread to spend another day traveling with me? He offered me a hesitant smile.

I clambered for something to say. "Morning. I didn't wake you, did I?"

My veil cat dropped her head between her paws as if to say, *Very smooth, Evelyn.*

He shrugged. "What were you doing?"

"I wanted to test the physicality of our connection." I cleared my throat. "What I described last night. I'm sorry if it disturbed you."

He looked contemplative but waved off my concern. "Did you get breakfast?"

I shook my head.

"Want to grab something before we leave? We should start early so as not to arrive at Compass Lake too late in the day." He offered me his hand to help me up. It was such an innocent gesture. I took it, even knowing I'd feel the spark between us crackle when we touched.

I put up a tough front, tried to convince myself I was immune, but I wasn't sure I could avoid this fire.

WHEN I REACHED for my veil cat after breakfast, I felt a shiver overtake me, but it wasn't enough to summon the flame—to push the shift over the edge. With the aid of another cinnamon candy, the shift was as easy as taking a breath. Ambrose's instruction had unlocked some door within me. My veil cat and I might not have been one, exactly, but we were aligned.

With this new level of control—even if it was assisted—my resentment of my veil cat lessened. I was still concerned about why a veil cat was my shifted form, but that wasn't her fault. It was my father's duty to explain. It also wasn't my veil cat's fault that she had been trying to tell me things I'd rather not understand about my feelings for Ambrose.

Thankfully, traveling as a veil cat and wolf meant that Ambrose and I didn't have to converse. There was really nothing to say to him anyway. I was attracted to him—maybe more than attracted—and still didn't want to deal with it. And he preferred to blame the magic connecting us for his physical pull to me.

The density of the forest increased as we approached the base of the mountain. Leaves and branches made for less visibility, like anything could be hidden here. Almost like how the details of my shift, or of how to wield my fire with more precision, the truths of how to unlock the rest of my Vesten magic unaided, were elusive. Ambrose's explanation had made a difference, quickly. But now that I knew it was within reach, I wanted to complete the cycle without candies given to train children.

Then I couldn't focus on anything but the climb. Compass Lake was nestled in the mountains—the perfect natural defense for the fae courts.

My legs burned as the climb steepened. We stuck close to the switchbacks, but just off the main path in case we encountered anyone. I wasn't used to running such long distances in my shifted form. Ambrose didn't seem bothered by it; his energy never wavered. When not nipping at my heels, he would turn the corners first to check for other travelers on the path.

Finally, we crested the pass, and I caught my first glimpse of Compass Lake. Each of the four fae courts had a house that sat around the perfectly circular lake. House, even estate, was an understatement. They were manors, each with their own individual style representing the court.

From our current vantage point, three of the four houses were visible. Only Norden House was tucked entirely away by tree cover. I had read enough to know that Norden House was like a stone castle. It was an austere building and an imposing sight, which I looked forward to encountering as we neared. Osten House was on the eastern shore. Instead of tall and imposing, it sprawled across the property like a sophisticated ranch. On the southern shore was Suden House. The only thing I could say from here was that it looked warm and inviting, which was not at all what I thought of when I considered the earth fae. The property was filled with trees, blurring the lines between Suden and our target, Vesten House.

I sucked in a breath as I took in the center of our court. Vesten House looked like an enormous log cabin. Some might have thought it simple, but I could tell from here that every detail of the house, every piece of wood used, had been chosen with care.

My mom and I, along with my father before he left, had lived in a one-room log cabin north of Sandrin. In my memories of the place, it was warm, and the rich wood walls were a symbol of peace and safety. Similar to the way my veil cat viewed the forest. Vesten House looked nothing like our first home, of course, but I had a hard time finding it imposing. I wondered if the woods represented a place of security to all Vesten.

The gray wolf in front of me turned as if to check my progress. I'd halted to survey the lake. This was my first time here. I hadn't thought much about that during our travels. Similar to my past thoughts on Vesten Library, Compass Lake was a destination I'd assumed I would never have cause to visit. It hadn't been a happy thought, just a fact. The seats of power for the fae courts were for ... fae. And not everyone believed I qualified.

An image flashed through my mind: me, moving to Compass Lake with Mom when I won the Vesten historian position. I wouldn't be arriving as a guest but as one of them, a half-fae they couldn't continue to dismiss.

I shivered and forced my paws forward. It was a beautiful dream, but the position wasn't mine, and wanting it, like wanting Ambrose, would only bring disappointment.

My thoughts crystallized into crisp focus on what we were doing here—how we'd break the blood magic between gods and Compass Points when Ambrose and I couldn't even deal with the magic connecting us. I followed the large gray wolf through the pass.

The sprint down the mountain was much easier than scaling it. I could avoid the pathways while chasing after Ambrose. We fell into this rhythm the rest of the way to the foot of the mountain. As we reached the edge of Compass Lake Village, magic sizzled within me. It was more alive than I'd ever experienced. On instinct, I reached for the fire without a candy. It ignited with barely a thought, and I shifted back into my half-fae form.

I didn't have time to enjoy my success. As I shifted, I stumbled under the sheer force of the magic surrounding me. It must be true what they said about this place, that it was the origin point for the fae, that this was a place of great power on the continent.

A solid form caught my arms, steadying me. I knew it was Ambrose by touch alone.

"The magic here is ... a lot," he said on a shaky breath.

His lip curled, and I knew instinctively that he'd caught my shift without the aid of the cinnamon ball. My skin prickled as I realized he knew me well enough not to draw attention to it.

"Have you been here before?" I asked.

"I've traveled here with my father, though I've never stayed in Vesten House. He always left me in the rented room in the village when he met with the Vesten Point."

Something about that story made me sad. I knew why it would be strange to bring a child to a meeting of court officials, but why bring him along at all if he were going to be left behind? It was another slight misconception corrected. I had assumed that with his position, Ambrose's father had introduced him at every opportunity—that he had paved the way for Ambrose's later success. Instead, perhaps he felt the same way I had earlier. Like Compass Lake and the surrounding forest were places where secrets were kept, even from him. Ambrose deserved to see what was behind the solid wooden door his father had kept closed.

"Let's go change that, shall we?" I smirked at him. "Lord Arctos said we should present ourselves at Vesten House."

He met my smirk with a grin, and we walked through the village gates. Compass Lake Village was all casual greetings and bustling activity. Lines formed at the more popular shops. The one with the most waiting guests appeared to be a bakery. Homes were peppered in between some of the businesses. Shoppers who had already procured their necessities disappeared into cozy cottages with flower-lined walkways.

No one gave us a second glance as we made our way through the village. It was so much smaller than Sandrin, but there was an energy here that underscored the importance of the destination. This was where decisions were made. This was the heart of fae society and magic.

My mind drifted again to what it would be like to arrive as one of those decision makers—as one whose knowledge of history and magic would guide the future of the court. It was a heady thought, one I worked to suppress for its intensity. Maybe that was why I didn't notice the person in my path and stumbled right into them. Hard.

Large, steady hands caught my forearms while a familiar scent filled my nostrils. It wasn't Ambrose's, though. The smell of fresh citrus was one I'd tried to forget. One I hadn't smelled in twenty years. When I looked up into this male's eyes, they were brown, not hazel.

His eye color was an exact match to my own. One I had studied for the first five years of my life.

I stepped back. The face was one I had tried to forget, but that was impossible. After all, Mom had kept his portrait on the mantle for years.

When we moved to Sandrin, she had finally relocated it into her bedroom—I assumed she had caught me glowering at it one too many times—but that didn't mean that the image of this male wasn't still burned into my brain. The male stabilizing me. The one I took careful, disbelieving steps away from.

My father.

24

Ambrose

Evelyn had fallen behind again. I couldn't tell if she was avoiding me or if the sights and sounds of this place overwhelmed her. Either way, she didn't need to walk next to me. If she wanted space, I wanted her to have as much as possible without the discomfort of our connection.

Things had gone too far last night.

It was like the moment she'd moved toward me, the moment she'd given me an inch, I'd taken a mile. My response was inevitable. In every scenario plotted—every outcome calculated—I hadn't considered *she* might be interested in *me*.

My wolf preened in my head, as if he'd suspected this all along.

But is she? With our magical connection, she doesn't know what she's doing.

And I'd taken advantage of it—like the worst kind of male.

Her legs had already been wrapped around me, and I was throwing us both onto the tiny bed at the inn, when I'd come to my senses. When I'd realized she didn't know the truth about our connection.

I'd gone over the facts obsessively since she'd confessed we were bound. From our individual intents, there was no way the magic could impact our emotions. I wasn't even sure blood magic could change a person's emotions. To my knowledge, there was only one type of magic that could do that, and it was a rare gift of the Suden Court.

But that wasn't the point.

The point was that, even if the magic wasn't influencing us, Evelyn thought it was. I had no idea how to explain that without embarrassing her. She'd never forgive me for such a thing. The way her cheeks had flushed last night when she declared that it was *good* that I'd touched her, as she explained what she'd learned about the magic—I almost salivated with want.

She did things to me. And my wolf.

I knew she didn't realize it. I hadn't understood the full extent of it until her reaction to our shared room at the inn. Finally, I knew what Vincent must feel like with his wind magic around Luna. He could never keep it in check when she was involved. My wolf had sensed Evelyn's anticipation, and for the first time in years, I'd fought for control. Evelyn probably believed that, too, was part of the magic connecting us.

My hand was in my hair, sending the strands in every direction while I searched the crowd for her. This was such a mess. I spotted her, but my shoulders tensed, and a growl loosed from my throat. A male was touching her. He held her in place like she had stumbled into him. I recognized that male. He'd followed us in the market for a few streets. I hadn't thought much of it. Compass Lake Village was the safest place on the continent. Not many would pick a fight in the presence of the fae leaders.

It looked like this male hadn't received that memo.

Brisk steps brought me toward the pair. Evelyn's elevated heart rate thrummed in my ears, urging me forward. Surprise and maybe fear widened her eyes, emotions so far from the lustful looks she'd given me last night. Who was this male?

"Evelyn." Her name alone drew her focus to me. I saw everything I needed to see there. Her teeth clenched, as if hearing her name flipped her fear to anger. I'd put myself between her and the male, not waiting for her reply.

"I think she's fine," I said. I gave her my shoulder in case she wanted something to steady herself against, but from her face alone, it was clear that she wanted space from whoever this was. She looked like a caged animal. Her control over her shift had improved drastically in the past few days, but the magic here could easily send her over the edge. She'd worked so hard to protect her secret. I wouldn't let this male and this place expose her shifted form. "I've got this, Evelyn, if you want to go ahead."

Finally, I made eye contact with the male in front of me. He hadn't fought me when I stepped between him and Evelyn. As I studied him, I thought I knew why.

His dark brown eyes were a perfect match to Evelyn's.

"I didn't mean to upset her." The male glanced over my shoulder. Or he tried to. He was short, and Evelyn used my body as a shield.

"Ambrose, I have to go," she whispered.

I nodded. My wolf whined, but the scent of her tension was palpable. She must be losing the battle with her veil cat. "It's fine, Evelyn. Do what you need to do. I'll let them know."

The male ducked under my armpit as he tried to see her again. "Evelyn, wait. I just want to—"

"No." She didn't stop to listen or make more excuses. She turned and ran.

I knew she would go deep into the forest. Thankfully, it surrounded this place. Within seconds, she disappeared into the lush greenery. Given the speed at which she retreated, I didn't think she had long before the veil cat took over.

The male moved to follow her. This time, I stopped him with a hand on his forearm. "She wants some space."

He tried again. "You don't understand. I'm her fath—"

I didn't need him to finish the sentence. Studying Evelyn Knowles was more than a hobby at this point. I could see the familial resemblance in this male's eyes alone. "I think I do, actually. And I think she's well aware of who you are to her. She's made her feelings on the matter clear."

He looked defeated, and a haunting desperation overtook him, but at least he didn't start after her again. "I've been looking for her everywhere—for both of them."

Well, that was ... unexpected. Against my better judgment, I didn't walk away. Part of me convinced myself I still protected her. It was my responsibility to ensure he didn't follow. In reality, I stood there unsure whether Evelyn would want me to hear whatever he said, or if she'd like to pretend we'd never encountered the male who sired her.

I couldn't help it. As with any piece of history that contradicted another, I had to know more. His words were not in line with what Evelyn had told me.

"You know her?" he asked.

I nodded.

He assessed me in a new light. "Are you her partner? Is she happy?"

This was the last thing I'd expected today. I'd woken up to the fresh scent of Evelyn's woodsy aroma coating the pillow beside me. I'd felt the tangle of our fingers before she slipped away, knowing without a doubt that I'd reached for her and she'd welcomed it. It was intoxicating to think that some part of her wanted me. Hope from the realization burned like a flame in my chest. I just wished I knew how to alert the rest of her to that fact.

But I was a researcher. If there was one thing I could do, it was study Evelyn with a dedication that bordered on religious devotion. I would test every method to determine if there was a way to make her mine.

Mine.

It was the first time I'd thought the word. Hearing her absentee father so casually assume I was hers—that I was in her life romantically—breathed new life into the dream.

This was ridiculous. I couldn't have this conversation with the missing fae father Evelyn had fled.

"I think it's up to Evelyn to decide what you know about her."

He let his head fall, but I saw the slightest nod, like he understood my response. "She doesn't even want to see me. I wasn't truly prepared for that outcome."

"Maybe you should tell her why that's unexpected to you." I sighed, feeling bad for the male. One look at the inward curve of his shoulders, at the way his clothes hung a little too loosely from his frame, told me he hadn't abandoned them. Whether Evelyn's mom was correct and it was the mist plague, or some other ill tidings, it didn't matter. The same damage had been done from Evelyn's perspective. He needed to repair that on his own.

He looked up at me, brown eyes shining with unshed tears. "When I woke from the mist plague, they weren't where I left them."

My heart twisted, and I wasn't sure if it was because Evelyn was too far away or because of the confirmation of his whereabouts. Evelyn's mom had been right.

"You were in one of the mist plague villages?"

He nodded. "The Compass Points awoke us months ago, but when I returned to our cabin, they weren't there. I searched the surrounding villages for news, but no one had any information. I am here to petition the Vesten Point for help finding them."

His eyes brightened. "He told me last time I attended court that he was selecting a new Vesten historian and they'd be able to help me locate my family."

The laugh that escaped my lips held no mirth. I had thought my and Evelyn's situation was a mess. She had confessed one of the ways she would use the resources of the Vesten historian position, should she get it, was to find her father and demand answers from him. Of course, she claimed it was for her mom, and her magic. Never for her. Never because she wanted to.

What would she do now that she had him here? Would she listen to learn that everything her mother had feared might be true? I knew without a doubt that his story was not mine to reveal to her.

I already knew too much. There would be no winning when she asked me about this later. I needed to get out of here. "I have to go."

"You'll tell her?" he asked, his voice filled with too much hope.

"I don't think I'm the one she should hear it from."

He looked longingly into the woods where Evelyn had disappeared. "What if she won't let me explain?"

I glanced away, unsure what to do. "Where are you staying? I'll at least tell her that."

"At the inn in the Vesten neighborhood."

"I'll make sure she knows where to find you." I turned on my heel and took long strides down the path before he could say anything else.

25

Evelyn

It figured that on my way to the most important meeting of my professional career, my father, who had been *missing* for twenty years, decided to appear.

Couldn't he have remained missing for a few more hours?

Goosebumps covered my skin before I shifted. It was the human equivalent of my hackles rising. For once, my veil cat and I were in stark agreement. I needed to get away from my father.

It was the first time I remembered that I freely chose to use the veil cat. She wasn't a burden in this moment but an escape —a partner in my flight. My veil cat's methods might have differed from mine, but as with her instinct about Ambrose, she understood things I couldn't voice. We were one, even if she was a little more overt in her communication style.

Some new connection snapped into place between us as we finally understood each other. Branches and bushes flew by as I ran. My heart pounded in time with the paws pressing me forward. I didn't fight her; she knew we needed to get away.

I wasn't prepared to see him.

A low hiss slipped free as I thought of Ambrose stuck there with my father. It wasn't exactly my finest moment, but Ambrose had told me to go. Maybe it wasn't his job to deal with my missing parent, but he hadn't seemed to mind the assignment.

Thinking of Ambrose reminded me I had somewhere to be. I could not miss this meeting. With everything else going on, the Vesten historian position hadn't slipped my mind. I needed to impress the Vesten Point while I was here.

In tune with my thoughts, my veil cat turned slightly so that we were headed southwest. It felt like we were headed back to my original path—toward Vesten House. I trusted her to get me where we needed to be. She'd appeared when I called, when I needed to get away from my father, no questions asked.

This must be what Ambrose meant when he said he and his animal were one.

I wished I had more time to consider the momentous occasion that this was. Trusting that she understood me, that we were in this together, was the key. Something in me knew I could shift at will now, so long as I continued to trust in our partnership. I sighed as I ran, wondering if it had really been that easy.

The path was just ahead, but I didn't want to sprint onto it in my feline form. I might have had an understanding with my veil cat, but I still didn't have the information I wanted about how she'd come to be mine.

Well, the one person who could answer those questions tried to talk to you...

He'd ambushed me in the street. How could he think that was the best approach? No "Hi, I'm your father, sorry I haven't been around for twenty years?"

I sighed again, knowing that literally nothing he said could have made me listen. I had thought that I was ready for the confrontation, that I had hardened myself against the sting of his abandonment, but one look at him, at the misery written plainly on his face, told me I was nowhere near ready to hear what he had to say.

My father was a problem for later. Now, I needed to shift back unaided again. I knew I could do it, but my heart raced as I worried it wouldn't work. Ambrose and Lord Arctos were sure to be there by now. They would discuss the options with or without me. My theories could help. I just needed a chance to present them.

If Ambrose shared all his ideas, he would be seen as the leader in our research. He'd get a head start with the Vesten Point and would be rewarded with the Vesten historian position. My lip curled in a snarl, exposing my teeth. Apparently, my veil cat agreed that we needed to shift as soon as possible.

I reached for my fire with force. *Please.* I pleaded with the veil cat—pleaded with myself. *We need to get in there.*

Was I talking to myself? Maybe. I wasn't really sure of the mechanics. I knew that I could accomplish great things if given the chance. This was my chance. The flame ignited the shift back to my half-fae self.

As I stepped onto the heavily trodden path, I couldn't help but smile. When I looked west, it wasn't so much that I knew where the Vesten House was on the map of Compass Lake, but I could feel the tug toward Ambrose. For once, the connection proved useful, directing me where I needed to go.

A quick jog down the path brought the house into sight. I sprinted the rest of the way, only stopping as I scaled the back steps of the house. The heavy wooden door was more intimidating than I'd anticipated. I knocked quickly, before fear overtook me. When the door swung open, the last person I expected to see was standing there.

"Why are you answering the door?" I asked Lord Arctos.

"You're late."

My hands were on my hips. "I had to take care of something."

"I see. You might as well come with me. They've already started."

I forced my shoulders back. I wouldn't cower under the weight of this green-eyed god. Had my timing been inconvenient? Sure. Could I have handled it literally any other way? Probably. But that didn't mean anything. It meant I was a bit hotheaded where complex emotions were involved. But the problem Lord Arctos and the Vesten Point needed us to solve wasn't a complex emotion—it was blood magic. It made sense to me in a way nothing else did.

Lord Arctos walked through the large house like he owned the place. His legs were so long that it was hard to keep up with him and take in my new surroundings. I might have told myself that I belonged in this conversation, but part of me was still shocked that I was in Vesten House at all.

I'm not even fae.

I stopped in the hallway, staring at the wall. A painting there had caught my eye. I knew I needed to stop thinking of my fae-ness in such black-and-white terms. It was time to acknowledge that I didn't have to conform to fae standards to contribute to the court, to the continent. I could make a difference exactly as I was.

The veil cat purred in my mind.

Maybe ignoring my fae heritage, and disliking this not-so-mythical animal I shared space with, was as detrimental as the fae looking down on my human heritage. I shook my head. I'd been staring at a painting of Compass Lake for too long.

Lord Arctos cleared his throat beside me. "The tour was given to those who arrived on time."

My glare was immediate, and there was a twinkle in his eye when he caught it.

"Is this the creation of the fae?" I asked.

The painting depicted four fae on the beach in front of Norden House. Each fae leader received a gift from their god. This was what we needed. We knew the blood magic in question had taken place at the creation. Would these gifts serve as anchors?

Lord Arctos nodded. I hummed in consideration and followed him the rest of the way down the hall. It twisted to the left, and I knew whatever room we were headed to would be facing the lake. He opened a set of double doors easily, as if they were little more than an inconvenience. The voices on the other side stopped mid-sentence at his entrance.

"Yes, Arctos, please just let yourself in."

The voice was wry, a tone quite similar to the one I'd used when the Vesten God had opened the door. The speaker was young—or, at least, he looked it. Who knew with the fae. His shaggy hair framed his face, making him look both windswept but still utterly put together. As I stepped into the room, his eyes tracked me, though he didn't meet my gaze. He was bent over a table, books open in front of him.

I took the opportunity to survey my surroundings. It was like the Great Room in the library, fully lined with shelves. A desk sat in the far corner, but the stacks of books and papers indicated it was more of a staging area than a place of work. I couldn't believe I was in the Vesten Point's study.

The male unfolded himself from where he leaned over the book. "I see you found our rogue researcher." He was tall, too, and lean, much thinner than Ambrose, but as he strode across the room, something told me that underestimating his power would be a mistake.

With a glance at Lord Arctos, the male offered his hand.

"Hello, Evelyn. I'm the Vesten Point, but you can call me Carter. I'm glad you could join us."

I stared at his hand for a moment too long. There was a power in this room that I didn't quite understand. It felt ancient and primal, and it hadn't been present with me and Lord Arctos when he ushered me back here, so I knew it wasn't the god himself.

"Well," the Vesten Point—Carter—laughed. "Usually, I'm the one accused of being taciturn." He made to pull his hand back.

I grabbed it quickly to shake. "I apologize, sir. And I apologize for my tardiness. Please don't take it as a lack of enthusiasm for the project, or a lack of ideas on solutions to your problem."

He laughed. "Carter, please. And I took it as no such thing." He gestured toward the table, and without looking, I knew that Ambrose stood there. I had known it the moment I stepped into the room and the tether between us loosened. The awareness had told me where *not* to look. I wasn't ready to see what he'd learned from being left with my father.

Carter continued. "Your colleague explained you had an unavoidable conflict. He assured us you'd join shortly."

Finally, I glanced up. Relief flooded Ambrose's features, and I didn't think it was solely from the release of the magical connection.

The Vesten Point continued, unaware of my turmoil. "We were discussing what Ambrose noted as one of your working theories. To discover if an anchor was used—"

"Because when an anchor is present, destroying the anchor removes the magic." My hand immediately moved to cover my mouth. Had I just interrupted the Vesten Point? I glanced at him to see what kind of damage I'd done—if he'd ask me to leave immediately or if I'd be allowed to at least collect my bag, which I presumed Ambrose had picked up when I dropped it. "I'm so sorry," I mumbled.

This time, Carter looked at me directly, as if my interrupting him had finally made me worthy of his attention. There were laugh lines at the corners of his eyes, and he was ... smiling. He glanced at Lord Arctos, who only shrugged in answer to a question I didn't understand.

"Yes, your point is correct." He turned to Ambrose. "Or, at least, I assume that is the point Mr. Yarrow was about to make."

Ambrose inspected me as he responded. He seemed to be searching me for something, but I couldn't tell what. "That's correct."

"And does an anchor have to be stated as such?" Carter directed his question more openly to both of us.

Ambrose still stared at me and didn't seem like he'd respond. I cleared my throat. Still nothing. I shook my head, needing to answer but unwilling to take credit for his idea. "Ambrose's recent paper hypothesized that any object with a connection to the magic could be considered an anchor."

Finally, Ambrose spoke. "It may have been my paper on anchors, but Evelyn was the one who suggested it could solve this particular problem."

"Interesting," Carter said. His gaze shifted between me and Ambrose, as if unsure who to direct his next question to.

I glared at the god standing beside the table. "Lord Arctos wasn't all that helpful when we asked about any potential anchors from the creation of the fae, but I noticed the painting in the hallway. Lord Arctos bestowed a gift upon the first Vesten Point, correct?"

Carter shot a glance toward the Vesten God. "He knows that—"

"My apologies, we rushed you right in here," Lord Arctos interrupted, before Carter could finish his thought. The Vesten God rambled on. "This is a sufficient summary for now. Carter must attend to a few things, but he'd be delighted if you'd both join him for the evening meal. We can discuss any tests you'd like to conduct with us while you're here."

I nodded slowly, glancing between the god and the fae leader. Carter looked as confused as I did.

Finally, Ambrose approached my side. "I put your bag in your room. I can show you to it."

Lord Arctos shifted into his bird form and perched on my shoulder. "*I'll let Mr. Yarrow give you that tour.*"

My glare was lost when Lord Arctos flapped his wing against the side of my face and flew to Carter's shoulder.

26

Evelyn

The warm weight of Ambrose's palm at my back was more distracting than I cared to admit. What had happened in there? We hadn't decided anything. Lord Arctos had cut off the one conversation we should have had. "What did you speak about before I arrived?"

Ambrose shrugged. "He asked about our work prior to this. I told him what I could of your papers and my history work at the library."

"You didn't discuss theories?"

He shook his head. "Not more than what you said. I didn't want to discuss the idea of working through the magic, since it would involve sharing our predicament."

I let out a sigh of relief. "Lord Arctos obviously knows, but I don't think he'll tell the Vesten Point unless we do. And I'd rather not tell him when our situation only makes us look incompetent with blood magic."

Ambrose's ears pinkened, but he nodded. "Every time I asked about anchors, Lord Arctos changed the topic."

That didn't seem right. It was part of the reason we were here. I only had myself to blame for not being there to witness it, though. If I hadn't lost my composure when my father showed up, if I hadn't shifted and run, maybe I could have combatted Lord Arctos's redirections.

I rubbed my forehead. It throbbed worse when Ambrose's hand dropped from my back. He said something about the house and the layout that I didn't quite catch. It wasn't as if I didn't trust Ambrose to relay our ideas. Astonishingly, I did. But that wasn't really the point. I wanted to have an impact on the direction of our court, and being in the room during the discussion was part of that. Mostly, I was disappointed in myself for missing out.

"What painting did you see about the creation?" Ambrose asked.

That brought me from my thoughts. "Lord Arctos didn't give you a tour?"

He laughed dryly. "Lord Arctos doesn't find me as entertaining as he finds you."

I wasn't sure what to make of that, but I knew, with Ambrose's knowledge of fae history, the painting might mean more to him than it did to me. I took his hand and pulled him in the opposite direction.

He sucked in a breath behind me, but as I tugged, he stumbled along. At some point, he must have decided to follow me, because no amount of force from me could drag Ambrose Yarrow anywhere he didn't want to go. He was too big. His hand was too warm and reassuring.

Wait. What?

No, I felt it—his hand reclasped mine like it held on for dear life. It was like I was an adventure, and he wasn't sure he dared to embark. His grip tightened as we followed the hallway near the entry.

"Do you feel the magic here?" I asked as we walked.

"The magic here feels ... heavier than elsewhere. Is that what you mean?" he asked. I had an image of him pulling his hand from mine to jot notes in his journal, but they remained intertwined.

"Not that. This is different. It's in this house, or maybe on this property specifically. The magic feels so old." I knew I wasn't explaining it right.

Ambrose tugged me to a stop. He shook his head. "I don't think I feel that. Describe it."

"I'm not sure I can. Ancient, primitive. Powerful. All I can do is describe it with single words."

Now his hand was reaching for his notebook. "When did you start—"

I waved him off and took a few more steps down the hall. "Don't worry about it. This is more important." When we came to where I had stopped with Lord Arctos. I pointed to the painting. "See? They were each given gifts."

Ambrose's brow furrowed slightly. He stepped closer to the painting and nodded.

"What if ... what if whatever this gift is could be used as an anchor?" My finger all but touched the image of the item being passed from Lord Arctos to the proud-looking Vesten female.

Suddenly, Ambrose reached out and tugged me toward him. His strong arms wrapped around me in what I could only call an embrace. "Evelyn, you're a genius."

I knew that. I was pretty sure he already knew that. But if this was what it took for him to say it out loud, I'd allow it. My cheek was pressed against his chest. He was solid, but not uncomfortable. His chin came to rest on top of my head. Something could be said of the way I fit so perfectly into the cage of him without feeling trapped.

My arms wrapped around his waist, and I nuzzled into him farther.

Oh, my gods. *I nuzzled?*

I cleared my throat, released my grip, and pushed myself back. Some part of me didn't want to go. But regardless of this win, nothing had changed since last night. He was unaware that the magic didn't affect us this way. And I knew that wanting things for myself was foolish. If anything, seeing my father this afternoon had been a stark reminder.

Desire brought nothing but heartache and anger. I'd wanted my father to return—apparently, I needed to change my position on that, because he had returned at the most inconvenient time, and I wasn't sure I wanted to hear his story. Or what about my desperate wish to go to the Vesten school? They hadn't let me in because I wasn't fully fae. Or when I'd wanted someone to teach me how to use my magic? No one would spare the time for a half-fae when I needed it.

Ambrose did. There was concern in his eyes as I met them, but he let me break our connection.

Wordlessly, I turned to focus on the painting. It was hard to tell what the gift given to the Vesten Point was. It was very small, even smaller than the other items pictured. One of them looked like a dagger. That must be what the Norden Goddess, Aurora, handed to the male fae, the first Norden Point. The other two items, from the Osten God and Suden God, looked like jewelry. Maybe a necklace and a ring? I peered closer. The item in Lord Arctos's palm was even smaller than the ring.

"Can you tell what it is?"

Ambrose leaned forward, careful to give me space now that I'd separated us. I was fully aware of his presence anyway. The shape of him, the heat that always surrounded him, it was something I was painfully aware of—though usually better at ignoring.

I caught his scent as he leaned closer to the painting. The

smell of pencil shavings and old books did something to me, and I couldn't pretend it had to do with the magic connecting us.

Something sparked behind his eyes, and I knew he figured it out. "It's the Vesten coin."

I racked my brain trying to remember what that meant. It definitely had something to do with Vesten history.

Ambrose kept speaking. "Each of the gods granted the new court leaders an item that could enhance their power. This item works even better than we first anticipated. The object is inherently connected to the magic."

While I'd known Ambrose would recognize the item, his answer brought a sudden exhaustion with it. Doubt swirled through my mind. I didn't know enough Vesten history to be here. This was proof that I wasn't one of them. Ambrose was.

My veil cat growled as my thoughts spun.

"Good. We should ask about it at the evening meal," I said before making my escape. "I'm going to head up to my room. Can you point me in the right direction? Or I can find the steward."

"I can show you." His spine straightened, and he gestured forward.

He spoke a little on the walk. I knew he only filled the silence, but the information he shared, more history of the house or comments on other paintings and artifacts on display, reinforced my worry. He surely thought he was being helpful, welcoming, but it reminded me how unprepared I was for this.

Ambrose glanced at me as he finished speaking of the second Vesten Point and the work he'd done to spread the Vesten across the continent. His brow furrowed, and I recognized the look. It was one he gave every experiment before declaring it complete. It clicked then what his endless chatter meant. He wanted to know if I was ready to talk about something even more foreign than Vesten history. He waited for me to ask about my father.

"Did he say anything to you?"

Although Ambrose wasn't privy to my thoughts, he clearly didn't need an explanation about who *he* was.

He nodded.

"Well?"

Ambrose stopped before a door on the second floor. He pointed. "Your room is here. Mine is right next to you." He smiled sheepishly. "Lord Arctos's idea."

Now he wasn't answering. What had my father said? "Ambrose."

He sighed and ran his hand through his hair. "He wants to talk to you."

"Yes, I think he made that clear when he ambushed me on the street."

Ambrose's hand didn't manage to leave his hair; in fact, it gripped tighter at the roots. This was my family drama. What had him so worried?

"He's staying at the inn near the Vesten cottages. He wants to talk to you."

"You already said that." What was he keeping from me? "Ambrose. If he said something to you, I'd like to hear it."

His ears pinkened. "I think it should come from him. If it's something you want to hear."

I considered my brief interaction with my father. He'd looked ... hopeful, but under my glare, as I realized who he was, his features had crumpled. What had he said? He just wanted to ... what? Explain?

"Ambrose, I deserve to know what you do. He's my father."

Ambrose's hazel eyes snapped to mine. I swear a glint of gold crossed them, the briefest snap of the wolf within. "He wants to explain," Ambrose said. "But I don't feel qualified to pass on what I heard. I don't want to repeat it if you don't believe it, and I don't want to seem like I'm endorsing it by doing so. You're right. He is your father. And you deserve to hear what he has to say if you want to, but you deserve to hear it from him."

"Fine." His reaction, his understanding, proved too much for me. It hinted at something too deep, too disastrous to reach for. "Thank you for the information. I'll take care of it myself."

He shook his head. "Are you alright? Do you want to—"

I turned the knob on the door. "Thank you, Ambrose, for explaining my absence and passing on the message, but as you said. This is my mess, I will deal with it."

"That's not what I—"

I didn't wait for an explanation. Ambrose was already too tangled in every other aspect of my life at the moment. I didn't need to add him to this. We were colleagues. We were magically bound. We were competing for a position on which we both seemed intent. Worse—I wanted more. I wanted him to go with me to talk to my father. I wanted his calm, reassuring presence when my father's words were sure to upturn all my carefully held beliefs. Which was precisely why I couldn't accept what I knew he would offer.

I would deal with my father on my own. Before Ambrose could say more, I entered the room and closed the door behind me.

27

Evelyn

With the door closed behind me, I slid down its face to sit on the floor. Ambrose spoke outside the room. He apologized. He offered to accompany me to my father's accommodations. Still I didn't know what to do with any of it. As much as I wanted Ambrose with me, I knew that was a dependency I needed to break. We would solve this magical connection at some point. I couldn't rely on him for things like this. I let out a breath when he finally grew tired of my lack of response and went into his room.

I needed to collect myself before our evening meal with the Vesten Point. In all my work, both personal and professional, with plants, I'd read a lot about the Vesten Gardens. I might not get another chance to explore. If a few minutes before the meal were all I had, I'd take them. It would give me something to focus on besides my current problems. If it meant I arrived at the meal separately from Ambrose, that was a fringe benefit.

The coast was clear when I peeked out the doorway. I slipped quietly down the stairs and let myself out the front door. The gardens were easy to find from there.

The natural beauty combined with the raw magic that surrounded me, and made the entire place spectacular. I adapted to the magic with every step, but the feeling from the study—that feeling of ancient magic—still lurked. It wasn't imminently threatening, just obviously lingering. I tried to ignore it as I wandered the garden paths.

It was called the Burning Garden. All the flowers that grew here were bright orange or red, so that when the garden was in full bloom in the spring, it resembled the Vesten fire. Technically, it was winter, but this area never seemed to get snowfall. The flowers weren't out, but greenery still overran the space.

The most prominent feature in the garden drew my attention—an aged willow tree, so large that I could slip beneath the branches and hide from sight. So, of course, that's what I did. That feeling of ancient magic was even stronger beneath its boughs.

I squeaked as I finished a loop of the tree and found a veil cat watching my progress. Yellow-green eyes flashed up at me. I faltered, unsure what to do. Before I could decide, the veil cat was gone, and the Vesten Point stood there.

"Sorry if I scared you." He glanced around the tree as if to see if anyone else was with us.

"What are you doing here?" I winced, realizing I needed to work on my tone. My hand was still at my chest, hoping that my heart wouldn't burst from my rib cage.

He laughed but still didn't quite look at me. "This is my garden. Some might ask what you are doing here. But I won't." His gaze finally met mine. "I think I already know."

"What does that mean?"

"It's odd, isn't it?" The Vesten Point circled me, the same way

I imagined the veil cat would. My veil cat remained silent, though. She wasn't on high alert, and part of me took that as a sign that I didn't need to be, either. "That you had to come here —to Compass Lake?"

I wasn't sure if that was a statement or a question, but I bristled anyway. If I hadn't traveled to Compass Lake, I could have avoided that entire debacle with Ambrose last night. Maybe I wouldn't have run into my father. I could have spared myself a lot of embarrassment, and a lot of needless emotional turmoil. "Lord Arctos said we had to come. He said we'd learned all that we could from the library."

Carter laughed. "Of course he did. I should have known Arctos was meddling."

"Meddling how?" I asked. The Vesten God was mischievous, but I didn't think he meant us harm.

The Vesten Point swiped his hand through the air like a cat lazily batting away a fly. "Never mind."

Silence surrounded us beneath the willow tree. I decided to fill it. Maybe I could make up for some of the missed conversation this afternoon. "We came up with an idea that we'd like to talk to you about at the meal."

"I'm glad to hear it, but that's not what interests me at the moment." He touched the tree and shuddered. "Why did you come to this particular spot?"

"I..." Well, I wasn't sure how to answer that. "I work a lot with plants. I'd read of the gardens and wanted to see them."

The Vesten Point seemed to be speaking to himself more than to me, but I was startled at his words. "So Mr. Yarrow said. He went on for a while about your tests on living things before getting to his tests on inanimate objects."

He had? I flushed, because a part of me knew, of course, he would. Whether or not he agreed with the methods, he'd provide all available information. Another part of me said this was different. That Ambrose was someone I could depend on to be there for me when the load got too heavy—like it had this afternoon. That part of me thought that maybe I could expect things from him.

The Vesten Point spoke as he leaned against the tree. "But what I want to know, Ms. Knowles, is what brought you to this particular spot in the garden."

Ambrose had said he couldn't feel the magic I described in the library, but I knew that was what had guided me to this place. It was a risk, but if I wanted answers, I needed to ask questions. If I didn't ask questions, I only had myself to blame for remaining ignorant.

"There is a magic here—it's old." I shook my head. "No, that's not quite right. It's ancient. And I think it guided me here."

"Is that right?" Carter looked every inch the veil cat he was. Moreover, with my response, he looked remarkably like a cat who had caught a particularly troublesome canary.

I nodded slowly, unsure what else to say. I didn't have other words to describe the magic. It wasn't flashy; it felt more like a well-worn cloak, always right where you needed it at the necessary time. It was by no means threadbare, though. Its stitches were just as tight as the day they were sewn.

Carter watched me. Then he asked the last question I expected. "Do you know how the next Vesten Point is chosen?"

"No," I nearly spat. The reaction was visceral. The idea that a half-fae would know this precious court secret was laughable.

The tilt of Carter's head was enough to give me pause. He studied me, not in the same way Ambrose did but in a way that told me he saw something I hadn't yet put together. And I hated being caught off guard.

"Let me enlighten you, then." He folded his hands behind his back and strolled around the tree. I briefly wondered if he had ever taught other researchers when he was Vesten historian. The tone of his voice took on that of a practiced lecturer, one fascinated with his own subject matter. "The Vesten Court puts a lot of weight on our animals—our shifter magic. Of course, fire is part of the shift, but it's the animal itself that the court reveres."

"Why is that?" I couldn't help but ask. He made this seem so informal, like we were discussing the weather and not secrets I'd never been privy to as a court outsider.

A brief smile curled his lip, and he shook his head, his light brown waves swaying with the motion. "I'll deny it if you say this in front of Arctos, but I'm pretty sure it's because of him. It's clear he prefers his animals above his fae form. Past court leaders wanted to ... emulate what our god found important."

"Ugh, he'd be even more insufferable if he heard that," I mumbled.

The gleam in Carter's eye told me I hadn't been as quiet as I'd hoped. "Indeed. Regardless, the court's value of the animal led to how Vesten Points are chosen."

My brow furrowed. "How so? Aren't the animals hereditary?"

Carter's green eyes lit up. "They mostly are, but that is also the animal's choice. Once an animal line establishes itself in a family, it tends to continue unless things go wrong."

I briefly thought of my father and the information I needed from him. No matter his reasoning for not being with us, he could at least answer the questions about my shift. We didn't have to establish a relationship for him to do that for me.

Carter spoke again. The words caught my attention. "Some animals don't follow the pattern, of course, like mine."

I thought that, at this moment, my veil cat would be uncomfortable. Carter's eyes flashed the yellow-green that was clearly his veil cat's. His animal observed this conversation with him. *The animal always knows.* Ambrose's words flashed through my mind. First, I wondered what he would make of this situation.

Second, I wondered how literally to take his comment about our Vesten animals.

Carter's veil cat couldn't know what I was, could he?

"What do you mean?" I asked shakily. My hand balled into a fist at my side. He couldn't know. That wasn't possible, but my own veil cat was mysteriously silent. She curled up, unbothered by this entire conversation.

"I mean that my father, Gabriel, he's not a veil cat shifter." He studied me carefully, watching for something in my face.

It was clear he wanted me to ask the obvious question. If nothing else, the researcher in me needed to know what he was getting at, even if we were treading on dangerous ground with my own secret. "Why is that?"

"The continent required a veil cat," he said simply. "The continent still requires a veil cat."

I shook my head, repeating his words. "The continent still requires a veil cat." It felt like he was withholding information, somehow. Before I could ask, he continued.

"When a new Vesten Point is required, the current one receives a message about what animal the court needs. You could imagine our past leader's surprise when he was told his successor needed to be a creature most thought mythical."

I coughed forcefully. He did *not* just say that.

"Everything alright, Evelyn?" He paced back around the tree while he tracked my reaction.

"Did you think that?" I asked. "That your shift was mythical?"

His lip curled into a mischievous smile. "An animal said to shepherd souls to the afterlife? Of course I thought it was mythical. That didn't stop me from turning into one, though."

It was ... reassuring to know someone else had the same experience I had. But no matter our similarities, I wouldn't tell him my secrets. Especially given this conversation, I needed to know more about the veil cat lineage from my father.

He held my gaze. "The continent needed a veil cat, and I was that veil cat. The Vesten Point calling is one of the reasons the animal might not follow lineage."

The intensity was too much. I blurted out another question. "Why did the continent 'need' a veil cat? What does this have to do with the ancient magic here?"

He smiled, albeit a little sadly. There might even have been disappointment there and gone before I cataloged it. "The Compass Points have been through a lot in the past months. Much was happening on the continent and outside of our realm that required the courts to come together. I won't go into the details now, but suffice it to say that ancient magic was important, and a veil cat was essential to rid the continent of the mist plague."

"Did you really travel between realms?" I asked with no caution whatsoever. That was what he had to be implying. This was the sisters' experience in the journal Gabriel had given us days ago. When they'd shifted into veil cats, they'd gone to another realm—beyond the veil.

"I do."

"That's the magic I feel, isn't it?" I paused but ultimately threw caution to the wind. The sense of ancient magic was too strong. Only a realm known to hold the spirits of the departed could feel this way. I took careful steps toward the tree's trunk. It was as if the magic emanated from here. I still didn't understand it.

"It is." He tilted his head. "You seem aware of its origin as well."

Before I could ask another question, he glanced over my shoulder. I didn't know what he saw through the willow tree's drooping branches, but something halted our conversation. "The others are here. We should meet them for our meal."

That was fine with me. I couldn't handle any more of the Vesten Point's piercing stare. My veil cat's lack of concern seemed to indicate it wasn't as bad as I thought, but it definitely wasn't comfortable. I would need to find my father to talk sooner rather than later. I also hadn't missed the Vesten Point's tense change. I'd asked him if he had traveled between realms. He'd answered like he still did.

Something was going on here, and I wondered how closely it was related to my and Ambrose's project.

28

Ambrose

Before heading down to meet the Vesten Point, I tried knocking on Evelyn's door again. It was a performative action. The tightening in my chest said that she wasn't in her room. She was somewhere out on the property, and getting farther away by the moment.

A sigh slipped from my lips, and a weight settled on my shoulder. "*A lover's spat?*" the Vesten God asked.

I wished. What kind of fight was this, exactly? A friends fight? A collegial dispute? I had no idea, and wasn't that part of the problem. "She went for a walk."

"*Of course she did.*" This time, the Vesten God's voice held an air of satisfaction rather than condescension. Like maybe he'd won some bet with himself.

"I was about to go downstairs to the meal. Are you coming?" I asked.

He flapped his wings into the side of my face. "*Yes, but I believe Carter wanted to eat out in the garden. I'll show you the way.*"

I shrugged and followed Lord Arctos out of the house.

Reading about the Burning Garden hadn't prepared me to see it. Immediately, my mind went to Evelyn and her constant experiments with plants. She would love to see this. I guessed she would soon enough.

"I should find Evelyn before Carter arrives," I started.

"No need." Lord Arctos had shifted into his fae form and strode with purpose as he called toward the large willow tree in the center of the garden. The way its branches hung like a curtain behind which one could hide was beautiful—although maybe that was too tame a word for it. I might not have felt the magic that Evelyn described earlier, but this tree embodied the ancient feeling she had described.

It didn't surprise me that she'd discovered additional magic here. She was intuitive with unique magic. Yes, she thoroughly tested her ideas, but she also had a knack for it. I wondered what that meant when it came to unique magic on Vesten House grounds.

A few of the kitchen staff arrived in the garden behind us and laid out a checkered blanket. Plates filled with rich-smelling food were spread across it: meats, vegetables, fresh-baked bread, and brightly colored fruits.

The sun had already started to set, and the night had a chill about it. I hoped Evelyn had some of the candies with her. There were some in my pocket, but I wasn't sure she'd want me to offer her one in this company. The garden would be a lovely place to take in the scenery of Compass Lake at its most quiet hour, but it was sure to get cold if she didn't use her fire.

"Are you two coming?" Lord Arctos called.

My head snapped toward the giant willow tree as I realized what Lord Arctos had said. *Are you two coming?*

Evelyn and Carter pushed the drooping willow branches out of the way and walked toward us—together.

They weren't touching. Not that it was within my rights to be angry if they had been, but something about the two of them looked ... informal. My metaphorical hackles rose.

"Calm down, Wolfy, it's not what you think," Lord Arctos said.

Maybe my hackles rising hadn't been metaphorical.

As much as the knot in my chest loosened at her approach, a different feeling I wasn't quite sure what to do with threatened to double me over. Evelyn laughed freely as they approached. Had she ever been that relaxed with me?

It's not what you think. But what did I think it was? More importantly, what did he think I thought it was? Now my head was pounding, but I had no time to tie myself further into knots when they met us at the blanket.

"Ambrose, Lord Arctos, glad you could join us. Shall we sit?" The Vesten Point gestured toward the picnic.

Us? What had I missed in less than an hour? Wasn't it only last night I'd been contemplating if Evelyn and I could be an *us*?

Evelyn moved with a fluidity I hadn't seen since she'd prowled toward me in veil cat form. Dark strands fell from her braid, and her shoulders lacked their usual tension. She looked more relaxed than I'd seen her in ages, and I wanted to know what had caused it.

I guessed I didn't have to wonder. Carter's languid movements effused ease. He might have been the most powerful Vesten on the continent, but he certainly didn't act like it. Maybe that was what unshakeable confidence did to you. He knew no one could hurt him, so he went through life without concern. It was the exact opposite of the way I approached things. Worry dictated my every move. I tried to think differently, tried not to let fear of what could happen control my actions, but maybe that wasn't enough. Maybe that carefree attitude would be better for Evelyn.

"Ambrose?" My name from Evelyn's lips snapped my attention to her dark brown eyes. It was clear from her tone that this wasn't the first time she'd said it. She offered me a dish from the basket. It looked like bread and some kind of vegetable dip. "Did you want some?"

Absently, I took the dish and placed the food on the plate in front of me. Lord Arctos and Carter seemed to be in a heated discussion. I took their moment of distraction to whisper to Evelyn, "Do you need one of the candies?"

She looked a little startled but immediately relaxed. "I can do it without them now, but thank you."

Evelyn was a quick study. "I shouldn't be surprised that you mastered this within days when it takes most Vesten weeks or months to learn."

I loved that her cheeks pinkened at that statement.

She tucked a loose strand of hair behind her ear. "Since I mastered those so quickly, I'd love to hear what comes next in these lessons."

"What are you two talking about?" Lord Arctos interrupted.

Evelyn's eyes widened with panic, and I knew she didn't want to air the fact that she hadn't been taught basic Vesten magic in front of the Vesten Point and god of our court.

I improvised. "Evelyn and I had an idea."

She stiffened but didn't stop me. Carter turned, and his gold-green eyes flashed. "Do tell."

"Well, we discussed anchors after our conversation in your study. We wondered about the Vesten coin and whether it could have served as an anchor for the creation of the Vesten. It was said to—"

Carter glared at Lord Arctos.

"What is it?" Evelyn asked.

"The coin was..." Carter started, and shot another angry look at the god. Then cleared his throat and tried again. "It was given at the creation of the Vesten, and even uniquely tied to the magic that was shared. It would have fit your definition of an anchor perfectly." He raised a glass of wine to his lips.

"Was?" Evelyn said. "*Would* have?"

It wasn't a good sign that the Vesten Point spoke about the coin in the past tense.

"Yes, unfortunately, the coin was destroyed. We needed it for something else. Something more important than this project. Its magic was well spent, but I'm afraid it can't be spent again. I'm sorry if that's what you came here to test. Lord Arctos was very aware of this. He could have told you in Sandrin."

I tilted my head, considering. It didn't surprise me that Lord Arctos was playing his own game in this mess. I wasn't bothered by it. He was direct in his misdirections. Mostly, I wanted to know what had been so important that it required the sacrifice of the Vesten coin, but I knew better than to ask.

Evelyn didn't. "What did you use it for? It might have been the only anchor."

"As of this moment, it's classified. Maybe I'll tell you some day," Carter replied.

Lord Arctos's attention traveled between Evelyn and Carter, a satisfied smirk curling his lip.

Maybe he'd tell her? When what? When she was his historian? Or worse, his consort?

Where did that come from?

Evelyn glanced at me, and I feared my wolf might have growled along with the revelation. I cleared my throat, hoping no one else had heard the noise, and turned to Lord Arctos. "Are there any other items that persist from the creation of the fae?"

"No," he said flatly.

"What about the artifacts for the other courts?" I asked, remembering the other items in the painting.

"Destroyed," Arctos said, waving his hand in the air as if to tell me to move on.

"All of them?" Evelyn squeaked.

He nodded.

She glanced at Carter as if he could provide more rational information. Unfortunately, he nodded as well.

"While a good idea—and, from Ambrose's paper, a proven method for breaking blood magic—I'm not sure anchors will work for this particular case," Carter said.

Evelyn glanced at me. I thought I knew what she wanted to say. She'd been noodling on the idea of the rope between us since last night. But I also knew Evelyn. She would never say it until she'd at least proven it could work in a test. The problem was that she and I were the only ones who could be experimented on.

She opened and closed her mouth. The sun faded from the sky, and with it, her decision to say anything about the idea. Was she afraid I wouldn't let her test it on me? I shouldn't be surprised that she would assume I wouldn't participate. My fear of what could happen presented as hatred toward her methods, but this connection felt like an extenuating circumstance. There was literally no way out without experimentation, and it would necessarily have to be on us, two living beings.

I would push myself on this. There was no alternative. I trusted Evelyn to test as carefully as possible. With my decision made, I wanted Evelyn to share her idea—I wanted her to know that we were in this together. We weren't out of ideas yet.

"Evelyn has another theory she's working on."

She turned to me, her eyes widening again. "Ambrose."

"Don't give up yet. She'll say it's not ready. She still wants to do some testing, but it's promising."

Carter glanced between us. "My father was right, you two

do work well together. I look forward to seeing what you come up with next. I have complete faith in the pair of you."

Finally, I picked up the bread and cheese left on my plate and took a bite. It was simple, but exactly what I needed after the day I'd had. I swallowed with a smile on my face, even as I felt Evelyn glaring daggers at my cheek.

29

Evelyn

After the meal, Ambrose and I trudged up the stairs to our rooms. I clenched my teeth the entire walk.

"I can hear you fuming," he said behind me.

We were almost to the door of my room. I could wait a few more steps.

"They needed to know you were working on another option."

I opened the door, grabbed his hand, and pulled him into my room. "And what gave you the right to mention it?" I hissed as I pushed the door closed behind his broad frame.

Ambrose's brow lifted. "We're ... colleagues. I couldn't let you sell your own work short."

Something twisted in my chest at the word *colleagues*, and it had nothing to do with the magic that connected us. Or maybe it had everything to do with it. It had everything to do with the fact that he still thought the magic made us feel things we hadn't previously.

"I don't know if I can test it appropriately." I didn't look at him. He was sharp; he knew what I meant. That was part of why I couldn't believe he'd said something. Testing it would mean testing on *him*.

"You can test it on us."

I froze. He didn't know what he was saying. "This wouldn't be the same as trying to work through the magic. Testing this would require applying more magic to our connection. It would be akin to Lord Arctos and Carter's test, which you called reckless. It's something I would never ask you to do."

He took a step forward, crowding my space so that I couldn't see anything but him. "You're not asking. I'm offering."

I sucked in a breath. "We don't know what it will do."

"I'm aware."

I licked my lips and tried to think of a way to explain it to him. To make him understand the risks he seemed determined to avoid. But the way he tracked my tongue sent a different heat flooding me.

This was out of control. I had to make him see. "Last time we didn't know the risks, we ended up magically bound."

"Not the worst thing that's ever happened to me by far," he mumbled.

His entire life was structured around avoiding risk. I couldn't let him do this. We would find another way. "You only think that because of the magic."

He laughed. Actually laughed, but it wasn't carefree and full of mirth. "Evelyn"—he shook his head—"let's stop pretending the blood magic can alter our emotions."

I wasn't breathing. Had he said what I thought he said?

His fingers were in the auburn strands of his hair as he continued. "You know it as well as I do. The magic may be inconvenient. It may be uncomfortable when we separate. It may force us to spend time together, but neither of our intentions involved manipulating emotions. I don't even think blood magic could do such a thing."

Ambrose must have mistaken my incredulity for fear. He stepped forward again and reached for me. Then he must have realized that wasn't something we usually did, and let his hand drop to his side.

"I didn't think you knew," I breathed.

"Knew what? Knew that this magic has been awkward, distracting, and a million other things, but that I'm thankful for every moment we've had together? Or that I've been studying you for weeks, but I loved every new fact and facet of you I've learned from this connection?" His last words came out in almost a whisper. "I'm not sure I would have discovered them otherwise."

A smile tipped his lip, and he continued. "Like knowing that you prefer vegetables to meat, and I am sure that it comes from your belief that blood-magic-grown plants can sustain the continent?"

Something wet hit my cheek, breaking me from my stupor.

"Or that when your hair is braided, that means you're in battle armor, and you're expecting a fight."

I laughed, but it was watery. "I wear my hair in a braid to the library every day."

"Exactly," he said.

Was I crying? How could he have cataloged such things? Then his face got more pensive.

"Or the lengths you'll go to not to burden others, not to make your problems their problems, even though I know for a fact your friends are trying to rid you of that habit." He'd stepped even closer. His long fingers wrapped around my shoulders slowly—so slowly—like he was giving me every moment to get away.

"Why are you doing this?" I asked, unsure why I was hot and cold at the same time.

He tilted his head in a way that had once made him look condescending but was now a teasing question all its own. A silent *you know why*.

"If you knew that the magic wasn't affecting our emotions, then why did you stop us last night?" I asked. He'd known, and he'd still said no. It was his right, of course. I just couldn't reconcile it with what I thought he was saying now.

"I didn't think *you* knew," he said on a sigh. "But of course you did. I'm sure you figured it out before I did. You didn't want to burden me with the knowledge."

The hint of what I'd previously thought was exasperation was now drenched in fondness—something I never would have learned about him without our magical connection. If I hadn't seen the way he spoke to his siblings. If I hadn't understood the way he teased them.

"I'd very much like to kiss you again, if we have all of that cleared up," I said.

His smile was broad, lighting up the room even though it was pitch black outside. "If I'm going to touch you, which I also would very much like to do, I think you should explore our connection again first."

I let my head hang in mock exasperation. "It's always work first with you."

His smirk was sinful, a look I'd never expected to see on the serious researcher's face. "I believe strongly in a work-and-reward system. Let's do at least one test, see if you can get comfortable enough to tell Lord Arctos and ... the Vesten Point something more concrete tomorrow."

He stumbled over the title *Vesten Point*, like he wasn't sure he liked it. I knew him to be one of Carter's biggest fans, and I was sure he'd be even more so when we discussed what Carter had shared about the tree—about how the position was chosen.

I was about to tell him, had opened my mouth to do so,

when his hand slid from my shoulder to my sternum. My skin heated with every inch he crossed. I could tell him later. Now, I needed to focus on this. The heat from his palm felt like we'd arrived at the reward without having done any of the work.

But that was the beauty of doing what I loved for work. It never felt like a chore.

"This isn't very calming," I noted.

He twitched, and I knew he wanted to reach for the notebook and pencil tucked away somewhere on his person. "I never said it would be. The first time you felt the connection, when I was trying to explain shifting, your heartbeat was erratic, your pupils were dilated, and I was sure you were going to flee at any moment."

Well, he'd perfectly described my general mental state around him—a wild animal prepared to bolt. This wasn't humiliating at all.

I reached to pull his hand away, to stop this before I embarrassed myself further. His fingers only intertwined with mine, and he pressed them both to the skin beneath my collarbone. His hazel eyes danced when I glanced up at him. "If you weren't so busy panicking, you would have observed that I was right there with you. My heart felt like it would break free from my chest—simply from the act of standing near you."

A sigh slipped from my lips at his confession. He knew what I needed to hear. Ambrose was with me. We would figure this out because whatever existed between us was more than an accidental bond. He knew the blood magic hadn't manipulated his emotions, and he wanted to explore whatever this was.

After research, of course.

"You're sure?" My eyes were closed as I searched for the rope of fire, but I didn't need to see him to feel his response.

"I'm sure, Evelyn." He squeezed my fingers where our hands were still locked together. "Tell me what you're feeling, and I will write it down when you're done."

I snorted. Of course he would.

It was still new, this feeling that I could push my fire magic without the candies he'd supplied. I didn't know what the limits were, but since my shift in the woods here, my magic and I seemed to have better alignment. My veil cat hadn't let me down. And I didn't think she would—she was me, after all.

The fire ignited within me, and I searched for the connection to Ambrose. It was simple with his hand pressed against me. "It's here."

I wasn't sure what he'd want to know about my exploration. Then I considered the notes I usually took of my experiments and decided to start there. I stoked my fire magic further. It wouldn't burn me, and inherently, I knew it wouldn't hurt him. "My fire magic is spreading to my every extremity, searching for the connection point. It's burning through me."

His proximity meant I could sense the way his muscles tightened at my words. What I had once considered mistrust, or a belief I was incapable, I now knew to be worry. He was worried about me.

"But in a good way," I reassured. "It's to my fingers, toes, head ... I haven't found the place where you intersect yet, but I can feel that it is here."

My flame coursed through me, and my lips curved into a smile. I pressed down on our still intertwined fingers. "Ah. I found it, it's right below this."

"Many fae consider that the heart of their magic," he said quietly. I knew from the careful tone of his voice that he was trying to tell me something he wasn't sure I had learned about my fae heritage.

I nodded in response, not needing more explanation at the moment. The concept was clear.

"The rope leads away from me, toward you." My fire scorched down the connection like a lit fuse, but it left no destruction in its wake. "Can you feel it in the same place?"

I opened one eye to peek up at him. He was smiling. "I think so. Is your magic crossing?"

"Yes."

"I think the closer you come, the more I'm aware." Even though I knew he meant the magic between us, I physically stepped closer. Our fronts were flush with one another, our hands still wrapped together and pressed against my chest. His smile broadened.

This time, when I found the *something* in the middle, I identified it. "There is a knot between us. This must be what Lord Arctos saw at the tavern."

Ambrose leaned forward. Even though there was no one around to overhear us, he spoke into the shell of my ear like it was a secret just for me. "Even before the blood magic, my fire burned for you at every opportunity."

I sucked in a breath, unsure of what to do with the confession. My magic acted up around him as well, but I'd chalked it up to my uncontrollable shift. When I pushed away the haze of his words, I continued. "I think I need to..." Burn it? Break it? Untie it? I wasn't sure. My fire wasn't burning the rope as it searched it. How could I change that?

"We'll have to sever it, but I'm assuming your fire isn't burning?" he asked, reading my mind.

"Correct."

"It's a level of control I'm not sure you have yet over your fire."

He stated it so matter-of-factly, so bluntly, that I couldn't even be angry.

"You have to think about the fire like you would a muscle you exercise. You can flex it to burn or not to burn."

"Can you feel the connection? It might be faster if you found it and tried."

He seemed cautious, so I moved our hands to his chest, knowing the closeness helped me feel it. His shirt was buttoned, though, leaving no room for me to ensure our clasped hands touched skin. Without much thought, I undid the buttons at the top.

"Evelyn..." His voice was more growl, now, than I was used to. It halted me in my tracks, even though I was two buttons deep and moving toward the third, my fingers stealthily exploring him as they moved.

We were still flush against each other, and it occurred to me that something hard pressed against my stomach. It hadn't been there before.

"Evelyn," he said again. I looked up at him through long lashes. Gods, he was beautiful. "My focus is elsewhere."

He didn't meet my eyes, like maybe he feared he'd let me down.

"We know what to try next. We shouldn't do it when you're distracted. It's an acceptable outcome for tonight." I rose on the tips of my toes again to bring my lips to his.

That was all the encouragement he needed. His hands were beneath my thighs, and he lifted me to him. My legs wrapped around his torso again with no hesitation. His kiss wasn't soft and exploratory like last night. This was Ambrose Yarrow at his most demanding. His lips quested with singular focus. Mine parted, wanting him closer—wanting him to achieve all his goals. A moan slipped from me as his tongue advanced, and I rocked against him.

"Evelyn," he hissed again. But he didn't appear to have anything else to say. The strength of his arms held me in place, and his tongue slid against mine with unyielding strokes. I met each one with a challenge, leaving us both breathless and smiling.

He kissed behind my ear—sucked and licked his way to the center of my chest, where our hands were intertwined. All the while, he walked us backward toward the bed.

Fear flooded me. Fear that once he laid me down on the

mattress, like he had yesterday, all this would end. Wanting Ambrose terrified me. Even when I knew he wanted me, too. Wanting Ambrose would surely lead to disappointment.

But why focus on the future when this—now—felt so right? The part of me that didn't want him to stop overtook the fear of the future. When his steps paused, I clung tighter and pulled his mouth back to mine to make my intent clear.

With a huff, we fell to the bed. His chin was on my chest as he looked up at me, his gaze half-lidded. "Don't worry, I'm not going to stop unless you tell me to."

How had I ever thought him dismissive and uncaring? He was so observant, so in tune with my thoughts. It was a heady thing to be the focus of this particular researcher's attention.

"I think we should continue."

He chuckled, but there was an exhale in it, a release of tension, like maybe he needed to hear that.

"The way you take notes should be studied," I said on a gasp. His hand ran the length of me, and his mouth moved to my breast. I arched into him as he lapped at me through my shirt. My curse only meant he noted my response and increased the pressure. Then he latched his teeth around my peaked nipple beneath the shirt. "Your attention to detail is exquisite."

"With the right subject, I can be very motivated," he said, moving to the other breast.

I kept going. He'd said so much earlier, so much I had yet to respond to. I wanted him to know that I studied him, too. "I love that you can't help but share your ideas with me. Like they're just sitting there, ready to burst from your brain, but you won't discuss them with others. No, you wait until we have a confrontation, then let them casually slip out."

He lifted momentarily to peel my shirt away. "Noticed that, did you? It's not worth discussing with others. No one else will find the one piece I'm missing like you will. Call it expediency."

His mouth met mine again in a low groan, and his hand roamed my skin when he laid us back down. This exploration was detailed and all-encompassing. He mapped my curves like he'd have to sketch them later, and he'd fail the test if he forgot a single one.

"Nothing about this feels expedient," I mumbled, mostly to myself as he buried his nose in my neck.

"No ... you are the one sentence in the book that makes it all make sense. The one that perfectly proves a theory and neatly ties up all the loose threads but I had to read a thousand pages to find."

I sucked in a breath while his fingers slid down my side, peeling back my leggings. My body was alight with the heat of our connection, of every flick of his tongue and every inch his hand quested toward my center. But I knew it was his words that ignited the flame deep within me.

"I'd read a thousand more if that's what it took to find you."

It was no hardship for him, of course. He loved what he did. But it stole my breath to realize he considered me with the same tender dedication.

I interrupted him then, and brought his lips back to mine. I needed to pour a little of what I felt, a little of what I still tried to communicate, back into him. If wanting things was standing on the very edge of a cliff, verbalizing my wants was jumping off and hoping I wouldn't splatter. Speaking my desire was the scariest part.

It isn't so scary with him.

Then his fingers circled my center, teasing, building, stoking, but depriving me of the friction I desperately craved.

"I've been dreaming about this for weeks," he confessed.

I swallowed. The words wouldn't come. Still, I offered him something real, something true. "You are the most stubborn, most attractive, most intelligent male I've ever met, and sometimes when I find you in the stacks, I just want to shove you against them and work out our differences with my tongue."

His fingers moved only inches, but it was precisely what I needed. My back bowed again as desire flooded me.

"You seem to enjoy my reward system." He kissed me hard as his thumb circled my clit, and his middle finger slipped into my heat.

"It's acceptable, but we should really..." He paused his plunges to curl his finger and a moan escaped my lips. I grasped for reason to finish my thought. "Continue testing."

"Oh, we will." His reassurance warmed me to the center of my being.

And then he returned to his task with the tenacity that made him the library's golden boy, even if only in my head. His mouth was everywhere, while his hand maintained a steady rhythm. He wouldn't be rushed. Every movement wound me tighter, and every slight tilt of his head was an acknowledgement of a discovery—of something that brought me closer to my edge.

I ran my hands across his broad shoulders. Having studied them from afar for weeks, I took advantage of the opportunity to explore unhindered.

Fire burned within me while his mouth traversed my body. I bit down on his shoulder, needing the grounding as he drove me to new heights. It would leave a mark, but he didn't seem to mind. I traced my tongue over the space to cool the sting, and he continued, frustratingly steady in his work.

"It was the wildness I didn't understand at first, but I think my wolf did. I considered it reckless, but it's not. It's a desire to know more, to understand more, to fight for change, no matter what box this continent tries to fit you into."

My back didn't feel like it could bow any farther. My hands dropped to the sheets, clawing in search of something, anything, for purchase.

"You remind me why I loved our field to begin with. And I'd be honored to stoke that wildness, to explore this continent, to push its limits, so long as it's with you."

I shattered against his hand, but he didn't stop. Fire consumed me, and flames burned through my veins, leaving me a pile of ashes. All the while, Ambrose was there—working me through my pleasure.

He pressed a lingering kiss to my lips, and when he tried to pull away, I cupped my hands against his cheeks to hold him in place. I'd never felt so seen, so exposed. Distantly, I knew his words were nonsensical. We were still competing for ... something. We wouldn't even work together for much longer.

I desperately wanted everything he offered, but giving voice to a desire so fleeting, so unattainable, would only cause heartbreak. Even knowing it would leave a mark, I could enjoy this while it lasted and attempt to protect myself from our inevitable separation.

When I met his gaze, it held only warmth, no disappointment at my lack of words. My hands slid to his shoulders, and I realized he was still clothed. My fingers found the remaining buttons, freeing him from his white shirt and tossing it on the floor. Then I rolled us over, positioning myself on top of him to undo his trousers, removing the last vestiges between us.

He reached up to caress the side of my face, and I leaned into it. My veil cat purred, and from the smile that curled his lip, I knew he heard it.

"Show me what you like," he said as his hands rested at my hips. I straddled him, positioning him at my entrance. I'd never taken control like this before in the bedroom. But Ambrose wanted to see where I'd lead, and I knew he'd follow with studious attention.

I closed my eyes and sank down. Inch by delicious inch, he filled me, my body stretching to accommodate his very welcome intrusion. My hands rested on his pectorals, his body my stabilizing force as I found the perfect angle and rhythm.

His fingers tightened around my waist, steadying me. "That's it. You know what you want."

I marveled at his words. How he once again knew precisely what I needed to hear. There was no hesitation now, no consideration of what the words would cost me in the future. They slipped out for him, the same way my desire to be Vesten historian had days ago: "I want you, Ambrose."

Some restraint in him snapped. I squeaked as he flipped us over. His movements echoed where I'd led, what I'd shown him, but as he took over, his thrusts were faster, harder, deeper. He drew forth the flame that only moments ago had consumed me.

Our breaths quickened together—my heartbeat raced, and fire burned in my chest. I glanced up to see his hazel eyes flash gold. Knowing that this satisfied all parts of him only pushed me faster to my edge.

I came with his name on my lips, and he followed.

He tried to roll away so as not to settle his weight atop me, but I wrapped my legs around him so he couldn't get away. I didn't know how long we lay there, but every moment we did, I felt cherished. My veil cat agreed. The image of her curled up in my mind like the most contented animal on the continent was the last thing I saw before drifting off to sleep.

30

Ambrose

In sleep, Evelyn reached for me, tangling every part of us together. First it was our fingers, and then our legs. She inched closer and closer to me throughout the night. I was more than happy to oblige until she inevitably woke me with more demands.

My wolf chuffed with contentment.

I had to convince myself this was real. That Evelyn was here with me, that we shared a bed—and not because of a shortage of rooms at the inn. I pulled our linked hands closer.

I could get used to this.

Of course I could. It was Evelyn. She was everything I'd never dared to dream of. I closed my eyes and breathed her in. Her scent was so distinct, so perfectly her—wildflowers and honey.

Still asleep, she nuzzled closer. I'd had her multiple times last night, but it was nowhere near enough. No amount of her would be.

Our connection transcended the magic that tied us together. Thoughts of the blood magic weren't as painful after last night. Something had clicked into place. She was *aware* that our intent had nothing to do with our feelings for each other. She had probably figured it out long before I did.

Saying the words aloud had been freeing. Even better had been the look on her face, the shared acknowledgement that there was something between us that had nothing to do with magic. Well, maybe a little bit—but not the accidental bond. My wolf and my fire reacted to her. I was now certain the same went for her veil cat and flame. Our inherent magics' draw to each other was further proof of what I knew: this thing between us was real.

The way we felt about each other might not be due to blood magic, but magical connections were why we were at Compass Lake. We needed to deal with our bond if our fledgling relationship stood a chance at success.

She had wanted me to burn the rope connecting us last night. While at the time I'd been too distracted to do so successfully, as reason returned, I knew it was necessary for multiple reasons. First, if we could burn our bond away, if that severed the connection, we could present it as an option to solve Lord Arctos and Carter's problem. Second, it was important that I decide for myself where I stood with blood magic. I could no longer let Father's view color mine. It was like a ray of sun peeking through a cloudy day, to know Evelyn pushed this opportunity to me. That she had faith in me to decide.

My eyes drifted closed, and I pulled our linked hands to my chest. The heat of our connection guided me. Previously, I'd been unable to find what she described—a more tactile manifestation of our bond. This morning, it was as if the fire inside me mapped the most direct path to her, and the rope she described was the bridge.

It was still hard to believe she wanted me. I wasn't sure I

had ever wanted someone as much as I wanted her. My love of history had driven so much of my life. I'd never found anyone who not only shared my interest but pushed me to discover more. Evelyn did so without even trying.

The Vesten Point's attention hadn't gone unnoticed. Even if Lord Arctos's response had been *It's not what you think*. It was still something. I wouldn't let it derail whatever this was, though. Evelyn was stingy with her wants, and she said she wanted me. A low growl escaped my wolf at the memory.

"Let's give this a try," I murmured to myself. At the connection point, my fire magic surged toward her.

It traversed but didn't burn as it worked its way to the middle. There was a knot there, just like she'd said. Though I had talked a big game last night, the enormity of what I would attempt rushed through me. This was not blood magic on inanimate objects. It wasn't even blood magic using plants. Testing anything on this connection was dangerous. It was blood magic at its most fickle. It was everything Father warned me against and everything I had been raised to fear.

The experiment that led to Father's impaired vision had been less risky than this. I knew I should be rightly terrified about what I was attempting, but this morning, I couldn't summon the anxiety usually present when working with blood magic.

I needed this. We needed this. I needed to choose for myself, and we needed to break the connection between us if we stood a chance at something real. We couldn't live our lives with forced proximity. I'd give the magic credit—it had known what it was doing with our unstated intents. It had pushed us to get to know each other, to stop assuming the worst. I didn't know if anything less drastic than this connection would have driven us past our entrenched positions on blood magic.

It had done its job. Now it needed to go.

My thoughts lingered more on giving Evelyn and me a

chance rather than fixing Lord Arctos and the Vesten Point's problem. Yes, I wanted the Vesten historian position, but it came with a whole host of responsibilities I hadn't yet prepared for. Conducting this experiment was a start, but did it mean I would press forward with blood magic study? I thought so, but how hard would Father push back against my decisions? Would I teach others that blood magic tests on plants were acceptable? It would take time to find the path I was comfortable with. I suspected Evelyn already knew what she would do with the position—knew the direction she would steer the Vesten Court.

There was really only one way to find out how all this would end. I turned up the heat on my flame and did what she'd asked of me yesterday, burning through the rope's knot.

We both required space to breathe, like our fires; oxygen fanned the flames.

"And what is that?" she asked hazily, voice still soaked in sleep.

I must have been talking to myself aloud. "What is what?" I asked carefully, hoping she could fall back asleep.

She squeezed my hand, still pressed to hers, against my bare chest. "The next phase of our relationship."

Everything.

I couldn't say that. I'd sound like a crazy person. "One where you long to see me, not because of magic but because you can't stand to be away from me."

Her lips curled into a soft smile in the morning light. The rays of the sun seemed to stop in their tracks as they fell into her dark brown hair. "That sounds nice."

I turned the heat up a little higher on my flame. The rope between didn't fray. My control of my fire was as absolute as my control of my wolf. This shouldn't be so difficult. I focused, breathing in and out as I tried again.

The heat intensified, and it felt like smoke poured from the rope, but the knot remained. Maybe Evelyn needed to be the one to do it? She had learned the other control we'd practiced together so quickly; she could learn this, too. Disappointment flared with my flame. The cause might have been my failure at this task, or it might have been thinking of the Vesten Court's failure of Evelyn. Even with her father missing, someone should have helped her with her magic. The Vesten needed to get past their discomfort of sharing information about their shift with those they deemed outsiders.

Thinking of Evelyn's not-so-missing father tied me in knots. We hadn't discussed that last night. I still thought I had made the right decision. She deserved to hear everything from him, not me. I hoped Evelyn would speak with him before we left. Who knew how long we'd be staying? This trip felt more and more like one of Lord Arctos's whims than a calculated requirement for the project we'd been given.

I jolted as a knock sounded at the door. "Mr. Yarrow."

No, not her door, my door. Someone was knocking on the door of the bedroom I was supposed to be in.

Evelyn's eyes snapped open as the knocking continued.

"Mr. Yarrow." There was an expectation in that voice that only the Vesten God had perfected.

"I can distract him, tell him I heard you leave on an early morning walk," she whispered.

Was that what she wanted? "I—"

"Of course, if you think Lord Arctos's sarcastic comments about us were his way of hinting at our repressed attraction, and that this trip was partially an experiment to see if he could help us along, I'm also fine simply answering the door and telling him you're here."

Gods, I loved her.

Oh, my gods. I could not be thinking that.

I cleared my throat. "The second one sounds preferable."

She smiled sweetly and slipped from the bed. I regretted that either action took her from me, but we were at Compass

Lake. Ostensibly, we had work to do. I pulled on my clothes while she did the same, then opened the door.

"Can we help you, Lord Arctos?" she asked, sticking her head out into the hallway.

I couldn't see his face, but I could tell from his voice that was precisely what he wanted to hear. "We, you say? Have you taken Mr. Yarrow captive in there?"

She huffed, and I was sure she rolled her eyes at the god. I had no idea where she got the courage.

I pulled the door the rest of the way open, summoning the same strength she had. "I can confirm I'm here willingly."

Lord Arctos's eyes danced with mischief. "I'm glad I've found you both. Carter has an errand to run. He wanted to know if you needed him for any tests before he left."

I was about to say we didn't need him. My test had failed; without it, we had nothing to test on the god and Compass Point. But at Lord Arctos's comment, Evelyn's spine straightened like she'd had a thought.

"We should have you two test one thing, if you have time." She glanced over her shoulder at me. "You were able to find the knot this morning, correct?"

Of course she'd noticed.

"The knot?" Lord Arctos's eyebrow raised. "If this is a kink, feel free to keep it to yourselves."

This time, I did see her roll her eyes. I answered her question with the necessary details: "I couldn't burn it, though."

She bit the inside of her lip like maybe she'd expected the response. "I think it's the location."

Why hadn't I thought of that? Part of Lord Arctos's reason for our trip was that location mattered with magic. Our current location meant nothing to our connection; it was the first time Evelyn had been here. "Compass Lake would be a location of importance to the connection between Lord Arctos and Carter."

She turned back to Lord Arctos. "We need you to test something at the lake."

The god looked giddy. He shifted into a bird and flew away without another word.

"I think that means he's going to collect Carter?"

She shrugged. "We should at least have them check that they have the same type of connection."

"You don't want them to try and destroy it?" I thought I knew where this was going.

"I'd rather test that part with us first, if you're still amenable," she said. "It feels unconscionable to test breaking it on a god and the most powerful Vesten of our generation."

I let out a breath. "I completely agree."

"So, you want us to stand in the lake and see if we can feel a physical manifestation of our connection?" Lord Arctos glared over his shoulder at Evelyn. He had collected Carter and brought him to the beach outside of Vesten House. The god didn't sound amused, but Evelyn didn't wither under his appraisal.

"That's right."

The lake was quiet and as still as glass. Was it like this every morning? I couldn't imagine a more peaceful way to greet the day, except maybe waking up with Evelyn Knowles in my arms.

"You must have missed my skepticism of your idea since I mixed it with sarcasm," Lord Arctos pointed out.

Evelyn's hands were on her hips now. "I did not."

Carter laughed. "She doesn't seem to care, Arctos."

Lord Arctos batted away Carter's words the same way he usually flapped his wing against my face. At least he acted that way with everyone.

Carter finally took control. "What kind of connection are we looking for, exactly?"

Evelyn glanced at me. While she had no concerns speaking to Lord Arctos of our connection, she was hesitant where the Vesten Point was involved.

"She doesn't want to admit that she and Mr. Yarrow, on top of being brilliant researchers, have also managed to magically bind themselves together while working on our little problem. She can describe what to look for in detail, but it will be a reflection of their bond, not ours."

I ran my hand through my hair. Lord Arctos could be correct. It wasn't that Evelyn was embarrassed by our relationship. She was embarrassed by our stupidity with blood magic. We were supposed to be presenting our best selves to the Vesten Point so he would select one of us for the Vesten historian position. It made sense she wouldn't want to air our magical blunders.

"Technically, Lord Arctos is correct," Evelyn stated matter-of-factly. "The connection between Ambrose and me is a rope, with a knot in the center. I imagine the magic grows over time. Yours will likely be something even more stabilizing."

Her words rolled over me, but they paled in comparison to the reminder that there was still only one Vesten historian position. I had pushed aside those thoughts this morning in favor of my and Evelyn's future. But would our relationship survive one of us being named historian?

This experience had helped me find my own perspective on blood magic, but I already had one on the court's history. I also knew Evelyn would consider it a betrayal if I didn't give the competition my all, if I didn't keep searching for the answers. Our relationship only stood a chance if we could continue to push each other—it was part of what had always worked between us.

We had to keep going. Not just because it would break our

bond, or because one of us would win the position, or even to fulfill the project Lord Arctos had assigned, but because it was what I loved to do. It was what she loved to do, too.

But could our fledgling … romance survive the Vesten Point's decision?

I swallowed thickly.

Evelyn glanced at me. She must have finished her explanation. Lord Arctos and Carter stood in the water facing each other.

"Should I hold his hand?" Lord Arctos asked.

"Do what feels right," Evelyn said with a smile.

I would do anything for that smile. I would even compete with her for something I knew she wanted. I would challenge her the way she challenged me. I would have to trust that she would want me exactly as I was.

31

Evelyn

They found ... something. In truth, I wasn't focused on Lord Arctos and Carter bickering with everything else flooding my mind.

I'd slept with Ambrose Yarrow last night.

What was I thinking?

My veil cat growled as she prowled back and forth in the recesses of my mind. Alright, so some of us knew what we'd been thinking.

Ambrose got me in a way no one else seemed to. Not only since our blood magic accident—he had for some time, he just hadn't known how to show it. Ambrose saw more than I wanted him to, but he didn't press on my points of discomfort. He waited patiently for the best time to intercede.

Our passions for knowledge intersected in a complementary way, when we weren't arguing over methods. Now that I understood his hangups, I knew his interest in blood magic was only further elevated by his complicated relationship with it.

All of it summed up meant that he pushed me to be the best version of myself—to own my place between fae and human.

I sighed. My mental summary did not make whatever was between us feel casual. Maybe the worst part was that I didn't *want* it to be, either.

This morning, when I had announced to Arctos that we were in the same room together, I'd conveniently forgotten that Ambrose and I were competing for the Vesten historian position.

It changes things, right?

My veil cat was silent. So much for the animal always knowing.

Last night had felt wholly ours, wholly separated from our blood magic blunder, the competition for historian, and even my father. I'd felt safe, desired, and empowered to want something for myself.

I'd even ignored my own warning that wants never quite panned out for me.

What did Ambrose think? Did he regret our time together?

I met his hazel gaze, and any doubt of his desire fled when the golden color of his wolf cascaded across them. He looked ravenous.

My thighs inadvertently squeezed together.

So, we wanted each other. We also both wanted the Vesten historian position. I rubbed my temple. Where did that leave us?

"Evelyn, are you listening to me?" Lord Arctos asked.

"I was not," I confessed with little thought.

Carter laughed, and it sounded light, carefree. So different from the weight of our conversation yesterday. He had shared more than he needed to, and I still wasn't sure I understood why. The secret of how the Vesten Point was chosen wasn't information widely shared with anyone, let alone a half-fae library researcher.

The Vesten Court required a veil cat shifter. How long would it require one? Carter had the ability to travel between realms. What did that mean for me and my veil cat?

After our conversation, I had more questions than answers.

Part of me still wondered if Carter telling me meant he knew I was a veil cat, even though he'd said nothing about it directly. I was running out of chances to ask the Vesten Point about the animal. But the Vesten had taught me the lesson as a child: only discuss your shift with your family. Even with my shift somewhat under control and the Vesten Point bringing up the topic of shifter forms, I still couldn't bring myself to ask. Especially since I now knew where my father was, it seemed most appropriate to ask him first. If he had no information, well, I'd cross that bridge when I came to it.

Lord Arctos repeated himself, maybe for the third time, and finally pulled me from my thoughts. "That young male over there seems to be staring at you quite intently. It seems to have raised Ambrose's hackles."

I turned where Lord Arctos pointed. The male wasn't young. Well, maybe he was by Lord Arctos's standards. He was the male I'd run from yesterday. The male Ambrose had seemed to indicate was waiting for me to visit him. Apparently, he'd tired of waiting.

"Oh, Stephen," Carter said, waving casually to the male.

I turned to face him. "You know him?"

Carter tilted his head. "Yes, he's the one who inspired me to fill the position of Vesten historian. He needed his family tracked down after waking from the mist plague. I wasn't able to do it myself with my other responsibilities."

I choked on ... nothing. The news was what I'd run from yesterday. When I'd looked at my father's face, some part of me had known he was miserable—I'd been too scared to learn why. Now Carter had casually dropped the fact I'd been dreading.

My father had woken from the mist plague.

It couldn't be right. I shook my head, even though it was exactly what Mom had said. My mind spun. How could he have gone to one of the villages that just happened to be taken by the mist plague? "Are you sure?"

"About what?" Carter asked.

"That he was a victim of the mist plague."

Carter cleared his throat. "Yes, I woke him up."

My cheeks flushed.

"Is everything alright, Evelyn?" The Vesten Point's voice was distant, though, like the fire crackling through my veins was now burning too hot for me to hear anything else. Only one thing cut through the white noise. Ambrose.

"That's what he told you," I whispered. "That's what you didn't think I'd believe."

He rested his hand lightly on my lower back, showing his support. "I didn't know if you would believe it, but I thought he deserved a chance to try and tell you."

I nodded, still in a daze. "Can you explain to Carter and Lord Arctos?" I might have understood why Ambrose didn't want to tell me, but I still wasn't sure I was ready to hear this from my father. It seemed like I had few options on the matter, though, with him standing on Vesten House property.

Slow steps took me away from the group and toward the male whom I might have judged entirely incorrectly. How could I have done so? I wasn't rash; I had considered carefully where his deliveries on that fateful day would have taken him. In fact, when I'd first gained access to a map at the Sandrin Records Office, I'd plotted the whole thing out. The mist plague had not affected any of the cities he would have visited that day.

Maybe he deserves a chance to try and explain.

I probably wasn't ready to hear it, but Mom deserved to hear whatever he would say. At the very least, I needed to communicate how to find her. I straightened my spine, like a warrior preparing for battle. I touched my braid, remembering what Ambrose had said only last night about it being my armor. The memory sent a flush of heat running through me as I crossed the lawn.

No matter what kept my father from us, it had been twenty years. I was entitled to my own feelings on that fact.

"Evelyn," he started. "I know your friend told me to wait, but I couldn't. I've been waiting for so long. If you need more time, that's completely acceptable, but I need to find your mother."

He took the words right out of my mouth.

"You didn't leave us?" I whispered.

He shook his head before I finished the question. "Never."

"But your route ... I traced it."

His head tilted, and then he seemed to understand the question. He opened his hand, and it held a diamond ring. "I wasn't making deliveries the day I went missing. I snuck off to buy this for your mother."

Suddenly, I was having trouble seeing. Something blurred my vision, but he kept speaking.

"I'm not sure how much you know about the fae, but we don't marry like the humans do. We take life partners, but it doesn't have the same ceremony—or the same symbolism as the human act of marriage." He rubbed his hand across his face. "And your mom had never asked, but especially with you in the picture, with your fire magic manifesting, I wanted to offer her something human for our family. It was supposed to be a surprise."

"You wanted to ask her to marry you?" Tears ran freely down my face now. "A fae wanted to marry a human."

He shook his head a little, confused. "Not a fae and a human. Me and your mom. But now, I don't know how long it's been—I gather it's been years. I don't know what her life looks like, or if there is still room for me in it, but I have to try. I'm sorry if this steps on your decision to speak to me, but you're my only lead to find her."

A whisper escaped my lips. "I needed you." And once I'd said one thing, I didn't feel like I could stop. "I needed you to teach me about my magic."

Something broke in his expression, and a tear slid down his cheek. "I'm so sorry. I never meant for this to happen."

Rationally, I knew that. The mist plague had been uncontrollable. A natural disaster that still impacted more families than just mine. Some for much longer. There were stories of those in the northeast who had awoken to find their families had passed away, because it had been hundreds of years since they fell asleep.

I knew I was lucky to hear these words, to have this chance, but I also didn't know what to do with them. They didn't change the fact that he hadn't been there. I needed time.

"Mom is in Sandrin," I said. "She works at Compass Books."

Hesitantly, he put a hand on my shoulder, not coming any closer. "Thank you. I assume you need time to digest what I said. I'm sure it's too late, but I'd be happy to tell you anything I know about your magic."

I nodded. "I'll be back in the city soon."

He glanced over my shoulder. I knew without looking that Ambrose stood behind me, just out of earshot, even if the others were going about their business.

"I'll make sure to leave word of how to find me with your Mom."

I didn't think it was a betrayal to say what I did next. In fact, I thought it would only speed along the happiness Mom deserved. "She's been waiting for you. Even when I told her it was pointless."

The words he wanted to hear landed, even as his face crumpled at my second truth—that I had not believed he was coming back. He nodded. "I hope to make it up to you. If you let me."

Then he turned and ran, too eager by half to get to Sandrin. I'd been too overwhelmed by his words, by what he said, by the decision to share about Mom, that I hadn't even thought to ask questions about my veil cat.

As he flung himself into the forest, he shifted. I saw his animal. He was feline, yes, but something in my stomach plummeted when it took shape. The cat that loped into the woods was all black.

He was a panther, not a veil cat.

32

Evelyn

I'd done the right thing, I'd sent Stephen—my father —to Mom. Still, my body shook as he sprinted away.

He wasn't a veil cat shifter. My father didn't have the answers I needed. It didn't matter that he hadn't been there. It didn't matter that Mom was right, and something terrible had happened to him.

He could not have helped.

I folded my arms across my chest as if to hold myself together while fixated on the precise spot where he'd disappeared. Moments, maybe hours later, that warm, reassuring hand was at my lower back.

"He isn't like me," I said.

Ambrose huffed an acknowledgment.

"He doesn't have the answers I need."

"Is it possible that you put too much expectation on that missing piece? He wasn't there for you when you needed his help, so you assumed he took all the answers with him?"

I lifted my palm to wipe a tear from my cheek, but Ambrose's was already there, his hand warm against my cold skin. He brought his finger with the captured tear to his mouth and licked it.

A giggle bubbled up inside me. "You are so odd."

"I'm not fond of your tears," he said. "But I'll need to make a note that they taste like sunlight."

I shook my head in stunned disbelief. "What does that even mean?"

He dropped his hand from my lower back, and when I turned to look at him, he had his secret notebook and pencil out.

"Are you—"

"I told you, I'm taking notes."

Then I snorted with laughter, and he smiled.

It was so easy—just this. Ambrose knew I would tie my mind in knots with what-ifs. So, he'd picked a ridiculous way to distract me from what I couldn't change. Just the two of us here felt nice. It felt like something I could get used to. I wished we had the luxury of exploring what was between us, without complication, for a while longer, but that wasn't the case. The fae leaders and gods needed their problem solved. The answer felt within our grasp.

Ambrose tucked his notebook back into his pocket and regarded me. "You think location is why we couldn't burn the rope connecting us?"

Of course he knew where my mind had wandered to. I nodded.

"The Vesten Library in Sandrin, then?"

"The Vesten Library," I replied.

We explained ourselves to Lord Arctos, who waved us away and said he'd meet us in Sandrin to check if it worked. It seemed like further proof that Lord Arctos had indeed been meddling, though I wasn't sure how. Our presence here had not been required. He had wanted us here for something, not necessarily to test our theories on him and the Vesten Point. It was a mystery, but it wasn't my biggest problem at the moment.

Carter was nowhere to be found, but ageless magic hung thick in the air around Vesten House. I hypothesized, with no small amount of disbelief, where he might have disappeared to.

He couldn't have gone beyond the veil, right?

For the first time, I wondered if I was actually asking my veil cat. If I was asking a question to which I already knew the answer. The veil cat that lived within my thoughts stretched deep on her front paws, as if she couldn't be bothered to participate in this internal discussion.

Ambrose and I had no reason to wait. We knew what we had to do next, so together, we walked toward the treeline behind Vesten House.

"You lead, I'll follow," he said.

I smirked. "I was thinking more along the lines of 'I'll run, you chase.'"

His ears pinkened, and his gaze darted away from mine as a low rumble emanated from his chest.

"I think your wolf likes that."

When he glanced at me again, gold cascaded across his eyes. "We'll give you a ten-minute head start."

A shiver shot down my spine, and I ran into the forest before I could think better of it.

Fire burned through me with each step. I didn't need the candy to shift. My veil cat and I might not have fully understood each other, but in this, we did. As I jumped, I shifted. The move was seamless, like I'd seen Lord Arctos do. One step, my feet left the earth; the next, my paws landed back on it.

I sprinted away, running through the trees beside the forest path. There was no time to slow down and congratulate myself. As Compass Lake Village and the mountain trail came into view, a howl echoed through the woods behind me. I was out of time.

My paws pressed me forward, skipping against the ground. The tug in my chest told me I was just far enough ahead of him to trigger discomfort in our bond. That was the distance I needed to maintain to win this game.

He wouldn't *let* me win, though.

If nothing else, I knew I could count on Ambrose for that.

We ran for hours this way. Clearing the mountain pass and sprinting down the switchbacks felt effortless with my focus wholly elsewhere. My heart pounded at every rustle in the trees. I imagined he'd somehow passed me and had doubled back to attack. It left me little choice but to keep sprinting. That rope between us stayed taut, even as I fled the foothills and ran through the thick woods toward the inn. I moved with a fluid grace I had yet to truly feel with my veil cat. Maybe being chased by Ambrose Yarrow was all I'd needed to understand how half-fae and veil cat worked together.

As with everything else between us, he pushed me to learn. Sometimes it was out of spite, but mostly, it was out of curiosity and a desire to do better. He pushed me to want.

That wasn't quite right. I wanted things: my mom's happiness, success in my career, and a sense of belonging in this world as a half-fae, but I didn't speak my desires. If I didn't voice them, then I wouldn't be embarrassed or disappointed when they didn't happen.

Silently wanting things might not sound powerful, but it was safe.

It was safe until Ambrose made me speak my truths—until Ambrose drew me to fight for what I wanted instead of letting it pass me by as another out-of-reach goal.

As if my thoughts summoned him, the rope in my chest loosened.

He was close.

We'd run all day. Exhaustion picked at every part of me that wanted to keep going, that wanted to win this game between us. Had this been his plan all along? Wait until I was at my most vulnerable to pounce?

The leaves shook in the trees.

It's just the wind.

I knew it wasn't. The rope between us was too loose, but the inn was in my sights, and I had no choice but to try.

A growl sounded—far too close.

Maybe I won't make it.

I pushed myself harder. My muscles burned, but nothing motivated me like the idea of proving Ambrose wrong. If I could make it to the inn steps without him, maybe he wasn't as good a predator as he thought he was.

The tug in my chest was gone completely. I couldn't spare a thought to consider how slack that rope between us must be. My legs were on fire, and all I wanted to do was sploot here on the forest floor.

That one distracted thought cost me.

One minute, I was sprinting toward the flickering lights of the inn. The next, I was rolling off course, through the woods, and a massive gray wolf tumbled with me.

Fur and limbs tangled together. It felt a little wild—what I'd always suspected lurked beneath the surface of Ambrose's golden boy persona. But even as we tangled together, I found his cautious preparation. Every time I flipped over him, his paws adjusted. He kept me safe even as he shattered my pride by catching me.

On the subsequent tumble, I let the fire burn through me and shifted. If I lost, at least I should get to tell him off. Gold flashed across his eyes, and on the next roll, he shifted, too. He conveniently landed on top of me, my body pinned beneath his weight.

"You were toying with me the whole time," I hissed as I wiggled beneath him.

He huffed. "I wish. You're fast when you want to be." He shook his head as if coming out of a haze. "How that's even possible, when I'm confident the only exercise you get is lifting books to a shelf above your head, I'll never understand."

"You're a library researcher," I pointed out. "Have you ever considered that your athletic activities are the abnormality here? What kind of historian has those shoulder muscles?"

The sinful smile was back. "Oh, Evelyn, I wasn't sure you noticed."

I laughed. "Yes, you were."

Any fight fled me as he leaned down to capture my mouth in a kiss. We hadn't had time to talk about last night—about what it meant, about the competition we still faced. My body decided all of that was irrelevant. Pinned beneath him, I wrapped my legs around his waist and pulled him down completely, desperate to feel his weight.

He'd known exactly what to do to stop my mind from spinning. It wasn't a distraction so much as another, more tangible goal on which to focus. He gave me so much and asked for so little. He seemed only to want more time with me. More time to learn about each other, more time to discuss our ideas, more time to grow together.

I wanted to grant him that, even when we severed the blood magic connecting us.

In the darkness of the woods, I saw him so clearly. His lips skated down my jaw, my neck, and I freed a hand to reach for him, slipping it inside his trousers.

"Evelyn," he hissed as his hips jerked. "We're in the woods."

My hand found his length and stroked him. His hips jolted forward with my movement. "Does that bother you?"

He canted his head in consideration. Then he buried his face in the crook of my neck. "You know, I don't think it does."

I continued to stroke him as he nipped and licked his way down my body. With his progress, his hips slipped from me. I reached for him again, but he held me in place.

"I've wanted to taste you for so long." His teeth were at the waistband of my leggings. My hips lifted automatically to help him achieve his goal.

With the first lick of his tongue across my center, my back arched from the forest floor. A desperate moan accompanied the movement. Ambrose's free hand slid toward my mouth. He paused for a chuckle as he offered it to me. "We're not that far from the inn, Evelyn. Bite down if you can't control yourself."

I sucked two of his fingers into my mouth in an attempt to toy with him as he did me, but at the next stroke of his tongue, I bit down—hard.

He didn't yelp; instead, his lips curled into a satisfied smile, and he continued his work.

"Better than I imagined," he said, pausing for a moment as the fingers of his other hand pressed into my center. He pumped them in rhythm with his tongue. Then he feasted.

Flame built within me, and my pulse raced like he chased me again.

But Ambrose caught me. He wanted to find me, no matter where I ran. With the thought, I shattered beneath him.

Desperate for more, I quickly freed him from his trousers. Lined up and ready, a single thrust granted my desire. My hips lifted to meet his, eager for a deeper connection. We moved together, challenge and response, a perfect synchronization to chase our shared pleasure.

My body heated, sensation built, and flames curled forth like a roaring inferno. Ambrose wasn't far behind. His forehead touched mine, and his eyes flashed gold when he found his release. We collapsed together, sharing panting breaths on the forest floor.

He studied me, scanning my features slowly as if he had something he wanted to say. Then, in the next instant, his face turned playful. "Do you want to bet they have two rooms tonight?"

I huffed out a laugh. "Don't even think about it."

He kissed me deeply before pushing backward, straightening himself, and helping me up. "It's like the law of nature. They will absolutely have two rooms at the inn this time."

33

Evelyn

As Ambrose predicted, when we greeted the innkeeper, she immediately provided two keys. I smiled as I felt the heat in Ambrose's attention. He let me lead, and I told her we'd only need one this time and slipped my hand in Ambrose's. Her brow arched as she glanced again between us. A knowing smile curled her lip as she handed me a key and told me that now she owed the Vesten God a favor. She didn't look too upset about whatever bet she had lost. And I was unsurprised to hear more of Lord Arctos's meddling, even now.

I'd never considered myself masochistic, but the way I soaked up every hour cocooned in a bubble of intimacy with Ambrose had me second-guessing. It was as if I had no fear of the future. I didn't focus on all that might happen next, or on what it could mean for us. I focused only on what existed between us now. In some unspoken agreement, Ambrose did the same.

With the sunrise, our responsibilities returned. We needed

to break the blood magic that connected us, and we both seemed confident we knew how. That answer would inevitably lead to the solution to Lord Arctos and Carter's problem, which would conclude with one of us named Vesten historian.

We would cross that bridge when we got there. In the meantime, our relationship wouldn't inhibit our research.

Ambrose might be cautious, and I might appear rash. He might know every fact about Vesten history, and I might understand blood magic, but beneath these surface-level differences, we held core similarities. The puzzle pieces had to be put together; neither of us would stop until the final picture made sense.

We left the inn early. With another shift, a final sprint west to Sandrin, Ambrose and I returned to the library. I was the first to reach the Great Room. An outside observer might have thought that we weren't racing, but they would be wrong. Ambrose and I couldn't *not* compete.

My favorite study carrel called to me across the room. It had only been a few days, but I immediately inspected my experiment. The rose and morning glory in the window were most certainly growing together.

Usually, the morning glory bloomed bright and big and beautifully, and completely overshadowed the rose. When I'd left, the stems had started to twine together. Part of me had worried this was a new way for the morning glory to strangle the rose. I was happy to see that I'd been wrong. The flowers didn't simply share space—their stems had intertwined to create a single, sturdier stem. The flowers had both bloomed. The red rose blossom and white morning glory petals were equally tipped toward the sun outside the window.

Anything is possible with blood magic.

If the flowers' connection was a mirror to mine and Ambrose's, I shouldn't be surprised that it had worked so well. I was glad that the Vesten Point said the anchor for their particular magic was no longer available because, in this moment, I knew the flowers were an anchor for mine and Ambrose's bond, and I *really* didn't want to destroy them. Since Lord Arctos and Carter said that path was unavailable to solve their problem, I saw no reason to explore it with ours. Another part of me hoped that breaking the connection with Ambrose wouldn't disrupt the flowers' newfound peace.

Maybe I also hope it won't disrupt our newfound ... something.

"Alright, Evelyn?" I turned to Ambrose, who had snuck up behind me again. The pot with the growing plants was in my hands, held out like an offering. I hadn't registered the emotions flooding me until I felt something wet against my cheek.

Ambrose's thumb was there. He cupped my cheek as he swiped away the drop. "I think they'll be alright. I'm sure you've already realized that they are our anchor. If burning the rope doesn't work, I do think burning the flowers would break the connection."

I sucked in an outraged breath.

He chuckled. "But we're not testing the anchor method, are we? We're testing your method, severing the connection at the source."

I punched him lightly on the shoulder. "You could have phrased that any other way."

He smiled. "Where would the fun be in that?"

"Are you ready to do this?" I asked.

He nodded. "Here?" He glanced down at the single chair in the study carrel.

"We should probably get the other chair from the closet to recreate the specific event."

"The event where you accepted a sandwich from me? The event where you shared your theories with me, even though we were ... are ... competitors?"

My stomach flipped with the acknowledgement I knew

we'd both avoided. I set the pot down in the window. "Yes, that one."

He returned quickly with the chair, and we took our seats. It was midday, and other researchers wandered through the stacks, but somehow it felt like Ambrose and I were alone in the library. Hesitation crept up my spine, and I couldn't pinpoint precisely why.

"You tried to do this at Vesten House, correct?" I asked, though he had already confirmed as much yesterday morning with Lord Arctos. I was pretty sure I was stalling.

His slight smirk said he understood too much, but still, he answered my question. "I could control the burn, but the rope wouldn't ignite."

"You should try it here."

His brow furrowed. "You don't want to try? I can teach you how to adjust the temperature of your fire. You learned so quickly with your shift, I'm sure you could do this with a few tries."

I smirked. "I'm sure I would, too. But if you're still comfortable with it, I'd like you to do it."

Heat flashed in Ambrose's eyes at my confidence. He was such a good teacher—well-practiced from helping his siblings, but he found the exact right ways to communicate with me, too. And I was a prickly student. I resented the fact that the information hadn't been available to me when I needed it. Ambrose had a point when he said I put too much weight on my father's absence. The responsibility of teaching me magic shouldn't have fallen on one person's shoulders. The Vesten Court needed solutions to help others in my situation find their way more quickly, more surely, than the roundabout path I had stumbled through. I wanted it to be easier for those who came after me.

My thoughts turned to Ambrose. He'd skirted how large a decision he'd made with his first attempt to break our connection. Blood magic on living things. Who would have thought? If anything, the severity of Lord Arctos and Carter's request seemed to have shown him there was value in the knowledge. I had already known he'd do great things, but how quickly he evolved his position with new knowledge gave me confidence he'd fit the Vesten historian position as well as I would.

And now I was back to thinking about our competition.

Emotions flooded me, emotions I wasn't used to dealing with. I'd gotten so used to letting the things I wanted pass me by. So used to not wanting anything to prevent further disappointment. Now, I'd ended up wanting two things that seemed incompatible with each other.

I wanted the Vesten historian position, but I wanted Ambrose, too.

My sigh was heavy as I rubbed my chest. We sat next to each other, but I could feel the flare of the magic between us. Part of me knew our fire and animals reaching for each other would remain. It was a symptom of our attraction to each other, not the blood magic. Still, I hesitated. "I am not sure I could destroy it. I'm feeling sentimental this afternoon."

He laughed. "You think I want to?"

I shrugged, unsure if I wanted to push to understand what his comment meant.

His hand closed around mine. "I'll do it because I know we're not exactly acting rationally at the moment. Before I do, I want you to know that this accidental bond was the best thing that has ever happened to me, Evelyn."

I saw the truth of his words in his hazel eyes. "No one has ever accused me of being irrational."

His lip tilted playfully. "That's not true, I used to do it all the time."

"You're the exception."

"I'll happily remain the exception to your every rule." He leaned forward but seemed to stop himself, as if he'd remembered we were in the library. Even the way he held my hand was likely pushing the limits of propriety here.

I wanted to stay in this space with him longer. After this, everything would change. Carter would make his decision. I glanced at my experiment in the window. I wanted to stay in the space where we grew together rather than apart. My wants blended as I imagined a world where I had both Ambrose in my life and the Vesten historian position. I had to assume that picture in my head allowed the words to slip out. "Save that for later."

Once they were out, I desperately wanted them to be true. But how could it be possible? I didn't know what I'd do if Ambrose got the position. Would he move to Compass Lake? It wasn't that I would begrudge him his success, but it certainly wouldn't make things easy for us. And if I got the position, Mom and I had talked of moving. Well, even that wasn't a guarantee anymore. Not with my father's return.

Everything felt up in the air, but as with our attempt to appease the blood magic, the only way out was through.

Ambrose nodded, his face resolute, determined. He knew as much as I did what my words meant. Knowing Ambrose, he was studying every tick of my jaw and narrowing of my eyes as I tried to will a future I couldn't see into existence.

The bubble we were in was about to burst. *But what if it doesn't have to?*

Our breaths were deep, and we finally stared at each other. "Do it now," I said.

He kept my hand wrapped in his as he closed his eyes. I followed, letting my fire find the connection point between us. Every time I searched for the rope that led from me to him, it was easier to find. My fire skittered along it to the center, to the tie that neither of us had been able to break.

His heat met mine at the impenetrable knot. I was proud of Ambrose for doing this. Everything about this test would have earned his father's disapproval. Not only had we accidentally bound ourselves together, but we'd tested breaking the connection—an unprecedented test, a test so rare the Compass Points and gods didn't know how to do it. Ambrose had avoided this kind of magic for so long. He thought his caution avoided any risk associated with blood magic—any connection to living things—but I liked to think I'd taught him differently. I'd taught him that there was always risk associated with blood magic. People were unpredictable, as we had learned firsthand, but I was confident in what he would do to break our connection.

Smoke drifted up from where his heat pressed into the knot. "It's fraying," he whispered.

My fire could sense the weakening magic. I squeezed his fingers tighter as he worked. My other hand rose to my chest, as if I could feel the break in our connection. I couldn't, but the tightening of my body felt like a warning—like something was coming, even if I wasn't sure what.

The tether between us snapped.

Ambrose gasped. We collapsed into each other's arms, forgetting again that we were in the library, forgetting that anyone around us could see. Our foreheads met softly, and we shared breaths, neither of us able to catch our own.

I just needed to know he was still there. My awareness of him was gone. That space in my chest where the discomfort had been seemed empty, like a well that hoped to fill with the first rain of the season.

"It worked," he whispered. He didn't even try to hide the lingering disappointment in his voice.

"I know." And I did. We could be more scientific about it. We could wait until we separated and didn't feel the insistent tug in the direction of the other to declare victory, but this test didn't require it. There was a bone-deep knowing that the magic had severed. As I put a few inches of space between us and studied Ambrose, I wondered if everything else we were building had been disrupted.

Only time would tell.

"Hi," I said.

"Hi," Ambrose replied with a dopey smile on his face. "Want to—"

"Your little knot—or whatever you were calling it—seems to be gone." Lord Arctos clapped his hands together loudly as he walked across the room. "Just in time. Carter will be here tomorrow for you to test it on us."

34

Ambrose

Lord Arctos's presence didn't allow time to process what happened. The magic had worked. I'd dissolved an unprecedented magical bond between two living beings—between a fae and half-fae. Discomfort stirred in my stomach, but I couldn't regret it, even if it was everything my father warned against.

Evelyn knew what this step meant to me. I was sure she was surprised I hadn't fought her harder on being the one to do it. Something warmed in my chest at how deeply she understood me. She'd known I needed to decide for myself the direction of my future—the direction of my experiments with blood magic. And she'd provided an opportunity.

My chest throbbed a little. It was odd not to sense the connection to Evelyn anymore. Did I miss it? Or was I worried about what the dissolution of the bond meant—what we'd have to face next?

One of us will be chosen for Vesten historian now.

Our gazes met and held, a million conversations dying to be had, but Lord Arctos's insistent cough behind us told me now was not the time for them.

"Yes, we broke the connection," Evelyn said, her brown eyes still on me.

Lord Arctos coughed again, demanding our attention. When we finally turned to face him, he had a hand on his hip and another gesticulating. "I'm a god, of course I can see you've broken the connection…" His head tilted as if questioning something else.

"You didn't give us much time," I said, "before having Carter follow us."

Lord Arctos's head snapped toward me. "Carter has other business to attend to in Sandrin, and we had the utmost faith in your capabilities."

His wry expression didn't signal that he had faith in *my* capabilities, but I decided to take his words at face value.

"What about the place of power? Isn't Compass Lake the location of importance for the magic connecting you?" Evelyn asked.

I felt my skin flush. That hadn't even occurred to me yet. Her mind was always working, and her attention to detail was impeccable. I wanted to tell her now and every day how brilliant I thought her. The weeks I'd spent not sharing that information had been wasted.

Lord Arctos waved her off. "We'll try here. The Vesten Library is important for the connection to Carter specifically. The blood magic connecting Compass Point and god may have started at Compass Lake, but the magic connecting me and Carter started here, the day he accepted that he would be the next Vesten Point."

Evelyn looked pensive.

I didn't get to ask any follow-up questions as Gabriel arrived at Evelyn's study carrel in a flurry of paper and a sweeping robe.

I had been so distracted I hadn't even seen him enter the Great Room. "Evelyn, Ambrose, I'm glad you're both here. There is something I believe you should know—about the Vesten historian position."

Next to me, Evelyn's spine straightened. I pushed my shoulders back, too, as if on reflex. If I understood her, which I liked to think I did, she'd been mentally avoiding this part as much as I had.

It was the first thing she'd told me she wanted. That was its own milestone for us. Then, as we'd grown together from our bond, I'd come to understand why.

Initially, she'd offered the reasoning that she would use the position to find her father. That was a moot point now, but it also wasn't the whole story. Evelyn had been inescapably shaped by growing up half-fae in a world where she didn't fit in. That was too generous—for nearly all of her life, the world had not wanted to acknowledge her existence.

While the Compass Points fought for change, it wouldn't happen overnight. It would take leading by example; it would take dogged determination to bring those who didn't fit the traditional fae mold into fae schools and courts. It would take careful direction that considered all angles, not just those of the traditional fae.

It would take someone like Evelyn in a position of importance to the court.

Her uncanny sense for other magics meant she would fulfill the magical side of the role with ease. Perhaps I knew more about Vesten history than she did currently, but, like learning her own magic, given time, I was sure she would catch up.

I stared at her with no small amount of awe. Then I studied her stance. I'd been lost in thought, but her hands were balled into fists at her side while Gabriel explained something she didn't want to hear.

"Ambrose, did you hear me?" Gabriel asked.

Evelyn's face was as white as a sheet. I'd been distracted for too long.

I shook my head.

"While you two were traveling, we received a review for the last paper you submitted." He cleared his throat with a careful glance at Evelyn. "That means that instead of you both having equal research submissions and publications, you are now in the lead."

"What?" That couldn't be right. The only person who reviewed my papers was Evelyn. She was the only one with the expertise. Yet, judging by the look on Evelyn's face, she clearly hadn't done it. Who could have provided a review while we were traveling?

The question was on the tip of my tongue. What Gabriel was saying didn't make sense.

Evelyn touched my shoulder—featherlight and unsure. It was so starkly different from all that we'd recently shared. Her face pinched, but the attempted smile was genuine. "Congratulations, Ambrose. That's great news." While I still stood in confused silence, she turned to Lord Arctos and Gabriel. "If that's all, I need to get to the tavern."

Gabriel nodded.

"We'll see you tomorrow morning?" Lord Arctos called after her. "I want you here when Carter arrives."

Evelyn waved over her shoulder. Theoretically, this was a gesture that conveyed understanding, albeit somewhat lax for communication with a god. Lord Arctos's gaze followed her, narrowing as she left the Great Room. I shared his apparent concern. She wasn't alright, and clearly, she didn't want to talk about it.

Still, I didn't think she'd skip meeting Carter. It was the conclusion of a project to which she was still assigned. She would want to see it through. Almost as bad, I didn't want to do it without her.

"Does the one paper make that much of a difference?" I asked.

Gabriel shrugged. "I don't speak for my son. But I do know you both came highly recommended. I don't think it's a secret that you excel at history and Evelyn excels at blood magic. Carter cares deeply about both disciplines, so he searched for other ways to differentiate. That was why he used the competition as a way to see if one of you set yourself apart."

Lord Arctos looked pensive but didn't add anything.

"I'm out of the loop," Gabriel continued, "but I gather you two worked together more than anticipated on the project."

"Let's say they worked together as much as anticipated," Lord Arctos replied.

Gabriel deferred. "Yes, well. Unfortunately, that means this paper is what he's been looking for. A way to set the two of you apart."

"Even if it's just a technicality?" I ran my hand through my hair at his silence, then asked the question that felt like a stone sinking in my stomach. "Who reviewed the paper?"

Gabriel grimaced, and that sinking feeling shifted to that of an animal burrowing.

"Gabriel," I rasped.

He sighed. "Your father."

A choked laugh escaped my lips. "My father reviewed my paper on the use of anchors for blood magic?"

He nodded. "He's entirely qualified."

I ground my teeth. "Oh, I know he's qualified. I also know his feelings on the paper. He'd contest every point. You're saying he approved it?"

"Yes."

"Excuse me." I nodded to them both and stormed out of the library to find him.

~

"WHAT DID YOU DO, FATHER?" I skipped the usual greetings as I entered the family apartment. Sasha and Timothy were at the table, eating. Metal clanged in the kitchen where Father cooked, and Mother carried a platter of pancakes toward the table.

"We're having breakfast for the evening meal," Sasha announced proudly.

I sighed. "I see that."

"Your siblings wanted to pretend they were at your apartment, since they hadn't been over there in three days," Mother said as she set the plate down.

In the kitchen, Father flipped another pancake.

"I need just a moment with Father," I said as I gave each of them a quick kiss on the forehead.

"I'm not sure what you're upset about, Ambrose," Father said as I entered the kitchen. He didn't have to see the pancakes to know when they were done. A small bell timer clanged every three minutes, signaling when to flip.

For a moment, I simply stared. Father and I might have disagreed on methods, but regardless, I'd let his caution guide me for far too long. If I wanted to prove myself worthy of the position of Vesten historian and be the scholar I knew myself capable of being, then choosing my own path was the first step.

This afternoon was only the beginning. I'd used myself as a test subject for blood magic. With the way Lord Arctos and Carter talked about the need to dissolve the bond between them, I could confidently say that the continent would be a safer place for my research. I only wished I had started thinking this way sooner.

"You didn't even agree with that paper," I said at last. "How could you approve it?"

Father waved away my concern. "I know you didn't want to do all that, you just needed the qualification."

Mother returned to the kitchen to collect another stack.

"James, how could you?" she said, clearly hearing our conversation. "You said you wouldn't interfere."

"I didn't. I checked the submissions when I was at the library a few days ago, to see if there was anything of interest."

Mother collected another stack of pancakes. "We will discuss this later. But for the record, that is the opposite of not interfering."

She squeezed my shoulder and left. I wasn't sure what else to say. Father had crossed a line. He had known what this would do.

"You could discredit me, of course, if it's so important to you," he said.

I sucked in a breath. That seemed drastic even for me. I believed in the paper, of course, but just because I knew Father disagreed with it didn't mean he wasn't capable of spotting mistakes. The question was, how genuinely had he searched for them?

"Did you think it drew the correct conclusion?" I asked.

He shrugged. "I think the test itself was unnecessary, but once conducted, the results were assembled sensibly."

Part of me wondered if I should be flattered by that response. That was as close to admitting he couldn't find fault with the logic as he would get.

He flipped another pancake and turned to me, brow furrowed and hands at his hips. "You thought I approved it just for the sake of doing so?"

"Well, yes," I replied. "You had no other reason to even read that paper."

"Other than caring about what my son spends his time on? Experiments we agreed he shouldn't be conducting." He waved the spatula at me. "It may have been convenient timing, I admit that, but I would never forge approval on an academic paper. I'd hope you know me better than that."

I sighed. Maybe I did? I no longer knew what to believe. At

the end of the day, I didn't like that this technicality was a convenient reason for the Vesten Point to choose me instead of Evelyn. It didn't consider what we each brought to the position. It reduced the decision to data points without context—now conveniently tipped in my favor.

"I'm sorry I didn't tell you sooner how much blood magic work I was doing, but I want you to know I chose to work on it. I should have been honest about that."

He turned back to his pancakes. "It's alright. You did what you had to. Now that you'll be Vesten historian, you'll have more control over what goes on there. You can point them in the right direction."

"That's not—" Suddenly, I was so tired, but I needed to clear this up. He needed to understand our differing opinions. "That's not what I'm going to do, Father." I ran my hand through my hair. "I'll expand our blood magic research. It's too important."

"The risk is too—"

"There is risk. I acknowledge that. Evelyn taught me ways to mitigate it. Part of our job is to learn these things so when others are in need, we have solutions to offer."

"It's dangerous."

I sighed. "I don't deny that. All blood magic is dangerous. But we've also proven it's necessary."

He looked like he'd say more, but I didn't want to hear it now.

"I have to go." I turned and left the kitchen. My siblings received a tired smile and a quick goodbye before I left the apartment. There was one more thing I could try.

35

Evelyn

Tears blurred my vision as I opened the staff door to Parkview Tavern. I grabbed an apron from the hook and walked down the hallway. I hadn't known when I would return from Compass Lake, but Seraphina had said to come into work when I could. I'd missed multiple days, and I didn't want to disappoint her now. This was one thing I could do.

The tavern had always been a safe space for me. Even as my academic career crumbled to pieces, I knew Seraphina and Parkview Tavern would have a crisp ale and a warm atmosphere waiting for me.

While it wasn't a guarantee that Ambrose's paper clearing the review process would grant him the position, it was not nothing. Carter and Gabriel said we were evenly matched. Once, that might have angered me, but now I saw it for what it was—we brought out the best in each other.

Ambrose loved history. He'd studied enough to know that blood magic played a vital role on the continent, even when the fae didn't acknowledge it. He didn't diminish the importance of learning more about blood magic's capabilities, even if he was cautious about it.

I knew Ambrose would do well as Vesten historian. That had never been in doubt.

The problem was how much I'd wanted it. I might not have loved history the way he did, but I respected it. I read it and learned from it. What we learned from history would shape our future. I knew I could help the Vesten Court learn from its mistakes and build on the changes that the Compass Points had started.

Before I arrived beside the bar, I swiped away my tears. Seraphina was mixing a drink, and Luna and Vincent sat on stools opposite her. The picture of the three of them together felt like home. Even with the tavern filled, the females' attention turned directly toward me, and something in both of their expressions shifted.

Luna stood before I could say anything, and she pointed to Vincent to take Seraphina's place behind the bar. Seraphina walked toward me, a look of concern furrowing her brow. She took my shoulders and turned me around, heading back down the hallway through which I'd just arrived.

"I think we need a consult," she said.

The tightness in my chest that had been there since Ambrose and I severed our bond finally released. Seraphina squeezed my shoulders, and Luna snuck by us to hold open the door.

"Are we going to stand in the water again?" I asked.

Luna glanced at Seraphina. "I don't see why we wouldn't. It has worked miracles in the past."

That was questionable, but honestly, I wanted to. And even though wanting things could lead to disappointment, my time with Ambrose made me think that maybe the risk—the dream of what could happen—was worth the potential disappointment.

That wasn't a theory I could test now. Now, I wanted to do something utterly ridiculous with my closest friends.

"Evelyn's choice," Seraphina said.

I pulled off my boots on my way toward the moat surrounding the tavern.

Luna squealed with glee, flipping off her slippers as she chased after me.

Seraphina removed her shoes as well and sat on the water's edge, letting her toes dip into the water while she played with the dirt on the bank. "What's going on, Evelyn?"

I didn't even know where to start. I must have said so aloud, because Luna replied, "What weighs heaviest on you?"

It was an interesting question. An answer slipped from my lips with little thought. "I think Ambrose and I are more than colleagues."

Maybe I would deal with this particular fact tonight. I didn't think I'd realized how much I was tying myself in knots over it. I was too good at pushing away my wants, but it made sense the more I thought about it. My feelings for Ambrose were inherently linked with the outcome of our contest. Both things I wanted were tied up together, and I didn't know what to do.

Luna squealed again with glee, but Seraphina's cool reserve urged me to continue.

"All the time together ... it showed me another side of Ambrose. The more I learned, the more I was drawn to him. We realized the magic that connected us had no hold on our emotions. So, the things we felt for each other were our own. And, I don't know ... things escalated from there."

Seraphina shook her head slowly before Luna could explode with joy at my statement. "And..."

She always knew. I didn't know how, but she always did. "Our feelings for each other don't change the fact that we both want the Vesten historian position. We're both qualified in different ways, and while we were gone, one of Ambrose's outstanding papers was approved for publication."

They glanced at each other, clearly unsure of the last part.

"It means he has a single mark ahead of me in our academic records. The Vesten Point only gave us our blood magic project as a tiebreaker, so to speak. The approval of Ambrose's paper means the tiebreaker is unnecessary. He is going to get the position."

They both nodded as if they understood. I wasn't sure they did. But I had more on my mind. "I found my father while we were at Compass Lake. He'd been searching for us just like Mom always said." I tugged at my braid. This part of my trip had been tucked into a neat little box in my mind. With Seraphina and Luna standing here, the truth pushed free. "I couldn't believe it. His insistence on finding me and Mom was even what pushed Carter to fill the Vesten historian position to begin with."

Luna twisted one of her white-blond strands around her finger. "Are we calling the Vesten Point Carter?" she asked hesitantly.

Seraphina glared at her. "Not the most important part of that story." Her attention returned to me. "This is good, right? You found him. You can ask him the questions you wanted to?"

I shook my head, tears rimming my eyes. Luna reached for my hand and held it with a steady reassurance. It wasn't like when Ambrose did it, but it was reassuring regardless. "I saw him shift. Our animals are not the same." I let out a heavy sigh. "He can't help me."

"I see." Seraphina nodded.

"That is a lot." Luna squeezed my hand again.

I wasn't even sure that was all of it. There was still whatever Carter had been trying to tell me about the tree on Vesten property. The fact that he'd shared so much about the Vesten Point position with me … it was something that few knew. Did that mean anything regarding my chances at the Vesten historian position? Did I want it to? I had so many pieces of information collected, and none of them made sense.

"What's next?" Seraphina asked, practical as ever.

"Next?" I sighed. "Tomorrow morning, Carter arrives. We'll finish the project, and then he'll make his decision."

They both nodded. "Do you want to do something tonight?" Seraphina offered. "I can kick everyone out, and we can hang in the empty tavern like we used to."

I sighed and shook my head. "No, if you don't need me to work, I should go see Mom. I sent Stephen—that's my father—to find her. I'm sure he arrived before me. I need to see how she is." My smile was watery when I glanced between them. "Thank you both. For dropping everything. For consulting. For listening."

Both females smiled like they wouldn't want to be anywhere else.

Finally, I glanced at Seraphina. "How about you? Do you still need to consult? Or have things cleared up for you?" She had been quite upset before I left, but we'd spent all our time talking about me. I wasn't sure if she'd spoken to Luna about it.

Seraphina's hand went to her pocket, as if to reassure herself that something was there. She didn't look at either of us when she replied. "It's not better, but I'm taking care of it."

Luna dropped my hand, moving hers to her hips. "Seraphina, what is going on?"

She waved away Luna's concern. "It's nothing, just news from home. They'll find something new and shiny to focus on eventually. I have to wait them out." Luna's brow furrowed, but Seraphina stood. "We should get back in there. Evelyn, I don't need you tonight, but I do think there is someone in there waiting for you."

I glanced at the tavern, unsure of what she meant. As we

put on our shoes and went back inside, I searched the room. Ambrose wouldn't have come here, would he?

My gaze landed on a table in the back—Mom's and my usual spot. She was there, and she was not alone.

Seraphina pressed me gently forward. "She asked if you were back when they came in. I'm not sure where you stand with him, but I know you can buck up enough to tell your mom you're home."

With tough love, she pushed me into the dining room. That was how I found myself standing beside their table. They barely glanced up, thinking I was Mina, but Mom gasped when she realized it was me.

"Honey!" She reached for my hand. "I'm so happy you're here. I asked about you."

I glanced at Stephen, who was seated across from her. His hand rested on the table. Clearly, he'd been holding Mom's until she reached for me.

"Have you eaten?" she asked. "We were leaving, but we can stay if you'd like."

I shook my head. "I'll grab something at home. I'm tired, I just wanted to find you."

They paid their tab. Mom didn't introduce Stephen or rave about his grand return, leading me to believe he had already explained our meeting. Something uneasy lingered between Stephen and me as he nodded in greeting. I did not know how to act around him. Honestly, he was as much a victim of circumstance as I was—I knew that—but knowing that couldn't close the hole left in my heart from the last twenty years. Thankfully, Mom seemed unaware of our awkwardness.

We left the tavern and strolled through the park. For the first time in my life, I was unsure of how to act with Mom. When Stephen had left—disappeared—I'd known how to comfort her. This felt more complicated, like one ball of yarn tangling with another. I had to sift through my emotions to find the right one to support her.

The love of her life had returned to her with the explanation she expected. It changed nothing about how I'd grown up separated from fae society and tradition, but it also wasn't all about me. I could be happy for her.

"Stephen said you weren't so happy to see him," she said. I hadn't noticed that he'd walked ahead, leaving us the illusion of privacy.

"I'm happy for you, Mom. Everything you believed was right. Something terrible happened, and he's been looking for you ever since."

"He's been looking for *us*, honey." She raised a brow as if the distinction were important.

I shrugged.

"Will you be alright if he stays with us?" she asked. "It's your home, too, and I want you to be comfortable."

I couldn't believe Mom was considering kicking out the male she'd waited twenty years for on account of my comfort. Then again, maybe I could—that was Mom through and through. I shook my head. "If you want to see him, which I assume you do"—I forced a smirk, but the twist of her lips said she didn't buy it—"he's welcome in our home."

She patted my hand. "Thank you, honey."

I noticed then that she wore the ring he'd shown me. How had I ended up so different from her? She loved fiercely and hoped deeply. She didn't let fear of looking foolish get in the way of her wants. Her life was an unapologetic song screamed at the top of her lungs.

It hadn't always been in her favor, either. She'd gone years without the male she wanted, yet still, she hadn't given up hope. Something bloomed in my chest for her. Just as quickly, heat flooded me—embarrassment at my behavior. I, not the world, had thought her foolish for her hope.

"Mom..." I started.

She patted my hand again. "It's alright, honey."

She already knew what I would say, but I wouldn't sleep well until I said it aloud. I wiped tears from my eyes. "I'm sorry. I'm so sorry I doubted. I just..." I picked through my feelings, trying to find the words I'd shared with Ambrose only days ago. "I just thought it would be easier to expect nothing. That maybe it wouldn't hurt so much."

Her smile was so soft as she pulled our slow walk to a halt. "I know, honey. I've always known. It was going to hurt either way. Having hope and believing in love doesn't mean you don't experience pain."

"Then why do it? Why bother with the hope if the outcome is the same? Why put your life on hold for the chance of what could be?"

Her hand glided up my arm, squeezing. "I didn't put my life on hold. That was the part I don't think you understood. I kept living, but I never found something equal to what I felt for your father. Romantic love is one kind of love. My life was filled with fulfilling relationships. The women at the bookstore, my knitting group, and ... you." She smiled at Stephen's back as we walked. "Your father was worth waiting for. I love him, and I knew he'd be back, but he also helped set the standard for the romantic love I wanted."

The sparkle in her eyes had me thinking of the gold light in Ambrose's, and I thought I might understand what she meant. There was something about Ambrose that sharpened my senses and pushed my limits, but it also showed me how far below that standard any of my past romantic partners had been.

I pushed Mom forward, knowing that even if I wasn't ready yet, she needed this. "Go, Mom. I'll be fine."

Mom gave me a glance over her shoulder and must have

seen some truth in my face. She took Stephen's hand, and we walked through the park toward the apartment.

36

Evelyn

Too much had happened too fast. With everything weighing on me—my father, Ambrose, the blood magic, the job—and with no simple resolution in reach, I slept like a rock. My brain must have needed to shut down.

And although I could no longer feel Ambrose's distance like a constant tightness in my chest, I thought of him anyway. We hadn't discussed the evolution of our relationship. But the things he'd said to me couldn't be misconstrued, could they? Ambrose was so careful with his words. He wouldn't say things he didn't mean, but maybe I was the problem. What would I do when he got the Vesten historian position? When he moved to Compass Lake?

We could mean the words we said. Our actions could be more than just passing time. We could care about each other deeply. I might even love—

I shut down that thought.

Life wasn't guaranteed to work in our favor.

The morning came too soon, and with it, the meeting with Lord Arctos, Carter, and Ambrose to complete the project. I arrived at the library at my usual hour. No one was there yet, and this return to normalcy almost felt calming. The study carrel across from mine sat empty, and maybe it was a little bit of that hope Mom tried to reinforce, but I left the chair there just in case.

I worked on my notes. We needed to get everything documented, and while I was sure Ambrose had pulled out his notebook and pencil once I left yesterday, I didn't want to miss anything. Documenting blood magic tests between living entities was supposed to be my area of expertise.

Time passed, even with my mind tied in knots. Eventually, the large double doors creaked, and Ambrose entered the Great Room. He looked tired, and his auburn hair was untidy as ever, but when our eyes met across the expanse, a small smile curved his lip. Something fluttered in my chest, and I leaned a little more on Mom's hope. Maybe we could make it through whatever came next.

As he walked toward me, the familiar large black bird flew through the closing door. He shifted in the way that I now considered showing off, where he waited until the last second before seamlessly striding forward on two legs.

"Good morning, Evelyn." Lord Arctos glanced around as if expecting something. When Ambrose finally made it across the Great Room, the god smiled. "Aren't you late?"

Ambrose's brow furrowed. "You sound like Evelyn."

The comment from Ambrose caught me off guard, and I laughed, wondering how distracted Ambrose was that he finally snapped back at the Vesten God.

Lord Arctos only grinned. Then they both turned to me. "Is the Vesten Point here yet?"

"I am." Carter and Gabriel, entered the Great Room next.

As they walked toward us, I tugged Ambrose to my side and

whispered, "Have we considered how we'll do this if they can't burn away the connection like we did?"

We knew how we'd broken the magic. And Carter had found something when they'd searched for a similar connection. I had been so confident up until this precise moment that this would work.

Ambrose opened his mouth, but before he could respond, Lord Arctos cut him off. "I'm sure we can figure it out. If not, I have a few tricks up my sleeve."

I decided to set aside the comment about tricks up his sleeve and return to a stalwart belief that this would work. We'd done this only yesterday. We knew how to complete the project. The most powerful Vesten alive and the god of our court could certainly replicate what we had done.

Ambrose's hand briefly swept over my arm, then dropped. The heat it sent through me was incandescent. It was a little voice in my head, reminding me that this thing between us was worth fighting for. And maybe I couldn't control the future, maybe circumstances would tear us apart, but right now, he was with me.

"Do we want to do this here?" I asked, searching the room. Based on my and Ambrose's tests, I didn't think there was a risk to the materials, only a risk to being observed. As if on cue, Landon and Tatyana walked in. They gave our group a curious glance.

"Let's move to the Restricted Section. I assume we don't have to worry about damages?" Carter asked.

"The risk is low," I said.

He nodded, and we moved to the room Ambrose and I had fought over entering. I held in a laugh, and the way his ears pinkened, I wondered if he was remembering that particular discussion, too. The restricted section was a smaller room but completely filled with books. All four walls were lined with leatherbound volumes, and additional shelving units created rows in the center. I couldn't imagine the value of the knowledge within.

With everyone repositioned, I glanced at Ambrose. He urged me to start with a small gesture. That flame flared in my chest—not one of a magical binding, but one of shared understanding, a language of gleaned gestures and noticed facial expressions that only we cared to decode.

"We broke our connection yesterday," I said. "We will walk you through the steps to do it yourself."

I urged Ambrose to speak next with a glance. We had come this far through collaboration. It felt right to finish the project that way, too.

Ambrose nodded. "Can you locate the connection between you again? I think last time you said it was more of … a bridge than a rope?"

Carter shared a look with Lord Arctos, and I wondered what hidden understanding lay within it.

"Once you find the connection, the next step is simple," Ambrose said.

"Burn it down." I smiled sweetly.

Lord Arctos arched a brow. "Really?"

Carter's brow furrowed. "The metaphysical representation of the magic can be destroyed … by magic?"

"Yes. Ambrose and I were able to separate yesterday. With no trace of the strain of our connection."

My words didn't feel quite accurate, and I saw the same reflected in the flex of Ambrose's hand. Part of me knew that had nothing to do with the blood magic, though. Ambrose and I were on a precipice. The next hour would usher in a massive change in one of our futures, and I wasn't sure this new and fragile connection we'd forged would be strong enough to hold.

"Which one of you burned the rope?" Carter asked.

"Ambrose did," I replied before he could hem and haw over it. It had been the right move. Ambrose needed to free himself from his father's beliefs. He needed to be allowed to experiment intuitively.

"Evelyn was the one who even discovered the rope and guided me to it. I don't think I would have found it on my own," Ambrose added.

Carter looked contemplative, but he gave a swift dip of his chin. "Shall we, Arctos?"

"I think I should get to burn it down," the god replied.

"As you wish." Carter sounded tired but fond. "If I tried to object, you'd just remind me of your godhood."

Lord Arctos hmphed, like maybe being granted the request so easily meant he no longer wanted it.

I sucked in a breath as they closed their eyes. It was odd watching them, having no feeling as to whether progress was being made. At least with Ambrose burning our connection, I'd felt the change to the rope as it happened. I studied their features. The careful furrow of Carter's brow and the softening of Lord Arctos's shoulders told me they searched their magic and found the connection. Pride filled me as they did. Pride that we'd developed this solution through our own experimentation and expertise. Pride that we had a solution to offer.

Gabriel drifted near Ambrose and me while the pair worked. "You two exceeded my already high expectations."

"It hasn't succeeded yet," I said.

Ambrose rolled his eyes fondly.

Lord Arctos called out at the same moment, "I've got it. Ready, Carter?"

"As ready as we're going to be."

This was the scary part. This was the leap into the unknown, with inherently unpredictable magic. My and Ambrose's connection had severed easily, but we'd also known the precise parameters of the bond. Lord Arctos had shared that most of the gods weren't aware of this connection, and the Compass Points were utterly in the dark.

I held my breath, letting it puff my cheeks. Even though the work they did wasn't apparent to our eyes, the temperature rose as Lord Arctos's used his flame. Neither he nor Carter flinched, but I could no longer ignore the sweat dripping from my brow. Ambrose fared no better when I glanced at him. He swiped his arm across his forehead and murmured, "It'll work."

I nodded. I wanted to believe that. Another part of me didn't want to get my hopes up. This connection between Compass Point and god had been forged hundreds of years ago. Who knew what really lay at its root? Who knew how hot the Vesten God's fire would need to burn to break it? Perhaps more terrifying—what if they did break it? Ambrose and I would have to face what came next.

A large hand wrapped around mine, firm, warm, reassuring. I glanced up at Ambrose and heard Mom's words from last night in my head. *Having hope doesn't mean you don't experience pain or disappointment.* The words were somehow a comfort. I had taken every step I could in preparation for this moment. I could hope, and I could deal with whatever came after.

As if the thought manifested the outcome we desired, Lord Arctos raised his hands in celebration and declared, "I've done it."

The temperature in the room dropped immediately. Any fire the Vesten God wielded must have been dismissed. Lord Arctos and Carter stared at each other, blinking as if unsure they'd really succeeded.

Suddenly, they were flung away from each other like a too-tight bow snapping.

"Ooof!" Carter grunted as he slammed against a bookcase.

Gabriel ran to where Carter had landed against the eastern wall, kneeling beside him. The Vesten Point sat up quickly and glanced at Arctos, in a similar position on the other side of the room. "You alright?"

Arctos pushed from the floor and glared at Ambrose and

me. "I notice I did not have anyone fawning at *my* side to see if I was alright."

"You keep reminding us that you're a god." I put my hands on my hips, deciding that if he could sass us, he must not be hurt. "You'll be fine."

He smirked and rubbed his chest. Carter did the same.

"I think it's gone," Carter said. "Which is odd, because I didn't really notice it was there before."

"It really does open up a whole new line of study for us," Ambrose said. "The hypothesis that all blood magic has some connective tissue. Like, even when an anchor is not employed, there is a magical tether that could be manipulated."

Lord Arctos stood. "Careful, Ambrose, that sounds dangerously like tests that require living things."

I snorted, and Ambrose flushed. For the first time today, I felt like I could take a complete breath. Ambrose was right. This was a green field area of study. Maybe it didn't have to matter which of us was the Vesten historian; we could work together and push forward this understanding of magic.

"Should we test that it worked?" Carter asked.

Arctos looked bored again. "I can feel that it did, but I think we have to wait until we return to Compass Lake to confirm fully."

"What about the others?" Carter asked. "They won't be able to burn the connection away."

"We'll have to test. I suspect each of their magic will have a way to destroy the connection. If not, I can do it through them with fire."

I swallowed. "You can inhabit them?"

Arctos smiled dangerously. "It's a last resort, I assure you. But as everyone keeps reminding me, I am a god." The twinkle in his eye was back.

Gabriel helped Carter up, and he approached us. "I guess we should discuss the future."

His words weren't quite formal, but I felt something ... zing through me with them. Excitement, anticipation, terror? Maybe all three.

He rubbed his chest again. "You two were exactly as Father described. Even better, I admit, than I was when I held the historian position. You had very little material to work with yet still managed to solve an incredibly complex issue." He cleared his throat. "While also contending with your own magical entanglements."

Ambrose and I both flushed.

"What I'm saying is that you did tremendous work. We can't thank you enough. Not just myself but the rest of the Compass Points when I share the news with them. I know we didn't give you the details, but suffice to say not all our gods are as benevolent as Arctos."

Arctos's chest swelled with pride.

"We need to ensure the Compass Points have full autonomy when it comes to their magic and their ability to rule their court."

I tried to remain calm, but as with our conversation beneath the willow tree at Vesten House, Carter was sharing much more than was necessary. At least this time it was with both of us.

"Now, I know Gabriel told you we would select one of you to become Vesten historian when this was over. Whoever solved the problem first." He looked fondly at his father. "You were equally set in qualifications when this started. And from my understanding, you've continued to rely on each other to solve the challenge, even though it pitted you as rivals. Evelyn's awareness of the magic led her down the path to find the knot. And Ambrose's depth of knowledge on fire magic dissolved the connection."

Carter finally glanced at Lord Arctos, who had his arms folded across his chest and appeared to be staring straight at me.

"New information has come to light," the Vesten Point said, "and we can't ignore it."

My chest tightened, and Ambrose stiffened beside me. This was it—Ambrose's recently approved paper set him apart. I wouldn't begrudge him this, even as my chest tightened in preparation for the news.

"Sir," Ambrose interrupted. "I think you'll find even more information has come to light. Evelyn had another paper approved early this morning."

I turned to gawk at him. The circles beneath his eyes suddenly made sense. Had he stayed up all night reading the paper I had waiting for review? My heart beat a little faster at the gesture.

Carter looked confused. He glanced at Gabriel for clarity.

Lord Arctos snorted and mumbled something under his breath that sounded like "lovesick idiots."

Gabriel finally spoke. "One of their equal qualifications was the number of research papers approved for publication. While on their trip to Compass Lake, another of Ambrose's was approved, meaning he had a slight lead. This morning, he submitted his support for Evelyn's most recent paper. Meaning they are once again equal."

Hairs on the back of my neck stood on end. Gabriel was providing way too much context, which meant...

Carter had had no idea the paper was an item of contention between us. If he hadn't even known about the papers, what new information could have come to light?

The quizzical expression on Carter's face smoothed. "I see. While it is admirable that you continued your daily duties over the course of this project, that is not what we need to discuss."

With a final glance at Lord Arctos, he said, "Evelyn is disqualified from holding the position of Vesten historian."

37

Ambrose

This could not be happening. I'd stayed up all night to finish reviewing Evelyn's paper. When Sasha had come over in the morning for breakfast, she'd found me half asleep at the kitchen table. But here, in the restricted section of the Vesten Library, the Vesten Point said none of it mattered? My wolf clawed at the confines of my mind, and I didn't have the necessary discipline to restrain him.

I had finished it. The paper was sound. Everything should have been equal again.

The Vesten Point's decision should be based on how he envisioned the evolution of the historian position, not based on a single item in our academic records.

"What do you mean she's disqualified?" Heat surged through me, and my wolf paced a steady line back and forth in my mind. I hoped it wasn't noticeable, but the way the others glanced at me, I was confident everyone could feel the tenuous hold I had on my magic at the moment.

With the Vesten Point's words, Evelyn had gone catatonic, but my question ignited a spark within her. Her spine straightened as if she were remembering every one of the experiments she had done, the papers she had written that had brought her to this moment. I hoped she remembered how much she deserved to be here.

Her hands balled into fists at her sides, and her chin raised. "Please explain."

Carter tilted his head and shot another subtle glance at Lord Arctos.

"I don't think he'll leave the room without an answer," Arctos drawled. "And I am sure she would tell him immediately anyway."

My brow furrowed. Were they talking about me? Why would I leave?

Carter glanced at Evelyn. "The answer is somewhat private, and for your ears alone." He glanced at me. "Would you prefer we ask Ambrose to step back into the Great Room? Or do you accept Arctos's assessment?"

Evelyn sighed, then dropped the pretense that we weren't in this together. Our hands had disentangled when Carter and Lord Arctos broke their connection. She gripped my hand again now and repeated herself. "Please explain."

At her move, the smile on Carter's face was so feline that the hair on my arms stood on end. Nervous energy flooded me; my heart raced as I wondered what he could have to say to her. How could she be disqualified from winning the position?

"It turns out, Evelyn, that your disqualification is the same as mine."

That didn't make sense. Carter had had to step down from the position when...

"Surely, you're joking," she said, putting the pieces together more quickly than I did.

"You may not have been as honest with me as I was with

you, but I assure you, I was serious when I said the court still requires a veil cat shifter to lead. What I didn't say was that it can no longer be me."

Fear flashed through her eyes at the mention of her shifted form. She shook her head slowly as Carter spoke.

"Did you not suspect?" he asked. "You didn't wonder why I told you information that only the court leadership knows, about how the next Vesten Point is selected?" He nodded even as Evelyn continued to shake her head in disbelief. "Yes, Evelyn, you will be the next Vesten Point."

I swallowed, finally making sense of everything. Of Evelyn's shift, of Carter's apparent fascination with her, of her attunement to the magic in nature. I'd known she was magnificent, but this was even more than I realized. I squeezed her hand.

"This can't be right," she said, shoulders pushing back as if she'd found new confidence with my touch. "How do you even know about my shift?"

Lord Arctos gave up the pretense of letting Carter handle this and moved toward us. "I *am* a god."

Evelyn sighed loudly.

Carter stepped back in. "Lord Arctos suspected. I had hoped that when we spoke at the willow tree, you would say something, but you didn't. In the end, your draw to the tree was enough for me. There are no other veil cat shifters on record, so it makes sense that the next Vesten Point would be half-fae—the only children not tested by the court." He shrugged and glanced at Arctos. "I also trusted the god, I guess. And you're not denying it, so I suspect he didn't steer me wrong."

Evelyn surveyed Carter, and it was as if I could hear the pieces clicking into place within her mind. She deduced something, but still, her following words were a question. "Why can't you do it? It has something to do with traveling beyond the veil, doesn't it? Through the willow tree?"

Now she took control of the conversation. She believed

what he said, although her last sentence had gone a bit over my head. I knew she would hold her own from here on out. She didn't need me. I attempted to slip my fingers from hers so that she could fully stand against these two powerful beings, but she shook her head without looking at me and latched on tighter.

I knew better than to think it was from any fear of them—any need for me to defend her. I could do no such thing. She'd proved her lack of fear of them time and again. The action said she wanted me here. She wanted me to stand beside her as she received more news that would forever change her life.

And I would do so happily—proudly—for whatever time I was granted.

Carter nodded in response to her questions. "Though I only became Vesten Point within the last few years, something happened when we freed the continent from the mist plague. It means I have commitments elsewhere. Commitments I've not been in a position to act upon because of the ones I currently hold to the continent. I've been slowly splitting in two, and then Lord Arctos pointed out that there was an easy solution—to find my successor."

"Where could you have commitments that are not on the continent?" I asked. I wasn't sure if he'd answer me, but with another glance at the way Evelyn kept me close, he seemed to decide it was acceptable.

"Beyond the veil," Evelyn said before he could. "That's what he was trying to tell me. He has commitments beyond the veil, and he can't be in both places at once."

He nodded.

"Do I get a choice?" Evelyn asked.

Carter smirked. "Only you can answer that. The call of the Vesten Point position is a real thing. But if anyone could fight it, it would probably be you."

I tended to agree with that assessment. Resisting the call of court leadership was unheard of in Vesten history. But I remembered how hard she had fought her veil cat—how long she had gone in between shifts with no control. Evelyn could do anything she put her mind to.

"Would you want to fight it?" he asked when she didn't respond. With a quick glance at his father, he continued. "Father believes that your aim with the historian position was to elevate half-fae in our society, starting at the heart of the courts. I think you could accomplish your aims much better as the Vesten Point."

She bit the inside of her lip. "What about my research?"

Carter looked like he understood that question all too well. "It's a different kind of research, but a no less important use of your skills. You have to understand history and magic to be able to guide our people in a new direction."

The way he said *our people* with no hesitation warmed me to him immediately. I had believed Carter was different, of course. Gabriel was the most empathetic fae I knew. But to hear the leader of the Vesten so openly include half-fae in his statement meant we were already on the right track.

With Evelyn at the helm, we'd be unstoppable.

She seemed to accept his answer. "What about the historian position?" she asked.

Carter laughed. "I'll let you fill it as your first act as successor."

Her lip tilted dangerously, and she turned to me. This was all going too fast. Evelyn would be the next Vesten Point? Did that mean she would move to Compass Lake? Of course she'd have to, that was where her duties would be. Would she ask me to come with her? And now she was responsible for filling the position of Vesten historian? How would she choose? What qualifications would she look for?

"Ambrose, will you accept the position?"

The current Vesten Point seemed to believe my response was a technicality he did not need to witness. "We'll leave you two to talk. I'll return to Compass Lake tomorrow. I want to talk to you again before I leave."

She nodded but called after Lord Arctos's retreating form, "How long have you known?"

He laughed and didn't look back at her as he replied. "Since the first time you told me to go away. Only a Compass Point could be so disrespectful."

Then they were gone, and Evelyn and I stared at each other in the restricted section. My mind looped through all the ways our lives had changed in what felt like moments.

Evelyn was to be Vesten Point.

That voice in my brain that always urged caution spoke softly. Did she really want me as Vesten historian? Her life had changed so rapidly. I didn't want her to think... "Evelyn, you don't owe me—"

"I would never ask you to be historian because I thought I owed you something." Her eyes narrowed. "I respect the position too much for that."

My lip tugged into a half smile. "The position, not me?"

She waved her hands in the air, likely at her wits' end. "Both!"

I discovered new pieces of Evelyn Knowles every day. Once, I'd watched her conduct an experiment that entailed trying to get a blueberry plant to grow. She'd been determined to use magic to ensure that there was enough food for everyone, even if growing cycles were disrupted. I'd known she considered it a stressful project; there were many newly awakened on the continent, and the food supply wasn't entirely ready for the surplus. Even then, though, her hands had been steady, her brow only slightly scrunched. She'd shown nearly no signs of the pressure she was under.

Now she did.

She paced the restricted section. Her hair had been carefully plaited when the meeting started. Every pass back and forth across the room had her tugging another strand free. She was unraveling before my eyes.

I found her strikingly beautiful as she showed me more of the real her. Usually, her movements were too practiced. I didn't like to consider it, but she clearly experienced stress reactions often, and was skilled at hiding them. But now, she was showing me without a second thought—and it was that knowledge that made me secure in her offer of the historian position.

This was my first peek behind the curtain, an offering of trust she handed only to me. And I was intoxicated by it.

No amount of Evelyn would be enough. This addiction I had to her would only grow, never reaching its peak. Anything she asked me to give her, I would.

So, I did what I did best. I pulled out my pencil and notebook and said, "Maybe we should take some notes on this particular situation."

38

Evelyn

Carter was right—I should have known. What an embarrassing first move as a future Compass Point, not realizing what he'd been telling me.

My veil cat licked her paw and swiped it across her face as if to say *We shouldn't be bothered, we had a lot going on.*

Which ... fair.

I had so much to do, so much to consider. So many things I needed to figure out, given how drastically my life was about to change. It was during times like these that making lists became a calming activity. And here Ambrose was, whipping out that stupid pencil and notebook, starting my work for me.

"We can start with easy items, like what to do with your current experiments," he said.

I snapped my head up to look at him. I'd been doing the same thing in my mind, starting with the easy stuff and working my way toward the items that would thoroughly tear me apart. I wanted to kiss him. I wanted to throw him against the wall of books and climb him like a tree.

His gaze met mine, and a sheen of gold slid over his eyes, like he knew exactly what I wanted and would happily oblige. But my and Ambrose's relationship was a whole separate list of things to consider. He hadn't accepted my offer to be Vesten historian. Did he not want the job? Or did he not want to be with me?

Before I could completely spiral, he tapped the edge of his notebook. "List first."

I halted my next pace across the length of the restricted section and tried to think.

"Job at the tavern," he said. "You have to tell Seraphina, and Luna, and hopefully you can give them some time before you have to move to Compass Lake."

I swallowed. So much for sticking with the easy things.

"Find a place to live at Compass Lake," he said. Then he scratched that off. "I'm sure you get rooms in Vesten House, right? What do you think the allowance is for adding plants to the Burning Garden? I'll make a note about transplanting your flowers."

I stuttered, unintelligibly. He had never seen the garden outside my and Mom's apartment. "How do you—"

His smile was warm like the sun, and I was a plant gravitating toward its life source. "There is no way you would even think to conduct most of the experiments that you do without having your own garden." He laughed to himself. "Not many people know that morning glories tend to strangle roses."

He had a point. My cheeks heated anyway at how much he noticed.

His lips flattened into a thin line as he started writing another item down. "Your parents? Finding them a place at Compass Lake?"

It was plural. What I'd realized yesterday was already a

foregone conclusion in his mind. Mom and Stephen were together. They wouldn't be separated again.

"Ambrose," I sighed.

He looked up.

"I'd really like to talk about the item you seem to be avoiding."

His ears pinkened. "Which one is that?"

I took slow steps toward him, and with each movement, my veil cat purred, hearing his heart beat a little faster.

"Well, this is a turn of events," I said, trying to sound playful. In truth, it probably came out more strangled and unsure than anything.

"What is that?" he asked, still writing furiously in his book.

"Usually it's *my* heart that's a scattered mess when *you* approach." I tilted my head to listen again. "Today, it appears we switched roles."

He chuckled as he finished the note. His gaze locked on mine as I took the few remaining steps across the room toward him. "Do you want to be the kettle or the pot in this particular instance?"

I tilted my head in question.

He pointed to my chest with the end of his pencil. "Your heartbeat is also currently a mess, Evelyn."

Dammit. I winced, finally evaluating myself.

"And mine has always been a mess when it comes to you. You have just ... previously decided not to notice."

I wasn't going to let him distract me from this conversation. "When you thought of the Vesten historian position, where did you want to conduct your duties from?"

His hand was in his hair before I finished the question. "Evelyn."

My name on his lips in that moment sounded like a prayer. I couldn't help but notice he didn't continue. I needed an answer. His family was here. His siblings were at his apartment every morning. I couldn't ask him to come with me.

It's not your decision to make for him. All you can do is ask.

And I knew that was right. I needed to wait for his answer. His focus was on his notebook. I had a deep desire to know what he studied. I gently tugged it from his hands. He let it go regretfully.

"I imagined the position here." He sighed. "In Sandrin."

White noise filled my ears. It was what I'd expected, but I hadn't been ready to hear it. I had dreamed of the position being at Compass Lake, but it was flexible. The necessary meetings were infrequent enough that one could travel for them. The core of the responsibility was in the documentation and research, which only needed one of the Vesten's most prestigious libraries. There were only two worth knowing about—the one we stood in now, and the one in Vesten House.

My eyes brimmed with tears, but they didn't spill over as I glanced at the notebook.

Ambrose had written down everything that he'd said aloud. He'd even added another item to the list that said *Determine what you want from Ambrose.*

The list didn't end there. It seemed he had continued with his own list at some point in my panic. The page resembled a pros and cons list. One column listed *Sandrin*, the other *Compass Lake*. He hadn't finished filling it out. The only item was in the Compass Lake column in his tidy scrawl. The tears rimming my eyes slipped free as I read it.

The privilege of loving Evelyn, if she'll let me.

A drop of water hit the page. My eyes were officially leaking.

I glanced up, meeting his patient hazel gaze, which softened as he watched me crumble.

"What about your family?" I asked.

He pointed needlessly to the notebook, to the item I knew

he was most invested in. "That will be on my to-do list to figure out ... if you have completed the final item on your list there."

I opened and closed my mouth and flipped back a few pages in his notebook as I gathered my thoughts. I wanted everything with him. I wanted him to come to Compass Lake with me. He seemed to know it. But once again, he seemed intent on making me voice those desires for both of us to hear and acknowledge. Could I do it?

Then I caught my name in one of the notes on a prior page. My thoughts scattered as I flipped to another page and saw it again.

I gave him a final glance, checking for permission, before falling headfirst into reading his notebook. He only gave me a small smile, seemingly unworried about what I would find.

Evelyn's sense of magic is extraordinary. In the Vesten Point's study, she feels magic that seems connected to something on the property. The range on the sense is better than anyone else I've observed. Need to discuss, maybe when I'm less distracted by her.

Then another one.

Evelyn doesn't seem to realize that I notice her in every room. (Explain in a non-creepy way). Is this due to the bond between us?

Added note: This persists even after the bond is dissolved.

I flipped farther back and found my name scattered throughout, even before our magical entanglement.

Ask Evelyn how she thinks about which plants or animals to test. Want to understand the selection process better.

To Do: Tell her why I don't do that testing as of yet; maybe then I will seem more like an anxiety-ridden mess than a jerk.

I laughed at the last. "I figured this one out." Then my gaze held his again, and everything I'd been trying to avoid by perusing his notes slammed back into me.

"You write about me a lot," I said, wincing as the words came out.

"I think about you a lot," he said with no hesitation.

When had he started doing that? When had he started saying things like that without worrying about the consequences?

"Evelyn, I know this thing between us is new and untested..."

I gave him a flat stare. "We were magically bound to learn about each other's lives while competing for a position we both wanted." I tilted my head. "With a meddling god cackling at us the whole time. I think it's tested."

He sighed. "Time will test it further, but with your news, there seems to be more pressure on it than you might have wanted."

I opened and closed my mouth again. That wasn't how I felt. I didn't feel pressure to ask him to come with me.

"It's new, but"—he ran his fingers through his hair—"it doesn't feel casual to me. It never did. If that's all you wanted, that's obviously within your rights. I just think you should know that I love you and would follow you if you want me to."

My heart skipped a beat, and I was sure he heard it. Had he just said that? He loved me? Wasn't that what I'd been trying to find the words to tell him?

Time slowed around us, and I knew everything I wanted was within my grasp. My hope hadn't been in vain. Ambrose wanted to give us a chance. All I had to do was tell him I wanted it too.

I reached up to cup the side of his face with my palm. It was an intimacy I would never tire of. I spoke the following words with all the hope in my heart, still scared of his response even though he'd already told me his answer. "I love you, too, Ambrose, and all I've been trying to spit out this entire conversation is a single question. It might not have been what you originally wanted with the position, but will you come to Compass Lake ... with me?"

As his chin dipped in assent, I pulled his lips down to mine.

Kissing him was all I wanted now. We'd still have plenty to learn about our relationship, and he wasn't wrong: it would be in a more public position than we probably would have wished. But I was better when he was with me, and I liked to think the same was true for him.

The soft press of our lips against each other turned into a heated exploration, and my temperature rose with each stroke of his tongue. Our fires seemed to reach out to one another, like licking flames searching for more to burn. An inferno of desire cascaded through me. I glanced behind us. The door was closed; Lord Arctos had shut it upon his exit. Intentionally? I decided to believe he owed us this.

"I've had a particular fantasy about this library and you for longer than I care to admit."

Ambrose hummed, urging me to continue as he kissed my neck and slid his hand down my side.

I walked us backward and pushed him into the wall of books. "You and me, against the books in the restricted section." I paused dramatically. "Without the proper paperwork."

His laugh was decadent. "The library doesn't have paperwork for having sex in the restricted section."

As if he checked. My body warmed at the thought.

He flipped us around so my back was pressed into the shelves, and he dropped to his knees. Every inch he peeled my leggings down had my breath hitching. "Are you sure—"

He paused his progress, waiting for me to continue. I couldn't catch my breath to do so. He glanced up, those hazel eyes rimmed in gold. "Do you want to stop?"

I glanced at the door. Knowing Lord Arctos, he'd probably locked it, too. I shook my head. "I don't want to stop. But if you're uncomfortable, we don't have to—"

He pulled my leggings down farther, exposing me to him. "I'm doing just fine. Haven't you heard? I'm as reckless as you are. I test blood magic on living subjects now." He leaned into my center. His nose slid against the curve of my thigh. "Heavenly."

With his first lick, my knees threatened to buckle. With the second, they shook. He pressed against my stomach, holding me in place against the shelf. With the third pass of his tongue, something in him snapped.

My fingers laced in his hair. I wanted to run them through it in the way he was always doing. My mind echoed his word choice—*heavenly*. I had no opportunity to speak the word as he feasted on me with a single-minded devotion.

He noted every hitch of my breath and shake of my legs to catalog my likes, my desires, and pursued them rigorously. I was a research project he seemed more than passionate about. He hooked one of my legs around his shoulder and pressed in farther, his fingers sliding in to fill me as my pleasure built. I had no time to think, no time to realize where I was or who might hear. Fire burned through me, and I cried his name with my release.

My breaths were heavy as he stood and kissed me. It was a heady thing to taste myself on his tongue. I licked at him, wanting more and unafraid, for the first time, to reach for it.

"Was there more to the fantasy?" he asked.

I nodded, pulling him close. Our tongues slid together, igniting another flame of desire as I worked to free his length from his trousers. "A lot more."

He chuckled as I brought us together. He pushed inside me in one heated stroke, my body more than ready for him. He nipped at my ear, and his words were a whisper. "We'll have to thoroughly investigate each part."

"I'm sure you'll have some ideas to add."

He smiled. "We do tend to bring out the best in each other."

And then our hearts beat in unison as we drove toward our shared goal. Together.

39

Ambrose

I'd meant it when I told her I would follow her. Nothing would bring me more joy. That didn't mean I looked forward to telling my family.

Moving to my own apartment had been necessary. I'd needed my own space, but I truly enjoyed the ease with which I could spend time with them. This would be different. It took a day and a half to get from Sandrin to Compass Lake. It was a world of difference from a few steps across the hall.

I took the familiar journey from my apartment door to my parents' now. Things between Father and me had been strained when I'd visited last night. Maybe he wouldn't even care that I was leaving.

"Hello," I called as I opened the door.

My parents sat at the table. Father ate, while Mother wrote in a ledger. Sasha and Timothy played with their toys in front of the sofa.

"Ambrose." Father looked up first. "We're glad you're here."

He sounded tired, like I felt. The night without sleep had caught up to me, which was too bad, considering the paper I'd reviewed had been irrelevant. Not that I hadn't enjoyed reading it. It just would have been more enjoyable during my usual workday at the library.

Mother closed her book. "We hoped you would come by today." She pulled out a chair at the table.

"I have something to tell you." My shoulders fell as I thought about what came next. Sasha and Timothy wouldn't be happy. As an adult, I needed to make decisions for my life, but that didn't mean they couldn't hurt.

"Us, too," Father said.

Mother put her hand over his and squeezed. It was only then that I realized Father didn't only look tired—he lacked his usual confidence. He pushed aside his plate, most of the food untouched, and folded his fingers together before him. "I'm sorry for how I acted yesterday."

I had barely sat in the chair, occupied, preparing my own side of the conversation. His words stopped me in my tracks. "Excuse me?"

His head fell. "I'm sorry."

Mother squeezed his hand again, and he continued. "I shouldn't have interfered in your work at the library. I shouldn't have been so hard on you about blood magic. If anyone knows the opportunities it can bring, it's me. It's why I studied it in the first place."

"But—"

"My fear overshadowed everything I knew," he said quietly, like it wasn't the single most radical thing I'd ever heard him say.

As the words sank in, I huffed out a laugh. "I understand that too well."

Father winced. "I fear that is my fault also. I should have

realized sooner how much my fears became your own—how much I forced them on you."

"What's made you realize them now?" I asked, too stunned to pretend things weren't exactly as he said. It had taken me a while to realize, and once I had, I liked to think I'd taken my own steps to determine my perspective, but still.

Mother patted his hand again. "We didn't like the way you left yesterday."

"Your mother pointed out how many lines I'd crossed in our single conversation. Not to mention my stops by the Vesten Library to check on you."

Something tightened in my chest. While nice to hear, this didn't change what I had come here to say. Father wouldn't find it so easy to stop by the library and check on me in the future.

"I need to tell you both something as well." My voice shook more than I cared for.

"It doesn't matter if you got the Vesten historian job or not, Ambrose. I hope you know that," Father said. He must have heard of the Vesten Point's arrival and misconstrued my news.

I huffed another laugh, considering my news was technically what he had wanted for me. I ran my fingers through my hair. "I did get the job."

Mother and Father froze. "We thought..." Father started.

I tilted my head in question.

Mother cleared her throat. "Why do you look upset if you got the job? Do you not want it?" A new set of fears flashed across Father's features with her words, like maybe he worried he'd pushed me into something I never wanted. I wasn't sure what to do with this introspective version of my father, but I'd tell him what I could.

"I do want the job, and as I said yesterday when we spoke, I plan to continue the study of blood magic. I've done my own test on living beings. I plan to do more."

Mother glanced at Father, and he nodded. "I understand, but then why..."

The news might not be public yet, but I knew it would be soon enough. Evelyn wouldn't mind me sharing this. "Evelyn and I are together. It's new but serious. She's to be the next Vesten Point, and so she's asked me to take the historian position at Compass Lake."

My parents seemed momentarily speechless.

"She's to be—"

"You're in a—"

Neither sounded condemning as they repeated my statements and digested my words.

"Who knew?" Father said with a bit of a laugh. "The fae really are changing." There was bewilderment still in his tone, but it didn't feel disrespectful so much as awed. And when it came to Evelyn, that was a feeling I knew all too well.

"We're happy for you, Ambrose," Mother said.

"Very much so. I read her papers, too, since last night," Father said. "Her work is brilliant. She has an understanding of blood magic I didn't have after a decade of study. I can only assume how much she keeps you on your toes."

My lip tugged into a smile at that.

"We'll miss you, of course," Mother said. Her glance veered toward my siblings, who had thus far ignored our conversation.

I let my head hang. "I know. Me, too. I wish we could all live at Compass Lake, but I know that's too much to ask. And I know I have to make this decision for myself. I'll visit. The position requires work at the Vesten Library. It's not like I'll never return."

Mother squeezed Father's hand again. "We've always dreamed of living at Compass Lake."

I straightened in my chair. It couldn't be that easy. But Mother continued. "I've actually been offered a full-time position by one of the Vesten collectors at the lake. They want me to manage a restoration project. It would cut down on my travel significantly."

"When? Why didn't you say something?"

Mother waved her hand. "I only received the offer this week. I didn't think we'd consider it with you at the Vesten Library, but if that's not the case ... we could move with you, if you truly meant you wanted us to."

I had been the one to champion Evelyn speaking her desires. Yet, somehow, I hadn't believed how powerful it was to state what I wanted. If a move to Compass Lake wouldn't inconvenience my family, I wanted them to be there with me. "I meant it."

Mother and Father smiled. "Well, that settles that."

40

Evelyn

Ambrose and I had similar steps to take next. We both needed to speak to our families. I didn't think his confrontation would be simple, but at least the prospective reactions of the participants were known to him. Stephen was a mystery to me.

I found Mom and Stephen in the apartment when I returned. The real words for his presence hadn't stuck yet. He lived with us. He and Mom were in a relationship. My missing father was missing no more. I knew it wasn't fair to blame him for what had happened. The mist plague had been a natural disaster. He'd done nothing wrong, and nothing could have prevented it.

Knowing that didn't diminish the ache in my chest that the years of his absence had caused.

Mom deserved this, though, and I was committed to trying. Maybe we could get to know each other as two adults, without the pressure of him being my missing father.

Today was a day for scary questions. A new one popped into my mind. Would he want that?

The title of my position might have changed, but my dream of how it should be executed remained the same. It might not have always been directly related to the Vesten historian position, but Mom and I had dreamed of moving to Compass Lake —together.

In my dreams, we would get a cottage in the Vesten neighborhood, and I would work at the Vesten House Library by day, and we'd share a living space and meals outside of my work. They had bookstores there, just like here. She had wanted to come with me. We were the only family each other had.

That had all changed now.

They were playing a game of cards in the living room when I entered. I cleared my throat, unsure how to proceed.

"I have news."

Both Mom and Stephen looked up. I'd never been shy about my accomplishments, but all of a sudden, this felt weird. Was it an accomplishment to have so much magic that I was deemed next in line to be Vesten Point?

Maybe? It might have also been something I was born with, and I had these two to thank for it.

They both stared, waiting for me to proceed as I considered this question. The memory of Ambrose's notes returned to me —the idea that he'd tracked the increasing range of my magical detection. That he'd noticed such things made my heart soar. It also indicated that the answer to my question wasn't so straightforward. The power that made me the next Vesten Point must be a little of what I'd been born with and a little of how I continued to test and flex my magic and grow my abilities. I wondered if Ambrose knew how much he'd helped me with the Vesten magic. For the first time, I wished I had a stupid notebook to match his so I could remind myself to tell him.

And now I had completely lost the thread of what I needed

to tell my parents. I cleared my throat, reorienting. "I didn't get the Vesten historian position."

"Oh, honey." Mom stood and was almost around the table when I realized how that sounded.

"Oh, wait, that wasn't the end." I tried again. "I didn't get the Vesten historian position, because I was disqualified due to being named the next Vesten Point."

Mom froze, her eyes wide. She didn't know much about fae society, but she knew that title. Stephen rose to his feet, a smile playing on his lips, his head tilting in question.

"What—" she started. "How—" She looked to Stephen for help. He glanced at me like he was unsure if I wanted him to intrude on this moment. I wasn't sure I did, but it was clear Mom wanted him there, and my next question would impact his life as much as hers.

I needed to attempt to clear the air between us first.

"I know it wasn't your fault that you were away from us," I said to Stephen.

Words wouldn't fix this, but it was a starting point. Our relationship would need time to evolve. The hurt I'd felt from his absence had rooted deep, but Mom wasn't the only one who deserved this. I thought about what I wanted: Mom happy, those who loved me close. If it hadn't been Stephen's choice to be away from me, he probably fit into that group, too. I needed to give us a chance to find out.

"I've told myself for the last twenty years that you didn't want me. I know it was my twisted form of self-defense, but it's still not something that will disappear overnight. But if you're interested in getting to know me as an adult, I'd like to know you as well."

I glanced at Mom. Her smile filled her whole face, so broad it looked painful. Her eyes were already watering as I continued.

"Mom and I had a dream of living at Compass Lake. We'd

have one of the cottages as our own. We'd be one of the first human families to live among the Vesten." I glanced between the two of them. Stephen moved closer to Mom, and she grabbed his hand for support, her knuckles white with how hard she squeezed.

"I know this is a little different, but I still need to move to Compass Lake for this position. I will live in Vesten House, but it would still bring me a lot of joy if you two would consider moving to the Vesten neighborhood anyway."

It wasn't easy, exactly, but the words flowed more freely. Every opportunity Ambrose had taken to press me on what I wanted ... they'd paid off. It was Mom and Stephen's decision whether they came, but I could tell them what I wanted and let them choose. That was progress.

Mom glanced at Stephen, her question written plainly on her face. It was a true testament to Stephen's commitment that he saw it, too. "If your mom wants to move and wants me to come with her, I will, happily."

I glanced out the window at the flowers that grew so high they were visible beyond the sill, and Mom flung herself at Stephen. Moments later, she threw herself at me.

"Honey, I don't quite know what all of this means, but I am so proud of you. I know you'll be able to do everything you dreamed of in this position."

I hugged her back and smiled at Stephen over her shoulder. "I think so, too."

My conversation with Carter before he left was simple. We'd have a formal announcement to the Vesten Court at the next meeting, which would be in ten days. He'd asked that I fully relocate by that time. I got the sense he had understated the urgency of his *other commitments*. The current Vesten Point was slowly tearing in two, and my running the court would allow him to be pulled in the direction of his preference—beyond the Veil.

He promised to help with my veil cat. He'd tell me everything he knew about the shifted form, including how to reach him when he left the realm. Something like fear spiked through me at the thought, especially after reading the journal's details of the passage.

Terrifying? Probably, but I wouldn't find a better teacher for this particular set of skills, and my veil cat trusted him. Which I now knew meant I trusted him.

"Did you decide on the historian position?" Carter asked with a glance over my shoulder. Ambrose had entered the Great Room as he asked. We might no longer have been connected by blood magic, but my fire magic burned for him at every opportunity.

I nodded. "Ambrose will take the position. He will fulfill the duties from Compass Lake. He won't be there quite as quickly. I believe he needs more time to help his family move."

Carter nodded like he had expected this response. "And what about your family?"

"My parents will also relocate to Compass Lake."

Again, he nodded. "Wonderful. I will see you soon, then."

Ambrose and I had cataloged the rest of my work. He would do most of it; no one else studied blood magic like we did, but he seemed eager for the new challenge now that he'd decided for himself to test on living things. He would also spend his extra time in Sandrin helping Gabriel find new researchers to train. I heard him advocate with all the authority of his new position that we should find someone with a particular interest in blood magic.

My heart was so full it might burst.

Now, we headed to Parkview Tavern. I'd asked Seraphina and Luna to meet me there. I'd been back in the city for less than forty-eight hours and everything had changed, but I wanted to prioritize time with my friends, especially if that time might soon be limited. I knew in my heart that Seraphina and Luna would understand. That didn't make it hurt any less.

Ambrose held the tavern's heavy wooden door open for me, and I stepped inside. We strode hand in hand toward the bar. I was so thankful for Seraphina. She would tell me a million times that it was nothing, but when I'd been unsure how to follow my dream and still make ends meet, she had given me the chance.

Tears prickled the back of my eyes as I thought of all she'd done for me. Ambrose squeezed my hand as if he could feel my heartbreak over this pending separation from my friends.

My gaze met Seraphina's over the bar. She stood the same way she had the first night we'd met. Then, the tavern had been empty, and she'd dared me to ask how she could afford to hire me as a waitress. Now, a small smile joined the stubborn tilt to her chin. She suspected my departure and wordlessly communicated that I didn't need to worry about her. Then her attention moved over my shoulder, landing on Ambrose. Her brow pinched when she spotted his hand, which was on my lower back, ushering me forward.

Luna twisted around on the stool in front of Seraphina. She tilted her head with interest at my and Ambrose's apparent intimacy, and she swatted at Vincent.

"I'm going, I'm going." Without further instruction, Vincent slipped behind the bar and took over pouring drinks for patrons. He smiled fondly at Luna as she took my hand and pulled me forward.

"Whatever it is, clearly, we need a consult." She dragged me away from Ambrose and down the hallway.

We were in the moat in moments, and words poured freely from my lips. Finally, I didn't require them to ask me questions.

I wanted to share. I told them about the Vesten Point position, about Mom and Stephen, and about Ambrose.

Tears streaked down Luna's face, but she seemed happy. She smiled, laughed, and hugged me with each part of the story. Seraphina's evaluation remained reserved, but even her facade crumbled when I told her that Ambrose said he'd follow me anywhere. And that he would move with me.

"We'll miss you, of course," Seraphina said.

"Ambrose offered to work my shifts at the tavern until you find someone else."

She waved her hand. "First, I'm not sure he could handle it. Second, I'm not sure if you've realized this, but I don't require either of you to run this place."

"I had noticed that, I just thought it was one of those things we didn't say out loud."

Seraphina's laugh was loud. Even Luna turned and swatted at her. "We were excellent contributors!" she protested.

"You were. You are. I love you both dearly. The tavern isn't the same without you, but it doesn't need you to run. Just remember that, so you don't feel any guilt while you're both off chasing your dreams."

I smiled. It was such a Seraphina thing to say. "And what are your dreams?"

"This place is finally making enough money to sustain itself. That has always been my dream. To have my own place for my friends and community to gather."

The tavern as a thriving community fit Seraphina like a well-tailored jacket, but I also didn't think it was the whole story. She'd been more than patient with me, though. I would let her share what had driven her to seek this community in her own time.

"We'll visit Compass Lake," Luna said. "I've always wanted to go."

Seraphina's brow furrowed, but she smoothed it before I

could ask a question. "When you're ready, we'd love a tour of Vesten House."

I smiled. "I'll be back, too. Carter said there is plenty of business that needs to be done in Sandrin for the court. It's part of the job to visit."

"We would love you either way," Luna said. "And we won't let you go just because you've been declared the second most powerful Vesten on the continent."

The door to the tavern opened, and Ambrose stepped out. "Vincent says he only knows how to make Solstice Sips, and he could use some assistance with something his sister ordered ... a Berry Blush?"

Seraphina hugged me tightly. "We love you so much. I'm so happy for you." Luna did the same as we stepped from the water and back into reality. They both returned to the tavern, leaving Ambrose and me alone on the riverbank.

"You'll have to explain these consults to me at some point," he said. "They seem very powerful."

"Female friendship certainly is."

He pulled me to him. "Still feel good about your decision?"

I stretched on my toes and pressed my lips to his. "Carter was right. It was never really a decision. I wouldn't have wanted to escape it." I paused. "I'm just glad that you're in it with me."

Gold flashed across his eyes as he nipped at my neck. "You lead, I'll follow."

The refrain of our relationship was one of strength. To lead, I leaned on him—to challenge my thoughts, to share his own. His support kept me steady, and his love filled the well in my chest that seemed reserved only for him. He said he followed, but we both knew we were stronger together.

Our trials were only beginning. The veil cat might have chosen me, but the fae court might not yet be ready for a half-fae leader. Our relationship would be tested in the spotlight of my position, but we grew together against all odds. Just like my rose and morning glory. Whether bound with magic or connected by our hearts, we knew how to strengthen each other.

And that was the love I wanted.

A love that sought to understand, appreciate, and help each other grow. That was the message I would pour into the Vesten Court. That was the hope with which I would lead our people into the future.

Want more in this world? Check out Compass Points to discover the love between fae court leaders that changed everything.

If you enjoyed Research with Rivals, please consider leaving a review on your preferred platform(s).

ABOUT THE AUTHOR

Jillian Witt reads more romantic fantasy than is strictly necessary and writes books she would love to read. Her stories unleash powerful women into fantasy worlds, usually turn enemies into lovers, and always offer an escape from reality.

When not reading or writing, she's enjoying all four seasons in Michigan with her partner and their dog, Loki.

instagram.com/author.jillianwitt

tiktok.com/@author.jillianwitt

ALSO BY JILLIAN WITT

For a full list of Jillian's books, please go to www.jillianwitt.com/books, or use the QR code below:

ACKNOWLEDGMENTS

Thank you so much for reading. Evelyn and Ambrose are so special to me, and I'm so glad you joined them on their journey.

A special thank you to all those who helped put the pieces of this project together. Even as an indie author, it takes a village. Adie, Isla, Elle, Katie, Hillary, and Nicola, thank you for your talent and support.

I'll continue to thank my mom for being my number one fan. Ian and Loki will forever be mentioned in my acknowledgments, even if they never see this page of the book (and Loki is a dog, so he can't read).

www.ingramcontent.com/pod-product-compliance
Lightning Source LLC
Chambersburg PA
CBHW020911310726
48980CB00011B/841/J

* 9 7 9 8 9 9 2 3 3 6 1 8 4 *